H E D D Y S I M M O N S

Do You Know
THE LANTERN MAN?

An Elmira Book Club Mystery

Heddy Publishing

This is a work of fiction. All of the characters, organizations, and events portrayed in this novel are products of the author's imagination. Any resemblance to actual events or persons, living or dead, is entirely coincidental.

The Library of Congress catalogue information is as follows:

Do You Know the Lantern Man: An Elmira Book Club Mystery.
Copyright © 2025 by Heddy Simmons.
All rights reserved.

ISBN
Paperback 979-8-9923441-7-2
eBook 979-8-9923441-3-4

Book design: Guy William Fulton

Acknowledgements

Thank you to Guy Fulton, who created the beautiful book cover. Thank you to Dave Peterson, who did a wonderful job wiring my writing shed with electricity so I could write in comfort. Thank you to those who patiently read *Do You Know The Lantern Man?* as beta readers. Thank you to Amber Cox of Better Than an Editor LLC and Dana Boyer of Dana Boyer Editing for being my editors. Thank you to Veronica Presley for her book layout expertise.

Chapter 1

For the Reading Club of Retired and Capable Ladies, it was a time of beginnings. The beginning of October. The prelude to a season ushered in with spiced lattes, hot doughnuts, and pumpkin muffins. The introduction of conversations about beginnings because that's what the club's chosen book was about, retired people trying new things.

The start of October was also the beginning of troubles with magic.

"I've got an idea." Fayette swung her right arm up and sideways in a dramatic gesture. The long nail of her middle finger just grazed Sheila's Royal Albert rose teacup, but the contact was enough to tip the cup askew. Amber liquid spilled onto Kitsy's book, laid open in the middle of the round café table.

"Holy buckets," Fayette said, managing to rescue the cup.

The three friends scrambled for napkins, mopping up tea before it could roll toward them. Fayette picked up the drowning book and worked to blot its pages dry with a paper placemat. She tried to shake off the tea till Kitsy and Sheila begged her to stop.

"It's a lost cause." Fayette's expression was petulant. Then she spotted her copy of the same book, dry and hardly used. She brightened and handed her book to

Kitsy. "Trade?"

Kitsy pretended to scowl in disapproval, but she accepted Fayette's tea-free copy of *The Magic of Starting Something New in the Age of Retirement.*

"Well, that's settled," Sheila said. "Now we can get back to our discussion."

Fayette Pinker, Kitsy Browning, and Sheila Fairlight started their tiny book club six months ago around a campfire at a retirement retreat. Several smores and a few beers into a moonlit conversation, they discovered they all lived in the same neighborhood, minutes from a café they each loved. Every month since, they gathered at Lucky Cup Café and Bakery in the tiny Pacific Northwest town of Elmira to talk about a new book.

"What was your great idea?" Kitsy asked Fayette. "Did it have to do with questions about the chapters?"

"What?" Fayette leaned back in her Amish Windsor chair. Dutch-crafted chairs and tables were signature pieces in the bright, cheerful bakery. The décor was simple, with local artists' landscapes on the walls, copies of famous paintings, white lace curtains in the windows, and tiny vases of flowers on each round, cherry-wood table. "Oh yeah." She reached for Kitsy's book. "The author says that learning something new is good for the brain, like how to juggle or how to play chess. You know, we grow new neurons when we try out a fresh skill. I got to thinking. What is something I wanted to do when I was a girl that I never got around to? Maybe we could all remember something we thought we'd do when we grew up, but it hasn't happened yet."

"Oh, la. You mean and try it out?" Sheila plunked her coppery brown elbows on the table in front of her so her pocket-sized hands could fold under her chin.

"Wow. That takes me back." Kitsy looked wistful. "We could pick something to do and then make a pact to support and encourage each other while we learn new skills."

"I've already started my list," Fayette said. "I'll get you another tea, Sheila. You want a refill, Kitsy?"

"Let's share a big pot of Darjeeling." Kitsy's blue eyes brightened in a face framed with silvery blonde, bob-cut curls. To her utter embarrassment, her husband Samuel still called her his Apple Tree Girl after a Hummel figurine they got for a wedding present 46 years ago.

At the front counter, flanked with display cases spotlighting piles of baked goods, Fayette ordered the blue-pot special, which included a fat, cobalt-blue pot of tea and a plate of pumpkin-spiced mini doughnuts. She was the tallest of the three, with a head of thick, steel-wool, gray hair, cut just long enough to put in a ponytail.

By the time Fayette poured the tea and passed out napkins, Kitsy and Sheila were already sorting through memories. Between tapping their pencils on the table in thought or looking up at the ceiling for inspiration, the women jotted down recollections of 55-year-old hopes, desires, and youthful aspirations. When the women reduced the doughnuts to one doughnut hole, Kitsy tore her list out of her notebook. "Okay, what have you got? Let's hand our ideas to the person to our right, and when we're done reading them, we can pass them on to the next person. Third pass and we'll have our own lists again."

"Well, alright, but I don't want you to laugh," Sheila begged.

"No promises." Fayette took hold of Sheila's list and handed her own scribbled notes to Kitsy.

And, indeed, there were snorts and giggles from each of the Retired and Capable Book Club ladies.

"Roller derby queen?" Kitsy chided Fayette who shot back with, "inventor of the world's best hot dog recipe?"

Sheila's notepaper had five things on it. Her parents

were immigrants from a Southern India Indigenous tribe. Tradition imbued every part of her childhood, so as a girl, she wanted to be a wife first and a mother second. Out of respect, Kitsy and Fayette stayed quiet about that. They knew Sheila was single and always had been. As a steadfast Lutheran church secretary for 42 years, there had been no family other than her parents, and they were now deceased. Their quiet friend also wrote down growing plants to make medicine and inventing trees that grew real strawberries, but Sheila's fifth aspiration stopped her friends short. Sheila's last item was on all their lists.

"Do I dare say this?" Kitsy trusted these women, but she still didn't want to come off as a screwball, someone whose elevator ran only halfway up, so to speak.

"I dare you." Fayette reached over and took the last doughnut hole. She wasn't one to leave leftovers.

"Well, you know how we said we would help and support each other in learning how to accomplish something new?" They nodded. "We could make this easy and all take up the same novel beginning. We could share the same learning experience. There is one thing we all wrote on our lists."

"It's pretty crazy," Sheila said, reaching to gather and reread their crumpled papers as though to reconfirm their shared ambition. "I don't know if it's even real. I don't think it is."

"It's the right season. It's almost Halloween after all." Fayette's mouth twisted into a devilish grin.

"How, though?" Kitsy extended both hands in front of her, palms up in a questioning gesture. "How does someone go about learning magic?"

"I can't get over how we shared anything on our lists at all, let alone this." Sheila shook her head. "When we were girls, we all wanted to study magic and become the kind of witches who use their powers for good. Is there a girl or woman in the world who hasn't at least thought of the possibility?"

"I tell you what," Fayette said. "We finished the book on new starts and beginnings, and we haven't picked a book to read for October. Why don't we each do some research on magic? Instead of meeting in four weeks, let's plop ourselves in these chairs every week, same time, same day, and share the books we find. It's a beginning. Who knows what we'll learn. Then, if nothing comes of it, no harm done."

"I guess I'd be afraid to check out books like that from the library." Sheila leaned into the table. "What would the librarians think?"

"You might have to drive to some used bookstores out of town," Kitsy suggested, half kidding. "Disguise yourself." Kitsy pictured Sheila in sunglasses with a flowered scarf wrapped tight over her platinum-streaked black hair and tied under her chin, but Sheila's point was well taken. Elmira was a small town, and people did like to talk. Superstitions and legends about the paranormal kept neighbors scandalized and entertained in most communities. Elmira was no exception. Besides, she doubted the public library carried many how-to books on magic.

"We all know the stories." Sheila looked out the Café window toward Elmira's city water tower, the highest point on the horizon between the town and the distant fir-tree-covered hills.

"It's been 35 years, but to some people it seems like yesterday." Kitsy followed Sheila's gaze and studied the so-called haunted water tower. "Three fourteen-year-olds climbed seventy-five feet to the water tower walkway. They sat frozen up there for five hours. When emergency crews rescued them, they claimed that a spectral dark figure used a wall of fire to block their way down."

"It's all kuku bananas." Fayette's tone tightened with indignation. "Those kids didn't want to admit what really happened. They froze up there and were afraid to climb down."

"Well, that may be, but everyone knows the story, and you know how tales like that heat up people's imaginations." Kitsy looked hard at Fayette and squeezed Sheila's arm. "Some city workers back then insisted they found scorch marks on the tower walkway, and a neighbor claimed she saw firelight on the tower that night."

"And there are stories about ghouls in the graveyard." Fayette stretched and yawned. "Are we supposed to believe those too? Every town has its ghost stories."

With her right-hand thumb, Sheila worried the handle of her teacup. "What scares me is that some people still speculate about which old lady in our little town might have been the so-called specter on the water tower, and that's when things get dodgy. There are always a few people who take things a step too far."

"Well, pluck a duck." Fayette swigged the last inch of tea in her cup and stood. "We can't let rumor mongers control us. Next Monday, then. Come prepared to share a book and a magic lesson." She gathered her black-leather biker jacket and helmet. "See you both over another blue-pot special." Fayette picked up the tea-sodden copy of *The Magic of Starting Something New in the Age of Retirement,* and on her way out, dropped it with a squishy *thunk* into the waste basket by the café's front door.

The rest of the book club followed. Neither Fayette nor Kitsy nor Sheila saw the Roseanne-Barr-look-a-like remove Fayette's soggy book from the trash and drop it into a plastic shopping bag. None of them paid any attention to this same woman as she practiced taking iPhone pictures of customers, including Kitsy, Fayette, and Sheila. No one noticed the eavesdropper as she filled scratchpad pages with speedy notes while they talked. After all, the magic of new beginnings was their focus, not the back of a square-framed, dark-haired woman seated at the tiny corner table next to theirs.

CHAPTER 2

Saturday before their next meeting, Sheila texted Fayette and Kitsy asking them for the dimensions of the books they were bringing. "I'm making book covers so no one else at the café will see what we're up to," she wrote.

Fayette let out a scornful "for pity's sake" as she read the text but remembered the words of her oldest daughter the last time they talked on the phone. Her daughter explained that Fayette's five-year-old grandson was a smidgin afraid of his grandma. "Mom, you hate it when people seem weak, but there's a broader definition of strength. It's okay for little boys, really anyone, to share their fears and feelings. Let him be vulnerable. Listen instead of scoffing when he's upset. You'll be surprised how fast he warms up to you."

Feeling a lump of resistance in her throat, Fayette wondered if her daughter was right. Was she a harsh judge of lily-livered character? She conceded that it wouldn't hurt to be patient with Sheila and go along with her safety measures no matter how pointless they seemed. Really, people got too worked up over what others thought of them.

Monday, the three women settled into chairs around a Polish-pottery, blue-rose teapot and a plate of maple cookies in the shape of fall leaves, and Sheila passed them their book covers. She'd constructed them out of sturdy, heavy-weight fabric. Fayette laughed at hers, which Sheila decorated with iron-on, fabric roller skates, and Kitsy crooned over her hotdog-patterned cover. Sheila finished her own cover with fabric-painted images of rosemary, sage, and lemon verbena.

Sometimes the café felt more like a house party than an eating establishment dedicated to separate tables and conversations. It was a favorite neighborhood hangout, so people tended to stand and talk or drift from table to table. This particular weekday, customers settled into intimate conversations at their respective tables, and members of the Reading Club of Retired and Capable Ladies found their favorite spot unoccupied.

After meeting at the same café haven for six months, the women gravitated to the corner table by the window, with its vase of orange carnations and peach gerberas. They felt at home under the framed copy of Girl with a Pearl Earring by Johannes Vermeer, lit by natural light from the window that looked out onto Elmira's Old Town Main Street.

"This is the first time we didn't all read the same book chapters for a meeting," Kitsy said, once they disguised their books under Sheila's snug covers. "I have no idea what you two discovered. I'm really kind of excited. I mean, the more I looked up books about magic, the more curious I got. I really had no idea what I'd find. Seriously, I've got a whole list of authors I want to explore, one at a time."

As it turned out, the book club women all chose different magic specialties to study, and although it wasn't planned, they each brought gifts for the other two.

Fayette placed her smallish book with its roller skate cover on the table in front of her and poked a finger at the spine. "Okay. I found this little gem in the neighborhood library box two streets down from mine." Her voice was loud enough for everyone in the café to hear. "It's all about spells and rituals on the home front."

"Shhhh," Sheila hissed, putting a finger to her lips. "The man at the table near the door is Pastor Fisby Parkinson from the Elmira Confess and Reform Church. He won't approve of what we're doing. He's serious about stamping out pagan beliefs. The man is like a spider with a fly. Once he's on to you, he'll eat you alive with prayer vigils and threats of exorcism. I know. A few people who came to Faith Lutheran were trying to escape his church. In the end, he never stopped harassing them. They all decided it wasn't worth the trouble, found jobs somewhere else, and moved out of town." Sheila hunched down and drew her hand-knitted, multi-colored scarf closer around her shoulders.

"Well, son of a motherless goat, we're not doing anything wrong." Fayette scoffed. "We're just learning something new, and we certainly don't intend to harm anyone. It's not against the law to read books."

Sheila sneaked a furtive glance toward Pastor Fisby's table. "See that woman sitting next to him, the one who looks a lot like Rosanne Bar on TV and keeps taking pictures of the customers? She's Darnelle Shipman, head of the Confess and Reform Women's Guild. Those ladies make it their business to convert and transform women who act in ungodly ways."

"Whatever that means," Fayette said with an air of brassy defiance, but she lowered her voice, nonetheless.

Kitsy was so engrossed in the pages of her book, cleverly hidden behind images of dancing hotdogs, that she missed most of the conversation. She heard enough to say, "Well, it's a pain, but let's err on the side of caution. My husband might be embarrassed if his wife gets accused of witchcraft by the Confess and Reform Women's Guild. What would my two grown children think, for that matter?"

Sheila breathed a grateful sigh. Nosy, prying church

leaders like Fisby and Darnelle gave her the creeps. She knew that her parents immigrated from India to escape religious persecution, and their history still felt raw in her memory.

Placing her book a safe distance from anyone's teacup, Kitsy whispered to Fayette. "I love that you found your book in a little neighborhood library box. Does that mean you get to keep it, or do you have to return it? What's it about?"

"I'm keeping it." Fayette kept her voice lower than its normal resonate alto, but heckfire, she was not going to whisper. "I put some paperback thrillers in the book box as a trade. This one's called *Recipes for Household Magic*, and I don't think anyone ever opened it before I nabbed it." She grinned. "I'm especially tickled by the garage chapter. You both know my garage is home to my Harley Davidson Street Glide, and I thought the spells for garage and vehicle protection might be worth a try. HOGs are a superstitious lot anyway. We're the first to call ourselves delusional. Why not add to the superstitions and wake up some garage magic?"

In her enthusiasm, Fayette raised her voice as she said the words "garage magic." The heads of Fisby Parkinson and Darnelle Shipman lifted in unison and turned in the direction of the book club table.

"Shhhh," warned Sheila.

Fayette tried to remedy the situation by raising her voice and announcing, "Yeah. In my garage I found a pamphlet titled *Churches Against Magic*. Everyone needs to read it."

"What's a hog?" Kitsy envisioned a couple of fat, pink hogs settled next to Fayette's motorcycle on a hay-strewn garage floor.

"Harley Owners Group, HOG," Fayette explained. "Elmira's got a group that meets every month. We call ourselves E-HOGS." Her voice trailed off as she caught sight of Fisby's hooded eyes staring at them from beneath a ridged brow and high forehead. A sharp widow's peak featured prominently at his hairline, perfectly centered under dark, slicked-back hair. Next to the pastor, Darnelle stared, too. She pressed her pointer finger hard against her lips as though in calculation of her next move, and her mascara-framed eyes burned with the intensity of a hawk assessing the right moment to swoop in on a vole. Kitsy and Sheila closed their books and focused on their teacups and cookies.

"How is your garden, Sheila?" Kitsy tried to bring normalcy to the conversation.

"It's just fine. I'm collecting dry fall leaves in bags to make into compost." Sheila wiped her mouth with a napkin to hide her worried frown.

And then pastor Fisby rose from his seat, eyes still on the book club ladies, and walked with resolute strides to their table, his dark brows raised like police batons. The tall, thin pastor stood over them in silence for an uncomfortable five seconds before speaking. "I couldn't help but hear your conversation, ma'am. I'd like to see this pamphlet you were talking about."

"Oh, dear." Fayette thought fast and flashed a quick smile Fisby's way. "I wish I had a copy. You see I was changing the oil on my motorcycle and spilled some. I laid the pamphlet on the cycle seat, and next thing I knew, the pamphlet was on the ground soaking up the oil. I had to throw it away. Interesting information about the dangers of believing in magic, though."

"Interesting indeed," said Fisby Parkinson in a low, warning voice. "That pamphlet surely listed our church as a beacon of truth against sorcery and conjuring. We work hard in my congregation to rid our village of even the hint of witching behavior. If you liked the pamphlet, you'll feel at home at the Elmira Confess and Reform Church. I'll look for you to visit one of these Sundays, shall I?" He took a short stack of business cards from his black clerical shirt pocket and counted out three.

"Pass one to your friends," he said to Sheila, who was closest, handing her the cards. The women couldn't help but notice the unusual length of his chard-shaped fingers and the large gold ring on his overlong thumb. A chunk of polished amber surrounded by smaller red stones inside a hexagon engraving adorned the ring.

Sheila slid cards to Kitsy and Fayette, but she wiped her fingers on the tablecloth as though Fisby's touch contaminated them. Her back was to the pastor, and her lips shaped a silent "no."

Kitsy spoke up. "Thank you for the invitation, pastor. Of course, we all have our own spiritual communities, but there might be a chance to call on you someday. Perhaps you would like to visit our places of worship as well." Her tone indicated that the conversation was over as far as she was concerned.

Sheila, Fayette, and Kitsy remained quiet as they watched Fisby and Darnelle pay for their refreshments and leave the café.

"That man sure knows how to take the fun out of learning something new." Fayette broke the silence and passed a clean napkin to Sheila so she could dab the moisture from her worried eyes. "I've never heard of Fisby Parkinson or his church. Why does anyone take him seriously?"

"Most people don't know much about him unless they go to his services or unless he's decided to single them out." Sheila frowned, remembering a time when the Lutheran pastor escorted Fisby from church premises and locked the door. "I know about Fisby from church scuttlebutt and from watching particular people try to escape him and his followers and their steel-edged evangelism. As a preacher, he mostly works behind the scenes, so you won't have heard of him, but I've learned enough about the man and his church to keep my distance."

Kitsy looked at Sheila's worried face and a shiver

ran down her own spine. Both Kitsy and Sheila jumped when Fayette struck the table with a fist and then grabbed a menu. "What we need is another blue pot special and to start over again. Do we want more cookies? I know. Let's get a dozen of Lucky Cup's Magic Halloween Donut Holes." She chuckled at that. "We'll ask for the Calming Combo. It's made of hibiscus tea with peppermint, orange, rose hip, and apple for calming. What do you think?"

Sheila offered a grateful nod, and Kitsy tendered a thumbs up.

Minutes later, cups filled with hot tea in hand, the women felt safe to talk about their new discoveries.

Kitsy nodded to Fayette. "You were saying about garage magic?"

Fayette leaned over a bag by her chair and drew out two items. She set the green and brown figures, complete with pointed teeth and clawed feet, next to the teapot. "It's called the dinosaur car spell. I already put a Velociraptor inside my motorbike seat, and I brought these two for you to put in your cars."

"What do they do?" Sheila stroked the top of an eight-inch, green and mustard-yellow, plastic Tyrannosaurus rex. Kitsy claimed the brown T-rex and patted its tan belly.

"Well, according to the household magic spell book, the dinosaurs are for protection. They keep bad vibes away from your car and defend the vehicle from danger. But these two don't have anything special about them, not yet. It's up to you to give them the power needed to keep you and your car safe on the road. I did it with my Velociraptor. You've got to do it for your T-rex."

"Will it work?" Sheila eyed her dinosaur's miniature, plastic claws.

"How in blazes do I know? This is an experiment in learning something new, right?"

"Stop being pigheaded and tell us what we're supposed

to do with these monsters." Sheila sipped her tea and narrowed her brown eyes at Fayette, exasperated with her flippant, intractable attitude.

"Yeah. Well. Listen up." Fayette realized that Sheila still blamed her for the scare they'd had with Pastor Parkinson. "This is what the book says to do. Set your dinosaur on your front dash. Then do some visualizing. See the dinosaur as a living, breathing, hunting creature. Envision yourself filling its body with energy, enough energy to protect you in traffic. Blow a big breath of strength and power onto your T-rex to protect your car from theft and break-ins, that kind of thing. The book said if your visualizations are effective, the protections will be successful. The strength of the magic is your responsibility."

"Is that another way of saying you've got to believe to make it happen?" Kitsy picked up her T-rex and peered straight into its left, reptilian, yellow eye. "Are you going to protect me from catalytic converter thefts?"

Sheila balanced her dinosaur on the palm of her left hand. She aimed a long sigh at the plastic toy. "I could use some courage. Our new project makes me nervous. I don't think we're doing anything wrong, but I'm afraid some people will think it's immoral to learn about magic. I'll keep this little guy in my car, and maybe it'll protect me from the Elmira Confess and Reform Church and Pastor Fisby Parkinson. Thank you, Fayette."

"Fiddlesniddle to Parkinson and his henchwoman. I've got Velcro strips somewhere in here." Fayette pawed through her backpack. "Stick them to your dinosaur's feet and you've got a car dash ornament with teeth."

Kitsy tucked Velcro strips into a shirt pocket. "And now it's my turn." She too had a bag beside her from which she pulled three shimmering, hand-sewn scarves. She wrapped the one made with pink shades around her own shoulders and handed an orange and gold scarf to

Fayette and a green and silver scarf to Sheila. "The book I found is called *Bewitching Sewing and Needlework Methods*. I got it online and had it delivered. It's full of ideas for making hand-sewn objects that promote positive power and protection and strength. Orange is for breaking down barriers, green is for changing directions and attitudes, and pink is for self-love. I figured we could each use a collection with scarves of every color."

"I'm enchanted." Sheila replaced her knitted wrap with Kitsy's scarf. She stroked the bright fabric around her neck. "I love the green garden colors."

"It looks fetching on you, Sheila," Kitsy said. "I'm hoping it helps you with one of the goals on your list, the one about finding a life partner. Are you ready?"

Sheila's blush told Kitsy all she needed to know.

"Something extra I did," Kitsy continued, "was to sew on witch-stitches. Inside each scarf on the seams, I embroidered three small cross stitches with pink thread and asked for protection and the ability to make good choices. The book said to say, *By these stiches three, my will be done, so mote it be. Let the wearer of this scarf be protected from harm and make right choices.*"

"I could certainly use help with 'right choices'," Fayette looked across the table at Sheila. "I do apologize for not listening to you about that Parkinson nut bunny. I really should have kept my voice down."

Sheila reached over and patted Fayette's hand, so surprised she thought her voice would crack if she accepted the apology. Cradling her dinosaur in the crook of her arm and wrapping her shoulders in her new scarf, she took a deep breath. "And now I have something, too." Sheila put down her T-rex and pulled a basket from under the table. "My contribution this week comes from my own garden. It's mint. I know you were joking about disguises last week, but I took your advice, Kitsy, and disguised myself in a baseball cap and reading glasses and went to a big, used bookstore in the middle of Olympia. I discovered a book called *Beetlebum's Compendium of Magical Herbs*. It's a perfect book for someone like me because it's for gardeners. I brought it home expecting to browse through it between chores, but once I opened the cover, I hardly moved from the kitchen table. I read non-stop until two in the morning."

Out of Sheila's basket came two brown paper packages for Kitsy and two for Fayette. The smell of mint, mixed with sweet aromas from the tea pot, triggered a rush of memories of boutique Christmas shops, mint ice cream, and the fresh flower section of a farmer's market. Fayette's mind drifted to a cold night on the pillion seat of a bagger motorcycle, her arms around the leather-clad chest of a long-haired adonis who smelled of orange and spice cologne. Kitsy recalled the fruity soap her husband Samuel used when they were college sweethearts. Sheila remembered a creamy cup of cocoa, garnished with a red and green peppermint stick. A certain handsome maintenance man delivered it into her hands along with a peck on her cheek at a church Christmas party nearly three years ago.

The women filled their lungs with spiced air to savor the moment.

"Smell and emotion are mapped in our brain as one memory," Kitsy murmured to herself, remembering a quote she'd heard somewhere. She lifted one of the little packages to her nose and closed her eyes. "What are these for?"

Encouraged by Kitsy's response, Sheila leaned forward, eager to share what she'd learned. "One package has dried mint for all kinds of purposes, including healing and protection. The other package has fresh mint to aid in magic and attract good spirits." She laughed. "The book even said you could put a mint leaf in your wallet or purse to lure money and prosperity."

"Well, who would ever complain about getting rich?"

Fayette, her square-jawed face framed in the orange and gold scarf, opened her fresh mint package, and chose a deep green, fragrant leaf. She sniffed at it in appreciation and then inserted it in a zippered pocket of her leather wallet. "Let's just see what happens."

They passed their magic-themed books around the table, so everyone got a chance to peek at some of the recipes, browse through directions for spells, and take note of advice for making useful items.

"As far as I can see, these three books are really just about helping people gain confidence, you know, feel some sense of control over the uncontrollable." Kitsy looked thoughtful. "Everything in these pages is about trying to build a more pleasant, safer life and to inspire loved ones to do the same."

"There are no recipes or projects or words printed in these pages that are for causing harm that I can see," Sheila agreed. "Even our Elmira Confess and Reform Women's Guild wouldn't be able to find a dark side in these chapters."

"Who knows what people like Darnelle Shipman might read into the dinosaur car spell." Fayette's tone was gruff and cynical. "Even the idea of dinosaurs might set some people off, you know, if they don't understand biology or evolution science, or if they see evil spirits in everything to do with magic, or Lord knows what else. Witch accusations have blown storms through communities for hundreds of years over much less than a plastic dinosaur in a car window."

"I'd bet anything that Pastor Fisby has his eye on us, now." Sheila's nervous fingers worked one end of her new scarf into a tight twist. "Somehow we've attracted his attention."

"I have a suggestion." Kitsy pulled a notebook out of her pocket to write down dates and times. "In light of the pastor's unwelcome interest, I think we should limit our magic research conversations to private, online Zoom meetings. And I'm up for a connecting once a week online and once a week in the café. We can bring our new books, hidden in Sheila's book covers, to share right here at this table. And we can keep our café conversations simple while we're looking through the books, limit our talk to everyday life and the books we've read together in the past."

"I wouldn't put it past Pastor Fisby to send out spies." Sheila sniffed. "Some people went through torture when the pastor targeted them. I for one think it's safer to meet in private online to talk about what we're learning."

Fayette exaggerated her best mocking eye roll. "I really hate feeling controlled by 'what ifs,' and I try to avoid paranoid thoughts, but if it makes you happy, I'll try an online meeting."

They gathered their new gifts, books, hats, riding helmets, coats, and bags. The meeting was over, and they would see each other in a few days online. Kitsy would be their Zoom meeting host.

"I'm set to search for more books," Sheila told them. "I loved browsing in that used bookstore, and I want to go back tomorrow."

"Well, yeah. Collecting another book might be just the ticket for me too. The possibilities for garage and kitchen and bedroom magic have my mind racing. I'm learning about the magical mindset if nothing else," Fayette said.

"Let's be careful, though. Look what this says at the end of the first chapter." Sheila picked up her garden magic book with its herb-decorated cover and proceeded to read aloud. *'Magic-summoning beginners are especially prone to setting loose energies that ricochet through their lives like negative ions after a lightning strike.'*

"Let's hope it's not thundering next time we meet." Kitsy laughed as she followed Fayette out the front door.

CHAPTER 3

Sheila parked in a lot two blocks from the multi-level, used bookstore, downtown Olympia. As she closed her car door, her side vision caught a blurred glimpse of her T-rex's toothy grin. Too bad he couldn't turn into a real dinosaur while she was gone and growl at suspicious loiterers. A couple of skinny, scruffy types in gray, hooded sweatshirts leaned against the brick wall of the nearest empty storefront. Sheila stuffed her shoulder-length, gray streaked hair into a Mariners baseball cap, put on her reading glasses, and pressed the automatic lock button on her car key.

In a matter of minutes, she felt secure, even sheltered in rows of bookshelves, where it was easy to forget about her car, dinosaurs, and the Elmira Confess and Reform Women's Guild. She ignored everything except the abundant collections of hardbacks and paperbacks, some upright and side by side in the chestnut-stained wood shelves and others stacked in piles on the floor. By the time Sheila got to the checkout desk, she carried four cookbooks, three used volumes of a paranormal mystery series, and two how-to books about practical magic. She couldn't wait to show Kitsy and Fayette *Green Witchy Gardening for High Magic* and the larger book *Wild Garden Craft*.

The tiny young woman with blue hair, red bangs. and

an over-active ponytail priced the books and proffered an encouraging smile in Sheila's direction as she tucked the two magical-methods hardbacks with the other books in a sturdy bag. "Good choices," she grinned. "I've got both of these in my green witch collection at home."

All Sheila could think to say was, "Oh."

The bag was heavy, but she only had two blocks to go, and Sheila enjoyed walking through the scramble of yellow, brown, and orange leaves on the sidewalk. Picturing her new books spread out on her kitchen table, a pan of cocoa on the stove, and her feet cossetted in a pair of thick, wool socks, Sheila couldn't wait to get home.

As she turned into the parking lot, flashing red and blue police cruiser lights sparked an adrenaline rush and set her heart to thumping fast and hard. Police lights always did that, but her stomach muscles tightened when she realized that the cruiser and two police officers blocked the way to her sage-green, 2016 Honda Accord.

"Sorry, ma'am. Is this your car?" The shorter, stockier officer pointed to her vehicle's broken back window and four car doors, open wide. Even from a distance, Sheila could see the empty space left by a pulled radio and slashed back seats void of belongings. Whoever shattered her back window also took her groceries, her umbrella, and who knew what else.

"Sorry to say your catalytic converter was stolen," the officer informed her. "The lot attendant called this in but says he didn't see it happen. You'll need to hire a tow truck and get the car to a shop to assess any other damages. These guys are getting cockier by the day. Usually, break-ins like this happen at night."

The second officer gave Sheila, who had yet to say a word, a paper form with the case number on it for her insurance records and a phone number for a tow truck. Then, the two men jumped into the police cruiser, turned off the emergency vehicle lights, backed out of the lot and sped away.

Sheila approached her car to better see the damage. Broken safety glass stippled the ravaged back seat, and the thieves cracked the front dash where they ripped out her radio unit. They even took her dinosaur. Instead of scaring thieves away, the grinning reptile seemed to have attracted them.

Remembering that she wore the scarf Kitsy gave her, Sheila clutched it for comfort. At least the crooks hadn't taken her bag of new books or Kitsy's gift. How was she going to get the car to a repair service and then get home? She wanted a friend by her side to help her cope, and the only person she knew who understood cars was Darwin Finnigan, retired maintenance man of the Faith Lutheran Church in Elmira. She hadn't talked with him since her last day on the job twelve months ago. How would it look if she called him out of the blue and asked him to drive all the way to Olympia to help her deal with her mess of a car? But in the desperation of the moment, she did it. She couldn't believe she did it. She called him. Yes, she'd stayed single all her life, but for close to eleven years, Sheila kept an enduring secret, one she shared only with her book group. She'd been in love with the church custodian and was too shy to tell him.

***

Back in Elmira, Kitsy struggled through her own misadventures. She ordered two new books online about magic, one called *Honorary Herbal Tea Charms* and the second titled *Teapots full of Tea Power*. Now it was time to prune the old rosehips from her Joseph's Coat, multicolored, climbing rose bush. Maybe she could dry some of the cuttings and make rosehip tea, something she'd never tried before.

Mostly, Kitsy was no gardener, but she did have one apple tree that her husband planted for his "Apple Tree Girl." She also had two rose bushes, which she struggled to keep healthy and spotless. On impulse, and without changing clothes or finding gloves, Kitsy grabbed pruning shears from the shed and started snipping. Before she knew it, her new pink scarf caught among the thorns. Joseph's Coat grew prickers that were longer, sharper, and more numerous than those on most domesticated roses, and before she knew what was happening, Kitsy was a prisoner. The rose bush trapped her face a finger's width from razor-sharp thorns. Barbs on other branches held both sides of her scarf tight.

"Hey, I feed you." Positive that she would look ridiculous to any passing neighbors, Kitsy kicked out at the base of the bush. "What if I cut you to within a centimeter of your life and make sure you never grow taller than my knees."

Still, the bush held the wrap tighter until, inch by inch, Kitsy extracted herself from the scarf, working hard to protect the fabric, but the thorns were relentless. They seemed to attract the pink cloth like static electricity. By the time she freed the wrap from the bush, thorns shredded it in several places, and sticky red smears blotched her face and hands from bleeding scratches. What about those extra cross stitches she sewed with care on the seam? What about the special words she recited to empower the scarf to protect the wearer from harm and inspire right choices?

Samuel, Kitsy's husband, took pity and made supper for them. He'd gone to the store for buns and hotdogs and opened a can of Thai peanut soup.

"Comfort food," Samuel said as he put dinner in front of Kitsy and gifted her with a new box of Band-Aids. Each time Kitsy dipped her hotdog in the peanut soup, she wondered at the mix of flavors. Not bad. Not bad at all. Could the combination inspire an original recipe for a new hotdog cookbook?

***

At the same time Kitsy waged war with her rose bush, Fayette's mind was on the mint leaf in her wallet. What if mint really did attract money and she could get enough to finally pay for her house and buy a car for when it was too snowy or rainy to ride the Harley? She wasn't going to let Sheila's fear of Pastor Fisby rule her life, so she went to the little bookstore on Elmira's main street, the one next to the Masonic Lodge and six blocks down from the bakery café. She didn't care if the whole town knew what books she bought. Inside Forever Reading Bookstore, everything looked faded as though a gray murkiness percolated the air, muting the colors of the book spines and the walls. Even the storekeeper seemed dusty and transparent as he led her to a back corner where he kept a substantial collection of books devoted to the paranormal.

"No rhyme or reason why, but the Confess and Reform Church hasn't found this corner yet," he chuckled. "I just put this collection together a few weeks ago."

"Do they harass you, the church I mean?" Fayette asked.

"They come in and try to tell me what I can and can't sell. I don't pay them much never mind. There's no law against selling books, but they want me to get rid of anything that has magic in it, even in the children's section. When I caught them stealing books to destroy, I finally had to call the police and ask a judge to issue a restraining order. Of course, the Confess and Reform Women's Guild works hard to discourage people from coming in. Their vigilance has hurt my business a little. I'm not too fussed, though."

He scrutinized Fayette with critical eyes that were cinnamon brown with peppery energy and frosted with heavy, white brows. "You're not one of them, are you?"

"No, sir. I'm here to explore. I'm curious."

"Well, that's just fine. I'm Lars Columbus, by the way. I'll leave you to your search. You have any questions, I'll be upfront reading the new Robert Vaughan western."

Fayette found several books on magic, but she returned all but one to the shelves, choosing to take home a compact hardback called *Jar Spells for the Ready and Willing*. She handed the book to Lars so he could slip it in a paper bag.

"I've got a friend who uses this book so often that she's needed the cover repaired more than once. I have a little shop for book repair and restoration, by the way." Lars nodded his head toward the back wall where Fayette noticed three doors, two extra wide and painted the same tan color as the wall. The third door was thin, tall, and dusty blue. She stared at the blue door for several long seconds, feeling drawn to the rose-colored, glass doorknob.

"*Look on every exit as being an entrance to somewhere else.'* Tom Stoppard wrote that in his book *Rosencrantz and Guildenstern Are Dead*. Ever read it?" Lars afforded Fayette with a knowing smile.

Fayette shook herself and focused on finding the right combination of five and one-dollar bills. Her purchase complete, she slipped *Jar Spells for the Ready and Willing* into her backpack. Unnoticed by her, the mint leaf fell out of her wallet and onto the floor during the transaction.

October marks the time of year in the Pacific Northwest when the spin axis of Earth points 90 degrees away from the sun. As a result, the earth, the wind, and the rain cool by several degrees. Fayette felt the cooling deep in her bones by the time she parked her Harley in the garage. Her hands and feet stung with cold. She hurried to close the automatic garage door, anticipating the warmth of her toasty breakfast nook. A bowl of hot soup would help, but she thought about pushing up the thermostat to seventy-five once she hung up her riding gear and settled herself for the evening.

"Bugger my toe," she muttered as she opened the door from the garage into the kitchen. The kitchen was as cold as the garage, and so was the rest of the house. Something was horribly wrong.

Two hours later, Marjorie, the local HVAC technician, explained the bad news. "I'll have to replace the entire ancient system. The damage? Maybe $7,000. Maybe more. In the meantime, I've got an extra portable unit in the back of my truck I can loan you, so you won't freeze tonight."

Fayette scratched her head at the news. What happened to the mint leaf magic and the possibility of attracting wealth instead of losing it? The only good thing about the emergency was meeting Marjorie, a woman whose hands and mouth were in constant motion. She wore what looked to be size eleven work boots, extra-large, blue denim coveralls, and a sooty, black-billed cap with lettering that spelled out *Margie's Heating and Air*. In the middle of a nonstop airstream of talk, Marjorie mentioned that she was a jammer on the town roller derby team.

"Good grief. I love roller derby," Fayette told her.

"Come by the rink during practice sometime. You can join us just for the fun of it. And we can always use more fans cheering on the sidelines. Elmira competitions are every other Saturday."

"I just might do that." Fayette closed the door to the frigid air as Marjorie headed home, lugging her toolbox to her truck. The tools and the truck reminded Fayette of her days as a locksmith before she retired. She too had a trusty truck, but Fayette filled hers with key-making and lock picking tools, ready for call outs at all hours to help people get into their cars and houses.

Left with a tiny portable heater for the bedroom,

Fayette would spend the evening in the kitchen with a wool blanket around her shoulders, next to the heated oven with its door open, sorting through her financial records to locate the cash she needed to reheat her house. It wasn't the first time she'd had to deal with a financial emergency. Over the years, she married, had three children, divorced and remarried. She finished raising her children on her own after outliving her second husband. Locksmithing was no ticket to affluence, but it kept the bills paid most of the time, and Fayette had loved having her own business. On those days when her heating worked, she loved retirement more.

Next to her lists of figures and budget numbers, the book she purchased a few hours ago about jar spells lay unopened on the kitchen table. Seeing its cover got Fayette to wondering. Did people ever use magic to unlock doors or safes or bank vaults?

Next day, after a few glitches with the Zoom address and six minutes spent trying to get everyone's audio and video working, Kitsy, Sheila, and Fayette at last stared at each other through computer monitors. Then the chattering started.

"Quiet," Kitsy barked in her class-come-to-order teacher's voice. She had, after all, spent 23 years as a second-grade teacher, honing and perfecting the stop-talking directive and the focus-on-me command. Her friends, though, could be more unruly than seven-year-olds. Everyone tried to tell their magic-gone-wrong stories at once, and no one heard much of anything. For a whole minute, only an occasional phrase came through with any clarity, such as when Sheila said, "They even took my dinosaur!"

Chapter 4

"Quiet," Kitsy repeated, her stern demeanor hardening. For a few seconds they just stared at each other's images. Sheila giggled while Fayette frowned.

"I suggest we take turns talking. Sheila, why don't you go first, then Fayette and then me."
Once Kitsy got them organized, and they finisheddescribing their mishaps, the book club members knew they botched something big time.

"It seems like we made things worse rather than helping," Kitsy said.

"Way worse." Sheila looked depressed.
"A complete goat rodeo," Fayette agreed. "But unexpected, good things happened, too. I mean you called Darwin Finnigan, Sheila. You actually called him after all these months, and he came right away. You two had a wonderful dinner in Olympia before he brought you back home."

"That's true." Sheila tried to keep her mouth straight, but her lips wanted to grin. "I've been thinking about that. It took a small crisis to move me in a new direction, you know, to do something I couldn't make myself do before."

"And you got invited to skate yourself into roller derby practices," Kitsy said to Fayette. "That has to be more than a coincidence, doesn't it? As for me, I'm experimenting with hotdog recipes, just one per week. I'm thinking of writing a hotdog themed cookbook."

"But why were the good things that happened connected with bad things?" Sheila's voice pitched up an octave. "I tried to figure it out by reading more in my gardening magic books, and I have some ideas, but what do you think happened? I wish we had an expert to ask."

"I don't know for sure, but my new book on jar spells got me to speculating." Fayette held up her book for the others to see. "The book explains that spells are not supernatural activity, not how we think about magic from fairy tales. They take skill to create. If they're done right, they tell the cosmos what we want. The cosmos receives the message and reacts to turn our spells into reality." She read from the book, " *'Spells are the determination and fortitude to use energy to bring about change.'*"

Kitsy chimed in, "Yes. My books say kind of the same thing, but I'm not sure if I get it. Do you?"

"Magic is more scientific than witches stirring newt eyes into cauldrons." Fayette wiggled her fingers in the air as though feeling for invisible forces. "That thing we call magic has to do with focusing our bodies and minds. It has to do with the fixed intentions we put into our charms. Spells are requests to the universe that move energy."

The women were silent for a long minute.

"I was thinking about my dinosaur and how he didn't protect my car at all." Sheila opened the hardcover in her hand to the page with the yellow bookmark. "This is what it says in one of my books. *'To do a good job with magic you have to have an open mind, sincere desire, strong will, patience, self-conviction, bravery to follow one's heart, and you've got to be mature enough to accept responsibility for your actions.'*" She closed the book with a solid thud. "If the dinosaur had anything to do with the car break-in, I wonder if it's because I didn't have an open mind or self-conviction when I blew my breath of energy on him, you know, like you told me to do, Fayette. I wasn't sincere. I was just playing."

"Yes. I was thinking the same thing, Sheila." Kitsy looked over at her sewing machine and bit the inside of her cheek. "I loved making those scarves, and I had fun sewing on the special witch stitches, but you're right, I just saw it as whimsy and 'what-if'."

Fayette puckered her lips in concentration. "I don't claim to really understand, but apparently, it's about physics. Even Newton's Laws of Thermodynamics and Motion help explain it."

"I never took physics." It was the first time Sheila regretted her limited science education. "Do I need to take a night class to get the hang of this?"

"Holy humus, I hope not." Fayette wasn't against night classes, but she would rather take something like Motorcycle Engine Repair.

"This is what my book says," Kitsy said. "Let's see if it helps. *In spell making, energy gets directed toward a goal, and it takes energy to direct energy. It's not just about a few words; it's about the right words, and it's about the conviction behind them.*" Putting down her book, Kitsy rubbed her chin, puzzled. "I can understand something not happening because the charm maker didn't put enough energy into it, but why would something bad happen as a result? It's true. Maybe I didn't take it seriously when I sewed those witch stitches onto the seams of our scarves, but I didn't think negative thoughts either. Why did my scarf catch in the rose bush?"

"Good gravy." Fayette narrowed her eyes at Kitsy's face on her screen. "You caught your scarf in the rose bush because you forgot to take it off, and you forgot to wear gloves, so the rose bush scratched you. I'm not sure that's the scarf's fault."

"But why did I forget?" Kitsy's tone was insistent, stubborn. "I always do things by the book. I follow the rules, and I anticipate what could go wrong and take precautions."

"My scarf didn't cause any problems that I know of," Sheila said. "I still love it. But your question is a good one, Kitsy."

"Mine hasn't done me any harm either." Fayette pulled at hers to show she was not afraid to wear it. "And about the mint you gave me, Sheila, I put a leaf in my wallet, but it's gone. I don't see how that missing leaf is responsible for my broken cooling and heating system. If it is, it would be on me. I didn't put much energy into asking the universe for more wealth when I stuck the leaf in my wallet. I wasn't specific about how big the windfall should be or what kind of wealth I wanted or where it should show up. From what I've read, magic requires some minimal change-in-consciousness and an extremely specific, carefully worded goal in mind. All I did was think, 'Won't hurt to try.'"

"Wow. I mean this magic stuff isn't something to play with, is it? It's going to take concentration and clear thinking if we want to avoid trouble." Sheila's face was a study in doubt.

"Along with the disasters, things happened that caused all of us to get closer to other desires that we have. So how did that happen?" Kitsy thought about her plans to write a hotdog recipe book and the ingredient combinations she'd been brainstorming, like red curry, peanut, and lemon ginger sauce poured over a hot dog on a brioche bun.

"Maybe it's about being responsible," Fayette said. "This section in the Jar Spells book caught my attention. It says, '... *there is a corresponding but opposing reaction to every action. You always pay a price for casting spells. The energy you expend is part of that price ... For the spell to be effective, you must give something for the energy you are creating.*' After reading that, I was thinking that maybe if we learn to be conscientious about what we're doing, the payment required will reflect our good purpose and right action. If we're sloppy about magic, then the price is more random."

"And if we're purposefully irresponsible or even ask for something cruel, I mean if we do something to cause harm, the price might be high for us and damaging," Kitsy added.

"Yeah. We'd grow a wart on our nose," Sheila suggested, causing them all to laugh.

"Do we want to try it again, or is it too dangerous?" Kitsy left her question hanging.

Fayette squinted down at her jar spell book and opened it to the page titled *Jar Spell Recipes*. Kitsy smoothed out a page in her tea magic book devoted to a recipe for improved mental focus.

"I'm ready to try something small and really study how to do it right," Sheila said with a nervous cough. "I don't want to give up just yet. My catalytic converter may have been stolen, but it was a fair trade for spending time with Darwin. We're getting together for dinner again this week."

"Yes. Something small," Kitsy agreed, and Fayette nodded.

"Next time we meet it'll be at the café," Sheila reminded them. "If we can't really talk out loud about magic, we can bring a written description of what we learn and pass it around."

Fayette, still irritated at having to be so cautious, ended their meeting with suggestions garnished with sarcasm. "Out loud, you can tell us about your date with Darwin, Sheila. Kitsy can describe some of her new hotdog recipes, and I'll keep you educated about roller derby practice. Our talk will bore the bejezzus out of any Confess and Reform Church spies."

CHAPTER 5

Sheila tore through the long, thin, cardboard box with enthusiasm -- and a pair of kitchen shears.

A delighted "oooh" escaped her lips as the carboard fell away and revealed three, sturdy, bleached-ash brooms, size large. The brooms were from a broom-crafter in New Mexico, who bound together long, straight, creamy branches of sorghum broomcorn to make stiff but flexible broom heads. It was the ash-tree handle that attracted Sheila to them because she learned from one of her gardening books that in the British Isles, ash is associated with divination and knowledge. Celtic Druids saw the ash tree as sacred, connecting the inner self to outer worlds, and as a symbol of creativity. The brooms would be perfect for a strewing-herb-ritual that Sheila wanted to try, and she planned to give a broom to each of her book club friends as a tool for clearing unwanted energy from home and workspaces.

Sheila mumbled to herself as she cut the carboard into small pieces to put in her recycling box. "Controlled consciousness for focus; having a specific goal in mind; having a sincere desire for making it happen; increasing energy by reciting a chant, or drumming, or singing, or dancing; expecting the outcomes to happen, and then letting it go by not dwelling on it." She thought of the dinosaur disaster again. This next try at magic, she was determined to do it right.

After propping two of the brooms against the wall next to her front door, Sheila took the third broom, her own, into her greenhouse. Her sixteen-foot by twenty-five-foot glasshouse was her pride and joy, something she saved for, designed, and had built only six years before. It was the kind of indulgence she rarely allowed herself, but with her parents gone and no children, she decided she could afford to make one of her dreams come true.

White-washed wood framing was a key feature in her Victorian design, but the greenhouse included a partial, red-brick wall on all sides topped with tall, wood-framed, self-tinting windows and a high-peaked roof made mostly of glass that was held in place by white-washed wood frames. A white Stonington cupula with a copper crown supported a striking, black-raven weathervane in the center of the rooftop. The weathervane creaked on stormy days like the bearings of a rusty-garden wind ornament. Gable end doors in front and back opened to the outside of her glasshouse, and inside were long rows of cedar benches along the walls for potted plants and seedling trays. Growing season was done outdoors, so some pots were empty, but others supported winter vegetables, such as tomatoes, lettuces, and climbing beans, and between the vegetables were containers sustaining the roots of cool-weather flowers. Sheila kept her benches and floors as spotless as possible. She wanted her glasshouse to be a tranquil haven, and it was. The cares of the world seemed to dissolve into the soil as she put on her gardening apron and lost herself in the work of growing things.

Toward the back wall, Sheila created a space for focus and experimentation. This was the place where she planned to try a simple, new spell. As she hung her broom from a wall hook, Sheila's phone rang. Her heartbeat quickened just a tad as she said, "Hello,

Darwin. How are you today?"

"Excited for tonight," he said. "We still on for dinner at the bistro and a movie at the theater?"

"I'll be ready at 7 o'clock."

"Great."

"Where are you?" Sheila listened harder to the voices in the background at Darwin's end. "I can hear someone shouting."

"Oh, that. It's that Pastor Fisby Parkinson from the Elmira Confess and Reform Church. I'm walking past the city park, and he's on a soap box about the evils of magic. He claims he heard some women in town talking about casting spells. He's harping on about sorcery. The pastor is also demanding that people report to him if they hear anyone they know discussing magic."

"I see." Sheila felt the clamor of alarm bells in her head. She could hear shouted phrases behind Darwin's words such as "wicked women" and "demon conjurers," and she wondered what Darwin thought about people who experimented with magic. Would this whole project to learn about the mystical realms ruin her chances at a more personal friendship with Darwin?

As she said goodbye, a worrying sensation took charge of her belly. Before the phone call, she'd been delighted with the brooms and eager to try out her new spell. Now she was less sure. She decided to make a pot of tea and re-read a few of the more encouraging pages in her new magical gardening books.

By the time her tea break ended, Sheila knew what she could do to protect herself from negative energies. She found a white, emergency candle in her utility cupboard and set it on the table next to her. Taking a deep beath, she lit it and looked with purpose into the flame, visualizing the light from the candle as energy that cleansed, cleared, and protected her from negative brainwaves and destructive forces. It took several minutes, but as the candle flame steadied her thoughts,

Sheila felt able to trade fear for calmness. What right did pastor Fisby have to spoil her happiness in learning something new? She was being careful to hurt no one. She decided to go ahead with her plans for the greenhouse charm.

Retrieving her gardening clippers and gathering basket, Sheila strode to her patch of herbs near the back fence. As prescribed in her gardening magic book, she stopped to clear her head and focus on feelings of gratefulness and caring for all creatures and for the plants in her garden spaces. As the anger dissipated, she could even visualize sending thoughts of forgiveness toward Pastor Fisby.

When she felt ready, she knelt to better appreciate her patch of rosemary shrubs, and reading from a piece of paper saved in her jeans pocket, she ran her left hand through the cool sprigs. "Rosemary, rosemary, your job today is to help nurture love and peace." Sheila felt the soft needle-shaped leaves at the end of the shrub branches and cut some rosemary twigs. She closed her eyes to focus on the spicy green aroma. She couldn't help it. Rosmary always reminded her of roast beef with onions. Rising from the ground, she approached her two red cedar trees that stood tall near her front gate. Repeating the ritual, she harvested a hand-full of moist, firm cedar greens.

With a basket of fresh cedar and rosemary in hand, Sheila headed to the greenhouse. Was she really going through with it? Images of her defenseless car and its slashed seats flickered through her mind like slides in an old-fashioned slide show. What a disaster, but despite feelings of hesitancy, her legs took her to the back door, with its welcoming dried flower wreath, and into her favorite place in the entire world. Sheila turned to the back wall, where a ceramic bowl and other ingredients sat ready on her workbench. It was time to *get back in the saddle*, as the saying went, and try again.

In the bowl she stripped and then mixed the rosemary with shredded pieces of cedar, sprinkles of salt and pepper, and a few tablespoons of cinnamon. As a baker, Sheila should have known better than to stick her nose right above the mixture and try to breathe in the strong perfume. Her sinuses protested and she sneezed, but all-in-all she was pleased. The blend certainly smelled ready for the strewing spell, an invocation that came from her newest garden magic book. It was a rite to help freshen her workspace and break up negative energy. The ritual involved strewing the mixture on the floor of the greenhouse and saying words to help guide the cleansing energy.

"For love and peace. All negative energy, leave me be. Let me create in peace."

Sheila worked to visualize the herbs purifying and cleansing her greenhouse. Pastor Fisby's face kept invading her thoughts, so she pictured him as negative energy scrubbed with a cloth from her windows. In the morning, she would return with her new energy-clearing tool, her broom, and sweep up the herbs. She would bless the herbs for their good strength and strew them at the front gate to rest in peace.

Satisfied with her efforts, Sheila went into her house to find something pretty to wear for dinner.

* * *

In the meantime, Fayette sprawled herself in the bleachers above the roller-skating rink.

"You alright?" Marjorie called up from the edge of the rink, both hands cupped around her mouth to form a make-shift megaphone.

"I'm good," Fayette called back, motioning Marjorie to go ahead and skate without her. In truth, she had wrenched a knee, and her leg muscles complained with the pain of over exertion, but as her speed-skating-adrenalin-high ebbed and slowed, Fayette felt the kind of satisfaction that only older people can understand. It came from the knowledge that, indeed, they were still capable of doing something others said they shouldn't. After an hour workout with the Atomic Energy Elmira Women's Roller Derby Team, Fayette could honestly say, "I wasn't half bad."

While she rested, the team on the rink continued to block and jam nonstop. For Fayette, it was enough just to sit and listen to the swish and rumble of skates on hardwood maple flooring, the wheels rolling all the faster with the best quality speed bearings money could buy. She closed her eyes to savor the moment. It was a fleeting moment because the cries of tiny mewing creatures brought her out of her reverie. Beings that mewed in a skating rink? Where was the sound coming from? Her eyes searched in the direction of pint-sized whimpers and wails, and she spied an abandoned cardboard box tucked between bleacher seats three rows down. Groaning with the effort, Fayette made her way to the box, her knee protesting every unsteady limp. She peered inside, and three sets of kitten eyes met hers. A wrinkled note explained all. "Kittens headed for the pound. Please help."

Fayette could imagine adopting one cat, but not three. She reached in to stroke their silky fur, and her warm hand seemed to calm the babies. The little black tuxedo kitten licked one side of her hand while the orange-striped tabby rubbed against the other side. The tubby little calico simply looked up with solemn green eyes.

"Well, I'm not going to just leave you youngsters to fend for yourselves," Fayette mumbled. "But you'll have to ride inside my backpack so I can get you home on my bike. The ride might be scary." Feeling disconcerted, she realized she'd called her house their home. And then she got an idea. It was a risky idea. Maybe a devilish idea. Would her book group friends ever forgive her? How would they react if next time they met in the café, Fayette gave Sheila and Kitsy a kitten?

She'd show them the chapter on animals in her *Magical Household* book. After all, didn't people who use magic have familiars, animal friends? And weren't cats often the familiar of choice for most witches? She'd show Kitsy and Sheila the page that explained how pets served as mediators between magic and the forces of nature. The magic practitioner and the familiar could sometimes form close bonds that helped strengthen magical energy. Surely, Sheila and Kitsy would see the importance of adopting the kittens. She'd be doing them a favor. She reached into the box, gently lifted the black and white kitten's left front paw and shook it as if finalizing an agreement. In Fayette's mind the matter was settled.

Fayette looked at the calico and remembered sentences from the book section on cats.

"A cat of three colors is exceptionally lucky and protects a house from harm."

The little black cat turned its face up to hers.

"A black-nosed cat brings wealth to its familiars."

The orange-striped kitten curled itself in a ball next to Fayette's dangling fingers.

"Orange or tabby cats are especially preferred by witches."

Smitten, she turned over the note in the box and wrote, *'Took kittens. Will find them good homes.'*

As Fayette located safe places in her backpack for the wiggling babies, she decided that the calico would go to Sheila, the orange tabby to Kitsy, and that she would keep the black tuxedo. The day before, Fayette got busy with a bit of experimental magic, making spell bottles for protection and positivity. She could sweeten the gift of kittens by giving the bottles to her friends.

Having gathered her coat, gloves, and helmet, Fayette

climbed the handicap ramp to the front entrance one limping footstep at a time, a pack full of wiggling kittens on her back.

***

A few streets down from Fayette's house, Kitsy studied her book on tea magic. For the book group ladies, she chose a recipe to enhance strength, courage, determination, and patience. To practice her magic, she decided to make a new scarf for herself, this time paying careful attention to her focus and intention. In her book on sewing magic, she researched things that could go wrong with spells. It mattered how the spell maker felt while she sewed. Being in the right frame of mind was important because being impatient, grumpy or uncentered could cause the intention of the spell-casting energy to change. The magic could sputter and fail. It could backfire, picking up negative emotions from the scarf maker, feelings of annoyance or impatience, or unsettled memories of getting stuck in rose thorns.

Kitsy arranged pin after pin along one of the seams for stitching, her mind so engrossed she was only half aware her husband entered her workspace. "Hey. It's a nice day outside. Maybe you want to get out of the house and see the sun, take a walk?" Hands in his wool jacket pocket, Samuel looked hopeful.

Kitsy thought to herself, *He seems to think I need exercise. I wonder why he doesn't mind his own business.* Realizing what she'd done, she stopped her pinning and recentered her energy. A walk would do her good. A break would help inspire a refreshed sense of positivity to her craft, and Samuel wanted to spend some time with her. What could be nicer than that?

"Let's go to the park," she said, smiling up at her life partner. A meander in the city park, with its beautiful fall colors, darting squirrels, and romping children almost always improved her mood. They grabbed coats and hats and strolled down the sidewalk hand in hand.

But it was at the park that Kitsy witnessed in person what Sheila heard in the background of Darwin's phone call. Pastor Fisby's words echoed around her from loudspeakers mounted on her special bench, the very bench she spent many happy afternoons reading quotes by Rumi or snippets from *A Course In Miracles*. Kitsy moved closer to Samuel as the pastor's denunciations triggered waves of judgment in her heart and mind. She judged the pastor for ruining her afternoon. His snarly voice and accusations darkened her spirits until the park seemed stark and unfriendly. "Find them!" Fisby yelled from the park podium. "Those who even dare to carry charms and talismans, point them out. Report them. They bring illness, discord, darkness. Those who try and manipulate the supernatural, cast them out of our town. They are traitors to hard-working, decent, American families."

Samuel laughed at the pastor's words. "What a crackpot, that man. I didn't know people like him still existed."

Kitsy slipped her arm under Samuel's. His amusement and easy sensibility melted the darkness Kitsy felt around her. Together they walked from the park to the ice cream shop down Main Street, near the Forever Reading Bookstore and the Masonic Lodge.

"Ice cream is magic." Kitsy licked her snickerdoodle-cookie scoop, balanced on top of a waffle cone. "Ice cream makes the world seem safe again."

Kitsy didn't try to finish her scarf or create a tea blend for her friends that day. She wanted to prevent any of Pastor Fisby's negativity from leaking into her intentions while she practiced even the smallest magical enchantments. Instead, she was eager to find ingredients for her tea spell at the local shops, and she visited the Forever Reading Bookstore for three special purchases.

Lars Columbus led her to the diary and writing tools section of his store and showed her his collection of vintage journals. Kitsy chose three blank books, each a distinct color, and each containing deckle-edged, handmade, cotton paper between soft, leather covers.

"Looks like you're planning to write up a storm," Lars teased.

"Yes. Me and two of my friends." Kitsy smiled at the storekeeper's attempt at a joke.

Encouraged, she returned home with her tea ingredients and her gifts. The author of her tea magic compendium suggested that everyone learning and practicing magic needed a grimoire, a regular notebook to write recipes and spells. It was in a grimoire that magic practitioners could keep track of formulas they tried and word combinations with which they experimented. A grimoire was a record of what worked and what went wrong. It was like a diary of progress made. The journals would be the book club ladies' grimoires, Kitsy decided.

CHAPTER 6

Sheila woke with a feeling that all was right with the world. Her dinner with Darwin had been as perfect as a date could be. The two decided to go out for a meal and a movie every Sunday night. And it was Monday, the day she met Kitsy and Fayette at the bakery. First things first, though. Sheila would finish her strewing spell. She would take her new broom, or besom, and sweep up the herbs and other ingredients left overnight on her greenhouse floor.

Excited to finish her new ritual, Sheila swallowed down a piece of buttered toast and gulped half a cup of strong coffee. The morning sun shone through low, pink, and violet clouds. *Red sky in the morning, sailors take warning*, Sheila thought, heading to the back door of her greenhouse. She lifted the ash besom from its wall hook and took hold of its handle. The wood felt warm and solid in her hands. As she swept the herbs into little piles, she sang a morning song she'd learned from her mother, adding her own phrases with words that blessed the greenhouse and the work she would do between its doors. It was a charmed start to the day.

In no time she poured the herbs and grains of salt into a small bucket using the dustpan, and she was ready to re-strew them at her front gate. With a happy flourish, Sheila opened the greenhouse door -- the door that led to the yard and gate.

At first, she didn't notice the still, twisted figure in black laying facedown near the bench that separated the walkway from the strawberry bed.

"Oh, la," Sheila choked out when she nearly tripped over the prone man in a long, wool coat. Where had those words come from? Until recently, she rarely said "Oh, la." That was something her mother used to say when something was funny or wrong.

Kneeling next to the body, Sheila dialed 911 as she checked Pastor Fisby Parkinson's wrist for a pulse. He had one. The man was still alive.

"I need help," she told the dispatcher. "There's an unconscious man in my yard."

The pastor's long, white fingers curled into the grass as though holding on for dear life. Sheila could see a band of skin around his right thumb that was two degrees whiter than the rest of him. A gold ring had covered that band of skin when Pastor Fisby confronted the book group ladies at the café a week ago. Today the ring was gone. She remembered its polished amber stone and smaller red stones set inside a hexagon engraving.

How long had the man been laying in her yard? She felt the coat. It was damp with dew, like the grass. Even though Pastor Fisby was silent and unmoving, Sheila felt a deep uneasiness being alone with him. She'd seen him make shambles out of the lives of people he decided were ungodly, much as religious fanatics in India inflicted turmoil in her parents' lives before they came to North America. He would try to destroy her life if he knew about her simple experiment in the greenhouse, and it was such a little thing. Sweeping herbs and singing for protection and good energy had made Sheila happy, and for those minutes with her handmade ash broom, she was secure and confident, emotions she had trouble feeling for most of her life.

Tears of relief filled her eyes when the emergency

vehicles drove up and parked along the sidewalk at the front of her house. With growing apprehension, Sheila watched as EMT's lifted the limp body onto an ambulance cot stretcher. The pastor's black tactical boots stuck out from the end of a blanket, hostile, like a set of binoculars focused on her.

"What happened?" an EMT asked.

"I don't know. I don't know why he is in my yard. I don't even know the man."

Feeling somehow responsible, Sheila followed the ambulance to Elmira Regional Hospital. After two hours and 45 minutes in the waiting room, a hospital attendant relented and told her that the hospital admitted Mr. Parkinson as a patient, that he was in a coma, and that doctors could not determine the cause. There were no bruises or other wounds on his body.

"We're running toxicology tests, but that will take some time. If we find the man's been poisoned, I'm sure the police will want to ask questions. Since you aren't a close relative, we can't allow you to visit the patient. There's nothing you can do. You might as well go home," the attendant said.

Sheila had just enough time to retrieve the bleached-ash brooms before meeting Fayette and Kitsy at the café for their weekly blue pot special. What would people in the café think if she brought in brooms as gifts? It was almost All Hallows' Eve, she reasoned. People everywhere were putting together costumes. Brooms were common Halloween props.

"Never mind about what people think about the brooms," Kitsy said once Sheila settled herself at their corner Café table, a bear claw pastry in hand. "What are people going to think when they find out that you discovered Pastor Fisby Parkinson comatose in your yard in front of your greenhouse?"

"Well, it just makes me mad. No one invited him to my home. He was trespassing. I haven't a clue what he was doing in my yard or why he lost consciousness. He certainly wasn't there when Darwin brought me home from our date at 11 o'clock last night."

"It's good to see you mad instead of scared," Kitsy said in a softer tone. "You're going to need some of that inner fire when the gossip spreads and people come up with all kinds of stories about you and Pastor Parkinson."

"I'm not saying I'm not afraid. I'm scared of Pastor Parkinson and the police, and I'm worried about what Darwin is going to think," Sheila admitted. "What if the whole thing turns out to be my fault?"

"I'm not sure what you mean."

"Well, what if the tiny spell I did yesterday caused injury to the pastor?"

"Nah. How could that be?"

Sheila described the strewing spell and her work to freshen her workspace and bring harmony and goodwill to the greenhouse, to break up negative energy.

"As I strewed the herbs, I said, 'For love and peace. All negative energy, leave me be. Let me work in peace.'"

"What's wrong with that?" Kitsy asked.

"It's just that I visualized the pastor as negative energy that I was cleansing from my thoughts and workspace. What if he tried to get into the greenhouse and my strewing spell caused him to get hurt?"

Kitsy laughed. "That would have to be some powerful magic. And it didn't work, anyway. The spell certainly did not cleanse the pastor from your thoughts. If nothing else, this incident put him more firmly in your head than he was before."

"Also,' said a voice behind them, "even if your spell somehow kept him out of the greenhouse, which I very much doubt, he didn't belong there in the first place. What was he doing on your property in the middle of the night? It's not your fault Pastor Fisby Parkinson invited himself to your yard," Fayette said. Kitsy and Sheila were so intent on talking that they hadn't seen her approach the table and listen with growing disquiet to their theories and guesswork.

They watched, curious, as Fayette settled two soft carriers on the table, removed a heavy backpack from her shoulders, and, with a groan, landed herself in a café chair.

"You look like I feel," Sheila told Fayette. "And I feel like I climbed over rubbly, sharp lava rocks for hours, lost in a lava bed with no landmarks in sight."

"That's very specific." Kitsy laughed at Sheila's description. "Did that really happened to you?"

"Once," Sheila admitted. "What about it, Fayette? You look stiff as a broomstick."

"Roller derby. My muscles have gone flat." With a pained expression, Fayette bent toward the table far enough for her arm to reach her jeans back pocket. She pulled out some papers and handed one to Kitsy and one to Sheila. The title of each paper read, *The Importance of Animals – Especially Cats - as Pets and Familiars in the Magical World.*

"Read," Fayette instructed.

Halfway through Fayette's treatise on why practitioners needed feline familiars, Kitsy heard a muffled wail and saw one of the carriers wobble.

"Orange cats are much loved by magic makers," Fayette said, nodding toward the carrier. "She's yours, Kitsy."

Fayette aimed her chin at Sheila and then to the second carrier. "Calicos protect our homes, and they bring luck. If anyone needs the little miss inside this carrier, it's you."

To Fayette's relief, the wide-eyed kittens so charmed the ladies that they forgot to protest. Her pack was extra heavy because she spent a fortune buying basic necessities for the babies. That way, she reasoned,

Sheila and Kitsy couldn't make excuses about not having supplies to take care of the fuzzy beasts. She needn't have worried. For several minutes, the three women forgot trespassing pastors, sore muscles, mismanaged magical experiments, errant rose bushes, broken HVACs, and stolen catalytic converters. In an instant they were in love with the squirming, purring kit cats.

"I don't know what Samuel's going to say, and I can't very well show him your research paper on familiars to explain why I said yes to this little gold-striped cherub, but there's no way I'm going to let her go now." Kitsy kissed the top of her new kitten's head while the little girl's paw grabbed at Kitsy's earring.

As Sheila and Kitsy returned the cats to their carriers, two uniformed officers approached their table.

"Sheila Fairlight?" The tall, redheaded officer looked between the three women.

"That's me," Sheila said, her voice thin and shaky.

"Ms. Fairlight," the curly-haired officer said, "You need to come to the station with us. We have questions about the assault on Pastor Fisby Parkinson."

"Assault?" all three women asked at the same time.

"Assault using deadly poison." The red-haired officer gestured for Sheila to follow them out the door.

"Poison derived from a plant we found in your garden," his curly-haired partner said.

Sheila got up, her motions careful and deliberate, using the table to guide herself toward the officers.

"We'll gather your things and take care of your new kitty." Kitsy was wide-eyed with worry.

"Then we'll come to the police station and wait for you." The entire circumference of Fayette's broad face looked pinched in irritation; if eyes could be weapons, hers would have directed a barrage of missile aerial fireworks toward the police officers. Fayette whispered something in Sheila's ear as she passed, causing the retired church secretary to smile for a brief second. She clasped Fayette's hand.

"Okay, okay," said redheaded cop. "Let's get this over with. Do you know which poisonous plant we found in your garden?"

"Poppy seeds?" Sheila guessed in a small voice. "Rhododendrons, chrysanthemum, lilies, elderberry?"

"Good, Lord, lady," curly-haired cop said. "How many poisonous plants do you grow?"

Fayette lifted her shoulders with impatience. "Think about it. Do some research, kid. Most plants, especially ornamentals, contain toxins."

"The one we're concerned with is called *Abrus precatorius*, according to the toxicology lab at the hospital." Redheaded cop consulted his notebook. "It's also called the rosary pea plant because some people make rosary beads out of the red seeds."

"Ms. Fairlight has two *Abrus precatorius* vines climbing up an arbor near her greenhouse," curly-haired cop added.

Kitsy cut in. "Did Pastor Parkinson come out of his coma? Did he say something about Sheila that makes you think she had something to do with his collapse?"

"He's still unconscious," redheaded cop said. "But Pastor Parkinson was discovered on Ms. Fairlight's property. That automatically makes her a person of interest. And, since the poison that made him sick grows near where he collapsed, well, that makes her even more suspicious."

"Look, guys." Fayette's tone was at first low and tense, but she attempted a friendlier, higher pitched appeal. "I suggest we order a blue-pot special and a cookie plate. Let's just sit around the table and go over this thing. You don't really have any evidence that points directly to Sheila, so why not do a preliminary interview right here where it's comfortable, and we can all help with ideas."

"Nice try," said curly-headed cop. "Nope. We go by the book, especially when it comes to something this serious. We need to interview Ms. Fairlight in an official capacity. We're not arresting her, unless she confesses, but we need her statement on record."

Chapter 7

The whole café watched the officers usher Sheila out the front door and into the police cruiser. None other than Darnelle Shipman, head of the Confess and Reform Women's Guild, observed the scene with the keenest of interest. "Those two friends of that Sheila woman are in on it too, I'm just sure." Darnelle's mutter to her tea-table companion carried to the quieter tables in the café. "Pastor Parkinson thinks they're practicing black magic. He said he was going to do something about it. Maybe that's why they poisoned him."

Fayette heard Darnelle's accusation and marched up to the woman. She pointed her first and second right hand fingers at her own eyes and then turned the fingers around to aim them at Darnelle. Then Fayette looked at both women and let out a throaty, "BOOO!"

Cackling, Fayette left Darnelle choking on tea that went down the wrong way. Her church companion's aghast expression seemed caked on her puffy face like clown makeup.

Returning to her own table, Fayette found Kitsy gathering their things. She handed Sheila's broom gift to Fayette and grabbed hold of her own ash-wood broom stick. Sheila had yet to tell them about the brooms and their purpose. With a painful heave, Fayette hoisted her pack on her shoulders and took hold of Sheila's cat carrier. Her own jar-spell gifts would have to wait.

"Let's put most of this stuff in the SUV. There's not a lot of room on your Harley." Kitsy was all business. "We need to present a uniformed front when we're at the police station for Sheila's sake. No messing around."

"Buggeration. Are you trying to tell me you didn't like my stunt with those shrill, rumor-mongering hypocrites over there?" Fayette turned her head toward Darnelle's table and spoke loud enough for the women to hear. Sometimes Kitsy had no sense of humor. Messing around, indeed.

The police station was across town. Kitsy in her SUV followed Fayette on her bike. They passed the streets leading to their own homes, the park, and the Confess and Reform Church, and they were about to pass the church rectory when Fayette took a sudden right turn and parked in the rectory driveway. Taken by surprise, Kitsy put on her brakes, pulled in behind Fayette, and opened her driver's side door.

"I'm just going to look in a few windows." Fayette's lips slid into a sly grin that forewarned mischief. "If the cops try and pin the pastor's coma on Sheila, then we need to find out what really happened to him. Maybe there are clues here at his house."

Kitsy sighed. "Fisby shouldn't have been trespassing in Sheila's yard, and we shouldn't be trespassing here, either." While Kitsy often admired Fayette's can-do attitude, flouting laws felt ill-disciplined, even wrong. Kitsy spent too many years teaching children to follow rules to feel comfortable about breaking them herself.

"I won't be long." Fayette motioned for Kitsy to back out of the driveway. "You can go on ahead, and I'll catch up."

Instead, Kitsy groaned, unfastened her seatbelt, and climbed out of her vehicle. "Let's get this over with. I'll take the back windows. You take the front."

They trudged up the walk to the house, a steel-gray

structure with white trimmed windows and a gable roof that needed de-mossing. Kitsy continued between the house and the garage through a covered walkway and on to the back. She surveyed the backyard, surprised to find a poorly-tended herb garden. The windows, she was relieved to see, were too high to reach, but the back door was another matter. It hung wide open. She climbed the back steps and peered into the house, knocking on the door frame in case someone was inside. Everything stayed quiet and still; not even a breeze rustled the garden plants and trees.

Fayette poked her tousle-haired head around the house corner. "See anything?"

"Can't see in, except the back door is open. It leads into the kitchen."

"Oh ho. That's not good. We'd better make sure it's closed and locked. Come to think of it, if we're being responsible, we'd better check inside to make sure everything is okay, you know, that a raccoon family hasn't moved in or that intruders or burglars haven't ransacked the place. It's the neighborly thing to do."

"I don't think …." Kitsy started to say, but she was too late. Fayette was up the steps and shouldering through the door and into the kitchen before Kitsy could say a word of protest. "Grrrrrrr," Kitsy complained to herself. She was set on staying outside as a lookout until Fayette called out, "Whoa. You gotta see this."

"Where are you?" Kitsy ventured one reluctant step after another through the kitchen, which smelled of stale liver and onions, and into a dark hallway, but she had no idea where Fayette had gone.

"In here," her book group buddy called from the first doorway to Kitsy's left as the hallway made a right turn.

Here turned out to be a kind of study. In the dim light, Kitsy could see the trappings of a workshop at one end. On a long metal table sat a collection of glass bowls filled with an array of beads made of plant seeds. Kitsy knew they were beads because some of them were strung on what looked to be six-pound fishing line. One bowl of beads in particular caught Kitsy's attention. The beads were a bright red, the size and color of lady bugs, and each bead bore one black dot. Someone, probably Pastor Parkinson, used the tiny drill bits on the table to pierce holes in the seeds, turning them into beads.

The workshop table was of little interest to Fayette. She motioned Kitsy to a corner near the curtained window, pointing out a rotating bookshelf and an open cupboard set over a rectangular table covered with a long, deep-purple, velvet cloth.

"What is it?" Kitsy whispered.

"Well, if my research into magic is accurate, what we've got here is an altar, and I don't mean a church altar. This is an occult altar. Take a look at the books on the other side of this bookshelf."

Fayette rotated the bookshelf, which pulled out of the wall and spun like a tall Lazy Susan. On one side were shelves of books on Christian philosophy. On the other side, the book titles referred to topics connected with magic and the paranormal. Newer looking books about helpful magic or high magic filled the upper shelves, such as *The White Magick Spell Book* by Didi Clarke, or *Backyard Witchcraft* by Cecilia Latarri and Betti Greco. For some reason, when an author's name was female, it was crossed out on the book spines with big red X's. An older collection of thick, leather-covered, and hard-backed tomes dominated the bottom shelves, ancient-looking volumes with dog-eared corners. The authors were mostly male. Their titles, such as *The Key of Hell* by Cyprianus, or *The Book of Black Magic* by Arthur Edward Waite, gave Kitsy a tight feeling in her throat because, even with her limited knowledge, these books seemed dedicated to harmful magic. Kitsy reached out to touch a pamphlet-sized book titled *The Book of Forbidden Knowledge*. With a shriek she pulled back and held her newly injured right hand in her left, examining her fingers and palm. She could see red burns transform into tiny, throbbing, blistery welts.

"Holy crap," Fayette said, as she eyed the burns. "Maybe you better go to the kitchen and run some cold water over that hand." She yanked her iPhone from a jeans' back pocket and got busy taking pictures of the books, the altar, and the workshop, while Kitsy, in pain, stood rooted to the spot. What did it all mean?

And then they heard them, footsteps in the hallway.

"Quick. Under the altar." Fayette pulled at Kitsy's corduroy jacket sleeve, managing to guide her down and under the altar cloth.

"Whoever it is knows someone is here," Kitsy whispered. "My SUV and your motorcycle are in the driveway."

"Shhhhh." The booted footsteps were close now, hesitating at the entry to the workshop room. From Fayette and Kitsy's limited point of view, the owner of the booted footsteps lingered at the doorway for an eternity. Kitsy's hand ached and her thigh muscles seared in their crouched position. Just when she thought she could bear it no longer, preparing herself to switch positions, the footsteps started up again, moving down the hall toward rooms that neither Kitsy nor Fayette inspected and never would, if Kitsy had her way.

They stayed under the altar cloth until they heard the back door close, at which point Fayette was out from under the altar in a flash. "I'm going to the front window to see who that was," she announced. Now it was Fayette's footsteps that Kitsy heard tromping on the wood flooring toward the front of the house and the big picture window near the main entrance door.

Crawling in slow motion from under the table, Kitsy used her left hand to grab the side of the altar table and pull herself to a standing position. She let out a frustrated groan, wanting to dash for the back door and her car and find relief for her throbbing hand, but instead, took her iPhone from her shoulder bag to take her own set of pictures. A book that burned people? What else was going on here? Curiosity spurred Kitsy to point her camera lens at everything in the room, including the tools, bowls of beads, and drills at the workshop table. She focused in on the cabinet above the altar, which contained candle sticks, a silver cross and stand, mortar and pestle sets, bottles with stoppers, jars full of unidentifiable substances, and a few sprigs of dried herbs. When she could think of no more picture possibilities, Kitsy stood in front of the rotating bookshelves and eyed the book that burned her. She felt a strong yearning to reach for it again, but that would be like playing with a black widow spider, an absurd, asinine thing to do.

From the corner of her right eye, she spied a pair of gloves on a bookshelf hook. Could she use gloves to handle *The Book of Forbidden Knowledge*? The gloves were a soft metallic green, the same color as the title of the book, and covered with scales - almost more lizard-like than alligator skin. With her left hand she put a glove on her right hand. The glove felt silky and cool on her skin, and, to her surprise, the ache of her burn subsided. Without the pain reminding her of danger, reaching for the book seemed logical rather than reckless. So, Kitsy, whose whole life had been about taking care, following institutional rules, and doing what was right, took hold of the thin black book with its harsh, dark, metallic-green title.

The Book of Forbidden Knowledge, by Johnson Smith & co, slid with ease from the shelf, but it was too slippery to hold with one hand, and Kitsy dropped it onto the altar. She would need two hands to grip the wily piece of literature. As she slid on the second glove, Kitsy heard Fayette's returning footsteps. For reasons she failed to question or consider, Kitsy used both gloved hands to tuck the book into her bag. She pulled off the gloves and stuffed them into her jacket pockets. A thought flitted through her brain that unnerved her. *Not only are you a trespasser, snooping in someone's house while they suffer sick in the hospital, but you are also a thief.*

"You will never guess who the intruder was." Fayette's voice was breathless, excited.

"Who was it?" Kitsy felt dizzy with the awareness that she and Fayette were intruders, too.

"It was that Lars Columbus. You know, that odd fellow who owns the Forever Reading Bookstore next to the Masonic Lodge. I watched him climb into an old, green, Chevy pickup parked on the street in front of this house. But he inspected your SUV and my bike thoroughly. He took a pen and pad out of his pocket and wrote something down before he left. I'm thinking it was our vehicle license numbers. Still, I took pictures of him getting into his pickup and got some shots of his truck license number."

"Let's get out of here," Kitsy begged, taking two steps toward the hallway leading to the back door.

"Yeah. Let's. First, I'll put things back the way we found them, and we'll skedaddle. We better take care of your burn, and Sheila may be needing our support right now at the police station."

As Fayette slid the bookshelf back into the wall with the Christian theology books facing outside, Kitsy looked at the palm of her injured hand. She could see no redness and feel no pain. The burn was gone.

If Fayette noticed a new lump in the bag that hung from Kitsy's shoulder, she didn't say anything. They tidied, wiped for possible fingerprints, and then closed the back door behind them as they surfaced from the shadowy house into the sunny, albeit cold backyard. Fayette took off with a roar on her hog, and Kitsy started the engine of her SUV, taking one last look at the house. When she first parked in the driveway, she had been a good citizen, having never even received a speeding ticket. Inside that house everything changed. She left the driveway a criminal. How could she help Sheila when she could no longer even look the police in the eye without wanting to confess? The tiny cries of the new kittens in their carriers intensified for Kitsy the calamity of the moment.

***

Elmira's police station was housed in a white-washed, renovated, 1960s gas station, which worked well because Javier Castillo, police chief and new father of twins, not only ran law enforcement operations, but was responsible for installing new brake shoes, overseeing oil changes, and engineering other kinds of police car maintenance. Everyone who worked for the city, population 3,632, wore a variety of job-responsibility hats, so the chief's mantra, which he said at least five times each day, was, "I don't have time for baloney or gibberish. Just take care of it."

The police department office manager, Andrea Strichter, was also the town water meter reader. The two police officers, curlyhead and redhead, shared duty with the night officer, who ended his shift by collecting garbage in a slew of Elmira neighborhoods. Elmira's dispatchers served as public information officers, as well as cashiers for city water bills and dog licenses.

"Be with you in a minute," said Andrea without looking up from her computer as Fayette and Kitsy entered the station. They stood side by side at the counter that separated the tiny waiting area from the hectic mechanisms of Elmira city government. Fayette brushed arms with Kitsy and then stood close enough to sustain the contact. Yes, indeed, Kitsy was trembling.

"Snap out of it," Fayette commanded in a hissing

whisper. "Sheila needs our support."

To Fayette's relief, a spark of anger flashed in Kitsy's eyes. "I didn't sign up for this, breaking into people's houses, almost getting caught." She scowled and folded her arms across her chest.

"Nobody did," Fayette shot back. "Yeah. We had a scare back there, but we also learned some stuff that might help Sheila."

Both women stayed quiet after that. Sitting across from one another over tea, talking about authors and plots, was one thing, Kitsy thought. Sure, they had different opinions about the books they read, but they'd never really argued before. She and Sheila both knew that Fayette was more adventurous than they were, but Kitsy in no way anticipated taking unlawful risks with the woman.

Never again, she thought to herself. And then a little voice in her head reminded her that Fayette had nothing to do with the theft of the book. That was all on her, Kitsy Browning, retired schoolteacher, and mother of two. Before coming into the police station, she'd left the stolen book in her bag and her bag in the SUV under a pile of newspapers tied together for recycling. The burn on her hand healed. She still couldn't comprehend how, but the book was dangerous, and what if it heated up and lit that pile of newspapers on fire? Kitsy shook herself. Fayette's words repeated in her thoughts. *Snap out of it.*

Meanwhile, in a corner of a back office, one door away from where Kitsy and Fayette waited, Sheila sat in a scuffed and scratched, solid oak, swivel bankers chair, likely part of the office furniture sixty-five years ago when the gas station was new. She'd answered as thoroughly as she could all redhead's and curlyhead's questions about finding Fisby on her lawn, only leaving out the bit about the sweeping spell.

The officers were courteous enough, just youngsters

from Sheila's 67-year-old perspective. When curlyhead spilled his coffee, speckling little brown dots over a pile of paperwork, he tried to salvage the papers using an old sweatshirt he grabbed from a mound of dirty laundry under his desk. When redhead blushed after getting a phone call, and curlyhead teased him for liking a girl, Sheila realized the two were still finding their way in life between boyhood and adulthood. She started asking them questions about their work and their hopes for the future. Before she knew it, the two poured out their life stories as though she was a favorite aunt, their tough-guy, police-officer brashness forgotten for the moment. Sheila discovered that redhead's name was Bruce and curlyhead's name was Noah.

"Yeah. We sort of knew about each other in high school," Bruce said, "but we really got to know each other at the academy. And then we took entry-level jobs here. We work together almost every day. No one knows more about me than Noah, not even my own mother."

"And it's good to have a work buddy like Bruce," Noah said. "In a small town like Elmira, people are suspicious of strangers, especially law enforcement strangers. They think they've got to be careful about what they say around us, so we don't get asked to parties, or to go deer hunting, or fishing, or much of anything."

"We can't find girls who will even consider trying us out," Bruce added.

The office door opened, and the police chief strode over to the interrogation corner. "What have you got?" Javier Castillo demanded of his deputies. "Are we ready for an arrest?"

Both deputies jumped to their feet. "No sir," Noah said. "We've got nothing to show for certain that Sheila Fairlight poisoned Fisby Parkinson or even knew the man."

"Then what the H. E. double L was he doing in your

yard, ma'am?" Castillo was almost shouting. "We found *Abrus precatorius* seeds in his pocket. Highly poisonous seeds, I might add, and they appear to have been harvested from your vines. Can you explain that Ms. Fairlight?"

"I just don't know." Sheila rolled her bankers chair a foot-length away from the chief whose black combat boots were only inches from her fur-lined Doc Martens. "I've never paid much attention to the seeds that come from those vines. They're a pretty red color. They fall to the ground and get absorbed into the soil like most leaves and seeds in my yard. As for Pastor Parkinson, I only know *of* the man. When I was the Lutheran church secretary, I remember him marching into our office, and I recall him having the audacity to tell Father Reynolds that his sermons about marriage equality were blasphemous, but I never had a personal conversation with him. I don't know why he was in my yard in the middle of the night, but to tell you the truth, it's creepy. Why was he there without my permission? I think he might have been stealing those seeds."

"I think you don't like the man, Ms. Fairlight." The chief's eyebrows rose past the brim of his Stetson-style, sage-green sheriff's hat. "Why is that?"

In that moment, Andrea the desk manager poked her head inside the office door and called, "Chief, your wife is on the line. The twins are both howling and fussy. She's ready to bring them to the station and leave them if you don't stop what you're doing and get over there, like you promised. You said you'd go home and give her a break. Sir, we don't need crying babies at headquarters."

The expression on Chief Javier's face changed from bad cop annoyance to baby daddy resignation.

"What do you want us to do?" Noah fumbled for the paperwork on Sheila.

"I don't have time for baloney or gibberish," Chief

Castillo shot back. "Just take care of it. As for you, Ms. Fairlight, don't think this is over." The chief turned his back to Sheila and strode across the room toward the exit door to the back parking lot. "Don't leave town, and consider getting yourself a lawyer. You are suspect number one in this assault. If the pastor dies instead of coming out of his coma, the charge will be murder. Even if the pastor comes out of this okay, I'm thinking of upping the charge from assault to attempted murder."

For emphasis, the chief slammed the back door as he headed toward his pickup.

Sheila sat frozen. How had this happened? Was she so useless at magic that something horrible transpired every time she tried to use it?

"Don't worry, ma'am," Noah said. "He's been like this ever since his twins started teething. He's sleep deprived. Bruce and I don't consider you our number one suspect. The trouble is, we don't have another suspect."

"Yeah. You're free to leave," Bruce told her, stuffing his interview notes into a dog-eared folder. "If we have more questions, we'll arrange an official visit."

Sheila rose from the chair and clasped the hands of each young man. "Thank you, fellas. And you're going to be fine. It'll take time, but you're bound to fit well into this little community. I predict by this time next year you will both have steady girlfriends, and you will be hosting your own get-togethers. Based on how you treated me this afternoon, you two know how to make personal connections with the residents, and that's important in small towns. People want to be able to know and trust their police out here in the country."

Bruce ushered Sheila to the front office where Fayette and Kitsy sat in silence, not looking at each other.

In the parking area, Kitsy opened her arms. "Come here and get a hug." She wrapped supportive arms around Sheila, and Fayette patted Sheila on the shoulder.

"The chief considers me their number one suspect. Why oh why did I ever start messing around with spell casting." Sheila let Kitsy lead her toward her SUV. "I might be charged with attempted murder, at the very least."

"I tell you what," Fayette said, "let's get your kittens into safe places at your homes and then re-start our meeting at the café. I want to hear everything and maybe decide a plan of action, but our furry friends must be way done with being cooped in carriers."

"Yes, lets," Kitsy agreed. "It's only twelve thirty, and I have something to give both of you. Let's meet at the café in an hour."

As Kitsy tucked Sheila into the passenger seat of her SUV, she wondered how Fayette managed to transport two cat carriers on a motorcycle. The babies yowled non-stop in the back of her vehicle. They needed attention. Kitsy averted her gaze from the pile of newspapers and what was underneath, relieved to note there was no smell of burning paper.

"I'll pick you up again at 1:15," Kitsy told Sheila once they pulled up in front of Sheila's house. From under the hatchback, Kitsy lifted Sheila's calico kitten in its carrier and the bag of kitten supplies. "Your car's still waiting where you left it this morning, so you can drive it home when we're done at the café."

Sliding back into the driver's seat, Kitsy called back to her own kitten. "We'll get you out of there in a jiff, little one. I'm taking you home." True to her word, almost as soon as she brought the kitten into the house, Kitsy made room in a craft closet, fashioning a bed for her orange striped bundle of energy. Using the supplies Fayette gathered, she put out food and water, and she positioned a litter box in one corner. Her tabby nibbled her fingers, pounced on a stuffed mouse toy, and, in a loud voice, demanded Kitsy pay attention.

"Hmmm. You remind me of a jar of orange

marmalade," Kitsy told her tiny girl, scratching the baby between her ears. "So that's your name, Marmalade. But I'm going to call you Marmy. Now, make yourself comfy and go to sleep, and I'll be back later to play."

A few streets over, Fayette's tuxedo boy, Max, already had the run of her house. Once she dropped her pack at the front door and hung up her helmet, she found the black and white whirlwind at the top of her living room drapes.

As for Sheila, her orange, white and black calico became Patches in a matter of minutes. While fussing to create a safe space in her guestroom for the enthusiastic fur ball, she thought of Fayette's words earlier that day and felt comforted. "A cat of three colors is extremely lucky and will keep a house from harm."

Good luck and protection were life ingredients that Sheila sorely needed.

CHAPTER 8

A sudden wind blew in dark clouds full of rain. *We rode on the winds of the rising storm*, thought Fayette, remembering a quote by Robert Jordan in his book about dragons. She locked her garage door before swinging a leg over the seat of her Harley.

By 1:40 p.m., the friends were back at their café table, mugs in hand, each looking softer, less stressed. There was something healing and blissful about spending time with kittens. Kitsy gave Fayette and Sheila their new grimoires, and Fayette's sparkling green and purple protection bottles made comforting centerpieces next to a pink-flowered teapot and plate of raspberry thumbprint cookies. Sheila shared copies of the strewing spell to go with the ash-handled brooms so they could use them for clearing unwelcome energy from home and workspaces.

"I love the positivity of all of our gifts," Kitsy exclaimed. "This strewing spell is about protection and peace. I can't see how it had anything to do with Pastor Fisby's illness."

"Except that he might have been a blast of unwelcome energy that got cleared away," Sheila pointed out.

"I really can't see it. We're just beginners, but as I said before, if he got in the way of an innocent spell, that's all on him, then." Fayette swished her fingers in the air as though to brush away a no-see-um. "Who knows what ill-will he brought with him to your garden." Fayette's pointer finger made passes over her iPhone, and she handed it to Sheila. "These are the pictures I took in Pastor Fisby's house."

"Oh, my soul," Sheila squeaked when she heard what her friends had done. "Now we're all going to end up in jail."

"Not you, too." Fayette looked between Sheila and Kitsy and shook her head. "Live a little. Seize the day as they say. Grow some moxie."

Two sets of smoldering eyes zeroed in on Fayette, and she shrugged as Sheila began her scroll through pictures of the altar and the books about magic. Fayette leaned over and pointed to the one titled *The Book of Forbidden Knowledge*. "We think this book burned Kitsy's hand when she reached for it." Fayette looked up and over to Kitsy. "How is your hand, by the way. I forgot all about it. Sorry."

Kitsy offered a weak grin, reluctant to talk about the injury. "It's okay. The burn was temporary and disappeared fast." She showed Fayette and Sheila her healed palm and closed her hand into a fist before putting it back on her lap. Fayette gave her a quizzical look and then continued to move through the pictures with Sheila. When photos of the workspace crossed the screen, Sheila drew in her breath.

"Would you look at that. See those bowls of red beads? I guess Pastor Fisby made them by drilling holes in seeds. Those beads are rosary peas, like the seeds that the police found in his pocket, the ones that came from the plants in my yard."

Fayette zoomed in on the red beads, each ornamented with one black dot. Behind the bowls of beads, they could see the drill stand and a miniature pile of fine dust under the tiny drill bit.

Kitsy's fingers flew over her iPhone keypad, researching information about rosary peas or the seeds of *Abrus precatorius*. Frowning, she read out a description. "'*These seeds contain abrin, one of the most potent toxins known.' It says here that 'people are concerned that felons, or terrorists, or unscrupulous dictators could use the seeds to commit biocrimes or biowarfare.'*" Kitsy paused, her eyes skimming the page. "'*The seed skins are a tough protection from the poison inside the rosary pea, but when the seed breaks or its skin wears off, you've got exposed poison. If injured human skin, say from a scratch, or cut, touches the broken seed, well, the contamination can lead to death. Even a prick on the finger when stringing drilled rosary pea beads might be disastrous.'*"

Sheila and Fayette leaned their heads together, closer to the phone, to squint at the tiny mound of dust under the drill bit.

"Who knew those vines and their little red seeds were dangerous enough to be used in warfare." Sheila wondered if she ought to remove the plants from her yard.

Fayette looked up from the iPhone picture and said what they all were thinking. "So, maybe the pastor poisoned himself while he was making these beads."

"He could have breathed in dust particles over time, or maybe he had a cut on his finger and touched some of the powder under that drill bit." Sheila cleared her throat to get everyone's attention. "I think we should show these pictures to officers Noah and Bruce."

"But we weren't supposed to be in Fisby's house taking these pictures," Kitsy lamented, "so how can we tell anyone about it?"

"But we've got to," Sheila said.

"I've been reading more chapters in my books about magic." Fayette straightened and waved her jar spell book in the air as though it was a flag. "I suggest a truth spell. If we're going to really learn something about magic, we need to use it when we need it. We need to stop playing around."

Kitsy and Sheila exchanged anxious glances. Sheila cleared her throat again. "Or we could tell officers Noah and Bruce what we suspect - that the pastor stole the seeds in his pocket. If I instigate trespassing and theft charges against Pastor Fisby, maybe the police can get a warrant to search his house. I mean usually they wouldn't search someone's house over a bunch of seeds, but they might this time because of the possible charges against me. That way they can find the seeds on their own without us having to say anything about you two being trespassers."

"I agree. Even if the police already searched the house, they might not have known what to look for when it came to the beads," Kitsy said.

"It's not a bad idea," Fayette conceded. "It might help strengthen your side of things if the police chief decides to arrest you. But I still want to try a truth spell on Fisby. He's not who or what he pretends to be." She showed Sheila more closeup shots of the altar and the two-sided bookcase. "I hate dealing with phonies, especially hypocrites who insist on setting moral standards for others."

"But, Fayette, there's always a cost to casting a spell," Kitsy warned. "I don't know how truth spells work, but I'm worried about the bad stuff that keeps happening to Sheila. What if things just get worse?"

Fayette gulped the rest of her tea, stuffed her gold-rimmed, leather-bound grimoire in her backpack, grabbed a handful of cookies to cram in her leather jacket pocket, and turned to leave. "I've got work to do, ladies. I need to move fast before hospital visiting hours are over." She limped towards the door, aching muscles still protesting her every move. She zipped her jacket and stepped outside before her two collaborators could do much more than say, "wait" and "don't be reckless."

"Oh la." Sheila twisted her paper napkin into a tight

bundle. "I'm afraid to even think what Fayette might get up to."

Kitsy gave Sheila's arm an absent-minded pat. She was just glad Fayette was on her own in whatever hair-brained scheme she'd begun. She, Kitsy, was well out of it. Marmy, her new kitten, and Samuel, her husband, came to mind. "It's time I go home and give my family some attention. Will you be all right, Sheila, because if not, you are welcome to come home with me."

"Thanks, I'm okay." As Kitsy talked about her family, Sheila was reminded of Darwin. What might he say if he knew the trouble she was in - if he knew she'd been dabbling in magic. Would it matter to him that the intentions of her experiments were benevolent, more about curiosity than anything else? She pictured his boyish features, the Sicilian good looks, and the soft, brown eyes that looked at her as though she was an earth goddess. The two were just getting to know each other as more than co-workers. Beginner magic wasn't something that came up in their conversations, and she hadn't told him about Pastor Parkinson's rudeness a week ago. Maybe Darwin already heard through the grapevine that Sheila found Pastor Fisby unconscious in her yard. What would he make of the situation?

"I'd better call Darwin and let him know what's going on," she said aloud. "Not the magic part, but everything else."

"Oh. Yes." Kitsy considered her friend's words. "I guess Samuel will want to hear the basics too, but you're right. He doesn't need to know about our experiments. He tends to be a bit of a fuddy duddy, despite being a folklore expert. He'd be worried about me trying magic stuff, and he'd wonder why we didn't choose to begin learning something safer like painting, or crochet, or chess."

"Or at least run of the mill magic tricks," Sheila said with an uneasy laugh. "You know, like pulling a coin out of someone's ear, that kind of thing."

Kitsy didn't add that Samuel would not be hearing about her escapades with Fayette inside the pastor's house. Nor would he hear about the book she took from the pastor's bookshelf. No one knew about the book. Kitsy felt around in her jacket pockets where she'd stuffed the special gloves. Yes. They were still there, almost weightless, like silk. She would have to deal with *The Book of Forbidden Knowledge* before the end of the day because there were things she needed from her bag, still under the stack of newspapers in the SUV. Her wallet and phone came to mind.

***

Across town, Fayette rummaged among the semi-precious stones in Brilliant Things, the local bead and jewelry supply store. She already had a few tiny pieces of blue-green amazonite in her gathering basket. Consulting her recipe, printed from an online website about truth magic, she read that amazonite acted as a talisman of honesty and trust and that it worked well with truth spells.

"Let's hope," Fayette murmured to herself.

Next, she needed minuscule shards or nuggets of howlite, the natural, chalky-white version, shot through with black veins. Apparently, elders in the magic world taught that howlite strengthens perspective and encourages mindfulness. Was mindfulness a necessary ingredient of truth telling? Fayette wasn't entirely sure what mindfulness was, but she knew it was a popular concept among spiritual and mental health counselors these days.

"Pish posh," she sniffed, and then stopped herself. Doubt and ridicule of the ingredients was sure to bring negative energy to her truth spell. She needed to focus on surety, intention, and optimism.

At home was a tiny bottle, already cleansed with smoke from burning rosemary and ready for the spell. After the stones, the last ingredient would be a piece of fragrant lemongrass for clearing energy blocks and raising spiritual sensitivity. She thought of the words she would say over the bottle before she sealed it with wax and fire.

Liars hither and Liars thither.
I ask our universe to help hinder.
Lies from leaving their lips and mind.
Let their words be joined to truth to bind.

Running her fingers through little mounds of turquoise, amber, yellow jasper, green agate, and white quartz, all gathered in wooden cubbies, Fayette moved through the store, intent on her search for howlite. The shop owner divided Brilliant Things into two parts. In the bead and jewelry section hung strings of vibrant stones along one wall. A second wall supported several hundred strings, hanks, and tubes of colorful, glass beads, sparkling with light from the front windows. Covering the wooden counters and benches, under the hanging collections of stone and glass, were trays and cubbies of hardened natural minerals. Below the trays and cubbies, the proprietor arranged precious stone and faceted gem displays in protected glass cases. While Fayette had no interest in making jewelry, she could imagine collecting jars of multi-colored stones and sparkling, faceted beads. Maybe someday when she had more time. Sorting through glittering glass and polished gemstones felt soothing, even meditative.

As she picked through shiny stones, some drilled for beadwork and others left whole for settings, Fayette lost track of time. She was unaware of the pinched set of eyes under low, deep, brow furrows that scrutinized her every move. Her watcher leaned against a counter in the other part of the store, a space devoted to old coins, watches, clocks, and antique jewelry. He was, in fact, the proprietor of Brilliant Things and had been for 36 years. This woman, he thought, who drove up on a wicked-red Harley, was surely not magic-world street smart. Her choice of stones was obvious. She was either making charms or gathering stones for luck, or she was intent on spell-work. This fusspot with her scuffed, black riding boots and worn-in leathers was either sloppy or new to the craft and too ignorant to disguise her intentions. Someone who knew better would buy more than a few miniature stones, or they would at least pretend to look at jewelry findings.

The proprietor's thin lips formed a smirk as he watched her consider tiny howlite pieces. Without a doubt, the woman intended them for magic. The man chuckled knowingly, but the chuckle caught in his throat. His nostrils flared in alarm at the sight of Fayette dipping her fingers into a bowl of the special beads he forgot to put under lock and key inside the display case.

The man's tall, lanky body straightened as he pushed off from the counter and strode in fury toward his curious customer. In a moment he was by her side, extricating her fingers from the beads and snatching the bowl from the counter.

"Excuse, me?" Fayette faced the man, incensed. "I was looking at those."

"They're not for the likes of you." The man's ferocity was evident in his dark eyes and raised, sharp chin, which he aimed at her in his displeasure. He was at least nine inches taller than Fayette's five foot seven inches, and he leaned over her, longish black hair straggling over his hollow cheeks.

"Well, what the heck are they doing on display if your customers aren't supposed to touch them?" Fayette squashed the urge to push this man on his keester and out of her personal space. "And I think I do want to buy some. Is there a good reason why I can't have a few?"

"There's a very good reason why you should never have touched them." The proprietor hissed out his words. "You obviously don't have a Y chromosome. These are for men only."

"And just how do you know I don't have a Y chromosome?" Fayette shot back. "Why would I need a Y chromosome to buy them anyway? It's not as though I don't know what they are or where they come from."

She did indeed know that these beads were rosary beads from a rosary pea vine. Their bright red hue and single black dot were a dead giveaway.

"I think I know who gave you these," she continued in a state of heated indignation. "And I'm sure I know where he stole them in the first place."

The proprietor switched from aggressive rage to still silence, regarding her with an ice-cold stare while stroking his close-cropped circle beard and goatee. He set the beads back on the counter and folded his arms across a leather-vest-clad chest. It was then that Fayette noticed his motorcycle attire. Like her, he wore riding leathers, right down to his shoes. He'd dressed his feet in black and white leather riding sneakers, the newest fashion in posh riding equipment.

"That Chieftain Elite Indian cycle in the alleyway is yours?" Fayette couldn't help but be impressed with the smoke metal bike she'd seen outside, even as its rider repelled her.

He didn't answer, just pointed to her gathering basket. "I'll ring up your purchases so you can be on your way." His voice was low, warning.

"Hold on, Elden," said a cheery voice behind them. "I couldn't help but overhear. The lady wants some beads that require a Y chromosome to buy. Well, I've got a monster Y chromosome, and I'd like to get some of those beads. How many did you want Ma'am?"

"Leo." The proprietor said the newcomer's name as a

statement, looking at the ceiling as though exasperated. "I've got your coins packaged and ready at the other register. You can pick them up there. As for the beads in question, they are exclusive, made only for members of a particular regional organization. I don't sell them to anyone else."

"Oh, la de da." Leo laughed. "You were always one for secret clubs and dark intrigue, even back when we started that Dungeons and Dragons club, what, forty years ago?" Leo turned his large, bald head in Fayette's direction and winked. "We go way back, Elden and me. Both of us thought we'd shock the grandmas in this town by tempting demons during those dangerous role-playing weekends. That was before D&D's reputation went from spooky nerdom to everybody's doing it because its good clean fun."

He's like a squirt of aloe vera on a burn from a hot grease spatter, Fayette thought, enjoying Leo's easy banter. The man had run interference before things turned to frick on a stick.

Fayette recognized Leo, though they were never formally introduced. He was an E-Hog, like her, and sometimes attended official meetings when the E-Hogs gathered to discuss motorcycle club business. Leo was one of those guys who could fill a Santa suit with ease at a Christmas bazaar, though his long, ragged beard had flecks of gray and auburn in it rather than being all white. He wore what must have been a size 3X, plain, gray sweatshirt over Carhart jeans, but his biker boots gave him away as a Harley rider.

When Fayette passed her gathering basket to Elden, he handed back the amazonite and howlite pieces. It was then that Fayette noticed the ring on the proprietor's thumb. Like pastor Fisby's thumb ring, a chunk of polished amber dominated the middle, surrounded by smaller red stones inside a hexagon engraving.

"Just take them. They're not worth ringing up," Elden

said, referring to the semi-precious stones in Fayette's hand. He glared straight into her eyes and raised his brows in a calculating stare, almost a silent accusation. The store owner's aggressive behavior confused Fayette. Did he treat all his customers as though they were the ugliest of pill bugs, pests to get rid of?

"Hold on," Leo said to Fayette. "I'd like to walk you out after I pick up my coins."

Fayette slipped the howlite and amazonite into her jacket watch pocket and gave the shop a once over as Leo retrieved his coins at the second register. For the first time, she spotted a woman in the store, a woman who was also looking at her. Curious how the woman seemed to blend into the background, as though she was part of the scenery.

When it was clear Fayette noticed her, the woman gave her a friendly wave, and then, to Fayette's surprise, she winked, pointed to Elden, and then, with the first finger of her right hand made the circular "he's crazy" sign next to her ear. This woman witnessed the whole aggressive scene and was on Fayette's side, so Fayette gave her a grateful thumbs up in response. About Fayette's own age and height, wavy, short-cut, gray hair framed the woman 's round cheeks. Her dignified, solid jaw gave her a sensible appearance. She looked like someone who would fit nicely into the Reading Club of Retired and Capable Ladies.

"Thanks for waiting." Leo was at her side, small brown bag in one large hand and two, root-beer-flavored lollypops in the other. He offered her one. Fayette, who took the lollypop, decided she liked this man who tried to buy beads for her. She liked Leo even more when they stepped out onto the sidewalk and he showed her his ride, a legend denim blue, customized Harley Softail Fat Boy.

"Hey. I spotted you at some of the E-Hog meetings." Leo watched Fayette run a hand over the engine cover of his iron horse. "I know you've got a bike." He beamed over at Fayette's Street Glide in approval. "Right now, I'm wondering if you'd want to ride the backroads together some Saturday."

"It's a possibility." Fayette gave Leo a one-sided smile. "I'm more than a little curious about that monster Y chromosome." Her grin widened as she handed him a card with her phone number, but she planned to ask around about him before agreeing to spend a day on the backroads with a virtual stranger. Fayette nodded goodbye and mounted her bike just as the front door to Brilliant Things opened, and Elden fairly pushed the other woman out of the store, turning the lock and positioning the closed sign.

"I need to talk with you," the woman said through the glass as Elden pulled down the blind. "When am I ever going to be able to interview that man," the woman murmured to herself. She shrugged in Fayette's direction, then shook her head and set off down the sidewalk toward town center.

As Fayette motored her bike back home, she gave Leo credit for bringing positive energy to a situation that might have left her seething. To complete her truth spell she needed to be in a good frame of mind. The strange confrontation with Elden over the rosary pea beads only hardened her determination to follow through with her plans. She would visit pastor Fisby's hospital room before the day was over.

CHAPTER 9

By dinner time, Fayette had a copy of her second truth spell in her left front jeans pocket and the fire-sealed spell bottle in her right front pocket. She'd left her leathers at home, having located the most boring outfit she could find in her small wardrobe, a pair of plain, loose-fitting jeans, tennis shoes, and a gray, wool, button-up jacket. Her book group friends often talked about how most people, young and old, disregarded women over fifty. Fayette counted on the invisibility of older women as she made her way to the hospital elevator that would take her to the third floor and pastor Fisby's room. She carried a clipboard that secured official looking paperwork so she could pretend to fill it out and, thus, avoid eye contact.

The elevator was empty when Fayette pushed the third-floor button, but it stopped on the second floor letting on two passengers, a broad-chested man dressed in matching gray scrub pants and shirt, and a tall woman in a business casual navy skirt and button-down blouse under a striped suit vest. Fayette busied herself with scribbling nonsense words on her clipboard as the woman advised the man on insurance expectations related to coma patients. "Mr. Parkinson's insurance company offers two more days of coverage for a private room, but after that we'll have to move him to a ward with roommates.”

“He’s showing signs of recovering,” the man said. “I anticipate he’ll regain consciousness soon. And we’ve determined his coma wasn’t induced by the poison directly. He suffered severe diarrhea over several days, which led to extreme dehydration. Unusual for diarrhea to cause a coma, but I’ve seen it before. Let’s just hope it didn’t lead to organ damage.”

The elevator doors opened to let Fayette out at level three but closed on the two hospital employees who were going on to level four. As soon as she stepped away from the elevator, Fayette was caught up in the frenzy of dogged, unwavering foot traffic surging through a busy corridor. Nurses, doctors, and orderlies zipped in and out of hospital rooms on the right side of polished linoleum flooring and visited staff rooms and patient monitor stations on the left. Her destination was room 321. In front of her was room 307, its door ajar so that she could see a patient’s front-side profile under a thin, white blanket, his arm fixed to a drip tube. Fayette heard the slow hum of some kind of monitor above his head.

Shuddering at the thought of ever being a hospital prisoner, Fayette kept her gaze intent on the clipboard and made her way past room 309, then 311 and on down the hallway. She was conscious of the rhythmic squeak of her tennis shoes on the shiny hall floor, but hers weren’t the only shoes making a racket. Plus, the noisy bustle of nurses moving mobile stands, beds on wheels, and dinner tray carts blended with the sounds of her own inconsequential movements. Her task was to squeeze close to the right-side wall and keep out of the way.

The door to room 321 was closed and the hallway curtains drawn. Fayette wrote something on her clipboard just to appear official, looked both ways, and then turned the cold, stainless steel doorknob.

She was in. It was time to do what she came for and then get out as fast as possible. Fayette couldn't help but think of squash plants as she considered Pastor Fisby laying still on a bed that lifted his head and shoulders higher than his torso and legs. Like an elongating squash vine, an intravenous line to his arm provided fluids and perhaps even medications. A monitor recorded his pulse activity and blood pressure. His eyes stayed closed, and his breathing seemed steady. Fayette remembered the saying that everyone looks innocent when they're sleeping. Pastor Fisby did not. His thin face, with its high cheekbones, sunken cheeks, sharp chin, and Roman nose appeared to judge even the air he breathed. The altar and bookshelf in Fisby's house came to mind as Fayette scrutinized the unconscious man. Who was Pastor Fisby, really?

"I've brought the tools to try and find out," she murmured to the room.

Where to put the truth spell bottle? Nothing in the room looked unattended. Someone would find the bottle in minutes during regular hospital procedures. The window. There were drapes covering the window. If she put the tiny bottle in a corner of the windowsill, even when staff opened the drapes, parts of the sill would stay hidden. It was the only possible place, so Fayette left her one-inch tall, fire-sealed glass spell bottle in the window corner closest to the patient.

"And now the spell," she said aloud to no one, pulling the piece of paper out of her pocket and drawing a deep breath to center herself. The spell came from a version of *The Book of Shadows*, which seemed to be a favorite within the magical community. Fayette practiced focusing the flow of energy toward a desired end. She worked to keep her intentions positive, prioritizing the goals of protection, good will, and causing no harm. If Pastor Fisby confessed the truth to bring himself peace of mind, then the truth spell would not harm even him,

Fayette reasoned.

She was ready. She spoke the spell to the room, but especially to the man laying before her in the hospital bed.

For those who want the truth revealed,
Opened hearts and secrets unsealed,
From now until it's now again,
After which the memory ends.
Those who now are in this house,
Will hear the truth from others' mouths.
It is done.

Fayette Pinker, newbie spell-maker, had tried. It was time to leave before someone caught her at the foot of the pastor's bed. The best course of action was to keep a sense of steady confidence and not worry about whether her spells worked. She would leave the hospital and focus on getting dinner, playing with Max, and doing a bit of online research about Leo and his legend denim blue, customized Harley Softail Fat Boy. She opened the hospital door to make her escape. As she slipped through the door frame, she looked back one last time at the bed and the patient.

Fayette choked. *Son of a bacon bit.* Pastor Fisby's black, bloodshot eyes were open and staring straight at her.

Fayette felt as though a clanging alarm clock went off in her chest as she stepped fully into the hallway and closed the door to 321 with a snap. *Not to panic,* she told herself. *Remember the way to the elevator, left, or right? Left.* She wanted to powerwalk her way down the hall to the spot where she could see the elevator doors. They opened just then and let someone out. "Judas Priest," she said aloud, rooted to a spot outside room 317. The tall, stiff form of Elden, the proprietor of Brilliant Things, headed in her direction. Fayette's hands still clutched her clipboard, and she managed to re-incorporate it as part of her disguise, focusing on her page full of nonsense words and scribbles. She turned her back on Elden and headed toward the other end of the hall, past room 321 again. Somewhere there was bound to be a stairway. For some strange reason, the hallway was quiet, no nurses moving equipment and delivering dinners, no hospital cleaning staff. Elden's shoes clicked like keys on a slow typewriter while hers squeaked like the sound of a rusty wheel bearing. *Click squeak, click squeak.* The clicks increased their pace as they moved closer to Pastor Fisby's room. The squeaks raised an octave as Fayette's shoes retreated in escape mode.

The alarm clock in Fayette's chest settled a bit when she spotted a staircase next to a vending machine at the end of the hallway. She was about to exit and slip away when her curiosity got the better of her. Was Elden going to the pastor's room? Fayette slid close to the vending machine and peaked around it. She was just in time to see Elden pause at room 321. He looked both ways before turning the doorknob, just as she had done. And then he was inside, presumably discovering that pastor Fisby was awake and no longer comatose.

Maybe, just maybe, Fisby and Elden hadn't recognized her. After all, they each saw her only once before, Fisby in the café when he demanded the pamphlet she pretended to have and Elden in Brilliant Things when he was so rude to her. Both times her dress was distinct, leathers with windblown helmet hair. Now she looked like one of the cleaning staff. Was her senior lady invisibility disguise enough?

Fayette's feet echoed on the metal stairway as she descended to the first floor and a way out. *Let it go*, she told herself over and over again as her feet touched each step. She needed to get the picture out of her head of Pastor Fisby's choleric stare.

In minutes, her knees hugged her saddleman seat as she filled her lungs with the fresh air of freedom. Fayette was back on her Street Glide, pushing the magic button to start her ride, and adjusting her brain bucket, a fancy term for helmet. She would reward herself with takeout from Red Curry Thai Palace and a mini chocolate cream pie from Midland Bakery.

As the bike took her further and further from the hospital, she felt the power and thrum of its 3750-RPM torque, 117-Volt twin engines restoring her confidence. A firm squeeze on the accelerator and she was speeding away that cold fear of being the subject of the pastor's stare. And then, the very thought of the soft, crazy, happy kitten waiting for her at home melted away the last of her anxiety. She was Fayette, motorcycle empress of Elmira once again.

Lars Columbus, owner and storekeeper of Forever Reading Bookstore, smiled with a nod as he watched her roar by his storefront window.

CHAPTER 10

Kitsy approached her SUV with slow reluctance and uneasiness congealed from fixated worry.

Her fear must have been easy to read because during dinner Samuel reached over and stroked her hand. "Looks like you've got something on your mind. Want to share?" He'd been introduced to Marmy, who took an immediate liking to him. The curious kitten sat on his shoulder, and Kitsy was startled to see a close match, Marmy with her ginger tabby hair and Samuel with his gray-streaked, red hair. Both had blue eyes, and both had whiskers - her hairs straight and horizontal, his short and mostly vertical.

Kitsy's smile was tolerant when Marmy jumped on the table to see if she could try some human food. With gentle patience, Samuel lifted her down several times before she got the message that dinner table food was off limits.

"You might have heard about the man who was found unconscious in my friend Sheila's yard," Kitsy said as explanation for being anxious and lost in thought. "Well, the police think she's a suspect, that she might have poisoned him. Fayette and I know that's not true, and we're trying to find out what really happened."

"Oh?" Samuel held Marmy at bay while he took a bite of chicken stew.

"Javier Castillo, our over-zealous police chief, seems to think that because Sheila was the one who found Pastor Fisby unconscious, and because she owns the land he was on, well, that makes her more than a person of interest. But the pastor was stealing the seeds from her yard that poisoned him. She didn't give him those seeds."

"Whoa. What seeds?" Samuel waved his fork like a conductor's baton as though to slow her down. "Start from the beginning." So, she did. Kitsy told him everything she could, leaving out her own and Fayette's adventures in Pastor Fisby's house and the fact that magic might be involved.

Samuel responded to her story with sympathy and a few thoughtful suggestions. After dinner, he retreated to his study, whistling. Even as he listened to an audio of a classic western, he whistled. Samuel had always been a whistler, which was why the door to his study was sturdy and thick to hold in the sound. After decades of marriage, he understood that whistling, while fun, is not always welcome. Marmy curled up near his elbow on a mound of papers in a wire basket.

With the kitten in good hands and the dishes washed, Kitsy could think of nothing else that needed doing. It was time to take care of the matter of her handbag and the stolen book. She had her supplies, a metal breadbox, the special gloves, and a flashlight. Already the sun was setting, even though it was only 6 o'clock. Fall, with its long, cool nights, was closing in fast.

Kitsy switched on her flashlight. Step one, remove the pile of newspapers for recycling. Step two, put on the gloves. Step three, open her bag. Kitsy made the quilted handbag herself only months ago, and, in no time, it became a favorite. It was a soft cream color with a print design of pink cherry blossoms and green leaves. The strap was just the right length so she could find things without removing the bag from her shoulder. Inside were all the amenities one might need when leaving the house. Also inside, rested a seemingly haunted and dangerous version of *The Book of Forbidden Knowledge*. Once she removed the book, Kitsy didn't think she could bring herself to use the carrier bag again because it would always remind her of her moral failure.

Reaching into the bag, Kitsy gripped a corner of the polluted book and lifted it out. Even inside the special gloves, her fingers warmed to the book's touch, and she could see a soft yellow glow turn into a harder, orange light between the book's pages. With a shudder, Kitsy fairly threw the book into the vintage, carbon-steel breadbox and snapped down the hinged lid. She secured the catch. Was the book itself making the heat? Was there something nefarious inside the book? What if some unwholesome thing lived in *The Book of Forbidden Knowledge*? What if it escaped from between the pages and managed to seep through the box's ventilation holes? Slapping the metal container, Kitsy realized that removing the book from her bag into the breadbox hadn't helped her feel any safer or at ease.

But at least in the metal box it won't burn anything up. Could she take it back to the pastor's residence and put the book back in his study? No. She wasn't brave enough to go back in that house alone and in the dark. Besides, by now the police might have gone to look things over. They would surely have locked the doors. *I just need to put the book in a place where I can keep an eye on it*, Kitsy thought.

After retrieving her wallet and cell phone, Kitsy locked her SUV and carried the box toward the outside kitchen entrance. Did she really want this thing in her kitchen? Before going inside, she lifted the box's ventilation holes to her eyes and peered in to see if the smoldering light between the book pages still blazed. The tiny holes allowed her to identify half of the book's cover but only because of a wispy glow from its pages.

Something shimmered on the cover, a moving picture of a rough hand coming out of mist or fog and holding an old-fashioned, lit lantern. The mist thickened over the image, darkening the light until there was nothing left to see.

Feeling lightheaded, Kitsy sat on the steps to her kitchen door, galvanized steel box at her feet. She needed advice. Books that heated up, glowed, and whose illustrations manifested as shimmering mirages were way out of her league, so she thought about Lars Columbus. Would he know anything about haunted books, or would he just think she was bonkers for asking? Then she remembered that he searched Pastor Fisby's house when they were hiding under the altar. Why had he been there?

"Oh, here you are." Samuel's voice called to her from the side gate. Kitsy's tense shoulders relaxed a smidgeon in response. "I wondered where you went." He helped her to her feet and opened the kitchen door. "Hot chocolate?" he asked.

Cocoa and the comfort of Samuel's company would, indeed, be welcome medicine.

Samuel had his back to her, and while he absorbed himself in pouring the chocolate, toasting English muffins, and recounting the plot of his new western, Kitsy found her large, lid-covered roasting pan in the shelf under the stove. To her relief, the breadbox and the special gloves fit inside. It was the best hiding place she could think of for the time being, that is until a wide-eyed Marmy jumped on the pan, pawed at the metal handle, and besieged the kitchen with a demanding yowl. Scooping up the kitten with one arm, Kitsy made sure Samuel's focus was the toaster; then she used her free hand to push the roasting pan back onto its shelf under the stove and slid the door shut. With the kitten still contained, she strode into the family room and settled herself in her favorite overstuffed, brown-velvet armchair.

Marmy struggled and escaped onto the end table that supported Kitsy's neat stacks of library books and her reading glasses. If Kitsy thought she could distract the kitten by taking her to a different room, she was wrong. Marmy scampered toward the kitchen as soon as Kitsy loosened her grip.

"She's pacing in front of the stove," Samuel reported as he brought in their plates of buttered muffins and cups of cocoa. "Do you think there are mice in that cupboard?"

Samuel, engrossed in stirring milk and buttering toast, had paid little to no attention while Kitsy slipped the breadbox in the pan, or he would have asked more questions. Had he taken the time to notice what Kitsy was doing, he might even have opened the roasting pan and the bread box to investigate.

"It's a kitten thing," Kitsy offered. As explanations go, it was lame, but Samuel nodded, already settled in his own chair, opening a book about Medieval folklore. Storytelling and folklore were lifelong interests, and even though he no longer worked as an English teacher, retirement only fired up Samuel's curiosity about old legends and myths.

Having finished her cocoa, Kitsy got up and re-entered the kitchen. She could see her fuzzy kitty pacing back and forth in front of the stove, stopping every few seconds to scratch at the lower shelf door.

"A kitten thing," Kitsy repeated to herself. Her words were truly an understatement. Marmy was obsessed with the contents contained in the breadbox; that was evident. Was it ludicrous to imagine this orange ball of energy getting the shelf door open, partially wrangling the roaster lid off the pan, and gaining access to the breadbox? Could the book harm Marmy if she were near it? Kitsy looked around. The potato bin would do. She pushed the heavy container against the shelf door and felt a little better.

There was one more thing. Kitsy returned to the SUV where the emerald-green protection bottle Fayette gave her settled in a crease on the passenger seat. She brought the gift into the house, secured the bottle on the counter, and made a silent request to the universe for protection. With all that had happened, sleep was bound to be a challenge that night.

Gathering up her wiggly feline, who grabbed at her hair with a wayward claw, Kitsy closed the door between the kitchen and family room and headed to bed.

CHAPTER 11

Sleep proved elusive for Sheila, who lay under three quilts in her four-poster bed feeling cold with anxiety. Patches was a rumbling, purring comfort, stretched out between the second and third quilt levels. Resting her arm alongside the lump that was Patches, Sheila went over the day's events in her mind for the hundredth time.

As soon as she got home from meeting with Kitsy and Fayette, Sheila called Darwin and asked him to meet her at the café for breakfast.

"Things have been going on in my life that I think you should know about," she told him.

"Well … I have heard rumors," he said. "It's a small town, after all, but I figure there's not a whole lot to them. I'm happy to lend a supportive ear."

Not only was Sheila nervous over what Darwin might think about her possible coming arrest, but something else happened after the phone call.

Finished with her dinner of boxed macaroni and cheese with a green salad, Sheila stepped out to her garden beds, curious about her rosary pea vines, her *Abrus precatorius* plants. She recalled buying them on a whim at a roadside nursery maybe ten years ago and hadn't given the vines much thought except to enjoy their luminous pink flowers and bright red seeds and to celebrate their healthy growth. They seemed to thrive on the steer manure soil amendments and were well established on the trellis she set up for them. She had no idea that some people made beads out of the seeds.

Before the sun finished setting, Sheila examined her vines, still full of feathery leaves, as the plants were semi-evergreen, typically losing many leaves before spring, but not all of them. She noted that the soft dirt underneath the vines exposed several large, deep boot prints. Vine branches were torn, likely from someone ripping off the brownish gray pods containing bright red seeds. For her own record, and to share with her friends, Sheila took pictures of the footprints and the damage to her plants, feeling a wave of resentment as she assessed the theft. Had the police even bothered to investigate her rosary pea vines? Did they know about the footprints? After all, the officers verified she had the plants in her garden, they must have spent time looking at them.

With a gloved hand, Sheila grasped a small broken branch to remove it. And then she saw it, dangling from a leafless stick behind the broken branch was a large gold ring adorned with a chunk of polished amber surrounded by smaller red stones inside a hexagon engraving. Sheila snapped picture after picture, wondering if she should retrieve the ring or leave it where she found it to show the police. How had the police missed seeing the ring? They must have given the bushes just a cursory once-over. Would they believe she discovered the ring on the vines, or would they think she planted it there to try and frame Pastor Fisby? Noah and Bruce would believe her, Sheila felt sure, but what about Javier Castillo, police chief?

Up above, a crow called to its fellows as they headed to their night shelter. The call reminded her that crows like to collect bright things. If Sheila left the ring on the vine, a bird or packrat or other creature might claim it before the police got around to investigating. She'd better keep it safe somewhere. Searching the ground, Sheila located a short, sturdy stick. Even she knew that getting her fingerprints on the shiny, smooth object was a bad idea, plus she loathed to touch it. With the stick she lifted the ring from the branch and dropped it onto a clean, folded handkerchief she carried in her jacket pocket.

As dusk deepened and the air cooled, Sheila gave up her investigation and carried the ring through her back door into her mud room. She turned on the overhead light and scrutinized the gold circle with its amber stone. Was it her imagination or did the smaller red stones form a grin that glinted up at her with malevolence? The ring felt ice cold in her hand even through the handkerchief. Spotting a battered, metal, chamomile tea container, used to capture spiders and stink bugs for tossing out the back door, Sheila made a bundle of the ring and the handkerchief and then stuffed them in the box, shutting the lid tight. She put the tea box on the mudroom windowsill and locked the back door. It was time to end the day, make hot tea from a new box of chamomile, and relax with her high-spirited kitten.

Patches made herself at home in only a few, short hours, claiming Sheila's favorite padded rocker for herself and spreading her toys from the bedroom to the sitting room to the kitchen. Tail high, she raced Sheila into the bathroom for tissue, into the bedroom for a pair of slippers, into the kitchen for tea, and then Patches sprinted ahead to take her place on the rocker.

"Okay, baby girl," Sheila crooned, massaging the kitten's silky head. "Just this once, mind you. I'll let you have the chair tonight, but in the future, I'll be the one to take the rocker." Patches opened her mouth for a full-fledged yawn, showing her entire bubblegum pink tongue and gums. She flopped on the fuzzy lap blanket and curled into a downy ball, watching through one slitted, green eye as Sheila reclined on the couch, reading her latest cozy mystery.

Minutes ticked by until Sheila finished the last chapter. The amateur female sleuth solved the crime and got a date with the hunky police chief to boot. All's well that ends well. Closing the book, she smiled with contented indulgence, noting that her rocker was empty, and that Patches must have gone to explore. A crash near the back end of the house brought her to her feet. Was the kitten all right? As she hurried into the mud room, Sheila could see Patches pouncing on an object half her size with such fierceness that it skidded across the floor, ricocheting off the shelves and a closet door. To her dismay, she saw that it was the metal tea box containing Pastor Fisby's thumb ring.

When the kitten hissed and growled at the box, Sheila removed it from the floor, but she wasn't quick enough. Patches reached for it, scratched Sheila's hand, and prepared to leap up her pant leg. *A few scratches are just part of raising a kitten, Sheila thought, but does Patches know what is inside the box? No. Couldn't be.* As she opened the closet to secure the metal container on a shelf, Sheila tried to shake the notion that her tiny feline buddy attacked the box with purpose and was not just playing. Her doubts turned to alarm when Patches paced in front of the closet door after she closed it, yowling and pawing at the wood.

Lifting the frustrated calico to her shoulder, Sheila stepped out of the mud room into the kitchen, shutting the door between the rooms, something she hadn't done for months. She wished she'd never seen the ring or that she had the presence of mind to leave it hanging from the rosary pea vine. What could she do to make things better? She thought of what her book club friends might say and recalled their gathering that afternoon around the café table. They had exchanged gifts, including Fayette's protection bottle. Why not? Sheila could ask for protection and place her friend's sparkling, sapphire-tinted, spell bottle on the counter near the mudroom entrance. As Sheila pulled the tissue paper from the apple-shaped bottle, the smooth curves and angles of the polished beach stones inside brought back childhood memories of summersaulting down steep, grassy hills and picking roadside blackberries.

"Thank you, Fayette," she breathed aloud.

CHAPTER 12

"And so, I'm suspected of poisoning Pastor Fisby, and the police chief pretty much vowed he would arrest me soon." Sheila looked for signs of discomfort or judgment on Darwin's face. She spent the last half hour explaining how she found the pastor in a coma near her greenhouse and how officers interrogated her in the police station after imprisoning her in an uncomfortable, wooden office chair.

"And those poor, lost boys," she said, referring to Noah and Bruce. "We really should try and introduce them to some of the younger people at the Lutheran Church. Maybe have a little dinner party for them."

"Well, yes. That's a steady idea." Darwin reached out his sizeable, calloused hand to cover her smaller, plumper hand, the one that wasn't holding her teacup.

As agreed, they started their day together at the café. They were early and the first of the morning customers, so they had their pick of fresh-baked, Scottish-oat and walnut scones, loganberry muffins, and apple turnovers.

"But Sheila. Don't you worry about me or what I might think. I've known you for more than twenty years now. There's no question in my mind that you couldn't hurt anyone unless you were defending yourself or someone else you cared about. Then, buddy. Watch out." Darwin laughed, that same chuckle that added *cream and sugar* to her routine days when they both worked at the church. "I remember some of those toxic parishioners you sometimes had to deal with. You know, Cicci, with the pet rat she carried around, who tried to tell you how to do your job even though she only came to church once or twice a year. Or remember Jackson, the tall guy with halitosis? He leaned over your desk and into your face at least once a week to gossip and complain about other people in the congregation. I saw how patient you were with the Ashtons. They demanded to be the center of your attention, constantly bragging about their oh-so special talents and achievements. You didn't poison any of them. You kept your cool."

"Oh la. Imagine you remembering all that." Sheila grinned. "Still, Fisby Parkinson is no angel, unless you count Lucifer. In fact, he's worse than the Ashtons, and some of the people he hounded over the years might still want to poison him. Lately, he's been nosy and interfering about my book group's reading material. Not that we invited him to talk about it with us, but he was listening in on a conversation and got his back up."

"Is that all? Who would poison someone for criticizing their choice in books?"

"Well, *I* found him unconscious on my property. He was poisoned with seeds that probably came from one of my plants. I can see why it looks suspicious." Sheila wondered if she should tell Darwin about the thumb ring she found that almost certainly belonged to Pastor Fisby.

A short bird warble drew the pair's attention to Sheila's satchel. It was her phone alerting her that she had a text message, but the bird chirps reminded her of how Darwin used to hum while he swept, mopped, and dusted the church floors.

"Do you still hum Beethoven concertos and sonatas while you work?" she asked as she reached for her phone.

"It's not the kind of habit I can break," he grinned. "Does humming bother you?"

"I always enjoyed …." Sheila broke off as she read the text. Darwin could feel her hand stiffen under his.

"Bad news?"

"I'd … say … so," Sheila said, one slow word at a time. "It's horrible." She looked up from her phone, dazed. "Someone kidnapped Fisby Parkinson from his hospital bed at about 3 o'clock in the morning. The hospital cameras recorded images of a hooded figure going into his room pushing a wheelchair. About seven minutes later, the figure came out again, pushing the chair with Fisby in it. The pastor was still dressed in a hospital gown with a blanket thrown over him."

"Someone took a man in a coma? Wouldn't he be dreary company and a whole lot of work to take care of?"

Darwin's cringe sense of humor was on the nerdy side, Sheila remembered, but usually forgivable. She managed a pale smile.

"Okay. Too witty too soon," Darwin said. "Apologies. What else did the message say?"

"Well, this is the worst part," Sheila continued. "Fayette … I don't know if you've met her before. She's in my book group. Anyway, she texted that she visited Fisby's room yesterday and left him a kind of …" Sheila paused, joining her hands in prayer fashion and pressing them to her lips. How could she put this in the best light? "Fayette was worried that Fisby would lie about what he was doing in my yard. She brought a kind of charm to his room, a kind of good luck charm that helps people tell the truth."

Darwin looked puzzled but nodded for her to continue.

"Fayette left the charm in Fisby's hospital windowsill. Anyway, the police found it when they searched the room. They matched prints on the bottle with hers. And now Fayette's a suspect in Fisby's disappearance."

"And since she's a friend of yours," Darwin interjected, "and since you're a suspect, too, the police might think you had something to do with kidnapping the preacher?"

"Well, I hadn't thought about it that way, but I guess you could be right." Sheila felt something constrict in her chest, and that Scottish-oat scone sat like a river rock in her stomach. What if the police brought a search warrant to her house and found Fisby's ring in the tea box? Would they think it was evidence of foul play? Should she just tell the police that she found the ring and show them the pictures she took, or should she go home and bury the box in the winter carrot patch?

"Trying to do magic just brings bad luck as far as I can tell," Sheila mumbled to herself.

"Sorry?" Darwin said. "Did you say something about magic?"

Magic, attic, static, plastic. Sheila tried to think fast.

"Tragic," she said as soon as she thought of it. "You know, one spot of bad luck can bring on a whole slew of mishaps, and it can start to seem tragic."

"You mean like bad things happening in threes?" Darwin offered. Sheila stopped looking at her phone and focused on Darwin, fascinated. He knew exactly what she'd said the first time, but he covered for her. This awkward, smokey-haired, broad-shouldered handyman, who could fix pipes, repair brickwork, and reroof a house, also knew enough to help a flustered friend regain her composure.

A crowd of customers had gathered, and several waited for tables.

"Look, Sheila." Darwin helped clear the teapot and stack the empty cups and plates. "If something comes up and you need company or assistance, or if the police start asking questions, that kind of thing, just call. I'm on your side."

CHAPTER 13

Fayette raced, pushing her skates faster than she could safely make the turn, headed for rink rash or worse unless she could manage a turn stop.

She'd come early to the rink, before it was open, and the manager, a young woman who thought Fayette looked a lot like her grandma, allowed her in.

"I need to work off some steam," Fayette told her. "I'll pay the usual rental rate and then some."

"Don't worry about it. I'll be in the back running account numbers. I'm Jennifer, by the way."

Speed and the feel of wheels under her feet helped simmer some of Fayette's boiling rage about the morning. The memories of what happened, the indignities, and the accusations compelled her to pump her skates even faster.

Fayette recalled how the day started in her cold kitchen. Her heat unit was still on the fritz, but she sat in front of the stove enjoying her first cup of Phantom Shuck House Blend when the police rattled her screen door and knocked loud enough to send Max scurrying under the table. As she peered out the front door curtains to see who was on her doorstep, one of the officers raised a plastic evidence bag. Inside was the tiny truth spell bottle Fayette left on the windowsill of Pastor Fisby's hospital room.

"Holy hen in a hat," Fayette said to Max, who waited at her feet. "What the frick are they doing with that?"

Ten minutes later, across Fayette's kitchen table, officers Noah and Bruce informed Fayette that she might be a suspect in the disappearance of Pastor Fisby Parkinson.

"You say you snuck into the pastor's hospital room because you wanted to leave this truth spell bottle so that a man in a coma would tell the truth about how he got poisoned?" Officer Bruce scratched his right ear, a nervous tick when he was unsure what to do next. "You're joking, right?"

Fayette narrowed her eyes at him, and to her surprise, Max sprung onto the table and swiped at Bruce's left ear, causing him to jump back.

"The police chief isn't going to like this report." Officer Noah raised his eyebrows in Bruce's direction. To Fayette he said, "Police reports have a way of becoming public. Are you sure you want to go on record as believing in truth spells?"

"I was trying to help my friend, Sheila. I wouldn't think of trying my hand at a truth spell if I knew the police were doing their job. Your chief has the wrong end of the stick about Sheila and the pastor. I did the only thing I could think of to set things straight."

"The thing is," Bruce said to Noah, "whoever steered Fisby out of the hospital in that wheelchair was tall and thin. These two women, Fayette and Sheila, well, they're not exactly tall or thin." The young officer cringed as he looked sideways at Fayette. "Sorry, ma'am. I'm not saying you're fat. It's just that you're not thin."

"The chief will say weight doesn't matter. The women could still be involved somehow." Noah cleared his throat, closed his notebook, and stood. "Ms. Pinker don't leave town, and I'm not just saying that as cliché police talk. Mr. Parkinson apparently came out of his coma last night, but he's still a very sick man, and without the right medical care, he could be in danger of getting sicker. We need to find him. You and your friend Sheila will be in a lot of trouble if you have anything to do with his disappearance."

Years ago, Fayette's college friends called her Archina Bunker, after the infamous Archie Bunker TV personality. That was because she never held back her exasperation. She hadn't changed.

"Police Chief Javier Castillo's buttcrack," she swore. "I don't even know Fisby Parkinson. I have no interest in knowing the son of a booger butt. I want as little to do with him as possible. Why would I kidnap someone who gives me the heebies jeebies?"

Noah stood with his mouth open, and Bruce had to turn his face away to hide his grin. He wrote in his notebook, "Police Chief Javier Castillo's buttcrack," so he could remember the exact phrase and spring it on Noah someday. When he recovered his composure, he turned. "Yes ma'am. You told us as much before. We'll just let ourselves out."

An hour later, after the indignities of being accused of kidnapping, and after the embarrassment of admitting she dabbled in magic, Fayette tried to speed her anger away on roller skates. That's how she found herself unable to make the next turn, flailing her way into an attempted stop. Quick skating stops were something she practiced when she was younger but hadn't done for years. A successful stop would require Fayette to scissor her legs, plant her back foot perpendicular, and drag it to a halt. She could also plow stop by spreading her legs wide and pointing her toes inward, using friction to slow her pace. Her body wasn't cooperating. Fayette wore a helmet, but she hadn't bothered with knee and elbow pads. She hit the cushioned rink wall full-on with enough force to spin her backward and downward.

For a minute, she lay on her back unable to breathe, feeling like a cracked engine head. Excruciating pain seared across her left shoulder, and Fayette knew, without a doubt, that she had broken her collarbone. She would need help sitting up, let alone getting her skates off her feet so she could stand. How long would it take Jennifer to find her?

Stuck on the ground with nothing to look at but the water and heat system pipes, crisscrossed over the ceiling, Fayette had little else to think about but her shoulder. Her break throbbed in rhythm with her heartbeat. For some reason, her greatest regret was that for several weeks she might not be able to hit the backroads and burn up miles with Leo. That kind of disappointment surprised and alarmed her. She didn't need a man in her life. Why was she so concerned about keeping a date with a bald, brawny, easy rider she hardly knew, one who togged himself up in a yeard, an untrimmed beard that took a year to grow for goodness' sake?

With an audible sigh, Fayette felt along the side of her left thigh where her fingers encountered bare skin through a tear in her jeans. Skidding along the floor usually caused those kinds of rips. Her leg skin was tender, likely from abrasions skaters call rink rash. She groaned. After several minutes of lying on the cold rink surface, Fayette wondered if she should call out. Too embarrassing, she decided, and instead closed her eyes and tried to focus through the pain and onto her breathing. Her mind wandered to the protection bottles she'd created. Her purple triangular bottle, filled with pretty pebbles, was at home. What if she'd brought it in her bag? Would the spell bottle have prevented her accident, or was Sheila right in thinking that fiddling with magic was the cause of the group's recent bad luck?

"Can I help you?" The voice was male, and Fayette jerked just enough to trigger a new wave of shooting pain in her shoulder. Her eyes flew open as she absorbed a flash of momentary panic. Leaning over her was none other than Lars Columbus, owner of Elmira's bookstore.

"Broken collar bone," Fayette breathed out. Even talking was painful.

"I'll call the medics." Lars took his phone from his pocket and arranged for an ambulance. Then he lowered his long, thin hips and legs to the floor beside Fayette to sit with her. For a few quiet minutes he looked off in the distance, as though sifting through memories.

"Magic is a funny thing," he said out of the blue, slipping his hands into the warm pockets of a houndstooth wool vest.

"What?" Fayette almost sat up in shock, but shrank back to the floor, her right hand steadying her left shoulder. Why was this man who made his living selling books talking to her about magic? Then she remembered that Lars Columbus snuck into Pastor Fisby's house the same day she was there with Kitsy.

"Don't be alarmed. Someone at the Elmira police department called me about your interview with officers Noah and Bruce and your truth spell bottle, someone who's part of our magical community. A few of us in the know already suspected that you and your friends, Sheila Fairlight and Kitsy Browning, are experimenting. Your bookstore purchases alerted me, and one of your Lucky Cup Café and Bakery servers heard bits and pieces of your plans. We've been discrete but on the watch in case something went wrong."

"How did you know I'd be here?" Fayette choked out the words, her mind spinning with fresh anxiety and a shedload of questions.

"I had no idea I would find you on your back in the middle of my skating rink. I'm half-owner of the rink and come by often to check on my investment. Lucky I decided to take a look-see at the rink itself this morning. But then, I don't believe in luck or coincidences."

Something Lars said niggled at Fayette's mind. Had

she heard right? Was she in shock from the accident and imagining things? Fayette needed to check. She tried to turn to see Lars' face but could only manage a side view of his austere profile. "Did you say magical community?"

Lars turned and stared at her with a mien of severity, his white Einstein-like hair, his pointed nose and chin, and his bushy eyebrows over glittering, cinnamon-brown eyes added fierceness to his bearing. He lowered his voice to a rumble. "The thing is, you three need help if you're going to keep conjuring and casting. We think you're capable of responsible magic once you learn how, but you've yet to prove it. You get your collarbone taken care of, and then I suggest the three of you plan an outing to the bookstore. The question is, are you smart enough to stay quiet about the magic community's connection to the Forever Reading Bookstore? Can we trust you?"

A clatter and the murmur of several voices at the double-door entrance to the rink interrupted the bookstore owner's disclosure.

"Okay. Your hospital ride is here." Lars spoke with an edge of warning in his tone. He stood. His lips pressed together in a stern line as he looked down at her. "Think about what I said. There's much more to talk about. Two small and distinct communities work magic in our area. One dabbles in the dark arts. One doesn't. You need to know the difference."

CHAPTER 14

While Sheila met with Darwin at the café, and while police officers Noah and Bruce interrogated Fayette about her truth spell bottle, Kitsy worked to block thoughts about a book in a bread box inside a roasting pan.

Her whistling husband, hand clutched around the handle of a whistling teakettle, dashed across the kitchen to fill mugs at the breakfast table. Samuel artfully positioned the mugs beside plates, which pushed up against containers of butter, jam, and syrup, as stipulated by breakfast place-setting etiquette. Kitsy watched with amusement as Samuel raced back to the stove just in time to flip pancakes, browning in two cast-iron skillets. Breakfast was her life partner's culinary triumph, and Kitsy knew to stay out of his way until it was served.

Samuel's choice of melody was a lively, old, British folk tune called Dashing Away With The Smoothing Iron.

'Twas on a Monday morning
When I beheld my darling
She looked so neat and charming
In every high degree
She looked so neat and nimble, O

A-washing of her linen, O
Dashing away with the smoothing iron
Dashing away with the smoothing iron
She stole my heart away.

Kitsy joined in, singing her own rendition of the song.

T'was on a Tuesday morning
When I beheld my darling
He looked so neat and charming
In every high degree
He looked so neat and nimble, O
A-cooking up his pancakes, O
Dashing away with the teakettle
Dashing away with the teakettle
He stole my heart away.

Samuel turned and winked at Kitsy. "Ready to try a new pancake recipe, madam?" He bowed and gestured with his free hand to the table and the serving plate stacked high with hot cakes.

Bacon and eggs accompanied the pancakes, which were light and buttery, and Kitsy cleaned her plate, a clear indication of a satisfactory start to her day. The smoothing iron ditty had a catchy melody that even she couldn't resist, so she let it go without a word as Samuel whistled stanzas of it every four or five minutes.

When the pancakes disappeared and breakfast talk wound down, Samuel took his whistling to his office while Kitsy washed the dishes and wiped down the kitchen cabinets. Marmy, with occasional low growls, stood guard over the cupboard holding the roasting pan and breadbox, the potato bin now moved back to its usual spot in the corner. Every tiny kitten growl reminded Kitsy that a relaxing, leisurely Tuesday was not in the cards for her because deciding what to do with the breadbox and its contents was her biggest priority.

With reluctance, she leaned down to open the cupboard below the stove, but before she touched the knob, her phone jingled a text alert. Procrastination could be such a relief. Better see who was contacting her. The reprieve was short-lived. Hers was the same message from Fayette that Sheila got at the café with Darwin. Fayette was a suspect in the hospital disappearance of Pastor Fisby because police identified her fingerprints on a truth-spell bottle, discovered near the pastor's bed and then bagged as evidence.

Kitsy slumped onto the kitchen floor in front of the stove and next to the orange kitten. Maybe Sheila was right. Maybe learning about magic would ruin their lives if they didn't watch out. Police now suspected both Sheila and Fayette of causing the misfortunes of Pastor Fisby Parkinson. If the police discovered that she, Kitsy, stole something from the pastor's house, all three of them could end up in jail. No more pancake breakfasts with a whistling Samuel. Oh, how she wished she'd never taken that book, and her regrets redoubled as she watched Marmy try to pull the cupboard door open with her pintsized claws.

"Where are you?" It was Samuel, poking his head in the kitchen door.

"I'm down here petting Marmy," Kitsy answered, not knowing whether to reveal anything to Samuel about Fayette or the breadbox or the stolen book.

"Gotcha. Just wanted to let you know I'm out the door and off to the post office. I'll be back soon." The kitchen porch door opened and shut, and Samuel was gone.

Kitsy sighed and looked into her kitten's bluer than blue eyes. "This might be the best time to get that book out of here and bury it in the woods. What do you think?"

Marmy climbed into her lap and curled into a comfortable ball. They sat there in companionable silence for a few minutes, that is until the whistling started. She could barely hear the sound, but it was the same tune that wafted through Samuel's lips all morning. This time, though, the whistling wasn't coming from her husband. It was emanating from behind the cupboard door, the one under the stove. Whoever or whatever whistled *Dashing Away With the Smoothing Iron* pulsated the tune as an uncanny dirge in a minor key. Instead of a happy ditty with a cheerful lilt, it became a spectral warning. And then the whistling shifted to a raspy whispering of words without tune.

T'was on a shadowy morning
When I beheld his darling
She looked so neat and charming
In every high degree
She looked so neat and nimble, O
A-trying to hurry away from me, O
Dashing away from The Lantern Man
Dashing away from The Lantern Man
I stole her life away.

Marmy yowled, her mouth wide open, tiny teeth framing her pink tongue. Her bright kitty eyes, round and dilated, stared up at Kitsy as though pleading. Kitsy lurched to her feet, clutching the distressed kitten in a protective hold. Her own heart raced as her breath quickened, and she backed away from the stove, bumping her waist on the cabinet corner, hard enough to raise a bruise. Was that smoke she smelled, something burning?

Before retiring from her schoolteacher job, Kitsy practiced monthly with her students how to run first, hide second, and fight last in an active shooter event. In time, the exercise became her go-to fear response. So, Kitsy did the only thing she could think of. She pressed Marmy to her chest, ran from the kitchen, and hid in the bathroom. Locking the door seemed futile, but she did it anyway and then sat on the toilet seat with its soft yellow cover. In a panic, she took stock of her hiding place. What was in the bathroom that could help her fight a spirit or ghost or some other unearthly thing inside a haunted book? What had it called itself? The Lantern Man?

Kitsy grabbed a basket containing smelly soaps in the shape of roses, dumped the soap bars without ceremony into the bathtub, and proceeded to collect possible weapons. What about Lysol? If it could kill 99 percent of all germs, couldn't it eradicate just about anything? The hydrogen peroxide bottle accompanied the Lysol in the basket. Maybe tweezers? The toilet brush? Did she have something like acid that would dissolve the pamphlet-sized book inside the bread box? A picture of old experiments came to mind where someone liquified pennies in Coca-Cola. But she didn't have Coca-Cola, and even if she did, it wouldn't be in the bathroom. Before she had a chance to put anything more in the basket, Marmy hopped in and stretched out, claiming the remaining space. As Kitsy stroked her kitten, she shook her head. Who was she kidding? She had no idea how to battle a haunted book or the cursed thing inside it. Was the specter even now lurking down the hallway toward their bathroom hideout? Was the creature still in the kitchen trying to claw its way out of the book? She had no idea.

Marmy dosed off, seeming at peace, so Kitsy relaxed a bit, moving to sit on the floor, her back to the starlight yellow wall, left of the door. Closing her eyes, she absorbed the solitude and focused on her breathing, using the calming techniques her yoga teacher recommended. Forty minutes later a rough tongue, like a little scrub brush, licked her chin and startled her out of sleep. She sat up straight, eyes wide. How had that happened? How had she dozed off through a possible attack? And then she remembered Samuel going to the post office. He had to be back by now. She, Kitsy, should have warned him. Did he hear the whistler inside the bread box? Was the whistler still trapped in the book, and if not, did Samuel get the brunt of the so-called Lantern Man's intimidations? Was Samuel hurt? Why oh why had she brought *The Book of Forbidden Knowledge* into their house? She'd put her husband and her kitten in danger.

Teary-eyed, Kitsy got to her feet. Maybe she was almost seventy, but she was limber enough to vault from the floor, even if she had to hold onto the bathtub rim to do it. Flinging open the bathroom door, Kitsy fairly ran down the hall to the kitchen. She'd manage whatever was necessary to rescue Samuel. Sure, he had some annoying habits. Whistling was just one of them. But he was her best friend in life, and she wanted to keep it that way. Through her storm of fearful and angry emotions, Kitsy remembered that Fayette sometimes referred to her as a milk-toast homebody.

"Humph," Kitsy said aloud. What did Fayette know? Her motorcycle-riding book buddy had yet to see Kitsy in action when someone she loved was in trouble. This specter, this apparition, this creep was in for a blast of wrath if he hurt a finger or toe or any of Samuel's body parts.

Bursting through the kitchen door, Kitsy braced for a fight, but her gusto fizzled upon hearing Samuel chuckle. There he was at the breakfast table in full research mode, books stacked beside him and pen in hand, scribbling in a notepad. Sitting across from Samuel was a tall, bearded, and decidedly dirty figure, sipping tea from one of her English, rose-embossed, China teacups.

"Well, look here." Samuel picked up one of his British folklore books and pointed to a paragraph on one of its pages. "It says in this section that The Lantern

Man was seen as an evil spirit trying to draw victims to their death in the reed beds and that lantern men, such as yourself, were lured by the sound of whistling. Is this account accurate? As a lantern man, what's your side of the story?"

Kitsy could see that Samuel, an avid student of old English stories, had his voice recorder going and a camera by his side. Her heart sank. The man in ragged clothes sitting in front of Samuel had to be the creature that haunted *The Book of Forbidden Knowledge*. Didn't Samuel realize that this fellow was dangerous?

For his part, Samuel would later tell Kitsy that he was in a state between disbelief and euphoria. Here was an apparition, Samuel said, who appeared from out of their bread box, who whistled folk songs, and who claimed to be from 17th century Britain. The temptation to assail him with questions about the old stories was too great to resist. So, Samuel, almost in a trance, asked The Lantern Man if he wanted tea and cookies and if he would be willing to talk about his own legend.

How had it all happened, Kitsy asked when they were alone later that night?

This was the story Samuel whispered to Kitsy hours later in the dark, their bedroom door locked, Marmy snuggled between them.

Samuel, it turned out, encountered The Lantern Man after returning from his errand to the post office. Whistling the smoothing iron tune once again, Samuel heard a repeating whistle. He'd whistle a phrase of the song, and someone would duplicate it. In short order, Samuel located the whistling echo in a cupboard under the stove, all the while keeping the whistle call and response going. Strangely enough, the response whistles came from a roasting pan that contained a bread box that contained a small pamphlet-sized book titled *The Book of Forbidden Knowledge*. As soon as Samuel lifted the bread box lid, pages of the book fluttered open. A shape inside a shadow launched from the middle fold and landed on the floor at Samuel's feet where it grew, transforming into human form. When all was said and done, the figure of the man, which seemed solid enough, finished growing at a height three inches taller than Samuel's five-foot, 10-inch stature.

The Lantern Man, as he called himself, was thinner than his surprised host. He wore clothes the color of house dust: breeches tied at the waist with a strip of cloth and tucked into knee-length boots; a frayed long coat stretched nearly to the ground and drooped on the man's shoulders over a faded button-up vest. The wool vest, probably brown at one time, fit tightly over a shirt that must have seen whiter days. Around the entirety of his neck, The Lantern Man had wrapped and knotted a smudged, faded, maroon scarf, with interlocking green stripes. Woolen gloves full of holes covered his hands, one of which tipped a Tudor flat cap, complete with a dingy, frayed feather sticking out the back. His other hand grasped a metal hook attached to a four-sided, tin-plated lantern, punched with holes for the light to come through. Even with the late morning sun filling the kitchen through east-facing windows, a glow visibly emanated from the crude, dented lantern.

"Uh, hello? I'm Samuel, Samuel Browning." He didn't know what else to say or do, so he stuck out a hand to offer a shake, but the travel-stained figure just stared, his eyes assessing slits in a sooty, lean face. After an awkward silence, uncomfortable for Samuel, at least, the figure straightened.

"I be The Lantern Man. It is your'n who whistled me free." The figure's voice was a throaty rasp that sounded metallic, like a hoarseness that develops from hours of shouting or roaring.

Samuel, of course, was awash in astonishment. As a folklorist, he recognized the clothing as 17th century traveling attire. When the figure introduced himself as

The Lantern Man, a spark of memory ignited Samuel's research neurons. The Lantern Man was part of old East Anglia folklore, native to the Wicken Fen and other places near Norfolk, Suffolk, and Cambridgeshire, England. What if this apparition really was a lantern man? What if the stories were true? And after seeing a shadow jump out of a book and become a man, Samuel's willingness to *believe* ratcheted to an unprecedented level. What if this strange phantom, as improbable as he was, could confirm or reconcile the lantern man mysteries? What if he had original, unwritten stories to tell?

In a haze of disoriented shock, Samuel settled the man at the breakfast table, made English Breakfast tea, got out the English tea set, and found a package of Scottish shortbread cookies. In short, Samuel did everything he could think of to make the visitor feel at home. Yet, a heavy silence permeated the kitchen for several moments after Samuel asked the dusty man to tell his story. To reconcile The lantern Man's taciturnity, Samuel tried to lighten the mood with a joke and chuckle. It was at this point that Kitsy entered the kitchen.

Heart beating fast, hyperactive from a deluge of adrenaline, she watched the uncanny guest regard her husband through shadowed eyes under furrowed brows. His clenched fists rested on the table on either side of the teacup and saucer.

The folklorist and the specter stared at each other for several, long seconds before the stalemate ended. Between the drooping, untrimmed mustache and the mottled gray beard, lips moved, and that raspy voice erupted once again. "Yfel oncunnan êow."

"Could you repeat that?" Samuel said. "I didn't understand."

"Yfel oncunnan êow."

Samuel grabbed a thick book beside him, turning

several pages, searching, and then turning pages again.

"I think you just told me in Old English that you don't understand me."

The Lantern Man nodded and then grinned, apparently satisfied.

That's when Kitsy made her presence known. She slapped her right hand against the counter and marched up to the breakfast table to lay a soft hand on Samuel's shoulder.

"Stop playing around," she told their visitor, using her sternest instructor voice. "You do understand Samuel. You understand modern English well enough to make new lyrics to an old song and whisper them through a cupboard door. You know what Samuel just said as he translated your Old English. You nodded your head when he said it in modern words."

"Eow âr hlêg scînl̄ æce ides," said The Lantern Man, his yellow-toothed grin widening. And then he smirked.

Samuel once more got busy turning pages in his Old English dictionary.

"What did he say?" Kitsy asked.

"You don't want to know." Samuel frowned.

"I said, you are a witch woman," came the hoarse voice of the man across the table, now pouring himself another cup of tea from Kitsy's best teapot and heaping his plate with chocolate-dipped shortbread.

Kitsy paled. How could this ancient man know about her recent attempts at magic? Or was he using a witch accusation to try and discredit and shame her, much as people often did to those who challenged them during the time and in the place of his origins, the time of witch burnings and hangings? He didn't know about her sewing and her scarf protection spells, Kitsy decided, or her grimoires, or her plans to blend ingredients using a recipe for tea that enhanced strength, courage, determination, and patience. The Lantern Man was simply being ugly, trying to scare her. Then she remembered that this capricious apparition was the only one who knew she stole Pastor Fisby's book from his house, the same book from which The Lantern Man escaped only a half an hour ago. She looked around to see where *The Book of Forbidden Knowledge* might be now. To her dismay, Marmy had jumped on the counter near the stove and was sitting in the bread box, on the book. It seemed the book was no longer too hot to touch. The kitten pawed at the strange, lightweight gloves nearby.

Samuel broke the unpleasant silence. "Sir," he said, "I know you call yourself The Lantern Man, but that can't be your real name. Who are you, really?"

"What sayeth those books of you'rn?" The man croaked out a laugh, shortbread crumbs flying from his lips.

Samuel studied one of his folklore books, looking between the index and several pages in a couple of chapters. "Well, according to folklorists, you were once called Will. Your name connects with the origins of will o' the wisps, which are lights that float at night over swamps and marshy areas."

A flash of sour bitterness further distorted the man's scuffed features. "I have seen neither swamp nor marsh for neigh unto 110 years. Me and me coal and me lantern be trapped in the pages of a book, burning, burning, but as to light, no. No blaese."

"Trapped in a book? That book?" Samuel pointed to the book under Marmy's petite but lethal paws. "How?"

"Tis a long tale," said The Lantern Man with a glower that extended to half-shuttered eyes and deep creases in his forehead.

"Tell it," Kitsy commanded, stepping forward to push her face close to his. She felt little patience for this creature, this man who didn't belong in her kitchen. If he told his story, perhaps he would reveal a way she could get him back into that book or at least out of their

118

lives.

"I heard that sorcerer talking, the one who owned me because he owned the book. He said female witches don't give orders to men." This time The Lantern Man's speech was in perfect modern English. He crossed his arms in front of his chest and leaned back to stare at Kitsy, his expression insolent and amused at the same time.

That sorcerer? Was The Lantern Man talking about Pastor Fisby Parkinson? Kitsy remembered the pastor's collection of conjuring books and his strange altar.

"Look, Kitsy is not a witch. You can get that notion out of your head." Samuel's voice was louder and tighter than usual. "And in this house, we are equals. I think you owe us your story. If I understand correctly, if it weren't for my whistling, you'd still be inside that book."

The man raised an eyebrow in Samuel's direction. "Are you a nursling or a man? You should send the woman away from this room." He wiped his dripping nose on his coat sleeve and reached for the last cookie. "I need more sustenance. Talking makes me tired, and I haven't eaten in more than one hundred years."

Kitsy sighed and gestured to the cupboards from her position in front of the stove. Her voice was hard in its vexation. "What do you want to eat?"

"Eggs. Eggs and bread, a table full of eggs and bread."

"Let me do it," Samuel insisted, getting up and reaching for the skillet. "I don't want him thinking you're some kind of domestic servant." Then Samuel pointed to the book in the bread box and mouthed the words, "Where did that book come from?"

Kitsy knew the game was up. "I'll tell you everything when we're alone."

A dozen eggs, a stick of butter, strawberry jam, and a loaf of bread later, The Lantern Man's hunger persisted. He wanted more coffee with generous portions of cream and honey.

"I've had better," was the thanks they got for all their efforts.

When they cleared the dishes and replaced the empty carafe with a fresh pot of coffee, Samuel sat down again across from their ungrateful guest. Kitsy chose to watch from a distance and settled herself on the kitchen counter overlooking the breakfast table. Her spouse turned to a fresh page in his notepad and then flipped on the voice recorder. He looked as harried as she felt.

"Okay, Mr. Lantern Man." Samuel's voice was less accommodating than before. He was losing patience. "Let's hear it. You tell us your story, or we take you to our local estuary, our bog down the highway, and leave you there. I can assure you, there are no cooked eggs or toast and jam in those marshlands."

The Lantern Man's eyes flashed as though stricken, but he bared his teeth, poured a fourth mug of coffee, emptied the rest of the cream into the brew, and added five spoons of honey. "I am a broken soul of the Wicken Fens," he said, beginning his speech in a hoarse whine, his smokey eyes darting between their faces as though looking for sympathy. He began his history with a difficult mixture of Old English, newer British English, and modern US English. Samuel turned up the microphone volume. Kitsy suspected he'd devote a few hours to recording, but he would take all night to transcribe the conversation, especially because he would have to translate half the words from older English to modern English.

Two hours later, when the specter of The Lantern Man, or whatever he was, finished talking, they were all three worn out from hard concentration. Samuel released The Lantern Man from the table, but the newcomer's presence meant Kitsy and Samuel were prisoners of a sort because they had to keep a constant eye on their wily guest. He spent the rest of the day shuffling through the rooms of their home, opening drawers and closets, examining their things, and eating, always eating. He kept his lantern close, within a few feet of his hands, and at no time did he let more than five minutes go by without touching it.

Samuel gave him clean clothes that fit him all right, except for the pants, which were a few inches too short.

"Can you watch him while I nap?" Samuel, who had managed most of The Lantern Man's caretaking, was dead on his feet by three that afternoon. "I don't trust him, so I want to be alert during the night hours while you sleep. Someone's got to watch him at all times, and I'll stay awake tonight by doing what I can to make sense of his garbled speech and his story."

"I don't know what I can do to stop him from doing just what he wants," Kitsy said. "And you know he has no respect for me. I'm a woman."

"Threaten him with the bog. He seemed genuinely afraid we'd leave him in a marshland when I suggested that's what might happen if he didn't cooperate."

Samuel closed his weary eyes and swayed on his feet. "I can't help but feel you know more than you're saying about that book in the kitchen." Kitsy sighed and then nodded as her husband continued. "So, while you're babysitting the marsh monster, could you write out where that book came from? I'll look at your explanation after dinner. We aren't going to get much time for serious talking today, but I need to know. How can an apparition or man, or whatever he is, appear from the middle of a book? Where does The Lantern Man belong? How are we going to get rid of him?"

By the time Samuel closed the door to their bedroom, assumedly taking off his shoes and sinking deep into a puffy quilt on their king-sized bed, The Lantern Man started roaming again. Kitsy watched, vexed, as he turned the handwheel on her sewing machine, fingered the thread spools on her thread rack, and unfolded her collection of colorful, printed cloth, leaving the yardage crumpled in a pile on the floor. He headed to her yarn stash. No way was she willing to try and untangle skeins of unraveled yarn once he got a hold of them. How to distract this unruly creature?

And then Kitsy got an idea. Would he take the bait? She marched across the hall from her sewing room and into their family room, just off the kitchen, where she and Samuel read in the evenings and where they sometimes watched a movie on their smallish, big-screen television. She grabbed a video DVD from Samuel's movie collection and inserted the disk into the player. With a push of a finger, she activated the DVD player and watched the opening scene flash on the screen of the first episode of the Original Star Trek series. It was called *The Man Trap*. Kitsy couldn't help but chuckle as she remembered the plot. A creature on an alien planet lures men away from other people and then sucks the salt out of them. The creature gets beamed onto the spaceship Enterprise where it traps the captain. Maybe the video would scare the jeebus out of The Lantern Man, especially if he thought it was real. Did he even come from a place that understood fiction? Did he know that most people considered *him* fiction? Kitsy wished The Lantern Man was fiction.

Squeezing her eyes shut for a moment, imagining what might be happening to her yarn stash, Kitsy gathered enough self-control to plant herself in her reading chair and pretend to watch Star Trek. She hoped The Lantern Man would be curious enough to wonder what she was doing and join her. Her handy notebook and a pen were within reach, so she began to write her explanation to Samuel about how the book containing The Lantern Man got into the house in the first place. Somehow it was easier to write out how she stole the book from the pastor's house than it would be to tell Samuel, or anyone else for that matter, face to face. She explained about the burn the book gave her and about the healing power of the special gloves, now on their kitchen counter. She ended her description with the words, "No one else knows, and I can't think what to do with the book or the thing that came out of it."

Sighing, Kitsy capped her pen and closed the notebook. She felt sleepy, exhausted, really. A hiss and a growl startled her out of the deep-breathing serenity of a catnap.

"Witch," The Lantern Man muttered. He sat on the edge of Samuel's reading chair, pointing at the screen. "She be a witch." On the screen lay a dead Starship Enterprise crew member, covered in red rings. If Kitsy remembered right, the alien disguised itself as a woman, one that the dead man remembered with fondness. That's how it lured the man to a secluded spot before killing him.

"Well, we witches have our alien ways." Kitsy didn't quite know why she said those words, but The Lantern Man's eyes widened, and he pushed himself further into Samuel's wingback chair, as though to put some distance between them. Encouraged by his discomfort, Kitsy raised her voice. "You know, Lantern Man, witches today are better than ever at wreaking havoc. Witch science has just gotten smarter and stronger. You have no idea what we can do."

The Lantern Man hissed again, his eyes wide with panic, making Kitsy wish she'd kept her mouth shut. What if he decided to challenge her? She knew diddly squat about magic. And then it was her turn to look scared when she saw what was happening on the little table near The Lantern Man's right elbow. There, his lantern glowed red, the metal so hot that the wood finish under it blistered.

"What in tarnation!" Kitsy shouted. "Get that lantern off the table. You're going to burn the house down."

On the television screen, another Enterprise crew

member lay in the dirt, his skin covered in red rings. The Lantern Man starred at the scene, frozen with horror, looking thin and tormented in Samuel's reading chair, but Kitsy felt no sympathy. She pushed herself out of her own wingback chair and marched her short legs to the kitchen to find the soft green gloves she'd stolen with *The Book of Forbidden Knowledge*. Thrusting her hands into the gloves Kitsy hurried to the family room and grabbed the glowing lantern off the scorched table. She fairly flew back to the kitchen where she put it on a cooking stove burner. An orange light pulsated through punched holes in the tin frame, and, for the first time, Kitsy realized the largest punctures outlined eyes, nose, and a grinning mouth, typical of fiendish, laughing faces on jack-o-lanterns. As she stared at the face, a small explosion seemed to take place behind the eyes. Flames rose inside the lantern, and she jumped as the heat popped and crackled like embers combusting on a campfire.

Mesmerized, Kitsy reached her gloved hand to the lantern door, meaning to open it, but Marmy yowled, jumped on Kitsy's back, and dug her claws into Kitsy's teal and gray wool sweater.

"Oww, you silly cat." Kitsy reacted in surprise and pain, her attention now on her furry spitfire. Was the kitten demanding attention, or was she protecting Kitsy from making a foolish mistake? What did kittens know about foolishness? Yet Marmy seemed to sense a great deal about the lantern, the book, and their unwelcome visitor.

Kitsy glanced back at the hot lantern. Flames appeared to dance within the metal box, and she could swear the thing's eyes and mouth moved as though leering and mocking her. The next second, Marmy launched from Kitsy's shoulders in alarm as an ear-splitting, adrenaline-spiking shriek issued from the family room.

CHAPTER 15

"Back at the scene of the crime, are you? Suspect one and suspect two joining forces?" Police Chief Javier Castillo stood over Fayette and Sheila, who sat on the edges of two waiting room chairs, impatient for hospital staff to process Fayette's paperwork. Exhaustion and pain constricted Fayette's already short fuse. Her arm was in a sling, and the pain killers only just kicked in. Minutes ago, Doctor Gottschall explained that it might take as many as eight weeks for her collarbone to heal fully.

"Can she ride her motorcycle, cook meals, do housework, go to the skating rink, things like that? Does she need someone to stay with her?" Sheila asked. She'd gone straight from the bakery tea shop to the hospital after getting Fayette's phone message. Fayette would need a ride home.

"She can do things that require only one arm," the doctor advised, "but motorcycle riding and roller skating are off-limits for at least a month."

"Thanks a lot," Fayette hissed in Sheila's ear.

"If that's your attitude, maybe I won't bring you hot dinners after all," Sheila shot back, but she only half meant it. Of course she would help her cranky friend get through the month. Sheila figured that if she had a broken collarbone, she'd be rude and ornery too.

After the doctor released Fayette to the front staff and hospital officialdom, she sat in a blistery silence on her rock-hard, metal-gilded waiting chair, still stewing on the news that she had to act like a feeble old lady for several weeks. So, when Police Chief Castillo walked over with his cutting accusation that the women poisoned and kidnapped Pastor Fisby, he unwittingly volunteered to serve as a lightning rod for Fayette's building fury.

The night before, Fayette, in a scorching mood in a cold house, plunged into an internet search about anger. She wanted advice on how to deal with her frustration over how the police treated Sheila. Max found space beside Fayette's mouse pad and began a careful wash of his two front paws.

"Well, I never," Fayette said after reading for 25 minutes. She looked at Max. "You wanna hear what I just found out?"

Max answered with a definitive chirp.

"Okay then. Imagine someone gets blamed for something they didn't do, like if I blamed you for licking the butter, but you didn't." Max sat at attention, watching every movement on Fayette's face. "Let's say the blamed person gets angry because they know they're innocent. I don't know about cats, but a lot of us humans believe that an angry person is probably a guilty person."

A yowl from Max seemed to demand an answer. "Well, yeah," Fayette said, reaching out to rub him between the ears. "But they've done some studies, you know, at universities. Turns out the opposite is true most of the time. Researchers discovered that the angrier someone got after being accused of something, the more likely they didn't do it. So, if you were human, and I accused you of licking the butter, and you got hot and angry, I would have to assume you didn't do it." Max yawned and turned to wash his tail. "Boring? Maybe this isn't new to you. It's new to me because most people don't think of anger that way. Most people seem to think rage is proof of guilt."

Fayette's conversation with Max was more than 11 hours ago, but in the hospital waiting room, her research was fresh in her memory. So, when the chief accused Fayette and Sheila of being "suspects joining forces," Fayette worked hard to control her anger and focus her annoyance on a statement she prepared for just such an occasion. She'd memorized it in case Castillo blamed Sheila for anything to do with Pastor Fisby. Now she was defending both of them.

"Like you, Police Chief Castillo," Fayette began, "Senator Joseph McCarthy often accused people without evidence, ruining their reputations and their lives. In the words of Boston lawyer Joseph Welch to Senator Joseph McCarthy in 1954, 'Until this moment I think I never really gauged your cruelty or your recklessness. You have done enough. Have you no sense of decency?'"

With her good arm, Fayette pushed herself to a standing position so that she could look the chief in the eye. So far, she'd kept her tone even but firm.

"Like Joseph McCarthy, you accuse us without evidence of crimes that you have no proof even exist. Chapter 22, section 223 of the nation's penal code states, and I quote: 'An aggravated false accusation is punishable by imprisonment for a term not exceeding 10 years.' If you go on like this, Chief, I may just charge you and then sue you for aggravated false accusations."

Sheila let her breath out in relief. She'd been holding it in since Fayette stood to face the police chief. What if Fayette lost control and used her good arm to push him?

As for the chief, he ran a brown hand through his thick, closely cropped, black hair and burst out laughing. "Bueno, Ma'am. Bonito speech, but I'm not buying it. I don't think my accusations are false, but even if they are, police officers are exempt from that law. They have to be. You're on my radar, Ma'am, and you will be until we find Pastor Parkinson, dead or alive, and determine how he was poisoned and who kidnapped him."

A shout across the room startled them all. "Bloody assassins. How dare you show your faces here."

Clad in sleek riding chaps slung low, Elden's long legs carried him in seconds to Chief Castillo's side. Towering above them, Elden glanced for a dismissive moment at Fayette and Sheila and then focused his attention on the chief. "Why aren't these atrocious women in jail?" he demanded, in a loud, carrying baritone.

"Sir?"

"It's clear that one of these nasty women poisoned Fisby and the other kidnapped him. Who knows what they've done with him? They may have given him more poison. What are you doing to find Fisby?"

"Settle down, Sir. We're keeping a close eye on all our suspects. We're chasing down all our leads. There's not enough evidence to arrest anyone, yet. And we don't call people *nasty* unless we have proof they deserve it."

"They're conniving, aren't they? They're suspects, aren't they?" Elden snarled, his muscled arms held stiff at his sides. "Don't let them deceive you, officer."

"You're under a lot of stress, so I'll look past what you just said. I repeat. We don't have the evidence we need for an arrest, but we're working on it."

"You've got video. I heard you telling your officers about it in the hallway upstairs," Elden insisted. "You've got it on camera that this woman (he gestured at Fayette) visited Fisby yesterday in his room. You've got a bottle, complete with her fingerprints, found on his windowsill. What other proof do you need?"

"Her body type doesn't match the body type of the person who removed the pastor from his room at 3 a.m." The chief sighed. "We have her explanation about why she was there earlier, as strange as it is."

Fayette moved in front of Elden and pointed a finger at his chest. "And I saw you. I know it was you visiting Pastor Fisby's room right after I did. Why aren't you a suspect? Why haven't they arrested you?"

Elden sneered down at her. "Because I'm Fisby's brother. I had a good reason for being there."

A memory flashed through Fayette's consciousness of the glass bowl containing red rosary pea beads, left on a counter in the Brilliant Things shop. Elden had snatched the beads from her. His close connection to Pastor Fisby further explained why he had them. The bright seed beads must have come from Fisby's workshop, and Fisby must have stolen them from Sheila's garden.

"I can see the resemblance, both in rudeness and facial features." Fayette couldn't stop herself from commenting. "Maybe police officers are exceptions to the laws concerning aggravated false accusations, but store owners are not exempt. Stop trying to blame us for your brother's misfortunes, Elden Parkinson, or you'll find yourself in all kinds of trouble you never dreamed of."

Elden's upper lip curled as part of an infuriating smirk. "You have no idea who you are talking to. You are a powerless wannabe about to be gobbled by smarter, more skillful opponents. Beware."

With that, he turned and strode to the hospital exit. The air stirred around him so that magazine covers and papers and even people's hair lifted, just a smidgeon, as he passed.

Chief Javier squinted after Elden's back and shook his head in puzzlement. "That man says the oddest things," he murmured to himself, looking at his watch. "Ay, caramba. It's time to give the wife a break para los niños." He nodded at Sheila and Fayette and followed Elden out of the waiting room.

"I think we can go now, too." Sheila grabbed Fayette's uninjured arm. "The hospital staff has your address.

They can send you the paperwork. I'm ready for lunch. How about you?"

"And after lunch, sleep, lots of sleep," was the answer.

As Fayette turned to follow Sheila, she recognized someone watching them near the public restrooms. It was the woman Elden pushed out of his shop yesterday, after Fayette met Leo. The same woman had watched Elden refuse to sell her a few rosary pea beads.

Fayette waved a finger at the woman, who smiled and waved back with notebook in hand.

"See that woman in the black wool blazer and red turtleneck?" Fayette pointed her out to Sheila.

"Oh, my, and she's wearing bib overalls under her blazer. I don't have any of those, but I love them," Sheila said. "What about her?"

"This is the second time she's witnessed me get in trouble with Elden Parkinson. I wonder why she's here?"

Sheila shrugged, and they made their slow way to the exit doors, one step at a time to keep from jostling Fayette's arm and shoulder. Once they were on the sidewalk, Sheila could see her recently repaired, sage-green, 2016 Honda Accord, with its brand-new catalytic converter and radio unit. It occupied a slot four parking rows away.

"I'm going to get the car and pick you up here. Have a seat on the bench, and I'll be here soon."

Fall leaves squished under Sheila's feet, smelling sweet and musky. She startled herself with the realization that she had yet to take time for a tour of Elmira trees in their orange, red, and yellow fall attire. So much had happened she barely noticed the changing colors, the crisp nights, and the shorter days. October was her favorite month, and it was half gone already.

As she neared her car, Sheila noticed a group of five or six people gathered around a tall, metal light pole. A man pointed to a poster taped to the pole. When she approached the small crowd, the pointer focused his gaze on her.

"It's her," he exclaimed, aiming his finger at Sheila. "She's one of the women in this picture."

The crowd watched as Sheila drew near to the pole. With so many eyes on her, she felt unsteady, and the trampled leaves near the pole were wet and slippery. The large poster hung right in front of her, its image stark, even hostile. She saw the message. Then it blurred, and the bottom seemed to fall out of the day. Someone had taken a photo of her sitting next to Fayette in the Lucky Cup Café and Bakery. The photographer snapped a picture just as Fayette caught Sheila's teacup with her middle fingernail the day the Reading Club of Retired and Capable Ladies met to talk about the book *The Magic of Starting Something New in the Age of Retirement*. In the photo, Sheila's eyes were wide with surprise, and her mouth formed a round O shape. Fayette's eyes scrunched into fixated slits; her jaw tightly supported gritted teeth. Tea spilling from the cup hung suspended in the air over Kitsy's book, which lay open in the middle of the table.

The photograph would have been something to chuckle over had the photographer sent it to Sheila on her phone. Fayette's and her own expression were farcical, and the situation a memory to laugh about. But something about the black-and-white starkness of the picture radiated creepiness and highlighted the women's expressions as somehow menacing. It didn't help that block letters above the picture spelled out the word *Witches*, with the word *Poisoners* printed below it.

"Oh, la," Sheila said, placing her right hand over her heart. She turned to race to her car, but her left foot slipped on damp leaves, and she went down, catching her fall with the palms of her hands. Tears stung her eyes, more from fear and embarrassment than from her skinned knees.

"This is ridiculous," said a gruff, young voice above her. She heard the rip of paper as someone tore the poster from the light pole. A hand touched her shoulder. "Ms. Fairlight, are you all right? Let me help you stand." Sheila looked up into Noah's face. He was out of uniform, but she recognized him as one of the officers who interviewed her the day before at the police station.

"Thank you, Noah. Yes, dear. I could use a hand up." Other hands in addition to Noah's helped Sheila back to her feet and assisted her in brushing the debris from her pants and coat.

"This must have been a shock," Noah said, gesturing to the torn poster on the ground, now wadded into a crumpled ball. He bent to pick it up. "If I see any more, rest assured I will remove and destroy them."

"But who …?" Sheila thought of Elden. Would he stoop so low?

"If we find out, we'll let you know," Noah promised her. "Can I help you to your car?"

By the time Sheila made it back to Fayette, the best she could do was maneuver the car catawampus to the curb in front of the hospital. She was too jittery to care. Fayette managed to climb into the front seat, and Sheila closed the passenger door and returned to her place behind the wheel. Should she drive? Her hands trembled from shock.

"I saw you fall." Fayette winced as she worked to maneuver the seatbelt over her upper body. "You've got a death grip on that steering wheel. Do you want to take time to decompress? We can sit in the parking lot for a while. Do you want me to drive? What happened anyhow?"

Closing her eyes, Sheila breathed in a lung full of air and then let it out, shaky and slow. "I've got a choice. I can either feel scared and helpless and guilty for even trying magic, or I can get mad and take control of the situation and maybe find some magic to help us get out of this mess. I think I know which option you would choose, Fayette."

"Where did this all come from? What happened out there between my bench and your car?"

"Someone put up a nasty, horrible poster about us," Sheila answered. "They called us witches and poisoners. But the worst thing is, they've printed a picture of us in the café looking like complete buffoons. It's embarrassing is what it is. Maybe there's some kind of spell I could use to have the embarrassment ricochet back to the person who made those posters."

"Posters, huh?" Fayette moved to face Sheila and winced with pain. "I think I know who took that picture. The days I saw her in the café, that Darnelle Shipman took hundreds of phone pictures of everyone. Get your hiney in gear and park this car right now." Fayette tried to motion toward the back window with her left arm, felt a sharp stab in her shoulder, and groaned. "Great galaxies. There's a line of cars ready to pick up other people. While we wait for you to get your shitickens together, I've got something to tell you. It's about what happened after I broke this bone but before the ambulance came. There is something we can do and there may be people who can help us."

CHAPTER 16

Holding onto the stovetop for support, Kitsy sank into a kitchen chair and put her head in her hands. Her adrenaline levels, high all day, left her feeling as though she'd gone through a washing machine spin cycle. But there was no rest for the wicked, as the saying goes, and The Lantern Man's shrieks increased. Kitsy felt sure that the neighbors might be calling the police as she sat frozen, too tired to respond, but the idea that the neighbors might think she and Samuel were in a dangerous domestic dispute got her back on her feet. After all, before that moment, the Brownings had always been quiet and respectful, the perfect neighbors. The idea that rumors might spread if the police arrived renewed Kitsy's motivation, and she fairly ran, banging through the kitchen door to confront The Lantern Man.

"Hey! What's going on? What are you going on about?" It was Samuel's gruff voice, the one he used when patience ran out. His nap was over, rudely interrupted.

I'm a poor excuse for a Lantern Man babysitter, Kitsy told herself. She joined Samuel standing over the tall, thin, craggy-faced being who held onto the arms of the reading chair as though they could save him. On the television screen, a new victim of the salt-drinking monster, sucker marks on his face, lay unconscious, maybe dead, in the hallway of the Starship Enterprise. The horror of it was too much for The Lantern Man.

"Get me away from here," he moaned. "Take me to the marshes if you must. But I can't go without my lantern. I must have my lantern."

Samuel reached to take the man's arm.

"Don't touch," screamed their guest.

Stepping forward and bending down, Kitsy clapped to get the man's attention. "Your lantern is in the kitchen. It was scorching the table, so I picked it up and put it on the stove where it wouldn't damage anything."

All three of them looked at the oval cherry and walnut side table with its delicate forest scene inlaid on its surface. Holly and maple wood trees and mountains, once bright and polished, were pealing back, singed and blackened, scorched by the lantern.

"Well, hell," said Samuel.

"How did you know?" asked The Lantern Man, studying Samuel with new respect.

"Know what?"

"That the lantern came from hell."

"Is that the story?" Samuel was quick to play along.

"It's a story people tell." The Lantern Man shook his head so vehemently that he dislodged strands of dark hair intermixed with gray, which fell into his eyes. "I read a story about myself one day. It was before that sorcerer conjured me into the book. The story was in a tourist guidebook someone dropped in the Fens. It said I had been a very bad person so that when I died, I wasn't allowed in heaven. But God and the devil gave me another life to redeem myself. Apparently, I was even worse in the next life, so bad that neither heaven nor hell would let me in. The devil condemned me to roam the marshes forever, but he gave me one piece of coal to keep me warm. That piece of coal is in my lantern, and it's all that I have in this world. The guidebook description concluded that without the lantern, I'd become a lowlier and more contemptable wretch."

"I wonder." Kitsy looked hard at their miserable, ancient storyteller. She turned to Samuel. "He says that's not his real story. If that's true, then the lantern isn't what he says it is either. It might be the very thing that makes him so loathsome, not the other way around. Maybe he'd be better off without it."

"You say people tell that story. What's the real story?" Samuel looked sympathetic, but all Kitsy felt was impatience. This man or creature, or whatever he was, reminded her of a few manipulative grade school kids she'd set straight.

"Don't people say you used the lantern to lure victims further into swamps until they were lost and drowned?" Kitsy's voice dripped sarcasm. "Maybe you don't deserve even a piece of coal." She noticed that the man's speech was devoid of British English and Old English. He knew perfectly well how to communicate in modern, North American English.

"I'm not the only one," whined the man in the chair. "There are other lantern men. Maybe the story in the pamphlet is theirs. It's not mine."

"Well, you'll get back your lantern only after you've told us your real story in plain, North American English so that Samuel, here, doesn't have to spend hours transcribing the garbled mess you dribbled out earlier today. And you will tell us what you know about Pastor Fisby." Kitsy saw an opportunity to make the best of a distasteful situation. "I'll cook up dinner while you sit at the kitchen table with Samuel and answer his questions truthfully and with words we can understand. That first interview was a sham. You know how to talk so that Samuel doesn't have to look up every other word in his Old English dictionary. Until we're satisfied you've given us an honest account of everything, in English we can comprehend, the lantern will remain on the stove."

On the TV screen, the Starship Enterprise doctor,

Bones, killed the salt-sucking monster, even while it shapeshifted into a woman he knew and loved.

The Lantern Man inched his way out of the chair and stood, his chest heaving, his eyes wide, full of trepidation. Samuel switched off the DVD player and then gestured to the TV screen, a puzzled frown on his face. "It's just a story-telling machine. Someone wrote that story and then people acted it out. It isn't real."

"No, sir. I saw it. I saw it was real." The Lantern Man turned to follow Kitsy to the kitchen and to find his metal box holding its piece of burning coal. To Kitsy's surprise, Marmy sat alert on the counter next to the stove and the flickering lantern, almost as though she was on guard. The little orange cat licked a front paw, flexing her sharp claws, and when The Lantern Man approached his lantern, Marmy hissed and then growled.

"Move on to the table," Kitsy commanded, "or we'll hide your lantern where you'll never find it." She kissed Marmy above her pink nose and whispered, "Well done, girl. Well done."

To Samuel she said, "I've got a hot dog recipe I want to try. I'll put together a salad and my new concoction and we'll have dinner within an hour. In the meantime, go ahead with your questions. This will save time, so you don't have to sort through those crazy tapes and notes from this morning."

Kitsy hoped that The Lantern Man would be more cooperative if she kept busy and stayed out of the question-and-answer session. She planned to have her turn, though. This spirit, or apparition, or specter had to know a lot about Pastor Fisby. After all, he'd been in Fisby's house for decades. Why was Fisby stealing rosary pea seeds and making them into beads? Why did he have an altar and books for the dark arts if he was a Christian pastor?

Equipped with his recorder and readied with notebook

and pen, Samuel conducted a second interview with The Lantern Man, while Kitsy mixed a maple syrup, Dejon mustard, and garlic sauce to pour over extra-long hotdogs nestled in brioche buns. If the recipe was a success, she would add it to her recipe book collection. In the meantime, Kitsy knew she had to contact Fayette and Sheila as soon as she could. The three of them were in over their heads. They needed to find help.

At first, The Lantern Man tried to eat his maple and mustard covered hotdog with his fingers, licking them to remove the sticky sauce. Then he copied Samuel's use of knife and fork to finish his second helping. "My tongue is bewitched." His voice emulated the darker tones of a whining basset horn, panting out complaining notes of distress, even fright. "It wants another helping. Foolish it is. The tongue knows not what it is eating."

"I agree. I want another helping too." Samuel laughed. "I think this combination is a winner. Put it in your book."

Both men held out their plates for more, Samuel with a satisfied expression and The Lantern Man looking dubious and awed at the same time.

Well, I'll be, Kitsy thought. *Maybe I'll call this recipe "A fool for hotdogs."*

CHAPTER 17

The Story of The Lantern Man
by Samuel Browning
and Alfred Dowsby

Following is a partial summary, in The Lantern Man's words, of the interview Samuel Browning conducted in the Browning kitchen. *Note: the appendix chapter at the end of this book contains a more complete version of The Lantern Man's story.*

Alfred Dowsby, known also as The Lantern Man, was born in 1616 in a herder's cottage within the Great Fens of East Anglia, England. His life began in an untamed country where the marshes, tidal creeks, washes, meres, and rivers helped rear him to be as wild as the land.

Like most of the Fenmen, my father herded cows and sheep. He fished and trapped birds when he wasn't chasing livestock. My brothers, sisters, and I milked the cows and made cheese and butter. We cut the tall grasses for hay, and we gathered peat for fuel and sedge and reed for thatching. My mother grew vegetables in the high places, where the rising waters in winter deposited soft, fertile silt.

Our life was fixed in the hinterlands on an isle often cut off from others during the winter. But in the summer, the waters retreated, and we had access to towns and villages, where there were cathedrals, churches, and abbeys, and all manner of marketplaces.

My mother was a cunning woman, a wise woman. People came to her for cures and advice to help them manage sickness in body and in heart. I knew about the Fen bogies, imps, familiars, and the spirits that lived in the marshes and meres. Sometimes, when everyone was asleep, and the moon was high, I went looking for them. I would see lights in the distance, dancing over the water and bogs. I'd follow the lights but couldn't catch them. Once I discovered an injured otter by one of the main paths. I decided that it must be the dying familiar of a fairy. I killed it with a stick.

The older I got, though, the more I felt drawn to the town of Ely. It is north of Cambridge and near the towns Witcham and Witchford. Our home place was slightly north of Ely, and a few hours away by punt on the river Ouse. I thought it was in town that I could make something big of myself. One day I went to the Ely market and stayed. After that, I only went home for special celebrations or to bring presents from the market. I was a young lad then.

By the time I left home, the draining of the Fens had begun.

My family was against the Fen drainers. We all joined the protests. I know that my brothers helped sabotage some of the dikes and pumps that were built. The Fen people made up songs and curses to taunt and scare the engineers and workers. My mother was among the women accusing the outsiders of witchcraft. Wealthy men from the cities were robbing the Fen people of their common area and of their livelihoods. They needed to be stopped. Drainage was big business. Its purpose was to create new farmland, not for local people but for major landowners, and it meant depriving Fen people of rights to fish and hunt.

My family and my neighbors were up to their knees fighting for their Fens, rebelling against changing the course of the rivers, struggling for their livelihoods. But I wanted in on the riches, and the drainers needed workers. I knew that the outlanders saw my people as heathenish yokels. I knew my people saw the drainers as diabolical. Both sides accused the other of witchcraft and sorcery. I was so set on making myself useful to the engineers and the rich landholders that - for food and money - I willingly warned the drainers when my people planned raids and protests. I pointed out the local Fen leaders.

Then one night, I heard some men laughing behind a curtain in the Abby. I heard my name mentioned, so I listened. They called me a worm, the lowest of low, a quisling, and a spy. And then I knew I was never to be one of them, never to become an estate holder, never to be brought into the royal fold. They had simply used me. My heart blackened. My mind felt hot, like the coal in a lantern, always burning, burning with hate.

It's true my people understood the importance of folk magic. They were motivated by a desire to maintain equilibrium and not to practice domination over the Fens. We knew of Fen magic. We knew of the Tiddy Mun as a peculiar Fen bogey. Our Tiddy Mun was a short goblin in a gray cloak who lived in the meres. Some said they saw him on misty nights. Occasionally, the flooding got high enough to reach the uplands. When that happened, cottagers, led by cunning women, marched outside during a full moon and chanted spells asking the Tiddy Mun to make the waters withdraw. It was a way of managing our environment with the help of a bogey.

I came to believe that I could grow in power and wealth with the help of the demons, fairies, and bogies, rather than with the help of mortal men of high social standing. Those men had one kind of power, but the magic folk had greater power. At night, I sought out the ancient supernatural beings who dwelled in the thick brushes and hidden places of the Fens. My mother was a cunning woman, respected by her community because her purpose was to help, never to hurt. My mother was a wise woman, not a witch, but I sought a different path. I wanted the power to punish the cold-blooded venture capitalists and their engineers draining the Fens. I wanted control over those who humiliated me. When I turned twenty, I sought out a diviner or sorcerer, wicca or wicce, female or male. It didn't matter to me.

One night, when there was no moon, I saw a fire in the distance as I punted through a marsh, dense with great Fen sedge. It was late fall, and the frogs were hibernating. All was quiet except the sound of my oar as I used it to feel a way through the reeds, making room for my passage. I moved closer to the fire, docking my watercraft at the foot of an island. As I climbed a short distance uphill, I could see a figure, a man cutting segments of his hair and throwing them into the fire. He picked up a shirt, tore it into pieces, and threw the sleeves and then the rest into the flames. Each time he added to the fire, it burst upwards in scorching surges, and then he talked the fire down, his voice soft and then loud and then soft again. I thought I recognized the full-sleeved silk shirt and the jacket of pomegranate-patterned linen that went piece by piece into the flames. They belonged to a draining engineer who was particularly eager for information about the Fen people. Remembering his false, covetous smile, I felt deep satisfaction at seeing his clothes burn.

By the look of the fire-raiser's hooded cloak, he was no benevolent wise man. He'd made his shroud from red, tanned leather, close-fitted with back and front hemlines plunging downward like the points of arrows.

A thread and needle artist embroidered the collar and hem with images of frenzied monsters. I was in awe. This was the kind of conjurer I sought, unshackled from the bounds of sympathetic humanity. Long brown hair, streaked with gray, straggled down his back in clumped strands. Pieces of cut hair hung uneven in front. In strange contrast to his unruly locks, the man trimmed his salt and pepper beard with even precision. His eyes mirrored the flames in the fire as he shouted and murmured, shouted and murmured long streams of words that I could not decipher. I watched, so fascinated that I was unaware of the four-foot-long black and yellow serpent that slid from the water and settled over my left leg. It was only a grass snake, but it surprised me, and I let loose a yell. The conjurer's head turned in my direction, but he kept on with his spell work.

The Teacher told me that night he was expecting me. My mother, he explained, was a descendant of the Wiffingas clan, though she did not know it. The magic that was strong in her passed to me. The Teacher said, 'Those rods she lights to burn away the malaria work sometimes, but not if my magic is causing the illness. Her magic is undisciplined and simple. Mine overpowers hers.' He told me he could help me control and focus my magical aptitude, but I must never question him if I wanted to stay with him. 'Never cross me, son, or you will live to regret it.' I didn't realize living to regret would mean lamenting my very existence, bemoaning even my birth, for hundreds of years.

The Teacher lived in a tall stone tower on his own island deep in the Fens. I slept in the damp basement underground, tending to the fires in the morning and preparing The Teacher's ingredients for his work each day. Many times, he refused to tell me the purposes for his conjuring. Often, he showed me how to gather ingredients, prepare them, and then use them in various rituals and spells. Sometimes The Teacher instructed me to use his rowboat and take items to Ely to leave on people's doorsteps or windowsills or to exchange at a market stall for goods or money. Some so-called gifts that I left on doorsteps had been commissioned. Some were from The Teacher himself to influence people's thinking, and, in that way, to direct political decisions. A few items were meant to cause punishment for a family. As I delivered the spells, I sometimes saw one of the dandies who used me in my younger years. I spat on the ground behind them and uttered spells to bring them misfortune. Then, when I was almost 30 years old, The Teacher set me free. 'You're ready, Alfred, to make your own future. But beware; if you ever try to use your magic in opposition to me or to counter my magic, you will wish you were never born.' I thanked The Teacher and left his tower with only the clothes on my back.

I set up shop in town as an accountant. Each night, when the doors of my shop closed, I descended to a basement I dug out in secret. It was damp, of course, like the one I'd occupied in the tower for eight years. You can't really expect basements in the Fen to be dry. But it made a good workshop for my real work. I began to manipulate my neighbors through magic. I worked magic to sway the clergy and bishop in the monastery and cathedral. In secret, I influenced the businessmen and engineers trying to make farmland out of the Fens, and the people who ran the weekly markets. When my magic required me to make talismans or potions that I needed to place near houses, chapels, or shops, I donned my darkest wool cloak and soft shoes and slipped in and out of night shadows as I made my clandestine deliveries. I tried to prevent the discovery of my spell receptacles because, when found, they fueled and intensified searches for local witches. When the witch hunters came to town, I focused my magic on spells I could conduct from my basement, but those were never as effective as spells delivered directly to the intended recipient.

One night, as I worked to insert a tiny clay spell pot into a crevice under the ivy near a prominent witch finder's residence, I felt a cold hand on my shoulder. The hand roughly spun me around, and the pot flew from my fingers and landed on the ground at my assailant's feet. The witch hunter, Hopkins, picked it up, and I muttered a short incantation under my breath. I knew I had one chance to save myself. If the spell worked, I could offer the right suggestion. I had to think of something plausible on the spot, and I had to think of it fast.

An idea came to mind, and I acted on it. 'I am a witch hunter, like you Mr. Hopkins. I have been tailing a known witch. He put this spell pot here. I assume it contains a spell that needs nullifying.'

I'm not sure the witchfinder believed me, but he played along.

'You are the accountant with an office down the street,' Hopkins said, twirling the left side of his long mustache. 'No one told me you are a witch hunter. What witches have you turned in for conviction?'

'None, yet, sir,' I said. 'I am new to this and want to make sure I have the best of proof.'

'What makes you qualified to identify a witch?' Hopkins' tone was surly and full of suspicion.

'I grew up with a cunning woman, my mother,' I confessed. 'She used magic for her neighbors' problems and to help cure people of sickness. I know some of the signs from her.'

'So, your mother is a witch.' Hopkins' eyes narrowed. 'She will be questioned and brought before the court.'

'No, sir. She is a wise woman, not a witch,' I was quick to say.

What had I done, I wondered, and how could I distract him from my family? I decided to take a chance. 'No, she's not a witch, but the man I followed tonight is one. He lives in a tower on an island in the Fens. He's the one you want to focus on. His name is Wehha, and he keeps alive the magic brought to this area through the earliest Anglo-Saxon rulers of East Anglia, the Wiffingas dynasty.'

The witchfinder's eyes widened with interest. Tracking down a witch connected with the Viking invaders of old would be a master coup.

'You must show me how to get to this tower and this witch called Wehha,' Hopkins said. 'If you take me to him tomorrow, I will have your mother watched rather than put in custody. But she will undergo examination and a trial at the Ely Quarter Sessions.'

The witch hunter regarded me with pursed lips nearly hidden by his heavy beard and mustache. 'I will commandeer a skiff and then find you at your place of business early in the morning. Be there.' He turned, then, and entered the place he rented.

I stood in the street, frozen, remembering the final words of The Teacher only months ago. 'But beware, if you ever try to use your magic in opposition to me or to counter my magic, you will wish you were never born.'

I came to the tower that night and woke The Teacher, explaining what happened and that men might come for him. I expected him to be angry, but I had never seen the true power of his wrath until the wee hours of the coming morning. He looked at me as though I was the lowest of worms or an insect he wished to crush under his heel. 'I warned you never to cross me,' he said, his voice at first cold and hard and then rumbling low, like the start of an avalanche. 'The searchers will never find me, and neither will they find you, Alfred of the Fens. When I finish this spell, you will be but a shell of a man, no longer human. Your destiny for as long as marshes exist on this planet will be to haunt the wetlands. Your only possession will be a lantern with a coal for a light, and as much as you might chase the people who come close, you can never be one of them. You are alone,

Alfred of the Fens. People will come to fear you, as they should. Not even your mother can trust you now, and no one should trust you in the future.'

'Is there nothing I can do to earn your forgiveness,' I pleaded.

'You are a traitor, full of avarice, caring only for yourself,' thundered The Teacher. 'Should you one day care enough to sacrifice yourself for the sake of another, then you might break from the torment you are about to begin.'

'I don't understand,' I said.

'I know,' said The Teacher.

And that is how I became The Lantern Man, cursed to carry a light in a metal box and wander the marshes. I came to hate humans and animals alike because they were free to live and free to die.

I spent more than 250 years wandering through the Fens, constantly moving as the drainers rerouted the waterways, set up pump stations, and turned the wetlands into farm country. I was a shell of my former self, no longer human, no longer feeling much that was good. My memories of my family and the people of Ely faded. For a time, my jealousy and anger grew to include every human in the world. I became ever reckless. I didn't care what happened to my victims, the ones who followed my light into the bogs and rivers. I relished chasing travelers with my lantern until they were lost and scared. No one cared for me. Why would I care for them?"

A note by Samuel Browing, folklorist: Over time, stories emerged about the man who carried a light, tempting people to follow him to their deaths in the reed beds of the Fens. His was often a lone light, shining over the darkness, luring people in. As the stories of The Lantern Man spread, so did advice for how to avoid him. Experts on the Fen wild areas counseled people not to carry torches or lights at night in the Fens because the Lantern Man followed such lights. Never whistle was another piece of wisdom because The Lantern Man runs towards a whistle and will kill the whistler if he can. Never mock the Lantern Man or he will follow you all the way home and try to torch your house. As one old man said, 'Hold your breath. If the Lantern Man is upon ye, throw yourself flat on your face and halt ye breathing.'

Alfred continues his story: *In time, my loneliness got the best of me. It had taken more than two and a half centuries to begin feeling remorse, even empathy and to wish I had a woman to love and a family to raise. As I began to wonder what it would be like to give rather than take, my piece of coal started to shrink. But just as I was learning to feel for others, and just as the heat of the coal in my lantern began to cool, a delegation of Wicken Fen neighbors visited the home of an ancient man called Wehha. By this time, he called himself a fiend hunter who could rid the countryside of unwanted creatures of the night. The people wanted lantern men and all manner of will o' the wisps to disappear.*

Wehha, my teacher, neared the end of an exceptionally long life as a conjurer and wizard. Since it was his spell that formed me into the monster I am, it was easy for him to commandeer my essence and imprison what was left of me into a smallish book, just published that year and sold in city bookstores. Wehha trapped me between the pages of 'The Book of Forbidden Knowledge' for a hundred and thirteen years, until you, Samuel, whistled me free.

Wehha had two sons. Their cunning mother left them as boys because she could no longer endure the cruelty of being with their father. I suppose she felt they were all better off without her, as Wehha degraded her day after day until she no longer believed she was capable of much. I understand she eventually took her own life. Wehha believed that women were less than human and that wise women of the Fen could never reach the knowledgeable heights of male necromancers and warlocks. He taught his sons his prejudices. Because they believed their father, and because they blamed their mother for leaving them, they, too, degraded women and their magic. Like Wehha, these sons are long-lived for humans. When Wehha died at the age of 537, the sons inherited their father's fortune as well as his conjuring tools and books. 'The Book of Forbidden Knowledge,' my prison, is part of one of his son's collections.

Wehha's sons brought their history, their conjuring tools, and their book collections to the Americas in 1983. East Anglia in Britain, their ancient birthright, is largely tamed. The wild energies of the fens and forests are shadows of their former glory, so the deep forests and powerful rivers of the Pacific Northwest, still full of untamed potencies, attracted the Wiffingas Clan descendants.

Pastor Fisby Parkinson and Elden Parkinson are Wehha's long-lived sons, and now that I am free, I plan to take revenge on them for the pain they caused me for more than 100 years and that their father caused me for nigh unto 388 years.

Chapter 18

By the time Alfred, The Lantern Man, revealed that Fisby and Elden were conjurers, and older than they looked, it was long past bedtime. Kitsy had a mountain of questions for the ancient apparition sitting in her kitchen, but most would have to wait. She did ask him one.

"As you told us more than once, you're a broken soul of the Wicken Fens. What can you tell us that's more useful? What do you know about the brothers that might be important to our safety and to your plan to get revenge?"

"Are you mocking me, again, witch?"

Kitsy remembered the old folk warnings about what not to do around The Lantern Man. Fen elders warned against mocking him, by all accounts, and she had been taunting him with a vengeance ever since he appeared in her kitchen. His rudeness and untidiness repelled her, but if she wanted his help, she would have to change tactics.

"No, Alfred. I am not mocking you. Your story touched me deeply, and I want to know how to help plan the best outcome for all of us."

The Lantern Man's eyes blazed for a moment on hearing his old name. Could he trust this strange woman? Alfred lived on the shelves of conjurers for more than a hundred years, listening to the talk of men whose father taught them to disdain women's power, but especially the energies of cunning or wise women. This Kitsy would be an object of scorn and contempt in Pastor Fisby's world, in Elden's world, and in Wehha's world. But then, these men would have belittled his mother, too, and she never hurt anyone.

"The brothers lead a male coven that they call The Guild of the Supreme Brotherhood of Manroots. One of its goals is to disempower Wiccan covens and female witches in whatever way they can. They detest that women generally lead Wiccan gatherings, and they are outraged that Wiccans value female strengths so highly in such groups."

"How do they try to take power from them?" Kitsy knew little about Wiccans or covens, male or female.

"They know how to use innuendo and gossip to lead non-magic people into fearing and hating people that the Manroots identify as Wiccan or witches. They direct people who will listen into doing their dirty work, and they use religion as a tool to motivate their unwitting followers. Some people listen to them, others do not. But at times, they also use dark magic, what my mother called low magic."

"Thank you for the heads up." Kitsy watched Samuel yawn and couldn't help mimicking him. "I hope we can talk more about this in the coming days. Now, I don't know if you need sleep, but perhaps while we sleep, you will welcome some quiet time on your own. I fixed the spare bedroom for you. There are books to read in Samuel's study and in the family room. Make yourself comfortable, and we will see you in the morning."

Samuel and Kitsy watched The Lantern Man, or Alfred, retire to their guest room to "sleep off bad company," as he put it. Samuel locked the kitchen door from the family room to safeguard the lantern. They could imagine the risks they took by not keeping watch over him, but exhaustion set in for them both. They would have to take their chances. Even in his early life, Alfred was concerned mostly with himself, willing to manipulate others around him for wealth and power. He'd been inept at it, but that didn't mean he wouldn't try again. On the other hand, he admitted to experiencing empathy, and he claimed he was learning from his centuries-long torment to suffer remorse. It was hard to tell if he was still re-discovering his humanity.

When Samuel joined Kitsy in their bedroom, he described what happened before the moment Kitsy burst into the kitchen, poised to battle the demon. After Samuel stopped talking, he let loose a weary groan, laid his head on his pillow, and closed his eyes.

"I am so sorry you are in the middle of this nightmare." Kitsy reached over and hugged Samuel tightly. "I don't know how you can forgive me, but I hope you do. I never should have taken that book from Pastor Fisby's house. I never should have been in his study. And now you are in the middle of something that is beyond imagining."

"Look." Samuel opened his eyes and sat up. "The Lantern Man, uh … Alfred, said he had the power to goad you into taking *The Book of Forbidden Knowledge*. He told me it wasn't exactly your idea to steal the book from the shelf and stick it into your bag. He wanted out of that house and away from Pastor Fisby. You were his ticket to freedom. I've been with you for 45 years, and you've never stolen so much as a drinking straw in all that time. It makes sense that he was at the bottom of the theft. He also said that if I hadn't been whistling, he never could have escaped, so I guess I can share the blame. We'll figure this out, but we can't do it on our own. Where does one go to find help transforming a demon?" Samuel heaved a sigh. "All I know is I'm desperate for sleep. It's been one of the longest days of my life."

Outside their bedroom door, Kitsy heard whistling from the hallway, the same melody for *Dashing Away With the Smoothing Iron*. Then the whistling shifted to raspy whispering, words without tune, the same hair-raising rhythm and echo she and Marmy heard early that morning coming from the cupboard under the stove.

T'was on a shadowy morning
When I beheld my tormentor
He looked deceitfully charming
In every high degree
He looked deceitfully charming, O
A-conjuring his curses, O
Dashing away with mad treachery
Dashing away with mad treachery
I'll get my vengeance soon

CHAPTER 19

'*Emergency meeting at the café, 9 a.m.,*' read the text from Fayette sent to Sheila and Kitsy.

Sheila, who was in her greenhouse when she got the message, slipped her phone into her gardening apron and re-focused on her *Green-Witch Magical Herbs* book. She wanted to find an herbal spell recipe powerful enough to end the embarrassment of being on that poster hung in the hospital parking lot. There were spells for protection and health, but not for particular ways to change specific circumstances.

"Gaaaak," she shrieked, tempted to throw the book out the window. The compendium contained plenty of descriptions of plants and their magical properties. "Useless," she said in frustration looking at the lists of plants that could be employed for such things as increasing fertility, attaining beauty, raising the dead, creating infertility, achieving invisibility, and other possible benefits. *Okay. So not entirely useless, just not what I need. I want exact directions for HOW to use them.*

Sheila wanted a recipe to stop people from doing mean things. She could find no ready formulas, so it appeared she might have to create her own. There were lists of plants that might help with her circumstances, such as halting gossip, assisting in legal matters, obtaining luck, strengthening mental powers, instilling peace and harmony, gaining protection, imparting strength, and promoting wisdom. Did she have the hutzpah to try designing her own recipe?

At breakfast she decided to be strong in her convictions and confident about her journey into the magic world. Taking control of her emotional state felt right to Sheila. She was, after all, a perfectly reputable woman who earned respect from the community after many years of church service. If someone was trying to ruin her standing by spreading rumors and putting up posters making her look ridiculous, well, that was their problem. Sheila would keep her chin up and her shoulders straight from now on.

"I refuse to be a scared little hummingbird," she said to herself. "No more. I will stand up to the likes of Pastor Fisby and Elden Parkinson. Stop with the doubts. Get a grip, woman."

***

Kitsy showed Samuel the message Fayette sent about the emergency meeting. They sat across from Alfred at the breakfast table, mostly concentrating on their oatmeal.

"Maybe Fayette and Sheila can help," she said to her husband. "I'll try not to be too long." She looked at their guest with his uncombed hair and thin, sharp elbows pressed into the table on each side of his breakfast bowl. He seemed more cooperative now that she stopped mocking and chiding him, but his mouth turned down; and his sullen eyes stared unseeing at the cream pitcher.

"Is there anything I can get you, Alfred, while I'm out?"

"The witch is talking to me," Alfred whispered, looking across at Samuel. "What more does she want from me?"

"For the fiftieth time, Alfred, Kitsy is not a witch." A pained expression seemed to age Samuel's tired face. "She's just asking if you need anything and if she can get it for you."

"If she were not a witch, she could not have heard me pleading with her to take *The Book of Forbidden Knowledge* from Pastor Fisby's bookshelf. If she were not a witch, she would not have figured out how to use the gloves and hide my book prison in her bag."

"I'll admit, Kitsy is something special, but more of a wise woman of old than a witch of old." Samuel reached over to squeeze Kitsy's hand. "If she had any magic powers, she would use them more like your mother did than like Wehha. So, what do you mean by calling her a witch?"

"I heard Fisby many times talking to his visitors about Wiccan witches, their belief in doing no harm, and their love of Earth. He preferred dark magic and the male witches of old. But perhaps the things he despised are better than bad. I am afraid of Puritan stories about envious witches of old, and your wife can be unpleasant. Which is she, an angry conjuror or a benevolent cunning woman? Is she a do-no-harm Wiccan witch of the new world? You see, Mr. Samuel, I know a wielder of magic when I see one. Your Kitsy is capable of magic. She has used magic."

"And which one are you Mr. Lantern Man?" Kitsy whispered, seething inside at the hypocrisy of Alfred's accusations. "Are you the envious, vengeance-seeking conjuror, or the wise man practitioner, or are you the do-no-harm Wiccan?"

***

A few blocks away, Fayette was just pulling a wrap over her shoulders, one-handed, when her phone rang. The caller ID read Leo Cagan. Was this the Leo of the denim blue customized Harley Softail Fat Boy?

"Hey, Faye," a gruff voice greeted her. "This is Leo, Leo from that day at Brilliant Things. How you been?" He stopped talking for a few seconds. "Stupid question isn't it. Word round town says you broke your shoulder and you're off your bike for a while. Anyway, I've been meanin' to call."

"Hello, Leo. You heard right. I've got my bike, and my roller skates corralled in the garage for at least six weeks. It's payback for flying around those roller rink curves too fast."

"Well, hell. Can I pretend to be an old church lady and bring by a casserole this evening? I don't mind sitting and sharing it with you and maybe challenging you to a game of Scrabble."

Fayette smirked at her kitten, pointed at her phone, and mouthed, *poor bastard*. "Just a warning, Leo. It's been 21 years since I lost at Scrabble. So, okay. I've got one good arm. Be here at 7 o'clock, and I'll set the table for dinner."

"You bet." Leo rang off.

If the rest of the day turned out to be like the day before, at least she had someone to do the dishes for her that evening, Fayette reasoned.

Half an hour later, a tall, thirty-something gentleman in a dark suit ushered her into the Lucky Cup Café and Bakery. Kitsy was already at their table, staring bleary-eyed at the ceiling while swirling tea with a spoon in her half-full cup. Fayette noted the bags under her friend's eyes and the harried tapping of a toe under the table. Had Kitsy seen some of the posters along the streets featuring Fayette and Sheila as bat-crazy witch poisoners? Is that why Kitsy put down her spoon and covered her face with both hands?

"What the corn nuts is wrong with you?" Fayette demanded, as she set down her own cup of blackberry tea and pushed a plate of hot-buttered ham and cheese biscuits in Kitsy's direction.

"Oh hi, Fayette. It's a long story." Kitsy removed her hands from her eyes and took a biscuit. "I've got some serious news, but let's wait for Sheila so I won't have to say it twice." She surveyed Fayette's bruised face and the sling on her left arm. "What was going on yesterday? How did this happen?" Kitsy gestured at Fayette's arm.

"It's this blasted old age," Fayette grumbled. "I was skating too fast for a 67-year-old codger and hit a wall."

They sat in silence for a few minutes, chewing on biscuits.

"Have you seen the posters?" Fayette asked.

"I haven't been out of my house for what seems like ages. What posters?"

Fayette tugged a crumpled sheet of paper from her pocket and held it up, folded. It was one of several that she'd torn off telephone poles on her walk from her house to the café. As Fayette spread out the shiny image, Kitsy choked on a bite of biscuit and felt the pain sear all the way down her throat. She almost cried out when she saw the image of her two friends, looking somehow clownish and devious at the same time.

"Witches and poisoners?" Kitsy said after swallows from a glass of cold water helped her recover from hacking down biscuit bites. "Hardly. Someone took this picture during a perfectly innocent accident, right here at this table." She shook her head. "You two are a thousand times more blameless than I am. I'm the one who should be on this poster, not you."

"What the bull Twinkies are you talking about, woman?" Fayette gave Kitsy a scornful look. "You're squeaky clean. You were near ready to go to jail just because you followed me to do a tiny bit of household investigating. What have you got to feel guilty about?"

"Who's feeling guilty?" Sheila added a pot of Ceylon tea and boysenberry jam tarts to their growing brunch feast.

"Kitsy thinks she should be on this wretched poster instead of us." Fayette motioned to the flyer.

"Oh la. Whatever for?" Sheila sat down and grabbed the last biscuit. She'd been up since 5:30 a.m., pouring through her garden magic books, and she was hungry. "None of us should be subject to the humiliation of being displayed around town on posters that accuse us of murder. For shame. We haven't done anything wrong."

"Well, that's not quite true in my case," Kitsy said, not meeting her friends' eyes. "I really have done something wrong, and I'm paying dearly for it. And Samuel is caught in the middle. He's paying for my mistake, too."

"What? Did you steal scrap paper from the library or something?" Fayette raised one eyebrow and curved her mouth into a sarcastic grin. "Did use the coffee shop bathrooms without buying something?" She guffawed at her own joke.

"For your information," Kitsy told Fayette, voice snippy and eyes narrowed, "I stole a book from Pastor Fisby's house. And it wasn't just any old book. It turned out to be a terrible, dangerous book."

Fayette sat stock still, her mouth frozen open in much the same O-shape of Sheila's lips in the ignoble picture featured on the poster. Sheila had a hand over her mouth, her eyes so wide the whites completely framed her irises. A sudden flash startled the women, and they turned to see that the young gentleman in the dark suit, the one who ushered Fayette into the bakery, had just taken a picture capturing Fayette and Sheila's surprised expressions.

"It was you!" Sheila and Fayette yelled in unison. They both launched from their chairs. Fayette was closest to the man and grabbed for his phone, but it was with her injured arm, and she groaned in pain.

"Darnelle Shipman took the first picture, not me," the man hollered back, hooting with laughter. He turned and ran through the tables and out the café door, Sheila and Fayette close on his heels.

"Damn it all to kingdom come," Kitsy said to nobody. "When am I finally going to get this whole truth-telling thing over with?" She wondered what was happening outside and worried about Fayette's injury. "Holy hell. That Fayette is one tough cookie." She pictured her friend in a sling chasing after the long-legged, young man. Then a niggle of worry tickled her mind as Kitsy recalled her own use of the words damn and hell. *And I'm starting to sound a lot like her.*

Should she go out and try to help them? No. Better to stay and guard their purses and bags. Kitsy would have fresh tea ready on their return. In minutes, the café door opened, and her two friends stumped in, breathless and looking wind-whipped and dejected. Fayette held onto the arm connected to her broken collar bone as though her limb was falling off. "Where's my ibuprofen," she said in a croaky whisper.

Sheila, limping, helped Fayette to her chair. "Are you sure you don't want me to take you home and put you to bed?" she asked.

"No. This is too important. I'll accept a ride home as soon as we're done here."

Kitsy poured more tea and watched Sheila and Fayette recover their breaths and their composures. Finally, Fayette closed her eyes, the pain receding, and Sheila straightened her scarf and combed fingers through her untidy hair.

"Spit on my biscuit, Sheila, you're a bloodhound." Fayette started laughing. "You stuck on his tail to the end. I thought you were going to climb on his pompous white Corvette bumper when he dove into the front seat and started the engine."

Sheila giggled. "I was ready to tackle him if that's

what it took, but I didn't have my shovel with me to knock him to the ground."

"I guess you can guess. He got away." Fayette turned to Kitsy.

"But I got his car license memorized." Sheila took a notebook from her purse and started writing. "MNROOTB123. It's got to be a personalized plate."

"I may know a lot more about motorcycles than I do cars, but that was a classic 1990s Corvette ZR-1. Hard to miss a ride like that. Did you see his ring?" asked Fayette.

"Just like Fisby's and Elden's rings." Sheila nodded. "I've got Fisby's ring in a cupboard at my house. I know exactly what they look like."

Now it was Kitsy's turn to look surprised at this startling revelation.

"Mustang Sally, aren't we all full of confessions today." Fayette started chuckling. Her chuckle turned into a contagious, uncontrolled hilarity of chokes and gasps, and Sheila and Kitsy couldn't help themselves. They joined her, and none of them could stop. Since the start of October, each day threw one novel trial after another in their paths, and they had resolved nothing yet, so it made sense to Kitsy that their stress turned into mirthful hysterics.

When they could look at each other without another laughing fit, and when they could breathe again, Sheila turned to Kitsy. "I think you were telling us something important about a book that you stole, and I still can't quite believe you did that, but you were interrupted, and I'd like to hear the rest of the story."

So, Kitsy told them everything, how an ancient spook haunted the book and how she and Samuel were trying to manage the spirit or specter. The Lantern Man had all the characteristics of a damaged and possibly dangerous fiend, or demon, or whatever was left of a bewitched human. "I don't know how to describe him except as a

lantern man," she said. "I don't know what to do with
him, how to help him, how to get him out of our lives."

"It's like you stepped into a horror novel." Sheila laid
her hands on top of her heart as if for protection. "And
he said he knew you practiced magic before and had the
capacity to be a witch? I guess this means that magic is
real."

They considered Sheila's words for a beat. *I guess
this means that magic is real.*

Fayette shuffled her feet, breaking the silence. "I think
it's time I told you what happened at the skating rink. It
might lead us to a solution to your problem, Kitsy, and
it might be a way to find help for what we're all going
through."

"A solution to my problem?" Kitsy tried to swallow
down a doubtful snort.

"Mother of butter, I hope so," Fayette said. "When
I was laying like a stuck squid on the skating rink, not
even able to sit up because of my bum shoulder, Lars
Columbus got down beside me while we waited for the
ambulance. You know what he said to me?" She looked
around the table, her eyes boring into theirs, expecting
an answer.

"That you're too old to be tearing around on skates
like a mad woman and that you ought to learn how to
slow down?" Sheila guessed.

"You're one of those killjoys who pop other people's
balloons," Fayette accused Sheila, shaking her head.
"No. He said, 'Magic is a funny thing.'"

"What was that supposed to mean?" Kitsy's voice
quickened with alarm, remembering that his were the
boots she heard tromping in and out of Fisby's bead-
making workshop when she and Fayette were hiding
under the pastor's altar.

"He meant that he knows about magic, and he's part
of a magic-practicing community here in Elmira. They
know about us. He invited us to meet them because he

said they could help us."

"Help us, how?" Sheila pointed the butter knife in Fayette's direction and waved it over the jam pot. "Are they hooked up with Pastor Fisby?"

"No, not Fisby. He told me to get my collarbone taken care of. Then, he said, 'I suggest the three of you plan an outing to the bookstore.'"

"Why the bookstore?" Kitsy pictured the bushy-browed proprietor and his collection of leather-bound journals.

Both Kitsy and Sheila leaned forward because Fayette looked so serious, and she actually lowered her voice. "Well, it was a little unnerving. He said, 'There's much more to talk about. Two small and distinct communities work magic in our area. One dabbles in the dark arts. One doesn't. You need to know the difference.'"

"Whoa. I think I know who dabbles in the dark arts." Kitsy remembered what Alfred, The Lantern Man, told them at the breakfast table. "The Lantern Man has lived in Pastor Fisby bookshelf, believe it or not, for more than 100 years. This morning, he told Samuel and me that Fisby and his brother, Elden, are heads of a male coven. That coven calls itself Guild of the Supreme Brotherhood of Manroots. One of its goals is to destroy the spirit of egalitarianism practiced in Wiccan magic."

"How did that awful book get into a bookshelf in our little town in the first place? Why Elmira?" Sheila grabbed the handle of the green, lettuce-ware teapot to pour a second helping. Distracted by Kitsy's story, she forgot what she was doing, and the Ceylon brew breached the sides of her gold-rimmed cup, spilling into her saucer. Kitsy reached over and steadied the pot.

"Fisby and Elden moved here from England." Kitsy filled Fayette's cup and set the empty teapot in front of her. "They brought the book with them, along with beliefs about strict versions of patriarchy from the middle ages. They are angry that women lead most modern covens and that Wiccans tend to value female powers more than masculine qualities in such groups. I really don't know what Alfred meant by female powers and masculine qualities, but that's neither here nor there."

"So, you think Fisby is a phony pastor, and he and his brother, Elden, are witches or conjurors or whatever, and they want to weaken female leadership in the magic community?" Sheila looked around the café, unsettled by feelings of alarm, which kindled a sudden hot flash. That man who took their picture surely must have been Fisby's spy. There might be others listening in. The safety of her little corner in her greenhouse came to mind. Newly devoted to garden magic, Sheila loved her light-filled, cozy space and all she was learning there about how to practice magic in positive ways. Would she be able to continue her work without interference?

"How do these dark-magic incels with suffering-savior complexes go about weakening Wiccan leaders?" Fayette leaned back from the table, her good arm supporting a clenched fist as though she was ready to swing into battle right then and there.

"Well, Alfred said he's heard them plan ways to manipulate non-magic people into fearing and hating suspected witches. They influence their church followers through innuendo, gossip, and besmirchment. We all read history. These are the same old methods from centuries past, but they often work." A dispirited grimace flashed across Kitsy's face, as though she was exasperated with the whole human race. "I think those posters are a means to triangulate his own church people against us. Pastor Fisby uses the power of religion as a tool to damage women's friendships and reputations. Most people in the town take little notice, but it only requires actions from a few people to cause serious crazy making. Alfred said the male coven also uses low or dark magic."

"That's got to be what Lars Columbus meant when he said there are two magic-practicing groups in the area, and only one uses the dark arts." Fayette thumped the table with her clenched fist, making the teacups rattle.

"Can we assume that when we see someone wearing one of those rings with the amber and red stones, they are part of the Manroot guild?" Sheila asked.

"Good thinking." Kitsy's eyes brightened with admiration for Sheila's deduction.

"You're onto something," Fayette agreed, picturing the ring on the thumb of the young man who took their picture only half an hour ago. "Which means, after today, the Manroots have another photo of us looking bat crazy so they can hang new posters all over town."

"I think I better tell Darwin we need to take a break until after this is over." Sheila bit her lip and shook her head. "I don't want him being ostracized and shamed because he's hanging around someone who people think is a murdering wild woman."

"Well, that's thoughtful of you," Fayette said with an edge of sarcasm, "but let's hope he's a better man than that. I for one will bean him if he decides to leave you in the lurch."

"Is it settled, then? Are we going to call Lars Columbus and meet with his group at the bookstore?" Kitsy was hopeful. Maybe there was help for them after all.

"I'll let you know when." Fayette was ready to go home and take a much-needed nap. "And I think you should bring that Lantern Man fellow."

CHAPTER 20

It didn't seem to matter how many of those blasted posters he pulled off poles, the sides of buildings, and storefront windows. More kept appearing. Darwin never saw anyone put up the ugly things, but sometimes he looked behind to survey where he had just been, and there they would be, new ones taking the place of the sheets he stuffed in the trash bag on his shoulder.

"Uncanny," he muttered, slipping his free thumb through his suspender on his way to the next poster. It was Wednesday, the day after Darwin had met with Sheila for breakfast at the café, and he was on a mission to get those horrific hate memos off the streets. Who would want to embarrass and hurt someone as sweet and gentle as Sheila? He couldn't imagine Sheila harming anyone, so what was the motive?

No doubt about it, he told himself. He'd been smitten by Sheila for countless years, and he wanted to help. He also didn't want to waste any more time waiting for something to happen between them. In the past few weeks, he'd loved their meals together. They were, on purpose and without pretense, getting to know each other, something he'd come to doubt would ever happen. Before they retired, they saw each other almost every day, but mostly just to say hello. Retiring meant no more contact whatsoever. Then, to his surprise, she'd called for help. She'd called him, Darwin Finnigan the Third, for help with her stripped and damaged car. And he'd been eager to do it. He was glad to be helping now.

Little did he know, but Darwin was under surveillance. Parked across the street with its motor running was a white 1990s Corvette ZR-1, complete with chrome hubcaps and a license plate that read MNROOTB123. More interesting than the car, was the man at the wheel with his dark-suited arm draped over the open window frame. Every few minutes, the young man lifted his iPhone to snap pictures of Darwin pulling down posters. The man zoomed into a closeup of Darwin's face and torso, squinting at the full head of wavy, smoke-colored hair, the well-formed nose, and the muscular upper arms and shoulders that supported a pair of suspenders over a blue and white button-down shirt. *Not a bad specimen for a fellow in his early seventies,* the photographer thought. Whatever did he see in that harpy of a woman he was trying to protect?

The photographer decided to plant a few seeds of uncertainty. He got out of the Corvette and crossed the street, adopting a casual gait as he pretended to window shop. When Darwin tore yet another poster from a tack on a signpost, the man approached. He leaned in as though to look at the poster in Darwin's hand and dropped a shiny bronze coin at Darwin's feet. He kept similar coins in his pocket for occasions just like this one. They were spell-made suggestion coins, which meant that if Darwin picked up the coin, the man could make a suggestion, just one, and Darwin's mind would absorb it.

"Hey, I know those women," the man said to Darwin as a conversation starter.

"Oh, yeah?" Darwin prepared himself for an indecent or disparaging remark. Some people reveled in opportunities to spread hearsay.

"Oh, wait. Is that your money there by your feet?"

Darwin peered down past his corduroy pants to the concrete under his scuffed, caramel-brown boat shoes. "I don't think so." He bent down to pick up the gleaming metal. As soon as Darwin had it in his fingers, the man seized his opportunity.

"Yeah. The shorter one, the one with the dark, straight hair, she goes through lovers like a NASCAR driver goes through cars. She uses up schmuck after schmuck and then tosses them out on their keesters. I guess that's why she never married."

"Where did you hear a rumor like that?" Darwin demanded, but the man was already crossing the street to his car, leaving Darwin to stew, and because he put the spell coin in his pocket, the man's suggestion would continue to simmer in Darwin's thoughts throughout the day and into the night. The uncertainty seed was planted.

***

In the meantime, Sheila, back in her garden shed, examined hanging bunches of dried fall herbs. Every year she dried leaves for cooking, but to her surprise, the same herbs turned out to be important ingredients in her garden magic books. Rosemary, chamomile, lavender, poppies, roses, bay, chives, mint, sage, thyme, tarragon, lemon verbena, wormwood, and yarrow were among the plants Sheila grew that she could use in several protection and health spells. She closed her eyes and breathed in the earthy, tangy scents of her drying bundles. As winter approached, this was the last harvest until next spring. Her herb garden would rest during the cold months.

As she tied together small bunches of tarragon, Sheila thought about Darwin, his soft brown eyes that looked right at her as she talked, his large, warm hand over hers. They chatted for hours when they got together, about anything and everything, her garden, his fix-it-shop, her new kitten, his old dog. She wanted him in her life, even to the end of their older years. "I refuse to regret not getting together sooner," she said aloud to her greenhouse plants. "I'll just be grateful we can enjoy each other in the here and now."

***

A few streets down from Sheila's, Kitsy eyed Alfred's lantern on the stove. Marmy curled herself on a tiny, soft blanket Samuel put on the counter near the lantern. He also moved Marmy's food and water dishes to the counter, encouraging the kitten's gumption as she took on the job of lantern guard. Alfred was wary of the little orange spitfire, even hissing at her and calling the cat "the witch's familiar."

"You promised, lady, if I answered your questions, you'd give me back me lantern," said the human form of a creature who had lived, if it could be called living, since the early seventeenth century.

Kitsy considered his plea and wondered what might happen if he had his lantern. Would he become even more obstinate and uncooperative? Would his lantern man side overpower his Alfred side? This cursed soul still had useful information about Fisby and his coven that might be critical to uncover.

She turned to confront Alfred directly and did a double take. The man had cleaned up with a new set of Samuel's clothes. He'd replaced his sour glare with a pleading stare. Was it possible, under all that dirt and anger, the Alfred version of The Lantern Man had some charm?

"There's another thing you need to do, Alfred." Kitsy decided that more experienced magic practitioners would know what to ask him and what to do with the lantern. "My friends and I are going to a meeting, probably this afternoon, and you need to attend. When you're there, you need to answer questions once again. We're connecting with people who might be able to help you. Together, we can decide what the best course of action might be."

Alfred's eyes seemed to redden, and his mouth twisted into a sour frown. He was back to looking like The Lantern Man. "This ain't right. That orange moggy with its devil claws is guarding stolen property, my stolen property."

Kitsy's iPhone pinged. Fayette's text message read, "Meet at bookstore 3 p.m. today." It was 12:35 p.m., and even though she'd just returned from meeting with her magic-experimenting book group, Kitsy didn't want to wait. Over the past few days, enough stress-hormone-cycles washed through her brain to keep her wired for weeks. She'd read that acute stress enhances long-term memory, but she didn't think she wanted to remember the last few days. Besides, stress was also a killer.

"Samuel, how are you doing?" Kitsy touched her husband's right shoulder. He'd been a soldier throughout this ordeal, not once blaming her or admonishing her for stealing that book. She thought he ought to.

"Alfred's been mostly quiet this morning. We did some barber work in the kitchen. I trimmed his beard, cut his hair, and found him a better outfit. After a snack, we watched *Dr. Who* on television so he could see what Britain looks like now, sort of, and I explained that the salt-sucking creature he saw yesterday and the Dr. Who telephone box, the TARDIS that travels in time, are just stories people made up and not real life. I mean, it's kind of a kick teaching someone who's more than four hundred years old about life in the twenty-first century."

"I'm going to take him to the bookstore at 2:30 and give you a break. There's a group of people we'll meet who know something about the paranormal. They might be able to help us."

"So, does this group of people practice magic?" Samuel's eyes implored her to say "no," and his facial muscles stretched into a worried expression. "I mean, after what's happened in our own kitchen, I have to think there's weird stuff going on in the world that I never believed real. Was Alfred right in saying you've practiced magic?"

"Just once, last week," Kitsy admitted. She could see her thorn-ripped scarf from the kitchen, hanging from the coat tree by the back door. "My book group agreed to learn about magic just for the month of October. It was supposed to be sort of an innocent project to practice a new skill. I was like you before we started trying it out. I didn't think much would happen. I was so wrong."

"And this group you're meeting this afternoon?"

"It's a group of Wiccans whose ethical foundation is to do no harm. We're hoping they can help us set things straight and teach us how to clean up our messes. They might know what we can do about The Lantern Man."

"Is Pastor Fisby part of the group?"

"No. He doesn't like Wiccans, remember? From what Alfred said, he's part of another group for men only, and it intends to dominate the magic world in the Northwest. If you recall, the members of Fisby's group do use dark magic, and they manipulate non-magic people to get what they want. I hope Alfred can tell us more about Fisby's coven so we can protect ourselves from them."

Kitsy described the posters of Fayette and Sheila that someone hung around town to cast suspicion on her friends. "I think Fisby and his crowd want to embarrass us and the Wiccan group so that we'll leave magic alone out of shame or fear. So, it's getting serious. I'm just sorry I dragged you into this."

"And Alfred thinks they don't like Wiccans because they don't like women in charge? Have I got that right?" Samuel pinched the end of his nose, something he often did when he was puzzled.

"I don't really understand either." Kitsy sighed and thought about the gender and history books she'd studied. "But it hasn't been that long since women couldn't get their own bank loans, have credit cards, work at much of anything except being teachers or secretaries or washerwomen." Taking off her sweater, Kitsy tried to cool down. Just thinking about gender inequality pushed up her metabolic temperature. "You know that some churches, even now, don't allow women to lead or teach men. It's only a matter of decades that separate us from times when women lost all control of their wealth and property to their husbands when they married and, of course, could not even vote. I suppose that Fisby, Elden, and those Manroot crazies are simply mixing old school, dark-age patriarchy with twenty first century patriarchy."

"I did some online research while we were watching Dr. Who." Samuel shuffled his feet as though uncomfortable with the conversation. "It's true that there's gender tension in the Wiccan community these days. Fisby isn't the only man who thinks female Wiccans have too much say in covens." He glanced sideways at Kitsy. He lowered his voice. "Are you a witch, then?"

"I don't think so. Trying one protection spell on a couple of scarves shouldn't make me a witch, should it? And, the spell backfired, so even if I were a witch, I'm not a particularly good one." Kitsy reached over to pat Marmy, ending her statement with a strangled laugh.

"This is a part of you I didn't know about," Samuel said. "It's kind of sexy and scary at the same time. Even after all these years, that spunky, creative, strict schoolteacher I married still surprises me."

Kitsy relaxed just a little at his words and kissed Samuel's forehead. Maybe they would come out of this okay after all.

At 2:30, Kitsy roused Alfred from his chair in front

of the television, where he was watching an episode of *Men In Black*. When Kitsy said they would walk to town, he shrank back. "They're going to think I'm one of those aliens. I'm not ready to be melted down."

"We don't have any alien hunters, at least not in Elmira."

They started down the block, a few people giving them second glances since they usually saw Kitsy walking with Samuel, not this tall, straight-haired stranger with his newly trimmed beard. Alfred found the smooth evenness of the sidewalks uncomfortable and stumbled several times. Kitsy advised him to walk on the grass beside the cement if that was easier. Two blocks into their stroll, she noticed a car a few houses behind, moving at a slow pace. Was the car following them? The vehicle was a sports car, an ochre color, maybe a Corvette? Kitsy was so intent on looking back at the car that she didn't see the woman coming in her direction. She walked right into Darnelle Shipman, head of the Confess and Reform Women's Guild. It was like running into a large sack of potting soil.

"Oh, so sorry, Darnelle. It's my fault. I was looking back over my shoulder and not ahead."

But single-minded Darnelle wasn't listening. Her laser-focused, hazel eyes, framed by long, black lashes, fixed on Alfred, her expression animated, even interested.

"Who is your handsome companion?" she asked, almost cooing. She flipped back a tress of wavy, bottle-black hair and moved closer to The Lantern Man. Kitsy watched, fascinated, as this short, stout woman in her mid-thirties, scanned Alfred's hands, perhaps looking to see if there was a wedding ring. Stepping away to give Darnell room, Kitsy took another, more discriminating look at Alfred. It occurred to her that since he'd lost access to his lantern, and since Samuel's shave and haircut makeover, Alfred's appearance was normalizing. How much human was left in him? How old did he look? He'd been close to Darnelle's age when he lost his human core and became The Lantern Man. Before this moment, Kitsy had thought of him only as ancient and vulgar. Apparently, Darnelle saw something else in him. Maybe there was more to Darnelle than Kitsy knew. In the café, the first time she saw Darnelle with Pastor Fisby, the woman seemed hard, cold, and judgmental. Today she projected Beanie Baby hedgehog. Go figure.

"Alfred, this is Darnelle Shipman." Kitsy remembered her manners. "Darnelle, this is Alfred Dowsby. He's a guest at our home for a few days."

"Hello," Darnelle said, offering her hand.

For his part, Alfred was speechless, motionless. "At least nod," Kitsy suggested in his ear.

He shook himself, nodded, and took Darnelle's proffered hand.

"Oh Honey, your hands are awfully cool. They need warming up. I've got a wonderful idea. I usually spend fall evenings in front of a backyard fire pit with a glass of wine and a bit of dessert. If you'd like to join me tonight, you could warm your cold hands in front of the flames." Darnelle gave Alfred a "come-to-me-boy" simpering smile. Kitsy sucked in her cheeks trying not to laugh. For being the head of the Confess and Reform Women's Guild, Darnelle knew a lot about picking up strangers and taking them home.

A blush spread over Alfred's cheeks, at least the parts above the beard, but Darnelle didn't wait for an answer. She drew a notepad and pen from a purse pocket, wrote something on the pad, ripped out the page, and handed it to Alfred. "Here's my phone number and address. It's just a block away. I'll be waiting, dear." With that, Darnelle turned to face Kitsy, raising her razor-thin eyebrows as if in challenge, and moved on down the sidewalk, her wide hips swaying. Alfred watched her go, his mouth open, and his hands holding his knees to keep them from buckling.

It was time to re-orient both herself and Alfred. Kitsy steadied Alfred and pointed him toward the Forever Reading Bookstore and the meeting with the Wiccan coven. As they walked, the rusty-colored Corvette continued to keep pace behind them.

In minutes, they passed the Masonic Lodge and found themselves in front of the bookstore. A sign on the door read *closed*, so Kitsy knocked. She glanced back to see if the car still followed and did a double take. Not one, but three Corvettes, engines idling, parked side by side across the street from the lodge. Next to a bright white, chrome-detailed Corvette, was the ugly coupé following her and Alfred, and next to that one a bright yellow, vintage model. "How very odd," she said to herself, feeling her shoulders tighten and the hairs rise on the back of her arms.

Chapter 21

A face peered at them through the bookstore entry curtains, and then the door swung open. If there were real fairies out there, the woman who opened the door would have to be one. A simple, mint green shift hung light on her small-boned, boyish frame. Black suede ballet shoes graced her tiny feet. If human ears could be pointed, hers almost were. Most striking were her delicate, doll-like facial features under a head of bright auburn hair, cut to within an inch of her head.

"Come in. My name is Estra," the fairy woman said in a voice that had Kitsy gaping in surprise. How could the here-be-dragons range of low bass come from the larynx of such a wispy creature?

Estra led Alfred and Kitsy between stacks of books and through a skinny, blue door to a back room. The space was large enough to accommodate a sizeable, oval, oak table with seating for at least twelve. Around the table was room to spare for mingling in small groups, especially near a refreshment table, and off in one corner was a well-used desk and a single, wooden office chair on wheels. Fayette and Sheila were already there, holding cups of home-grown apple cider and looking over the titles of well-worn books squeezed tight together, some stacked on top of each other in a ceiling-high bookshelf.

Kitsy recognized Lars Columbus, the bookstore owner who sold her the grimoire journals a few days ago. He ushered them in and closed the door, but in minutes re-opened it, bowing, and stepping back for a tall, older woman to enter. Exquisite was the right word for her, with her high cheek bones under umber skin, bright, friendly brown eyes surrounded by deep smile lines, and gray, wavy hair pulled back into a generous bun. Kitsy reflected that this lady radiated a special type of calm energy, discernable only in some older women.

"We can begin. Please take your seats," Lars announced. "Our coven priestess has arrived."

Three members of the Reading Club of Retired and Capable Ladies, The Lantern Man, and six Wiccans settled around the table, all eyes on the priestess lighting a corn-yellow, pillar candle in the middle of the table.

"Let us center ourselves by closing our eyes or focusing on the candle and start our meeting with a supplication to Earth energies." The coven leader's words played like a marimba in Fayette's ears with low sweet tones.

Earth Mother help all around this table
Earth Spirits help each of us
with patience and strength
to see what is truly vital
to think and speak without selfishness or fear
Help us
with wisdom
with courage
with faith and compassion
with being truly human in spirit and heart

She ended the devotion with direct scrutiny of Alfred and repeated, "With being truly human in spirit and heart." The Lantern Man, who refused to close his glowering eyes during the invocation, looked away.

To the rest of the group, the priestess said, "Welcome guests. Welcome all. I am Abigail Winterwild. We six are The Waterleaf Fen Circle." She gestured with her hands to Lars, Estra, and two women and a man that Kitsy, Fayette, and Sheila had yet to meet. "Time runs short, as usual, but let's begin by going around the table and introducing ourselves. We'll tell our names and, as a start, share one thing we love doing. Maybe we should say something about our religions of choices. For you who are new, the members of this circle don't see our Wiccan practices as organized around a religion. We see them more as spiritual, shaped around Earth energy."

The priestess took the time to give each person sitting at the table her direct attention and a nod. Then she picked up a small, carved, apple wood stick. "This is our talking piece. We pass it around the table from speaker to speaker to signify who has the floor." She held the stick in both hands, bowed her head to the stick for a silent moment, and began her own introduction. "Hello. I am Abigail. I love to sit on my bench below my willow tree and feel the breezes through the leaves as I finish the New York Times crossword puzzle. I am Ba'hai."

Next in line was the bookstore owner. "We've all met. I am Lars Columbus. These days, my greatest pleasure is riding my mountain bike on the trails in the nature reserve. I am interested in many religions and haven't settled on one in particular." Lars smiled at the fairy woman sitting next to him, handing her the stick.

"Hello. I am Estra, and I take pleasure in making homemade egg noodles on rainy nights. I am Christian, and I am also a neuroscientist and cognitive linguist. I study the effects of lying and liars on brain circuitry and mental maps."

Estra passed the stick to a round-cheeked woman with long black hair. "Hi. I am Lucinda. I adore getting my big family together for humongous tamale dinners. I am

Catholic." Lucinda described herself as a 40-year-old Hispanic American madre and real estate agent. "And I do love to cook." She flashed them a bright smile complete with a friendly wink.

A slender woman dressed in tight jeans and a peasant blouse took the talking stick. "I'm Gilda, and I spend time after school growing a little herb garden and watching movies with my friends and boyfriend. I also work at a bookstore in Olympia." The youngest coven member with the multi-colored hair and swinging ponytail, nodded at Sheila. "I remember you bought books from me a little while back." Gilda told them her parents were Arab immigrants from Iran and that she was Muslim." She rolled the stick over the table to the next Wiccan member, who snatched it up before it could fall off the edge.

"Hey. I'm Seth. In my spare time, I make costumes for cosplay conventions. I study Native American spirituality, but I don't belong to an official religion." Seth was pasty white, as though he spent the bulk of his time in a basement without windows. Sheila didn't know lenses could be as thick as the ones in Seth's eyeglasses.

It was The Lantern Man's turn, and Kitsy held her breath, waiting for a possible disaster. She'd noticed his was the face that the coven members kept staring at. They seemed to sense his vulnerable and dangerous energies. From Kitsy's description of him, they knew his experiences were outside of conventional categories, and they were curious.

The Lantern Man sat on the edge of his chair, fidgeting as though ready to bolt, but he managed to clear his throat. "I am Alfred." He got the words out with a rough growl. There was a long pause, but the coven members just waited, smiling. "I used to love gathering flowers and berries to give to my mother. I used to be British Anglican." A tear slid down Alfred's left cheek, startling Kitsy.

"Welcome, Alfred," the coven members said in unison.

They greeted each of the newcomers in turn as Fayette described her motorcycling trips, Sheila spoke of her gardening, and Kitsy talked about sewing and her hot dog recipe project.

Introductions were done, and the hard work started.

"I'm sure you all noticed the three Corvettes that followed the newcomers to our meeting place," Lars said. "The Manroots are playing out the harassment and intimidation phase of their plan. Things will escalate soon."

"Not again," sighed Gilda. "This is so repetitive it's boring."

"I agree that the Manroots can be tiring," Abigail said, her voice soothing. "But we've got three possible victims to help protect, maybe four." She glanced over at Alfred. "The focus of Manroot attacks are always the Waterleafs in the end. We all know that. Our vigilance is necessary for as long as we are here, and they are there."

"Yes, ma'am," Gilda said, nodding her head toward Abigail. "I'm in. You know I'll help."

"First, we need to gather information about our guests," Abigail continued. "Each of you in turn - Fayette, Sheila, and Kitsy - tell us what has been happening these last few weeks. You women experimented with magic. You triggered some interesting events, and the energies you released are still ricocheting in your lives. When you finish with your stories, we will tell you what we know about Pastor Fisby, his brother Elden, and the other Manroots. Then, we need to start planning defensive action, but also a strategic offense to their coming attack."

"Are the protection spells renewed for our meeting place?" Lucinda Gonzales stood.

"Lars does a renewal every morning, but there's no such thing as too much protection," Abigail said. "Let's take a break and enhance our shields for the sake of complete privacy."

Sheila, Kitsy, and Fayette stayed quiet and still. They watched with interest as each member of the coven took time to breathe, center themselves, cleanse themselves with candle smoke, and then concentrate on protection duties in different areas of the room. Their invocations always included respect for and entreaty from the sources of Earth-based energies and entities. Fayette recognized several protection spell bottles, much like the ones she made for her friends. Before the meeting, someone placed them in strategic positions on the floor in corners and on shelves. Kitsy noted how Seth spent time over the tea, heating more water, talking to the tea mixture, and heaping spoonsful into two, fat, brown-Betty teapots.

Familiar with the aromatic plants in her own garden, Sheila recognized the smells coming from wreaths of dried dill and sage that hung above the three doorways leading in and out of the room. She was excited to see Gilda perform a sweeping protection spell using a corn broom and a mixture of dried herbs.

Seth poured ten cups of tea and distributed them around the table. When he finished, the coven members took slow deep breaths. Each sat in front of a steaming teacup to hear their guests' stories.

Kitsy was the last of the three friends to talk. But she faltered, and her voice shook when she saw the coven members cross their arms over their chests, bow their heads, and close their eyes soon after she began her explanation of how Alfred came to be in her home and what she knew of his story.

"And so, my little kitten, Marmy, guards Alfred's lantern until we figure out what to do." In halting sentences, Kitsy finished her account of the last few days, afraid she might have understated the hopelessness of Alfred's story. Next to her, The Lantern Man sat stiff and still, hands clenched tight in front of him on the table, his eyes focused on his lap. Kitsy noted the muscles in his legs tensing and releasing, tensing, and releasing. Was he preparing to flee?

When the coven members unfolded their arms and opened their eyes, they avoided looking at The Lantern Man. Kitsy wondered why Abigail did not ask Alfred to speak. Instead, she announced the start of another break. "Refresh your tea, and Lucinda brought Mexican shortbread cookies and galletas de piloncillo."

"Oh la," Sheila said, releasing her own tension and making them all laugh.

Everyone stood, stretched their legs, and then coven members greeted the newcomers one by one.

"If you are serious about learning the craft, we can mentor you," Lucinda told Fayette. "Based on your elder vivacities, you obviously have inborn qualities for using Earth energies, and we can help you create beneficial spells for the sake of the common good."

For a few minutes, Kitsy stood alone, concerned that bringing The Lantern Man may have put everyone in a dangerous position. He was a spirit removed from his own time, cursed to lead people into danger. Maybe she should take him and leave. She felt a tap on her shoulder and turned to find Abigail bringing her a fresh cup, filled to capacity, with Seth's protection tea.

"We will help you," Abigail said, "but it will get worse before it gets better. Alfred has choices to make. His choices will determine his future, and they will affect those around him, citizens in this little community of Elmira, and those of us who are part of the bigger struggle between magic for good - what we call high magic - and dark magic, which we call low magic. As he makes his choices, we must be vigilant in building up our protections, especially you."

Kitsy hadn't meant to spill tears, but there they were, springing from her eyes so that she had to wipe them off with the back of her right sleeve. "What have I done?"

Abigail put a reassuring hand on Kitsy's arm. She opened her mouth, about to say something, when a scream pierced through the closed door to the bookshop. It was the kind of screech a bawling cat would make confronting an enemy feline, a coyote, or an owl. They heard a long, drawn-out moan that rose in pitch and ended in a hair-raising shriek.

Lars rushed to the timeworn, blue painted door with its rose crystal knob, and threw it open. They all heard the glass entry door to the shop slam shut, like the retort of a firecracker. Then Lars rushed to the front where a sizeable, orange cat growled, its fur raised on its shoulders and back and its tail looking like a four-inch wide, bottle scrub brush.

"Hey there, Cathbad, old man, what's wrong buddy." Lars knelt to calm the cat, who continued to pace, hissing at the store entry. A second cat, a sleek black and white tuxedo, vaulted three short bookshelves and approached the orange tabby. "Freya, thanks for coming." Lars reached out and stroked Freya's back. Freya rubbed her head against Cathbad's forehead three times, and he quieted while she washed his ears.

Fayette, Sheila, and Kitsy looked at the felines and then at each other. "Catsandratsandelephants," Fayette murmured. "These are spitting images of our new kittens, Max and Marmy."

"What about Patches?" Sheila asked.

Lars chuckled. "You guessed right. You are meeting the parents of the kittens you took home, Fayette. These two gave me permission to pass their latest offspring to you, all three of them, as companions and helpmates. Treat them well, and they will become loyal and special friends."

Fayette didn't know whether to feel tricked or

grateful. She decided to feel both.

Turning back to Cathbad, Lars asked the cat, "What did you see, my mate?"

Seth pushed through the onlookers and knelt beside Lars and the cat. "I believe, Lars, that it was that Lantern Man fellow. He's disappeared. I'm guessing he escaped while we busied ourselves with cookies."

"Our protection spells were making Alfred itchy. I could tell," Gilda said. "I don't think he could take much more."

"Oooh." Kitsy let out a cry. "I should never have brought him."

"You could not have kept him prisoner for long," Abigail soothed. "He was bound to escape your watch sooner or later. But he will try to come back to your home for his lantern. I suggest you bring it here where we can find a safer place to hide it. Without contact with that piece of coal he keeps in that metal lamp, he is awakening to his humanity. It would be better if he and the lantern stayed separated for the present."

Lars backed Abigail's words with his lower pitched, more gravelly resonances. "Marmy is an exceptional cat, and she will try to guard the lantern as best she can, but she is but a kitten. If Alfred succeeds in taking it from her, she will feel great shame. It's too early in her life to put such a big burden on her little shoulders."

Kitsy took out her cell phone and made a call. "Samuel, something has come up. The Lantern Man disappeared during our meeting at the bookstore. The people here say he'll be coming to the house for his lantern. They volunteered to hide it for us. Could you bring it to the front door of Forever Reading Bookstore?" She listened for a quarter minute and then said, "Yes. In a way, it is a relief. No more babysitting. But he could still hurt someone, so there's reason to worry." She tapped her phone to end the call. "Samuel says he'll be here in five."

Most of the group went back to the meeting room. Lars and Kitsy waited for Samuel. He arrived carrying the lantern inside an extra-large-sized Kentucky Fried Chicken bucket. *A smart disguise*, Kitsy thought. Cathbad and Freya wound around his legs, sniffing his pants and shoes, investigating the scents of their baby girl, Marmy.

"Would you like to join the meeting, Samuel?" Lars raised a hand and motioned toward the thin, blue door.

"Kitsy will tell me what it's about. I think I'd like to walk the streets around here and see if I can find a trace of Alfred."

"Be careful." Kitsy gave her husband a worried peck on the cheek.

Lars locked the front door while Kitsy watched Samuel out the window. His loping stride took him toward the parked Corvettes. She crossed her fingers that the three Manroots, who were chin-wagging while leaning on the hood of the white car, would not know him.

When Lars and Kitsy returned to the meeting room, closing the door behind them, Fayette spoke up. "Look. I'm confused. A couple of you told me a little bit about how these Manroots cause trouble for you and want to hassle us. You've said that Pastor Fisby and his brother are part of their group. But I still don't understand why they want to wound our reputation and run us out of town. Who are these men?"

"Let's sit down," Abigail instructed. She lit the candle a second time and said the invocation, fanning the candle flame until it smoked so she could waft the smoke in all four directions. Then she closed her eyelids and breathed in. When she opened her eyes, everyone was silent, waiting.

"A long time ago, before the larger Wiccan community started only seventy or so years ago, witches, wise women, cunning women, wizards, wise men, and sorcerers rarely met as part of organizations. They learned their crafts from individual teachers, often their mothers and grandmothers, fathers and grandfathers. They rarely met in what we call covens. Much of the healing in communities was done by women who understood herbs, childbirth, and illness. Women made potions, tended the sick, and acted as midwives. It was these women who often became the focus of witchcraft accusations, and because eighty five percent of those burned and killed in the European witch hunts and trials were women, the notion that witches are women is pervasive. Common belief has feminized the type of work that healers once did, and for good reason."

"But I'm working on my healing skills and I'm a dude," Seth interjected, grinning and lifting his teacup as though toasting the circle.

Lars nodded. "The Wiccans of today are part of a new legacy of witchcraft, started by a man named Gerald Gardner, who used the old word that meant a feminine witch to name his new belief system. Witch comes from the Anglo-Saxon, Old-English word wicca, perhaps pronounced witch-a, meaning female healer, magician or sorceress. It was only later that the word *witch* became associated with the devil, and that was because Puritan Christians invented stories of fear about cunning women and wizards."

Standing up, Lucinda pointed across the table at a large painting of a serene young woman wearing a soft, cotton tunic, bent over a wooden worktable. In the painting, the woman dipped her hands in a bowl of fresh, green leaves, her eyes focused on an ebony stone mortar and pestle. "It's a self-portrait by Gilda. She personifies a more typical Wiccan student."

Breathing out a sigh of pleasure, Sheila thought of her own worktable and the pungent aromas of herbs hanging in her greenhouse.

Lucinda's melodic voice continued her description

of history. "Our Wiccan tradition is new, starting in Britain and the Unites States only decades ago, and the beliefs and practices attract mostly women. We promote equality of the sexes and sacredness of the female form. What we call Dianic Wicca, focuses on women's power and energy. The movement is not against men, it is simply not centered on men. Witchcraft, today, may be a woman-centric practice, but it still exists in a man-centric world. Our Wiccan covens focus on women as leaders, teachers, and practitioners. Men are often in the minority of our gatherings."

"We see that as okay in a world in which men still dominate leadership positions in most religions." Lars spread his arms wide as though to embrace his fellow coven members.

"The Manroots disagree." Estra's low tones rumbled in Fayette's head, causing her to startle and take notice. "They feel," Estra said, "that what they call hardness and war, which they believe are male energies, should be just as important or more important than the female energies of love, softness, and care for Earth. They feel demoralized when the focus is on what they perceive as female energies, on life-giving and life-enhancing forces, and on recognizing the importance of Earth, which the Manroots feel is weak.

We do not believe that male and female energies are so black and white, so separated from each other. But most of us in the Wiccan community feel that patriarchy is a system that has done much harm in the world. Patriarchy creates an imbalance. To rectify this imbalance, we see it as good and wholesome for women to lead."

Leaning toward the candle, its flame constant at the midpoint of the table, Estra blew a strong even breath its way. The flame flickered and elongated, recentering the group's attention. Her voice lowered to speak her next words. "The Manroots are a regional group. Most members don't live in Elmira, but they force their will on smaller covens of Wiccan practitioners to weaken their communities. Manroot guild goals include bringing back patriarchy in full force to show the Wiccans that they are not to trifle with male-centered goals. As Lucinda explained, they see the male and the female as dichotomies rather than understanding that male and female energies are more complex than simple hardness versus softness. And there have always been more than just male and female genders. Wiccans understand that for each sex, and for each individual, the aspirations should be more about balancing energies. Seth, as a male Wiccan, what can you add?"

Seth grinned, took off his glasses, and winked at the three newcomers. "In my case, I learned my skills from a Wiccan mother and a Wiccan father. Respect and balance were keywords in my household. Tensions came up, but my parents worked to resolve their differences through communication. My father is Euromerican. My mother is of Cherokee descent. Traditionally, the Cherokees respected women as leaders before the Europeans came to the Americas. They were, and still are, matrilineal.

My mother's grandmother taught her about the different advantages women had in traditional Cherokee relationships. Those advantages served to equalize women's status. As my mother said, sometimes situations arose that would tip the scale in favor of female or male authority, but the goal was always to achieve balance. Everyone needed to respect all genders. So, you see, I grew up practicing balance. Being Wiccan, with women leaders, seems natural to me. The Waterleaf Fen Circle is a coven with a priestess leader, and often the priestess's co-leader is male. Currently, our co-leader is Lars."

The hinges of the thin, blue door with the rose crystal doorknobs squeaked as the door swung open about five inches, causing Sheila to startle, as though coming out of a trance. Tails fixed straight up like flag poles,

Cathbad and Freya sauntered in, heads held high. Both jumped onto the meeting table and took their places on either side of Lars, who reached to scratch them behind their ears.

"Lars, can you tell Fayette, Sheila, and Kitsy a little about yourself?" Abigail smiled at Lars, and those around the table could see gratefulness and respect in her expression.

"If my story helps you understand our coven and its goals, I am happy to tell it," Lars said. "I'll start by saying that I was raised on a Kansas cattle ranch. There were few women in my life. The Manroots would certainly have approved of my male-centered upbringing. I went to college, but I had no direction, so I quit just in time for the draft board to call me up and compel me to military service in the Vietnam War. In July 1968, my B-52 crashed in Central Quang Binh, the most southern province of North Vietnam, where the United States was conducting mass bombings. I was the only survivor of the crash. All I could do was bury my fellow soldiers, and then, for several grueling weeks, work my way through the mountains. My goal was the East Vietnam Sea where I might find U.S. Navy ships and a way home.

"By the time I wandered into the Annamite Mountain Range, I was starving and almost naked, my clothes in shreds. A tribe of cave dwellers called the Ruc found me and hid me. The Ruc were foragers then, and still are today, when their government allows them to re-visit their caves during pilgrimages. They fed me, clothed me, and nursed me back to health. It was with the Ruc that I learned about magic. I helped them hunt and gather, learned some of their music, and watched their spiritual rituals. A Ruc shaman taught me how to conjure protection spells. He drew power through his relationship with animals and plant life. I spent a year with the Ruc, and if the North Korean military hadn't rounded them up and forced them to start farming, I might have spent my whole life with them. Had they known I was there, those soldiers would have shot me, so the Ruc kept my presence secret, and as they were marched away from their caves, I left them and made my way to the sea. On the beach a lookout on a Navy ship spotted me. A skiff from the ship picked me up, and I returned to the States.

For a long minute Lars remained silent, and Kitsy thought that his face was a study in grief. Was he mourning the way the North Koreans demanded the Ruc become farmers rather than foragers? Perhaps she could ask him one day.

"My experiences taught me that magic is more than a fairy tale." Lars reached out to stroke Cathbad and then Freya. "Since then, I never stopped studying the uses and beliefs of mysticism throughout the world. Of course, I became a Wiccan, whose premise is to do no harm and to recognize and respect the natural world. I work to avoid using magic for self-serving power or for dominance."

Abigail rose from her seat and bowed to Lars, then to Seth, and around the table to each of the coven members. She faced Sheila, Kitsy, and Fayette and spread her arms as though to enfold them. "We live according to ideals that we believe are important to protect and defend. We simply want to be left in peace to practice our craft. Not all, but some witch-practicing men see our existence as a threat, so we must continually repair the damage they do and help strengthen safeguards around us and around those who might find themselves in the middle of the conflict. And now that includes you three."

She sat, then, and looked around the table. "What should we do, my friends?"

Estra snorted. "We've got to give these three some training. I recommend organizing lessons."

"We need to hide that lantern as soon as possible."

Seth rubbed his hands together over the steam from his tea. "I'll make sure that's done."

"It would be helpful to know more about the Manroots' plans." Lucinda bit her lower lip and turned her head toward Seth and Lars. "Our men will have easier access to Manroot meetings."

Gilda stuck her iPhone in her jacket pocket and picked up her teacup as though ready to go. "I want to know where the pastor is hiding. We need to help clear Fayette and Sheila of hurting him. I'll ask around."

Freya and Cathbad jumped from the table as Lars scooted his chair back. "Some of us should keep an eye on The Lantern Man. That's a group project."

Abigail stood. "We need to enhance and increase our work to provide protections for ourselves and the community." She clapped her hands together three times. The coven members chanted a final devotion. Lars blew out the meeting candle, and the gathering was over.

Fayette looked at her watch. She still had time to get home and set the table for casserole before Leo arrived.

CHAPTER 22

Having left Alfred's lantern with Kitsy's new friends, Samuel walked away from the bookstore to see if he could locate The Lantern Man. Not that he really wanted to find him, but it seemed like the responsible thing to do. Was there some kind of classic car show going on? In front of him, were three Corvettes, each from a different decade. He stood back to admire the gleaming cars. Their drivers were deep in conversation and took little notice of Samuel. What he wouldn't give to have a red-hot car with a turbocharged engine just once in his life, but wasn't that a cliché craving for men in their middle or older years? If there was one thing Samuel tried to avoid it was being cliché. As he trudged closer to the Corvettes, Samuel paid little attention to the men's conversation until the name Fisby popped up and plucked a neuron in Samuel's consciousness. Like a bear smelling halibut pieces hung to dry in a smoke house, he fixed his attention and zeroed in on their low, barely audible murmurs.

"Fisby's called a meeting for tomorrow night."

"He's doing alright then? Heard he was kidnapped."

"Naw, something's up, but Fisby's good. The police think those two sea hags poisoned him and took him. The whole town won't give those biddies the time of day by the time we're done with them."

"Good," said the third man, whose thinning hair and beard, large nose, and low forehead reminded Samuel of a Neanderthal. Not that he had anything against those ancient humans. It was just a resemblance. The man snarled in disgust.

"That's all we need is more women working magic. Everyone have the details of the meeting?"

"Basement of the Light in The Darkness Church, 6:45 p.m.," said the hat-wearing man in his houndstooth jacket.

Samuel decided it was time to walk past the men and their Corvettes. He'd heard enough to be concerned, even scared, for Kitsy and her friends. What had they done to raise the ire of these men? According to Kitsy, very little.

Picking up speed, he hiked off a measure of mounting anxiety, looking for traces of The Lantern Man in alleys and backyards. Nothing. Several blocks and street crossings later, Samuel returned to the bookshop where the SUV waited, and hopefully Kitsy. He tried the front door, and, to his surprise, it opened. In the back he could see his wife and the bookstore owner looking over a stack of hardbacks. The orange Tom and the black and white tuxedo followed him as he strode past bookshelves to join them.

"Samuel, what's wrong? You look as though the house burned down, or a burglar stole your book collection." Kitsy wrapped an arm around his waist.

"Kitsy, I don't understand how you and your friends got yourselves in a situation so far over your heads that you've got people gunning for you. I don't mean literally gunning. I do mean they are out to hurt you."

Lars put down the book he held and stepped closer. "What have you heard?"

Samuel repeated the conversation between the men with the Corvettes.

"These are people who gather as a coven from

throughout the Puget Sound and Seattle area," Lars said. "If I thought I could get away with it, I would go tomorrow night. I've been to a meeting before, and they know it. They don't want me back. They're on the lookout for me. Maybe I can get Seth to step in."

"I'll go," Samuel said. "They don't know me from Adam. If they're putting together a plan that might hurt Kitsy and her friends, I want to know about it."

Lars was thoughtful. "It's possible for you to go, Samuel, but extremely dangerous. I wouldn't want you to try it alone. All Manroots attend meetings disguised under dark purple robes, so dark they're almost black. Deep hoods hide their heads, and they wear masks. But they have two items that identify them as members of the Manroots. You can't get into a meeting without them. One is a special thumb ring. The second is a keyring decorated with red and black rosary pea beads."

"Sheila has Pastor Fisby's thumb ring," Kitsy announced. "She found it hanging from one of her rosary pea vines. But Samuel, I really don't want you to put yourself in that kind of danger."

"I have a thumb ring or two and some robes as well." Lars thudded the nearest wall with the side of a fist and looked unseeing past the Brownings; squinting creases framed his eyes; his chin jutted forward in thoughtful concentration. After several seconds he spoke. "Knowing what the Manroots plan to do could save us time and a whole lot of trouble. Would you feel better, Kitsy, if we find a second man to go with Samuel? I'll coach them ahead of time."

"But who? If those men can conjure dark magic, what would they do to Samuel if they discover him?"

"We'll take all the precautions we can," Lars said, "but Samuel, you've got to be very sure you want to do this. I wouldn't encourage you except the information you gather could be more than helpful."

"Hey, if I can deal with The Lantern Man, I can

handle a couple of male witches, right?" Samuel tried to smile at his own joke, but all he could manage was a bent upper lip.

"Sleep on it," Lars cautioned. "No one will fault you if you change your mind by morning."

Inside their SUV, Kitsy and Samuel stayed silent as they made their way home. Kitsy kept her eye out for signs of Alfred. She blinked twice at the steel blue motorcycle with shiny chrome handlebars parked in front of Fayette's cozy, sky-blue bungalow. The rugged cycle leaned on its kickstand crossways to the white-trimmed porch and the gabled roof. Who owned a bike like that, and why were they visiting Fayette at dinner hour? *Is it any of my business?* Kitsy asked herself.

Back at her bungalow, Fayette set dinner plates, cloth napkins, and glasses of ice water on her wooden booth table built into her breakfast window nook. She even managed to pour a salad kit into a cut-glass serving bowl to accompany the casserole. Over by the kitchen sink, Leo unzipped his well-worn, insulated food carrier and lifted out the steaming Mexican casserole. Fayette could make out layers of tortilla chips, cheese, spiced meat, salsa, and refried beans. She closed her eyes and sniffed in appreciation the spicy tang of cumin and chili pepper, mingled with the aroma of hot, melted, cheddar cheese.

"Holy Cheezits," she said.

"Got a surprise." Leo lifted the lid of a second insulated food carrier and brought out two bottles of locally crafted, light-lager beer. "I'm off the heavy stuff, but this is a treat for a special occasion. Plus, it goes great with my casserole."

They slid onto the sturdy wood bench seats across from each other. Fayette's left arm, cradled in its sling, still felt like an iron weight pulling on her tender shoulder, so Leo got no protest from her as he served both plates. She dug into the refried beans and crunchy chips and salsa crust with gusto, groaning with pleasure.

"You like?" Leo's weathered face crinkled with pride.

"You can cook for me anytime." Fayette moaned again.

"That'd be my pleasure," Leo said. "I've been meaning to call for a few days and finally had a good reason. Someone at the E-Hog's meeting said you'd injured yourself."

"Yeah. I get it. I meant to set up a riding date with you, but a lot's been going on." Fayette took another bite, this time aiming her fork at the tender ground beef smothered in Mexican spices.

"So, I've heard, Faye. Whatever did you do to piss someone off so bad they posted pictures of you all over town? And, hey, that picture doesn't do you justice by a long shot. Took me a while to recognize you on those trash sheets and realize you were the one accused of poisoning that nagging pastor."

"It's a long and tedious story, Leo. But you can bet my dill-headed winker toss that neither Sheila nor I hurt a soul. Sheila is the other woman in those pictures."

Fayette stopped eating and surveyed the man across from her with his open, generous face and foot-long, platinum beard streaked with gold. Right then, he looked like real friend material, but how would he react to learning about her recent misadventures and the craziness of trying to use magic? Plus, she promised the coven members not to reveal to anyone the existence of the Waterleaf Fen Circle.

"Dill-headed winker toss? I never bet on those." Leo laughed and Fayette joined him. "All the same, I can't help but believe you, Faye. And I'm sure the E-Hogs are behind you all the way. Several of us pulled down posters for a couple of hours today. I can't think how someone managed to get so many scattered to so many locations."

"Much obliged." Fayette picked up her beer bottle and saluted Leo with it. "It's been one thing after another, and I haven't had time to even think about the bad publicity."

Halfway through their bottles of beer, Fayette and Leo forgot the posters and spent the rest of dinner sharing bits and pieces of their history. Leo revealed, while stroking Max, that he had been married three times. At age 48, he decided he needed to stop jumping headlong into bad relationships. "I determined to get my head on straight and work on mellowing, or as some people called it, growing up. That was twenty years ago."

"And how did that turn out?"

"I'm settled enough to have some honest buddies who watch out for each other. I hope I've matured enough to take up with a lady friend and not make a mess of it. I found a woman who's got me interested."

"Oh, yeah?" Fayette put her right hand over her heart in mock surprise.

"Yeah. I even made her casserole. That's a big step. Never done that for a woman before." He grinned across at Fayette and winked.

Fayette noticed that Leo had a tell. His slow laugh, easy banter, and straight-backed, heavy stride were indicators of a man with confidence, but once in a while, he revealed tiny hints of self-consciousness. When that happened, he grabbed the ornament at the end of a silver chain he wore around his sunburned neck. With his thumb and second finger, he rubbed the decoration for just a moment or two.

"What's that around your neck?" Fayette asked.

"What? Oh, this. It's a St. Christopher medal."

"Rider protection." Fayette nodded.

"Well, we're all superstitious, us bikers," Leo laughed. "And this medal was a gift from a special friend. I wear it to remember him as much as for safety."

"Never turn down protection. I had a set of gremlin

guardian bells on my bike until last week. Can't think what happened to them. But since I can't ride for a month, I've got time to try and find them. They were a gift, too."

"I'm wondering if you need more than bells, Faye." Leo squinted out the kitchen window. "For starters, why is that guy looking over here with binoculars from inside his 1990's Corvette ZR-1? He's parked across the street from your house. I've been watching him since before we finished our beers."

"Well, flapdoodle." Fayette leaned closer to the window glass. "That's the same car that followed me on my walk to the bookstore this afternoon. What's he playing at?"

"Want me to drag him out of that open window and get him to talk?"

"Really? You'd do that?" She considered him for a long minute, feeling her shoulders relax a grateful half inch. "I don't think it's a good idea, Leo. He'd have reason to call the police and get you arrested."

"Yeah. It was a joke. My window-dragging days are probably over. But it's not right, me leaving you alone with him out there. Has he got something to do with all those lousy posters?"

"Probably."

"Want to tell me about it?"

"There's nothing I'd like better, but if I did, you'd run like mad and never look back." Fayette leaned over, reached across the table, and tapped Leo's chest. "It's just too weird. And I still want to know more about that monster Y chromosome you bragged about at Brilliant Things."

Leo's whole face lit up and he beamed. "When your shoulder heals, and we can hit the road, I'd like nothing better." He peered out the window again. "Have you got a place for you and Max to go tonight? Cause if you don't, I'm happy to sleep on the couch to make sure that

198

creep out there doesn't bother you." Max rose up on his back paws, put his front paws on Leo's shoulder and licked his nose.

"Max is a big fan of that idea." Fayette chuckled. "But asking you to stay over is way too much for a first get-together. I'll call Sheila. She's one of my book group friends. She might want some company, too. She's got a guy in another Corvette following her, and she lives alone, too. She's also got Patches, Max's sister. They might like seeing each other again."

"Something stranger than fiction is going on here," Leo said. "I respect your need to keep it to yourself. After all, you hardly know me. But I'd like to help. I'm gonna see you safely to your friend's house, and then you call if you need something."

Sheila was glad for Fayette's company. The yellow Corvette sat idling across from her front yard, driving Patches to distraction, and causing Sheila to imagine she saw moving shadows everywhere as the night darkened.

"And Darwin's not answering his phone," she said, her voice strained.

Leo hefted Max's carrying cage inside Sheila's front door, and Fayette unloaded her backpack and an overnight bag from the taxi Leo called for her. He'd followed the taxi on his Fat Boy.

"Thanks for the casserole and heroic company." Fayette gave him a one-armed hug.

"I'll call in the morning to make sure things are good."

After the front door closed, Fayette peeked out the window. She could see Leo and the Corvette driver staring each other down. It was at least twenty minutes before Leo turned over his engine and rumbled on down the street.

CHAPTER 23

"Think we should call the police?" Fayette waved her phone toward the front door. "Now the Corvette that was outside of my house is here too."

"Yeah. In case something happens in the night, the police should know these Manroots are harassing us. Maybe officers Bruce and Noah can drive by every hour at the very least. Are there laws against following people in your car and parking outside their houses?"

"There teetering-teapots should be."

"Well, I'm so glad you called Fayette. I was beside myself." Sheila pressed her arms to her sides, her constricted shoulders raised high. "And look at those two kittens. They make no bones about being glad to be back together." Patches and Max raced lickety-split down the hall and up the short staircase, skidding around corners and leaping over each other, first the calico in the lead and then the tuxedo.

When Sheila phoned the police department, the dispatcher directed her call to Noah, who was on night duty. "Hmmm. That sounds bizarre, kind of sinister," he told Sheila after hearing her story about the Corvettes. "You bet I'll pass around your house a few times, maybe ask those drivers what they're up to and direct them to leave. They're in the wrong if they're stalking or harassing. Sometimes that's hard to prove, though."

Turning to share what she'd learned from Noah, Sheila saw that Fayette was busy putting bright-colored bottles on the windowsills and near the doorways of the front room. Each time she placed a bottle, she took deep, cleansing breaths, and whispered a few words.

"Protection bottles," Fayette explained when she saw Sheila staring.

"Oh. Good thinking. I still have the one you gave me near the back door."

"I've got one more to put back there." Fayette took her bag, now almost empty of bottles, to the other end of Sheila's house.

Since sleep didn't seem like a possibility, the women decided to put together a jigsaw puzzle, spreading the pieces of a farm scene on the edges of a folding card table.

"So, who's this Leo guy?" Before he left, Sheila had time to look over the barrel of a man perched on his Harley. She approved of the way he had Fayette's back.

"I barely know him, but it feels as though we're good friends already. He brought me dinner tonight and right away got shuzbutt-concerned about that white Corvette."

"I like that he's willing to stand up for you, Fayette." Sheila paused. "I just wonder why Darwin's avoiding my calls. I hoped to at least hear his voice, you know, and feel comforted."

A knock at the door made them both jump. Sheila put her hand over her heart as though to slow its pounding. Fayette stood, grabbing the neck of one of her taller protection bottles, and turning it into a possible weapon. "Who's there?" she yelled.

"It's the police. It's Noah."

"Thank, God," Sheila breathed.

Fayette strode over and opened the front door.

"Hey, ladies," Noah tipped his hat. "I see you're in the middle of trouble again. I'm not sure I'll ever figure you two out."

"I can assure you, Noah dear, that my main goal in life is to garden, read library books, and live in peace," Sheila said.

"What's with the Corvettes?" Fayette's voice prickled with irritation.

"Well, the men told me they were just meeting to admire each other's cars and talk engines and tires and bucket seats. I explained they were making the neighbors nervous, and they should take their car-meet somewhere else."

"Do you believe them?" Sheila tilted her head to the right and scrutinized the young cop.

"Naw. But they're gone for now. I'll keep checking your street, though."

"Noah, Fayette and I really appreciate your help. Got time for some coffee?"

"I don't. Got to get back to the station. There's one more thing. Coming up the walk, I could see something strange near your front gate. I shone my flashlight on it. There're two lemon halves with burning sticks poking out of the centers. Wanna tell me what those are?"

"Great God in the foothills," Fayette said. "That doesn't sound good."

"I'll bet those men in the cars have something to do with it." Sheila's voice shook just enough to get Noah's attention.

"Is this something like those truth spells Fayette said she performed in Pastor Fisby's hospital room? Are those guys playing around with magic, too? Man, I thought people your age were too old and smart for crazy stuff like this."

"We'll take care of it, officer." Fayette ignored his last statement as they said their goodbyes to Noah. She was deep in thought about a chapter in one of her new books dealing with curses. When someone left you a lemon with burning sticks in it, they were trying to make your life go sour. If she remembered right, there were ways to squelch a curse like that. In the morning, she would call Abigail and Lars, but she could do her best to counter the curse in the meantime.

"Sheila, I need salt and sugar, a lot of both."

Sheila scurried to the kitchen, returning with a five-pound bag of sugar and a canister of sea salt.

"We need a flashlight." Fayette closed the kittens in one of the bedrooms and then peered out the front door and down the walk. In the grass near the gate there was, indeed, a strange little lump.

With hesitant, uneven steps of trepidation, Sheila approached the lump. Noah was right. Someone assembled two lemon halves and stuffed them with slow-burning sticks. Sheila bent to look closer.

"Don't touch anything," Fayette warned. "First we need to surround the lemon halves in a circle of salt." She handed Sheila the sugar and spread the whole cannister of salt around the lemon halves. "Give me the sugar." Fayette dumped all five pounds of sugar crystals on top of the lemons, completely burying them.

"Contain the curse within the circle," she chanted. "Instead of lives gone sour, change the intention to lives gone sweet, transforming lemons to lemonade." She repeated her words three times and then clapped her hands together twice. Without another word, Fayette led a shaking and unsteady Sheila up the walk and back into the house, closing the door and locking it. "Curses of curses, I did the best I know how. We'll call the coven in the morning and get expert advice."

CHAPTER 24

Even though Sheila and Fayette were sure they would never sleep that night, they both woke at 8 a.m. from deep slumber, Sheila in her bed with Patches at her feet and Fayette on the pull-out couch with Max in the crook of her quilt-covered knees. Only once in the early morning was Fayette startled out of her dreams. Max stood at the front door, hackles raised, an unpracticed growl issuing through tiny, sharp teeth, but Fayette could see nothing from between the curtains except the shadows of Sheila's trees, fence, and gate.

In the morning, she understood Max's warnings. The men returned and kicked apart the lemons covered in sugar and surrounded with salt. They installed a second curse.

***

In the Browning household, Kitsy arose early after a fitful night. She thought she heard something in the kitchen at about 3 a.m., but when she got there, she found nothing and no one, only the door to the back lawn was open. "For Pete's sake." Re-positioning both locks and checking them twice, Kitsy was grateful she'd left Marmy cozied up to Samuel, so the little bundle was safe inside.

"It must have been Alfred after the lantern. He realized it's gone, and he left." Samuel slid an 8:30 a.m. cup of coffee across the counter to Kitsy. "Where does a lantern man go in the middle of the night? What does he do without a place to live?"

"From what I understand, he spent at least 350 years without a place to live," Kitsy mused. Then she described looking out the front window after securing the kitchen door and seeing the ochre-colored Corvette parked across the street.

"That's harassment," Samuel growled, a storm of angry frown lines distorting his usually calm face.

Kitsy noticed the change in her husband. "Are you really going to that meeting tonight? I wish you wouldn't. I'm worried about what might happen."

"I want to help," Samuel said. "I can't just sit around and watch strangers follow you and your friends and attack you. I won't go unless there's someone with me. I'm thinking I'll ask Sheila's friend, Darwin. He would understand the situation, don't you think? He's known Sheila for a long time, and from all you've told me, he's cared about her for years."

Kitsy folded her arms across her chest in concern. Here was this bookish folklorist, English teacher, her life partner, wanting to protect and defend, and she couldn't help but feel appreciated and cherished but worried about his safety.

"If you're bent on doing this, how can I assist?"

"I talked to Lars before you got up. He's got a replica of a beaded keychain, you know, one of the things we need to get ourselves into the meeting. He doesn't have the beads to make more. Does Sheila have more of those rosary pea seeds, and is there a way to make them into beads?"

"Let's walk over and ask her. She only lives a few blocks away, and I could use some down time checking out the leaves and dry grasses. I've hardly paid attention to the changing fall colors. I feel like I'm missing out on the season."

Before they started out, Kitsy picked up Marmy and stroked her fur. "Thank you, sweetheart, for guarding that lantern. It was a lot to ask of you." Marmy offered a quick chirrup and gave Kitsy's hand a gentle nip.

Samuel and Kitsy's house was at a Bobbins Way address. Two blocks south was Twinkle Can Lane, the street Sheila lived on. As the walking pair rounded the corner toward Sheila's Craftsman home, they stopped in their tracks and stood staring. A small crowd gathered a block down the street right next to a parked police car.

"That's near Sheila's house," Kitsy told Samuel with a tight whisper.

As they approached, Kitsy could see several people she recognized, and she pointed them out to Samuel. Officers Noah and Bruce were there. Fayette, Sheila, and Lars were there. Kitsy drew Samuel's attention to a sullen and downcast Darwin, standing off to the side, away from the crowd.

The *potato, potato, potato* rhythm of a Harley passed the couple, and a mountain of a man drove up on his bike, parking it in front of the police car. He dismounted with a huff, waved to Fayette, and joined Darwin, away from the center of attention.

"I think I'll go meet Darwin," Samuel said. "Maybe you can find out from Fayette and Sheila what's going on."

As Samuel approached Darwin, he heard the biker introduce himself. "Yeah. I'm Leo Cagan, a friend of Fayette's. You?"

"Darwin Finnigan. I know Sheila."

"What's going on over there?" Leo waved a meaty hand toward the crowd. "I was here last night, staring down a guy in a yellow Corvette. He'd parked his car right here on the street. Maybe I should have insisted on staying. Glad to see Sheila and Fayette look okay."

206

"A Corvette and you?" Darwin straightened, and he gave Leo a suspicious once over. "What … was Sheila partying with a bunch of men? Just how often does she have men over anyway?"

"You've got the wrong end of the stick." Leo backed up a step. "This Corvette fellow was a trespasser and not friendly. I suspect the police are here because of him."

Samuel strode over and offered his hand to the men, one at a time. "I'm Samuel, married to Kitsy over there. So, there was a Corvette here last night? We had one in front of our house too, an ochre-colored one."

"Yeah. Something's up, but Fayette won't talk. She and I had dinner at her house, and a man in a white Corvette kept his eye on us through binoculars the whole time. I brought Fayette here to spend the night so she wouldn't be alone. When we pulled up, a yellow Corvette sat idling across the street from Sheila's house, taking up not one, but two parking places."

"And that white Corvette showed up right after you left." Fayette walked over to Leo and put her good arm through one of his. "So, we had two Corvettes out here until Officer Noah came and asked the drivers to leave. He's here now because one or both of those stalkers left something threatening behind and then added to the mess later in the night."

"You sure they weren't Sheila's boyfriends?" Darwin's voice was uncharacteristically high, his words clipped.

Fayette laughed. "You've got to be kidding. Sheila? Boyfriends? You're the only man she ever talks about, and let me tell you, Darwin Finnigan, she talks about you a lot. Get a grip, boy." Fayette gave Leo's arm a final squeeze as she looked Darwin over. The man was rubbing his temples with the fingers of both hands. To Fayette, Darwin looked like a man working hard to wake up from a deep sleep. With a sniff, Fayette left the men to join Sheila again.

For his part, Darwin kept shuffling his feet, reaching his hand into his pants pocket every few minutes to find the special coin. As a man who fixed broken things in his backyard shop, Darwin rarely felt broken himself. From the moment he'd stopped tearing down posters the day before, something felt missing. Even in his sleep he'd worried over a strong urge to polish the coin between his fingers to make things whole.

"Strange stuff is going on." Samuel shook his head. "I don't think the three of us know the half of it, but it sounds like you two are clued in a little." He proceeded to tell Darwin and Leo what Lars had explained the day before. The Corvette drivers were part of a group set on stifling women's Earth-based, leadership powers. "Those busters, and others like them, are into the dark arts, whatever that means. For some bizarre reason, part of their agenda involves harassing Kitsy and Fayette and Sheila. They call themselves The Guild of the Supreme Brotherhood of Manroots, and they've got some kind of secret gathering scheduled tonight. I've decided to crash that meeting, and I'm looking for someone to go with me."

"I've seen some weird stuff in my life," Leo said, "some of it supernatural crap, but what have these women been up to that would cause this much commotion? It's a real mind bender. No wonder Fayette kept mum about it."

Darwin rubbed his temple a second time, trying to clear his thoughts. "Sheila's a person of interest in a poisoning, and Fayette's a suspect in a kidnapping. And you say that all this connects to a group that despises women who use magic? I literally can't wrap my mind around it. If I went to this meeting, I might start to understand. I think I better go with you."

"Yeah. Count me in too," Leo said. "I can't think of anything worse than hanging out in my cabin feeling like a putz for not going."

The three men, who'd only met each other a quarter of an hour ago, shook on it. Samuel collected their contact information and pointed out Lars. "That's the man who's going to help us get ready."

They could see Lars and Noah were in deep discussion, the officer taking notes.

"So, what the mother bear are they looking at?" Leo tried to move closer and squint at the subject of interest but there were too many bodies in the way. Kitsy broke away from the circle of onlookers and joined the men. "What's going on?" Leo asked after Samuel introduced her.

"Apparently there were some men in Corvettes loitering in front of the house last night. They left the remains of two awful curses. Fayette tells me the first one was a curse to cause people's lives to go sour because it included lemons."

Darwin snorted, drawing Kitsy's attention to his face, which appeared to curdle right before her eyes. Kitsy had seen pictures but never formally met Darwin, and for a moment she wondered what Sheila saw in him. Right then he looked like a bitter, old man. She cleared her throat and continued. "Well, Fayette and Sheila surrounded the lemons last night with a circle of salt, and then Fayette dumped five pounds of sugar on top of them. She said it would sweeten and reverse the curse so it would produce a different kind of energy. People affected by the changed spell would be able to make lemonade out of lemons, sweetness from the sour. Inspired solution, right? But then the culprits came back and built a new curse."

"Curses?" Darwin bent his knees and then held onto them with both hands. He looked as though he might be sick.

"Hey, buddy. I know it sounds crazy, but with the couple of days I just had, I could almost believe anything." Samuel reached over and gave Darwin a friendly slap on the back.

"Not much surprises me anymore after decades of watching people get in and out of trouble." Leo looked up at the sky to watch a hawk circle over some nearby fir trees. "Some fortunate endings seemed nothing short of miraculous. Some of what happened made me think evil is a real thing. I'm keeping my mind open on this jumble till I know more."

"But I always thought Sheila was a faithful, God-fearing woman. How could she be involved in evil curses, or anything else to do with bad magic? And what about all those men she entertains at night?" Darwin looked over at Sheila, and Kitsy could see bewildered hurt in his tired eyes.

Puzzling how to help Darwin and not drive him away, Kitsy moved closer to look him square in the eye. "Two things, Mr. Finnigan. First, there is no way that Sheila entertains men at night. I don't know where that came from, but it's poppycock! Second, do you want the real story about why two men in Corvettes harassed Sheila and Fayette last night and why there are two piles of cursed objects next to her gate? I'm willing to fill you in if you've got the patience to listen."

"Fill me in, too," Leo said. "If I'm going to that meeting tonight, I think I need the scoop on why I'm there."

"Do you want to help me explain, Samuel?" Kitsy believed her husband's account of his experiences would add credibility to the story.

The four of them sat down on the grass, trying to get comfortable while Kitsy, and sometimes Samuel, explained everything they knew about the last two and a half weeks. Kitsy described the book club's pact to try something new and their experimentation with magic. Samuel told Leo and Darwin about The Lantern Man, and he laid out all he knew about the Manroots coven and its purposes. Both Kitsy and Samuel left out the existence of the Waterleaf Fen Circle. They vowed to guard the coven's secret, and they kept their promise. Instead, Kitsy assured Leo and Darwin that Fayette and Sheila knew people who could help them undo most of the chaos caused by their reckless attempts at magic, people like Lars Columbus.

She finished with these words. "You are the only man Sheila ever talks about, Darwin. She's careful and kind. You can get it out of your head that she spends time entertaining other men."

Darwin responded by putting both hands to his ears. He rubbed the sides of his head with fierce pressure as though his head tingled, as though something pulled hard at his brain in two painful directions.

"Okey Dokey …," Leo said, looking confused about this side conversation with Darwin. He shrugged his leviathan shoulders. "How do we get ready for this Manroots meeting?"

"As I said before, that's our man over there." Samuel pointed to Lars. "Thing is, we need some stuff to get ourselves into the meeting, special thumb rings, robes that hide our faces, and key rings made with red and black beads from a rosary pea plant. With the thumb ring that Sheila has, we've got enough, but Lars doesn't have any rosary pea beads to help us put together the coded key rings that we need. Sheila might be able to help us with that. After all, it was her plants that provided Fisby with the beads in the first place."

The gathering in Sheila's yard dispersed once Noah and Bruce jumped into the Elmira city patrol car and left the scene. Kitsy, Samuel, Darwin, and Leo moved to join Sheila and Fayette, who were watching while Lars, with gloved hands, lifted handfuls of material from the curse pile into a lead-lined box, including a knife plunged into a cow's heart. Fayette told Kitsy that the Corvette drivers had likely installed the bloody heart next to the sour lemon curse after the women had gone to bed.

"They are both serious curses," Lars said to Sheila and Fayette. "I'm taking no chances, but putting sugar on top of the lemons was a brilliant reversal of the negative with the positive."

It turned out that Sheila's rosary pea plants had finished producing seeds. Fisby, it seemed, harvested the last of the fresher seeds on the vine. All that remained were seeds that had been on the ground for a while, molded and faded by the fall weather. Sheila retrieved Pastor Fisby's ring in its metal tea box and handed it over to the men. They had rings and enough robes but still had the problem of finding rosary pea beads.

"Elden sells them in his Brilliant Things shop." Leo turned to Fayette. "Remember how he wouldn't sell them to you because you don't have a Y chromosome?"

"How could I forget." Fayette sniffed.

"I don't recommend buying beads at Brilliant Things," Lars said. "Elden is always there minding his shop. He'd think something was up if one of us asked for the beads."

"There are beads inside Fisby's house." Kitsy's voice was a whisper. Everyone knew, now, that she and Fayette had sneaked in the back door and how she took the book with The Lantern Man in it, but she was still ashamed.

"And those are seeds stolen from my vines after all," Sheila pointed out. "I don't feel bad about stealing them back."

"The question is," Lars said, "is the pastor using his house as a hideout? Does he have the house under surveillance? Since his kidnapping, are there cameras installed to monitor visitors and trespassers? Lastly, what kinds of spyware might be on that place since the three of us investigated his workshop the day he collapsed? I checked when I was there that day. No cameras then."

"So, where do you think he's hiding out?" Sheila heard from Noah that Police Chief Castillo wanted an arrest soon. She was afraid she might be behind bars by evening if the officers decided they had enough evidence against her.

"As to that, I can only speculate. We need more to go on." Lars lifted the lead box to take to his truck. "The meeting tonight might give us a place to start. In the meantime, we need to make sure you three women get some quality magical aptitude training."

At the words 'magical aptitude' Darwin groaned and grabbed his knees again. Lars scrutinized the man, from his scuffed boat shoes to his pallid face and gray-flecked, curly hair. Something wasn't right. He noticed that Leo was close to Fayette, and Samuel had his arm around Kitsy's waist. Darwin, however, kept several feet of unfriendly space between himself and Sheila. By the worried way she glanced toward him, Lars surmised that Sheila was fully tuned-in to Darwin's coolness.

"Darwin, is it? I'm Lars Columbus, owner of the downtown bookstore." He shifted the lead box to his left side and extended his right hand toward Darwin, inviting a friendly shake. Darwin relented, and as their palms met, Lars felt the tingle of a hex in Darwin's large, rough fingers. Someone had infected this bewildered man with unsolicited magic. "You're a friend of Sheila's, I understand," Lars said, probing.

"I was until I discovered she's a cougar who uses men." Darwin glanced sideways at Sheila, hurt and disappointment etched in the creases around his eyes.

"Who told you that?"

"A man on Main Street when I was pulling down those ugly posters of Sheila and Fayette. He came right up to me and said he knew Sheila and that she goes through lovers like a NASCAR driver goes through cars.'"

"Did he give you anything?"

"No. He didn't give me anything. He did point to a coin he thought I'd lost. It was on the ground, but when I picked it up, it wasn't like any coin I'd ever seen before. Here. It's in my pocket."

The builder-fixer-handyman stuck his right hand into his pants pocket and pulled out a quarter-sized piece of toast-colored metal. Darwin offered it to Lars, who slipped on a spare set of rubber gloves before taking it. Close examination showed that the coin was low quality, made from melted bronze poured into a cast. The mold for the coin included imprints for the words *Whisper Coin*. Lars realized that the stranger on the street subjected Darwin to a suggestion spell. Judging from the hard expression on Darwin's face, he was still under the spell. Was this what they called a "teachable moment"? Lars decided it was.

"Sheila, Fayette, Kitsy, can you come stand by me for a minute?" Lars motioned the three friends over.

Feeling numb, and more than a little shellshocked about Darwin's suspicions and his admission, Sheila complied, careful not to look in his direction. Her two friends stood by her side.

"Lars, it's been settled. Samuel, Leo and Darwin have agreed to attend that Manroot meeting tonight." Kitsy pointed to each man as she said their names, so Lars would know who they were.

Squinting, Lars studied the men and then nodded. "I want you to know the dangers of being in the presence of men who aren't above using Earth powers for self-serving purposes. You three men are new to the idea of magic as a reality, and that means you may be feeling a whole range of emotions, including disbelief. That's normal. But disbelief means you are less likely to take what you are about to do with enough seriousness. You might think that something you consider unreal can't affect you."

"I've seen enough the last few days to be concerned,"

Samuel interjected.

"Glad to hear it. You can help Leo and Darwin."

Lars reached out and put an arm around Sheila's shoulders.

"In the meantime, one of you is already under the influence of Manroot Guild mischief and doesn't know it. What happened to Darwin, here, could happen to any of you, and it might still if you aren't careful."

Turning to the three women, Lars asked Kitsy and Fayette, "Be honest, now. What kind of woman is your friend Sheila? Acknowledging that we all have weaknesses, does she sometimes tell falsehoods? Can she be insensitive to the feelings of others? Is she sometimes self-centered? Does she have a flock of man friends who come by to spend the night? Is she what some people refer to as a cougar, reeling in young men as well as old?"

Kitsy, her eyes flaming as though lit by a match, aimed a glare at Lars. She steeled herself to defend Sheila. Fayette let out a squawk which turned into gasps of laughter.

"You've got to be kidding." Fayette said when she could breathe.

"You're wrong on every count," Kitsy snapped.

"And yet, Darwin here thinks otherwise. He believes Sheila entertains strings of men, eating them up and spitting them out. She's a user and abuser of men, old and young." Lars threw out the accusation and waited for a reaction.

"Is that what you think?" Sheila turned toward Darwin, a pounding like drums bruising her heart and a gray fog filling her brain. What had she done to ever give him that impression?

"I know it's not true, Sheila," Lars said in a soothing voice. "But I wasn't the one subjected to the power of a deep lie caused by suggestive magic. Darwin is under such a spell, worsened by this lie token." He held up the coin for the group to see. "It's called a whisper coin, and it carries a spell that makes its holder believe a lie told by the one who made the coin. Since the lie that Darwin believes is hurtful to women in general and Sheila in particular, I'd say the conjurer is part of the Manroot Guild. Know that when you attend the meeting tonight, the Manroots will subject you to similar lies. You may be vulnerable to slander spells. Resisting deceptions is a test of your strength in a gathering where leaders encourage and expect anti-woman stereotyping and falsehoods."

"But what are we going to do about Darwin?" Kitsy had her arm around Sheila, whose shoulders stiffened like old fennel stalks. Sheila tried to focus, but her throat and eyes strained with the work of holding back tears.

Fixated on his feet, a stubborn set to his brow and lips pressed together, Darwin said nothing. Kitsy got the impression that the man was in a daze, only half aware of his surroundings.

"Darwin, old man." Lars stepped closer to the tall fellow standing separate from the others. "You'll need to stay home tonight. You're in no condition to go to a meeting where the man who cast that spell is sure to be. You've got some sorting out to do."

"I don't mean about tonight." Kitsy stamped her right foot and swallowed a sob. "What do we do right now to help mend things between Darwin and Sheila? She waited years to get his attention. She really cares for him. Now that's all ruined."

"Melting the coin will help, but only so much. Seth Green, who you met at the circle meeting yesterday, has a casting torch. We can take the coin to him to destroy." Lars regarded Darwin with a grim set to his lips. "But Darwin's going to have to do the rest. He'll need to recognize his part in believing the lie, experience true regret, and be able to apologize to Sheila and mean it." Lars turned to Sheila. "In the meantime, your job is

216

to come to terms with your feelings, which I imagine include a whole array of emotions, not the least of which is a sense of betrayal from someone you trusted. I think our coven priestess, Abigail, can help you, along with your good friends, here."

A large, swelling tear gathered speed as it slid down Sheila's left cheek. She took a deep breath and let it out in a lengthy sigh of tired resignation. It had been a long night and a longer morning. For that matter, it had been a long life, a life of patient waiting. Perhaps the wait had been for naught. She glanced Darwin's way, but he was looking at his hands, so Sheila lifted her chin, straightened her back and turned away.

"How can I help get things ready for tonight?" she said in a small, resigned voice. "Now that the sour lemon curse is cleared away, and the knife and cow's heart are locked in a box, let's go in, have some coffee, and sort out jobs and a plan."

As Leo, Samuel, Kitsy, Fayette, and Sheila filed through Sheila's front door, Lars led Darwin to his vintage, tea-green, 1955, 3100 Chevy pickup, with its artillery-style wheels, chrome caps, and refurbished, stainless steel brake lines. The pickup was an indulgence Lars allowed himself without apology. They settled onto the distressed brown leather bench seat and were off with a roar to find Seth and melt the whisper coin. On a normal day, Darwin salivated over vintage pickups, but he barely noticed the gleaming banjo-style steering wheel or roomy dashboard. He could have been in a dumpy school bus van or a Hummer H3 for all he cared. Despite the speeches everyone made, and as much as he tried to let go of his suspicions, Darwin couldn't shake the notion that Sheila had been using him. It was as though the suggestion spell flipped some kind of cognitive switch and rewired a mind map in his brain. He would need some kind of brain re-calibration to recover.

"You know, fella, if you don't get your head on straight, you're going to lose her." Lars geared down to turn onto the gravel driveway to Seth's family farm. "That would be a terrible shame."

CHAPTER 25

Pastor Fisby's thumb ring cast an ominous shadow on Sheila's kitchen table where the three women and Leo and Samuel gathered. Their priority was to find more rosary pea seed beads so Samuel and Leo could get into the Manroot meeting.

"Samuel and I can nab the beads from Fisby's house. We'll make a quick entry and get out of the building in a dirty minute." Leo started toward Sheila's front door to get to his bike.

"Stay put, Mr. Cagan. I'm going with you." Fayette's fierce countenance warned Leo that her participation wasn't up for negotiation. "For one thing, I know where to find the beads. I've been there already. Besides, what if the police show up? They don't know you from Batman or Judas Priest or Marlboro Man. They've already met me. They know I think magic is real and that I'm likely to do madcap things in the name of it."

As Samuel, Leo, and Fayette prepared to burglarize Pastor Fisby's rectory, it was Kitsy's job to help Sheila get much-needed rest, so she pointed Sheila to her bedroom. "Go take a nap."

After tucking a soft quilt around her friend, Kitsy would try to think up possible lantern man hideouts. She could only imagine the kinds of disturbances a specter from the Fens of East Anglia might trigger in an unpretentious American town like Elmira. Could he manage an intersection and crosswalk? Would he leave the gas pumps alone at the filling station? What if he followed people onto the city transportation van and freaked out when it started up? *Stop*, she told herself. *It's either stand here and brainstorm improbable troubles with lantern men, find something helpful to do, or go with Fayette to Pastor Fisby's.* But Kitsy never wanted to even drive by that house again let alone go inside, so she stood on the porch and wished Samuel, Fayette, and Leo luck as they left on their mission to retrieve rosary pea beads from Fisby's worktable.

Fayette boarded the back of Leo's motorcycle. With her left arm in its sling, she had only her right arm with which to hold onto Leo and steady herself in the pillion seat.

"She just can't help herself," Kitsy murmured, signaling her disapproval of Fayette's recklessness with a resigned shrug.

Samuel gave Kitsy a quick squeeze as he left the house.

He climbed into the driver's seat of Sheila's car, turned over the engine, and readied himself to follow Leo's lead. *What have I got Samuel into?* Kitsy thought, but she could swear that her life partner relished the adventure, matching the roar of Leo's whack-the-throttle by gunning the engine of Sheila's modest sedan. Most days, he liked nothing better than spending an afternoon with his books and sorting through unending folklore and history puzzles. Lately, Kitsy was witnessing a new side of him as he stepped in to help uncover Manroot Guild secrets. He'd already delt with a hard-bitten, paranormal creature from the past, and seemed to take her magic experiments in stride. Had he been bored with retirement and not realized it? Had she?

"Lead the way, Captain!" Samuel yelled from his open window. Leo blasted out of the parking place with

Samuel peeling out as a close second, leaving rubber on the asphalt that might require explaining once Sheila woke from her nap.

"Don't let Fayette fall off," Kitsy called after them.

Looking in on Sheila, Kitsy noted the orange, black, and white kitten mound, a little body curled in the crook of Sheila's knees. Patches raised her head and eyed the human visitor, and for some reason, Kitsy felt compelled to nod at the cat, just a small forward movement. To her surprise, Patches lifted her white chin and blinked two apple-green eyes in acknowledgement. Max kitten-walked sideways into the room in an arched-backed stance. Spying Patches, he leaped onto the bed, achieving a direct landing on top of his sister. In seconds, the two baby felines were dashing down the hall, crashing into the bathroom door and catapulting onto a soft-pile, wool throw rug that slid into a rolling book cart in the living room. Kitsy sprinted to catch the cart before it hit a standing Tiffany lamp that looked genuine, a real antique.

***

Several streets away, Fayette, Leo, and Samuel parked on the other side of a wooded lot from Pastor Fisby's house. They planned to walk through the grove of young fir trees, which ended along Fisby's back yard. From the edge of the woods, they would assess ways to enter the house.

As they approached their destination, Leo picked up a stick, which he pointed at the grey-painted back wall of Fisby's abode. "Got any ideas for how to get in there?"

"It's my business to initiate break-ins." Fayette curled her right hand into a fist and used it to deliver three, no-nonsense thumps on her own chest. "I was a locksmith for two decades, and I was dang good at it. Once a locksmith always a locksmith."

"Hey ho. Well then, I guess it's Samuel and I who'll keep watch while you breach the lock." Leo looked at his newfound friend with admiration. Life had shifted into higher gear since connecting with Fayette.

But the lock didn't need picking. Indeed, the back door was ajar, like it was when Fayette and Kitsy pushed it open only days ago, the day that Kitsy stole *The Book of Forbidden Knowledge*.

Stepping with caution into the kitchen, Fayette held her arm out to stop Samuel and Leo from moving past her. Voices carried down the hallway from Fisby's study. A finger to her lips, Fayette motioned the men closer to the voices so they could listen better.

They heard a man's gruff and throaty intonation first. "Look closely at that altar. Read the titles of the books over the ritual knife. Fisby is not the righteous man of God you thought him to be. He is not even true to his own depiction of God."

"Do you mean he practices magic?" They could hear dismay in the woman's voice, which tightened from shock to anger. "Do you mean he practices *dark* magic?"

"The darkest," the husky voice agreed. "I am one of his victims, one of his father's victims."

"But he betrayed me too, then." The woman wailed, her lamentations a mixture of angst and ire. "When I met him, I was learning about healing crafts. I studied ways to use herbs and the power of the moon for making medicine. He threatened to tell the world that I practiced witchcraft, that my friends would turn against me if I kept studying. Together we burned my books and my herbs. I followed him to his church and believed his teachings. I trusted him when he said my work was wicked."

"Trust neither Fisby nor his brother Elden," the man said. "They lead a coven bent on weakening the power of women."

"How do you know all of this?" The woman's tone

became more moan than wail.

"Because I was privy to countless conversations for many years. I was Fisby's prisoner for decades. I only just escaped a few days ago."

"Yes. You told me about that. Where is the SOB now? I want to strangle him." The woman's voice sharpened, and Fayette, Samuel, and Leo heard something heavy hit the floor.

"Whoa, whoa. Let's not tear the place up just yet. There are things I need to find for the work I need to do. That's why we came."

"You're so secretive sometimes. Can't you tell me at least a little about what you're planning to do? Is it something to punish Fisby? Are you going to kill him?"

Samuel, who was behind the other two, stepped back at these words. Leo's and Fayette's eyes met. He mouthed the word *insane*, and she nodded.

A raspy guffaw insinuated itself into the listeners' ears. "No. I won't kill him. Something worse. Something he and his father did to me. An eye for an eye."

Fayette shuddered. Yes. Some things could be worse than death. There was no doubt about it. But what did this man intend for Fisby?

And then, Leo, who leaned closer and closer to the hallway to hear better, lost his balance, and fell into the kitchen stove with such force that it rocked. An empty, stainless steel tea kettle on the front burner fell crashing and rattling onto the tiled floor. Wincing, Leo looked toward Fayette, expecting a face full of disappointment. Instead, she snickered and then held her bad arm tight, trying to keep herself from laughing out loud; but restrained and snorting laughter is contagious, so that Samuel and Leo had to look away to control their own urges to laugh. Even as the figures of a man and woman marched with determination toward them down the dark hallway, the spying trio couldn't stop snickering.

"You!" It was the woman's voice, accusatory.

"Why are you here?" The man's voice cut into their spontaneous mirth.

Fayette wiped a sleeve over the tears streaming down her face, gasping to control her hilarity.

"Alfred?" Samuel wheezed for breath, working hard to regain his speaking ability. He turned to his fellow spies. "Leo, this is Alfred, The Lantern Man, the one who went missing yesterday."

Leo looked bemused. "The fellow who carries around a piece of coal?"

"And I recognize this woman." Fayette waved her lock pick at the shortish woman whose thin, sharp nose pointed up at Fayette like an accusatory finger. "She is Darnelle Shipman of the Confess and Reform Church."

"Kitsy told me that Darnelle invited Alfred to come over last night to sit around a firepit and have wine and dessert," Samuel said, surprise in his voice. He turned to face Alfred. (Seeing another man wearing his own Shetland Aran wool sweater and his own dark-wash jeans felt unnerving.) "You took her up on it, did you old boy?"

"We had a lovely evening," Darnelle cut in, her tone clipped and schooling. "Alfred and I talked for hours and hours, so long that it seemed rude for Alfred to wake you and your wife by going back, so Alfred stayed over." She put her arm inside one of his and pulled him close. "We became fast friends, bosom buddies in one night. I've never met anyone quite like Alfred. By the time breakfast was on the table this morning, I knew he was a brilliant, unusual, fascinating man, someone I don't want to let go of."

"I've waited a long time to meet a good woman," Alfred told Samuel, an edge of defiance in his blunt statement. "I've never had the pleasure of knowing anyone quite like Darnelle. I believe she might be the redeemer of my soul."

"Woah." Leo's bushy eyebrows raised high on his

forehead as he rubbed his chin with strong, thick fingers. "I've heard of whirlwind romances, but this one vaulted faster than the speed of light."

Samuel reached out to grab Alfred's arm. "Old boy, how many women have you courted? You never mentioned a girlfriend or wife in your life history yesterday. Are you sure you don't want to take this slow and easy?" He turned toward Darnelle. "What does he mean 'redeemer of my soul'?"

Instead of answering Samuel, Alfred's eyes focused quizzically on Fayette's lock picks. "Are you looking for me? Is that why you are here?"

"We were worried about you." Samuel frowned. "We didn't imagine you would return here, though. We thought you'd want to stay away from the place Fisby imprisoned you for so long."

"I have a plan. The tools for my plan are here." Alfred licked his lips, not meeting Samuel's eyes.

Fayette scrutinized this peculiar creature, whose emotions seemed to change as fast as a two-year-old's. Between the fingers of his closed left fist, she could see the edges of a piece of paper with scribbled lines and what might have been a tiny jar.

"And Darnelle needed to see this ugliness." Alfred's upper lip curled in disgust as he gestured in the direction of the pastor's library and workshop. "Fisby is a conjuror, full of malice inherited directly from his wretched father."

Darnelle choked, and a look of tenderness softened Alfred's eyes as he regarded his new companion, her face a study in grief and then anger, grief and then anger. Fayette noticed too. Darnelle had been a loyal follower in Fisby's church, giving time, energy, and devotion to his causes. Discovering his deception must feel like betrayal.

For his part, Samuel could see Alfred really did care for his new girlfriend. At Samuel and Kitsy's kitchen table, Alfred described his change of mind near the end of his long exile in the fen marshlands. Alfred recalled his dream of finding a life partner and ending his misery. Perhaps he'd decided to waste no time now that he was free from the book and separated from the lantern. Whatever the reason for jumping into romance, this strange man part demon seemed on his best behavior, less likely to snarl, less caustic. What would Kitsy make of this turn of events? Samuel scratched the back of his neck in bewilderment.

It dawned on Samuel that when this individual was Alfred, he was Robert Louis Stevenson's Dr. Jekyll. His mouth turned up at the corners, his eyes softened, and his jaw relaxed. When he was The Lantern Man, he was Mr. Hyde. His lips frowned, his eyes protruded, and his jaw clenched.

Darnelle, in the meantime, turned to face the three kitchen crashers, regaining her characteristic abrasive demeanor. "Why are you here?" Her acidic tone scolded Fayette, Leo, and Samuel as she looked them over; her nose wrinkled as though smelling fermented silage. "Alfred lived here for many years, but you are trespassers." She took her phone out of her pocket and held it up to her face as though preparing to take pictures.

"Darnelle, stand down. Your Pastor Fisby took valuable seeds from my friend Sheila's yard," Fayette said, sounding exasperated. "We're here to reclaim some of what he stole." She pushed past the couple in the hallway to get to the blood-red, rosary-pea beads before Darnelle could prevent her from entering Fisby's workshop.

Darnelle started after Fayette, but Alfred's next words distracted her. "I want my lantern back, Samuel Browning. Make no mistake; there will be a reckoning if you fail to return it to me. I am a partially free man now but still bound to the power of the lamp. If I am to become whole again, human instead of demon, I need the lantern returned to me for a proper severance."

"Hey. I'm sorry. I don't know where it is. Other people hid it for safekeeping. It's no longer in our home." Samuel watched a flash of anger cross over Alfred's face and then settle as smoldering rage in his eyes. In moments, stress lines deepened, eyes hollowed, and thin lips turned down into a bitter sneer. The visage in the hallway transformed from a gentler Alfred-in-love to yesterday's pestilential lantern man. Samuel stepped back, knocking into Leo who had started following Fayette down the hall.

"Steady, man." Leo braced Samuel's shoulders to keep the two of them from falling into a knife rack on the wall. The Lantern Man's eyes, now clouded with animosity, shifted several times from the knife rack to Samuel and back to the knife rack.

"You'll never get yourself severed from that lantern if you decide to hurt people," Samuel said, eyeing The Lantern Man and nodding toward the knives. "If I remember your story right, it's by protecting people, sacrificing yourself for another, that you will gain your freedom. Isn't that what your teacher said?"

A growl, low and warning, arose from The lantern Man's throat. "What if The Lantern Man does not want to die? What if he would protect himself from Alfred?"

"Alfred?" The soft fingers of Darnelle's small, plump hand wrapped around The Lantern Man's upper left arm. Her other hand, tentative, rubbed his forearm. "What is it my teddy bear?" The growl shifted to a soft moan. To Samuel and Leo's surprise, The Lantern Man's eyes glittered with unshed tears, and it was Alfred whose arms circled Darnelle, pulling her close into a long, lingering kiss. When the kiss went on for more than a full minute, even Leo looked uncomfortable.

"Thank you, my love," they heard Alfred whisper into Darnelle's ear. "You saved me. You saved me from myself."

"What is this, a teen house party?" It was Fayette, returned from Fisby's work room. She reached into her jeans pocket and pulled out a handful of scarlet beads to show Samuel and Leo, then she turned to Alfred and Darnelle. "Congratulations on finding true love, but in the name of beknighted toad spawn, keep it to yourself, will ya?"

Wanting to see the library and the altar they'd heard about, Samuel and Leo moved to step down the hall toward the workroom.

"No time," Fayette whispered. "We gotta move fast. Someone just motored up the driveway on a Chieftain Elite Indian motorcycle and parked out front. It's got to be Fisby's brother."

They all heard the screech of a screen door opening and the sound of a key in the living room front door lock. In seconds they became five bodies in flight, bruising themselves and each other in their tussle to get out the back and into the woods before Elden could see them.

CHAPTER 26

"What's next?" Leo was still breathing hard as he took his place next to Fayette and Samuel sitting side by side on the hood of Sheila's car. They felt safe with a wooded vacant lot as a buffer between them and the house they'd just fled. They felt safe until the front grill of a classic 1990's white Corvette crested the lip of the steep hill in front of them. The slow speed of the car as it passed Leo's bike and Sheila's car seemed deliberate to Fayette. She recognized the driver as the young man who used his cell phone to take an unflattering picture of herself and Sheila in the bakery only the morning before.

The Corvette decelerated almost to a stop, and Fayette could see, thrust out of the driver's window, a hand holding a cellphone. Another picture? She was ready to spring at the car, grab that phone, and stomp the holy bologna out of it, but too late, the car sped up, and all she could do was pull out her phone and get her own picture, a photo of a shiny chrome bumper exhibiting the car license MNROOTB123.

"That turkey buzzard is the one who keeps collecting horrible pictures of Sheila and me to put on posters for the whole town to ogle at." Fayette glanced sideways at Leo and Samuel. "Now it looks like he's including you two in his slander campaign."

"That's okay." Leo grinned. "I'm confident I look like a badass in that shot he took. I gave him my best smile." Leo bared his teeth between wide, curled back lips. "It's my dominance sneer."

"Is that what that is," Fayette teased. "I thought maybe you were passing gas."

"Give me a break, woman. I just saved your butt in that preacher's house, and this is the thanks I get?"

"If I remember right, you're the one who crashed yourself through the woods first, leaving the rest of us far behind." In truth, Fayette was grateful for the way Leo and Samuel kept Darnelle and Alfred talking while she filched beads from Fisby's workroom. As a result, they all had a better idea of what Alfred was up to, and they had the red rosary pea beads that the men needed. They were almost ready to pass as coven followers at the gathering of the Guild of the Supreme Brotherhood of Manroots.

"What I can't figure out is how Mr. White Corvette knew we'd be parked here so he could take our picture," Samuel said. "Does Elden Parkinson know we were in his brother's house?"

"Mr. White Corvette just happened to see our vehicles parked and kept driving by, waiting for us to get back to them," Leo proposed. But somehow Samuel didn't think it was quite that simple. If the Manroots-in-Corvettes were following them, and always knew their locations, how would he and Leo manage to go undetected to the Manroot coven meeting?

"Just the same, I'm checking all our vehicles for tracking devices." Samuel got on his knees and then his elbows to scan the under belly of Sheila's car for a GPS tracker. "Darn. I need a flashlight to see anything."

Fayette and Leo ran their fingers over every inch of Leo's bike. Nothing.

"You're new to the team, a wildcard." Fayette grinned up at her new buddy. "Maybe they only just noticed you. Didn't know till today that they needed to track you too."

"Maybe. Maybe not." Leo's eyes squinted hard at Fayette, the lines between his woolly brows creased more in confusion than exasperation. "What kinds of madcap stuff are you into, woman?" He'd turned the escape from Fisby's house and the picture-taking episode into a joke, but now he seemed serious. "Kitsy and Samuel sat us down in the grass this morning and explained some of it, but I still can't wrap my head around how you even attracted the attention of these goons? This morning, I heard words thrown around like curse, magician, dark magic, coven, protection spells, and Wiccans, and that doesn't even cover half the list. I'm not judging but fill me in with your version of events before I disguise myself as some kind of druid to rub shoulders with a bunch of conjuring weirdos who might just be dangerous. I feel like a lamb to the slaughter."

Fayette grabbed Leo's arm and pulled him down next to her on the grass near the sidewalk. "Hey. You barely know me. I'm not your motorcycle mamma, just someone you met. I don't expect you to go tearing off to put yourself in danger for my sake after only one meal together. That shouldn't happen until after the second meal." She laughed. "You've been more than generous with your time and your help. I'll hold nothing against you if you want to back out of tonight's meeting. Leo, you're right. These people are bullies and fouler than hardboiled liver on moldy buns, pardon my English. I'm only just starting to figure out why they're attacking us."

Fayette paused, thinking hard and reaching into her pocket to feel the red, rosary beads. "In truth, we're members of a book group just farting around. We thought we wanted to learn a little about magic, just to try something new. That's all. Turned out we're a trio of silly neonates playing with fire. Our antics somehow threatened the pastor, his brother, and a host of male witches, and that's as surprising to me as it is to you."

"Can you wave a white flag, if you know what I mean?" Leo reached through the grass to grab Fayette's hand and then thought better of it. After all, they'd only had one meal together.

"It's too late. My back is up. My hackles are raised. It's war now that I know these men are trying to suppress women's power, magic and otherwise." Fayette's lips pressed together in a fine line, straight as a sharpening file.

They sat in silence for several seconds, watching Samuel use his phone to google 'best places to put tracking devices in a car.' As Samuel got down on his knees again, and reached to feel under the passenger seat, Leo cleared his throat. "Yeah, tonight, I'll be a Harley big dog mingling with Corvette chick-car deviants. My misogynist days are over, that is on the days when I know what misogynist means. I'm really just an old hippie. You know, love and peace and equality. The idea of men playing games with people's heads in a church, just to belittle and control the female half of our human population, it ain't my idea of fair play. I'll do my part. It's better than staying home feeling like a deserter and wondering if Samuel got through it okay .... alone."

"You're one loyal scout," Fayette said with a short chuckle. "But I'm grateful. Help me up if you will. Looks like Samuel found something."

Samuel held a one-and-a-half-inch black box, complete with magnet. "It's a GPS tracker, alright. Found this under Sheila's driver seat, tucked into the upholstery."

"Flaming heck. Does that mean there's a tracker on my bike and your SUV, Samuel?" Fayette held out her hand for the tracker. "What if you're traced to the meeting tonight? They'd know right then and there to look for you, disguise or not."

"You can bet I'll go over the SUV until I find it." Samuel shook his head, brows furrowed. "I'm not taking that kind of chance. Whatever you three did, you and Kitsy and Sheila certainly attracted Fisby and his Manroots' attention. Curses planted in people's yards, spies in Corvettes, whisper coins, trackers on all our cars. These busters mean business."

Leo walked over and executed a second examination of his bike. Nothing.

"What do we do with this thing?" Fayette gave the GPS tracker back to Samuel. The little black box marshaled the undivided attention of each of them, sitting like a grenade on top of Samuel's open hand.

"I'll throw it in the woods." Samuel lifted his arm, ready to send the GPS flying.

"Wait." Leo pulled at the end of his beard. "We could use it to our advantage. I don't know exactly how, yet. But we could put it on something else, and if we put it on the right thing, we might be able to confuse them."

"Like on the county bus for seniors," Fayette suggested, "or on one of the city police cars."

"That'd be a hoot." Samuel grinned, closing his fingers around the device and sliding it into his jacket pocket. "But you're right. This little gadget might be something we could use later. It doesn't hurt to take it with us and keep it in Sheila's mailbox or high up on one of those sidewalk streetlights until we have a plan. They'll just think Sheila has her car parked in front of her house. They won't know we've discovered the GPS beacon. That way Sheila can use her car without them following her."

"And if it turns out you've got one on your SUV and Fayette's bike is bugged, we'll have a few more devices to use as decoys," Leo said.

Fayette sighed. She could no longer ignore the ache in her collar bone that throbbed in rhythm with her heartbeat, a throb that increased in intensity as the day wore on. "Your neighborhood biker mamma's gotta get home for a nap," she admitted to the men. "I'm done in." She thrust the hand of her good arm into her watch pocket and let her fingers scoop out the dozen or so red beads collected from Fisby's worktable. Grabbing Leo's larger, fleshier hand, she let the red beads with the single black dots drop into his palm. "Be careful with these and be safe tonight."

"I'll take you home," Samuel said. "A car ride will jiggle your arm and shoulder less than trying to grip the back end of a Harley."

CHAPTER 27

A gusty wind blew in darkening clouds and packed them tight in the evening sky. Under the banks of threatening rain, elements of another kind of brewing storm gathered as a succession of vehicles found spaces in the parking lot of the Manroot meeting place, the Light in the Darkness Church. Dominating the lot was an assortment of muscle vehicles, including several Corvettes, gray and black monster-sized pickups, and a collection of cold-metal themed SUVs, the kind that imitated police patrol vehicles.

At exactly 6:25 P.M., just about sunset, two robed and caped figures climbed out of Leo's mid-sized, gray pickup, parked toward the back of the concrete-walled parking space. His truck spent most days in his garage, so few people recognized it. Just for the evening, Leo borrowed a stray set of plates from his antique license collection. He chose a matching pair of royal blue 1965 Michigan plates, since people tended to think citizens of Michigan were mostly a quiet, law-abiding sort.

"Time to mask up," Samuel said, as he and Leo met at the front grill of the truck. Two hours of training with Lars that afternoon had them feeling a mixture of confidence and trepidation. "Cognitive dissonance, that's what it is," Samuel told Lars. "Having strong conflicting feelings about what we're about to do."

Lars explained the Manroots' disguises, ritual formalities for entering the building, and what to expect during the meeting. "You can see from how this group harasses Sheila and Fayette just how serious they are about asserting their power. Let me assure you, they've been relatively tame so far. They can play a much dirtier game once they decide someone is their enemy. You don't want them to find out who you are or why you're there."

Remembering Lars' words, Leo took particular care to disguise his beard, tucking it into a turtleneck under his cape. Lars equipped him with a plain, black Bauta Venetian mask, with its classic long, pointed chin that covered the rest of his facial hair.

"How's a fellow to breath under this," Leo complained, his mask secured. "What do these Manroots have to hide? Odd that they're too chicken to let each other know who they are." He turned to face Samuel, who stared back at him through his red, gold, and black Bauta mask. "Creepy," Leo muttered.

"A daily sight in Venice in the 17th and 18th centuries," Samuel said. "Can you picture a street littered with people wearing this very costume, people throwing on black capes and masks to protect their identities so they could mingle with anyone they wanted and avoid judgement?"

"I can just see someone trying to ride a motorcycle with this getup." Leo snorted and then shifted his cape and pulled on the sleeves of his robe trying to ease his discomfort. The ring on his right thumb bit into his skin, but there was no time to change its size. It was the very ring Sheila found caught in her rosary pea plant, Pastor Fisby's ring. Samuel wore a matching ring on his thumb, adorned with a chunk of polished amber surrounded by smaller red stones inside a hexagon engraving. They both carried key rings ornamented with a circle of five beads, each red with a single black dot.

Leo locked the truck, and they turned to make their way toward the double, stone-gray, metal doors that were the basement entrance to the church. Five vehicles away, a figure, dressed much as they were, stumbled over the hem of his robe and fell to his knees. A woman with a mop of bottle-black hair jumped out of the nearby pearl-white van and ran to his side. She helped the dazed man to his feet, lifted his Venetian mask, gave him a concerned kiss, then replaced the mask and brushed dirt off his robe and cape.

"Isn't that The Lantern Man's girlfriend?" Leo adjusted his mask to see better.

"Well, well, well. Guess we're not the only party crashers." Samuel watched Darnelle Shipman return to her van while Alfred, The Lantern Man, limped his way to the closed metal doors.

"Wonder what those two weirdos are up to…" Leo mused, trying to process everything he'd learned about the mysterious Lantern Man.

Samuel shook his head, "He's out for revenge, that's for sure. Did you see how he eyed those knives on the wall in Fisby's house? I thought he might grab one. We're better off if he doesn't know we're here."

"Agreed."

They made their way through the parked trucks and SUVs toward the entrance. With the side of a closed fist, Leo knocked out three sharp bangs on the right door and a softer rata-tat-tat on the left, just as they'd practiced that afternoon with Lars. The left door, the one with the lock, opened two inches.

"Show your rings," a hoarse voice croaked out, opening the door another foot. They did as told, holding out their thumbs for inspection. The beam of a flashlight illuminated their hands. "Show your keys," the voice ordered. Samuel and Leo took their key rings from their pockets, making sure to display the red beads on their palms. "Enter," the voice said. "You know the rules."

Lars warned them that all but the top Manroot leaders kept their voices raspy as part of their disguises, so Samuel cleared his throat. "We know the rules," he stated in his own version of voiceless laryngitis. Leo bowed his head to show he concurred. The door opened wider, enough for them to slip through, one at a time.

Inside, Samuel and Leo stood to one side, waiting for their eyes to adjust in a room that was darker than the parking lot. Shadows enveloped the large basement where all was dim except for wall sconces, glowing like firelight on three floor-to-ceiling brick pillars set against the far, right wall. Polished floor tiles reflected flickering light from the sconces in three yellow circles. Samuel thought of dancing will-o'-the-wisps. He admired the golden, fir-slatted, curved ceiling and six cedar posts separating the middle of the room from the left and right sides. Leo felt as though he was inside an old wooden ship, not a church basement.

They were both intrigued by the geometric tile pattern on the floor, which joined caramel and coffee-colored right triangles, and which proved dizzying to those trying to focus. To one side, below a small stage, black-painted wooden chairs waited empty in rows for the meeting to begin. And within this murky setting, upright moving figures in dark purple robes, sorted and resorted themselves into small groups, stepping with care as though to avoid touching or jostling each other.

Leo, who missed his dinner, looked around for refreshments but saw nothing resembling food or drink. When all this was over, the first port of call would be Hamburger Heaven Drive In.

"Shall we join the shuffle, or go sit in those chairs and wait for the meeting?" Samuel whispered.

"No clue," Leo hissed back. "What if we sit in the wrong chairs? What if these Manroots have assigned seats?"

"Lars didn't talk about assigned seating." Samuel

whistled a short, nervous rendition of Twinkle Twinkle Little Star under his mask. He reached inside his cloak where he'd hidden an iPhone in a robe pocket. He'd set his phone to record, so his only job was to push the "on" button through the purple cloth. Leo was primed to do the same with his phone.

At that moment, one of the figures stepped on stage, clapping his hands for attention. The figure leaned a standing microphone toward his mask. "Take a seat, gentlemen," he commanded, not bothering to disguise his voice. Then, as Lars Columbus predicted, Elden Parkinson removed his face disguise.

"Remember the Manroots creed. We protect Manroot leaders and their identities. We do not repeat names of leaders outside of coven meetings. Some of you know each other. Some of you do not. That's as it should be. All of you know your leaders."

"Manroot leaders and their identities will be protected," the men's voices repeated in raspy unison as they located their seats. Leo and Samuel found places in the back row.

"Keeper of the creed, start the meeting." Elden bowed in the direction of a man in the shadows, waiting near a cedar pillar. The caped figure stationed himself in front of the microphone, and Elden stepped down, striding toward the back of the room. This new figure kept his mask firmly in place and spoke as someone with a serious case of bronchitis. "Let us begin the meeting with the reading of The Creed of the Guild of the Supreme Brotherhood of Manroots. Repeat after me." So began the hoarse chanting of the entire Manroots assembly.

We are here to restore men's leadership.
Male mystery is about strife, warfare, and death.
Dominance is male.

"Louder," the leader shouted. The assembly repeated
the creed in roaring voices, stomping their feet at the
end of each statement.

Grim, prickly silence followed the creed. No one
moved.

Just when Leo thought he could no longer hold back
a sneeze, the tintinnabulation of a small bell sounded
behind them. Elden walked along the chairs as though
in procession, ringing the bell until he stepped onto the
stage.

"Welcome, fellow Manroots," he said in the same
voice he used in his shop. He was Elden, male witch,
and second in command of the Manroots guild. "We
called a special meeting, and you graciously responded.
Something has happened. If we seize the moment, we
can cause great harm to the female energies of magic in
our region, including to the disgraceful Waterleaf Fen
Circle of Wiccans."

Sycophantic whistling ensued from several cloaked
Manroot members.

"Where's Fisby?" someone asked in a grating voice.
"We heard someone poisoned him, that maybe he's
dead. Why isn't he here?"

"Fisby is fine. Let me lay out the facts for you so we
can plan. Right now, the Elmira police and the members
of a few local churches are keen on arresting and
punishing two neophyte, female witches for poisoning
and kidnapping Fisby. We can use the situation to
build fear. If we take advantage of the rumors, we can

galvanize enough Elmira citizens into suppressing female Wiccan influences here."

Elden raised his left eyebrow to signal that he knew things the rest of them didn't. "Fisby is in hiding. But our spies recently identified three women who experimented with magic and who need punishment. To their credit, they are more powerful than they realize, so this is the time to destroy their interest in witchcraft by damaging their reputations before they learn the craft. And we can take down the Wiccan circle as we crush these women. If we crush Elmira's Wiccans, the tiny circles in other towns will lose energy as well."

A figure in the second row stood, speaking through a microphone held up to his mask. To Samuel's surprise, the device acted as a voice changer, broadcasting the man's words in a robotic tone. "We're still putting out posters accusing two of the women of poisoning, kidnapping and murder. Some of us are stalking the two old broads, and we installed two curses in the yard of the woman called Sheila Fairlight. These rookie witches have done little to fight back except pour a sack of sugar on a curse. What makes you think they have any power at all? After all, they called on the Wiccans to take care of the curse."

"Fisby." Elden simply named his brother in answer.

"What about Fisby?" Someone else called out. "Where in hell is he?"

"Fisby ended up in the hospital a few days ago, as you know. The doctors found poison in his system. What you don't know is that Fisby was harvesting rosary pea seeds from the garden of the woman called Sheila. It was before dawn, and he decided to investigate her greenhouse. As he touched the door handle, a force blasted his body backwards. The power of the blast knocked him out, and he lay there in the grass for several hours before the ambulance came. He tells me that magic caused the blast, a spell to drive out negative energy. The woman Sheila must have cast the spell."

Leo and Samuel sat stiff and upright in their high-backed wooden chairs. Leo's right knee jiggled up and down like a piston attached to a rotating crankshaft. Samuel fidgeted with the hem of his cape sleeve. Leo's new girlfriend and Samuel's life partner believed they had misdirected their attempts at magic, that the spells were ineffective or had resulted in fiascos. But maybe there was more to their magical energies than anyone knew. What if they weren't failures at spell casting after all?

"What about the poison?" It was the man with the voice-changing microphone.

"There are no spells that I know of that can poison someone," Elden said. "Fisby never ate anything on the woman's property. We think the poisoning may have happened while he made those rosary pea beads, the ones you all carry on your keyrings. Those seeds can be highly toxic. The blast may have intensified poisons he already had in his system."

"One blast. It's not much proof," said a man sitting next to Samuel.

"There's more." Elden stood taller; the set of his jaw hardened. "You see, I'm the one who kidnapped Fisby from the hospital. The woman called Fayette Pinker was in his hospital room before I got there. She cast a truth spell, and she left a truth spell bottle in the room. When Fisby woke from his coma, he couldn't stop talking about us, the Manroot Guild. No matter how much I shook him and yelled at him, his tongue wagged. His confessions were constant. He was about to blow his cover as a pastor. He was about to reveal our existence as a coven, our methods, our goals. I did the one thing I could think of. I bundled him out of the hospital and hid him. Only in the last twenty-four hours has he been able to hold his tongue. That woman, however ignorant, directed a powerful truth spell. Both those hags are more formidable than they know. That's why we need to shut them down forever. And we need to do it now before they realize their potential."

"And the third woman?" asked the man sitting next to Samuel.

"Her powers are undetermined," Elden said. "We must assume she is as dangerous as the others and act accordingly. For your information, her name is Kitsy, Kitsy Browning." A cold chill locked in on Samuel's neck and shoulders, and the hairs on the back of his head bristled in fear for his wife. Next to him, Leo's head buzzed, a symptom of shock. For just a moment everything in his vision lost color. People around him and the room transformed into shades of gray. He realized the situation was far more serious than Fayette knew. "This is unbelievable," he muttered.

A figure at the left end of the second row appeared to hunch low, as though trying to disappear in his seat. He pulled his cloak hood tighter around his mask. Could that be The Lantern Man, Alfred? Leo wondered if this talk about Kitsy and her friends made Alfred feel edgy. Why was he at the meeting?

"So...." the man next to Samuel mused. "You want us to make plans to destroy the women's reputations and relationships and drive them out of town. But as part of the plan, we take down the Wiccan group at the same time."

"Exactly." Elden nodded, a sideways grin playing on his thin lips. "I suggest breaking up into groups, each group with different purposes. We need to hammer out our line of attack. We've already got an alliance doing the posters. We need a second group of Manroots who have special connections with churches and can be guest speakers. They'll be able to whip up phobia of female witchcraft and magic. We know which congregations lend themselves most to fear and exclusion."

"We need a group to work the police angle," the

man sitting closest to the stage said. "They suspect the women as kidnappers and poisoners already. We need ways to motivate people in the town to pressure the police. Let's get those women charged and arrested."

The figure sitting directly in front of Leo stood. His rasp was deep and guttural. "Let's not forget our own powers to use black magic. We must establish a coalition that others can consult about using spells to intensify the fear and deepen the anxiety. I'll give you an example. The woman Sheila has a man friend. I used a spelled suggestion coin on him after I caught him tearing down our posters. He's of little use to Ms. Fairlight now. He heard me loud and clear as I told him a rumor I made up about her. Lies are powerful. They're hard to erase from the mind. He, of course, started having doubts about her. He couldn't help himself. The spell-coin hardened those doubts. He isn't pulling down posters for her anymore."

The group clapped in approval, not the usual kind of appreciative clapping, not a group of individuals each clapping at their own pace and rhythm. This applause was choreographed beats in unison, one, two, three, four, stop. As the clapping died away, the man who gave Darwin the suggestion coin continued. "The woman we aren't sure of, Kitsy Browning, has a husband. We need to find a means of creating division between them. As for Fayette Pinker, it would seem she has a new friend, someone who grew up around here. Some of us remember him from high school, Leo Cagan. We need to put him out of commission or help him see that Ms. Pinker is bad news. Lies backed up with magic might help us get that job done."

"Yes. Let's form a group to help make the best use of our craft," Elden agreed. "And that group can make plans for how to destroy the Waterleaf Circle as we upend the lives of these three female usurpers. Our speeches to the congregations, our pressure on the police, our posters, and our magic must include actions and messages that connect the three women with the Wiccans as enemies."

Elden motioned for the keeper of the creed, waiting beside the cedar pillar. In his hands was a large salver holding five smaller trays of tiny plastic cups containing a dark liquid.

"Brothers in blood. Drink to our creed. Drink to our brotherhood," the keeper shouted. In unison the Manroots repeated his words twice. Samuel felt trapped in a den of copperheads, with their rasping, guttural disguised voices.

The creed keeper brought the trays to the beginning of each row of seated Manroots. As soon as the first person in the first row stood and lifted one of the trays, the row of robed figures stood, and the tray passed from man to man, each taking one of the tiny cups and each lifting his mask just high enough to pour the liquid down his throat. Row by row the men performed the same ritual until the fifth row, the one that included Samuel and Leo. The last tray made its way to Leo. He lifted his mask just enough to slip the tiny cup underneath and let the liquid pour down his beard. Lars Columbus warned Leo and Samuel that the Manroots might pass the cups and that they contained human blood. "The Manroots get the blood from people called sheep," Lars told them. "These sheep are paid to donate their own blood for use in rituals."

When the last cup reached the last Manroot, the coven members sat.

"Four groups, four corners," the keeper of the creed announced. "Meet to devise your strategies. When you finish, report your plans to your leader, Elden. He will inform Fisby of our work. The defamation group meets in the back right corner. The manipulation of churches group meets in the back left corner. Pressuring the police group meets in the front right corner. The magic consultant group to destroy the Wiccans meets in the front left corner. Take your chairs with you."

"I'm thinking police," Leo said, voice raspy.

"I'll do churches," Samuel said, catching on to the idea of splitting up for more information. He poked Leo's shoulder and nodded towards Alfred, heading toward the magic consultant group.

They watched The Lantern Man settle his chair a little outside the other chairs, now gathered in the dim left hand corner at the front of the church basement. Groups were already talking so Leo hoisted his chair off the ground and headed toward the front right-hand corner where the police-pressure group met. That left Samuel with the group focused on churches. As he settled his chair near the circle, the robed and caped figures scooted to make room for him. Introductions were never part of Manroots meetings. There were no small group leaders. The men simply started talking.

"Most of us know the drill, here," a long-legged, black-shoed man rumbled. "We're all part of some church or another. We've all given the odd sermon or talked about the dangers of female witchery."

"Think we should try to expand our scope to some of the churches that haven't welcomed us in the past?" The idea came from a hefty fellow whose bushy brown beard stuck out on both sides of a white Bauta mask; its painted eyes turned down on their sides to convey sadness.

"No reason to," the first speaker said. "Not all Christian churches welcome our message, but we've got enough churches under our thrall to spread gossip. People will remember the words we use to label the women. If we repeat the words over and over, our brands for the women will spread. Once we can lodge the words and the innuendos into enough people's minds, suspicion will grow. Even if most people reject our message, they will begin to absorb some of our descriptions of these women."

"Yeah. No one can accuse us of defamation if we don't use the women's names," said a short man with a greasy voice. "But we can refer to the posters. We can hint that there is a circle of witches meeting in Elmira, and we can blame them for any unfortunate things that happen in the town."

A man further down the circle of seven cleared his throat. Samuel noticed the callouses on his hands that indicated labor with rough tools. "Compare the dames to vile animals," he said, pushing out air and breathing air back in a whistling wheeze. "That way people feel disgusted with them, repelled. It won't matter if the women are proven innocent of hurting Fisby. People will still remember them as revolting animals. It's how human brains work."

"Snakes, vermin, rats, hyenas, maggots, that sort of thing," agreed the man on his left. "We need to choose one or two labels to repeat often when we talk about the three wannabe witches and the Wiccan circle."

Samuel never got the chance to find out which vile words they would choose to describe his wife because a loud cacophony of angry shouts and the jarring thuds of chairs crashing to the floor brought them all to their feet.

Over in the left-hand corner at the front of the church basement, bodies pushed and shoved, their capes flying and robes flapping. Angry voices, no longer disguised, called out to other groups.

"We've got a spy, here."

"Don't let him get out of the building."

"Catch that rotting snake."

"Watch out. He throws fire."

It's the magic consultant group, Leo thought. You don't suppose ....? Squinting through the dark, Leo could see several Manroots dashing after the usurper, but with everyone running, they lost track of their target. Some stopped long enough to help their fellows smother flames that burned the bottoms of their robes.

"Time to get out of here," Leo said, though nobody heard him. He headed toward the back door, hoping that Samuel was doing the same. They needed to get gone before the Manroots organized themselves and found a method to root out intruders. Leo could see that robed men posted themselves on either side of the two metal doors leading to the parking lot. They were there to question Manroots before letting them resume the chase outside. He thought about times when he and his biker buddies needed to get out of a situation fast. Talking their way out had never worked. It was now or never. He filled his chest with air and charged, yelling, "Geiiiit Hiiiiiiim!" As he passed the guards, he realized he wasn't the only deserter. Two figures followed, repeating Leo's battle cry. "Geiiiit Hiiiiiiim!" Together they burst into the parking lot, hands raised as though wielding swords, capes billowing behind. Leo's impromptu performance convinced the masked guards the three escapees were Manroots, fervent and hungry to hunt their prey.

To Leo's relief, one of the two "extras" ran with him to the gray truck, jumping into the passenger side once Leo got the doors unlocked. It had to be Samuel. But what about the third man? He glanced over to where Darnelle parked. Yes. There were two people in Darnelle's van, and it was already leaving the lot, squealing its tires to make the turn onto the street. Time to follow. Leo started the truck engine and trailed Darnelle's van, noting in his rear-view mirror that one of the guards stood wide-legged, taking an iPhone picture of their back end and writing something in a notebook.

"Good luck finding us," he said to the mirror. To himself he muttered, "I gotta get this truck back in the garage right now and switch license plates." His voice lowered in disappointment. "Hell. No stopping to get dinner at the Burger Barn."

In case someone got wind of their location on the highway, Samuel stripped off his mask, cape, and robe so he would appear to be the regular, everyday fella he really was. While Leo sped as fast as he could without drawing undo attention to the truck, Samuel helped him take off his mask, remove the cape, and slip the robe down to his waist. Red, drying blood caked on his beard, but otherwise, he was himself again.

"I'm going to take the back way, in case we're being followed," Leo said as they approached the turnoff to a country road that came out close to where he lived. "If you spot a Corvette or monster truck in the distance, we can slip into a quick hiding place. I know this road well. It's a favorite for biking solo away from traffic."

Samuel seemed to deflate as his adrenaline levels eased bit by bit. He turned in his seat, shoulders stiff, hands balled into fists, keeping his eyes fixed on the road behind them. They stayed silent for the first five minutes, each knowing there was much they had to discuss but wanting to avoid the dirty business for a while longer.

"No rest for the wicked." Samuel finally broke the hush. "As soon as we get into your house, we've got to write down everything we can remember before it fades away. Lars's orders."

"I'll make hamburgers," Leo promised. "And fries."

"Find a hideout. There are high beams about a mile behind us. I think we should play it safe." Samuel's voice tensed. In seconds Leo extinguished his lights and turned the truck onto a pullout surrounded by a thicket of small fir trees. He was able to squeeze the truck into the brush where they could view the vehicle as it passed but stay camouflaged in the dark. Four minutes later, the lights of the vehicle approached. Samuel laughed, his chest and neck relaxing. "It's an old farm truck half rusted away. Can't see one of those Manroot minions driving something like that." But then they saw another car hanging close to the tail of the ancient truck. It was a white Corvette, driven without lights. Leo swore as he watched the Corvette's lights turn on just long enough for the sports car to pass the truck and speed on down the road, lights extinguished again.

"They didn't take any chances," Samuel said. "They're patrolling all the roads to Elmira."

The two fugitives sat for a while, Leo conjuring images of big, juicy hamburgers, Samuel wondering how life had changed so fast in so short a time.

"Okay." Leo broke into Samuel's ruminations. "I've got an idea. We don't know if that Corvette will park along the road to watch for a truck like ours with Michigan plates. I've got another set of plates somewhere in here. I'm going to switch out the plates right now, while we're out of view. I've got a tarp in the back that we can pull over the top of the bed to make the pickup look a little different. I've even got a bumper sticker in the glove box that we can plunk on the back by the tail pipe, so the truck won't fit the exact description of the one they're looking for." Leo turned, reached under his truck seat, and came up with a couple of dented plates. "Anything else you can think of to beef up the disguise?"

Samuel inspected the truck cab and scanned the shadowy forms of trees out the window, searching for anything that might help. It was dark outside and even darker under the trees. Tiny water droplets gathered on the windshield from light rain.

"Mud? Maybe there's mud out there around the tires we can use to smear across the truck doors and hood. We could cut some brush and have some of it stick out from under the tarp."

"We gotta move fast, though." Leo grunted to himself. He realized that his pickup, once home, would need to stay hidden, encrusted with mud for several weeks before he could chance a trip to the car wash. And the bumper sticker would have to come off. It was a picture of a black crow against a yellow background and the words *Throw Bread On Me*.

"I'm not clear about what this bumper sticker is trying to say," Leo told Samuel as he reached across and pulled it out of the glove compartment. "It was a gift, so I didn't throw it away, but, if I don't know what it means, it doesn't belong on my truck, so this is temporary." He located a couple of mini flashlights under the truck registration envelope in the glove compartment. "Let's go."

They piled out of the cab, working as fast as two tired men could, both showing little enthusiasm for picking up handfuls of mud and smearing it on slabs of metal. In his toolbox, Leo found a hand saw for cutting spruce and Douglas fir branches from the young trees surrounding the truck. Samuel artfully arranged the limbs, so they stuck out from under the blue tarp, which Leo secured with bungee cords. Car license plates replaced and secure, Leo finished off his work by mudding the truck bed gate, leaving the replacement Arizona plates mostly clean and visible. The Michigan plates were royal blue. These new plates featured a light blue skyline over a desert scene. That ought to be enough to keep people guessing.

With mud-caked shoes and a sweater wet from rain, Leo felt ten pounds heavier climbing back into the driver's seat. Getting the truck stuck would be the last straw, but he backed the pickup out from behind the trees with the help of Samuel's flashlight directions.

"Bloody hell, there better be some sneaky devil waiting on the side of the road to appreciate our artwork," Leo growled to Samuel once they were back on the road. "I want the satisfaction of confusing the malarky out of someone."

Laughing, Samuel looked down at the mud drying on

his hands and knees. "That would be a fitting end to one of the creepiest, confusing days I can ever remember."

A Manroot in a vintage Corvette did stake out the backroad to town, taking pictures of every vehicle that passed. But Leo and Samuel didn't spot him, nor did they see the flash of his camera as he took a picture of their truck speeding by, muddy streaks and all.

Chapter 28

Three ceramic mugs, crowned with coffee filters inside cones, waited for hot water on Leo's tiny side counter. It was 7:30 in the morning. Samuel, who spent the night on Leo's couch, sat bleary eyed at the old-fashioned, enamel topped table. Kitsy and Marmy stayed the night at Sheila's, so it made sense that once they got the truck in the garage, he and Leo kept working on their coven meeting notes for as long as it took. It took till 1:12 a.m.

"What's holding up the coffee, anyway," Samuel muttered, missing his own kitchen and his daily pancake ritual.

Leo was in even worse shape. Having eaten one too many hamburgers the night before, he spent several post-midnight bouts in the bathroom trying to settle his stomach. Nothing, not even coffee, appealed to him. Sleep was his highest priority. And still Lars pounded on the front door at 7:15 a.m. with no mercy. If Leo's stomach turned at the sight of the pastry box in Lars' hands, Samuel welcomed the assortment of muffins and croissants from Lucky Cup Café and Bakery.

"There's been another curse attack," Lars told them. "Fayette this time."

Leo shot to his feet, adrenaline having electrified a sudden surge of energy. "I better get over there."

"Not now." Lars held out an arm to restrain him. "The

Waterleaf Circle is handling it. Right now, you need to fill me in about what happened last night. What's in the works with these Manroots? The curse attack on Fayette indicates to me that they're executing their plans directly, no delays."

Sentence by sentence they went over their notes with Lars, adding missing details in the margins when he asked questions. As they read out what they'd heard and seen, Lars kept his hands folded together under his chin, nodding at certain details, forehead wrinkled like the top of an old, leather shoe. When they got to the part about the unusual power behind Sheila's protection spell and Fayette's truth spells, Lars chuckled. His eyes sparkled with appreciation; his bushy brows danced like coconut shavings frying in hot butter. But then his face clouded, and he shook his head when they disclosed the Manroots' plan to spoil Leo and Fayette's new relationship and Samuel and Kitsy's marriage.

"Whoa, stop. Have you thought about this? How are you going to deflect magic-heavy words and charms meant to ruin your connections with Fayette and Kitsy? Darwin's in a bad way because of the spell-coin. That talisman hardened suspicions that the Manroot Guild conjurer put into Darwin's mind. He desperately wants to get back into Sheila's good graces, but he can't let go of those nasty doubts." Lars looked each of them in the eye for a long moment, his eyebrows no longer dancing. "Don't assume you can handle things when they make their move on you. You're going to need protection. Even with Wiccan shields, it's going to take strong determination and character to repel a magic-laden power of suggestion."

"Damn, that's low." Leo said. "These bastards are genuine scum, the lowest of the low. What kind of men are so afraid of a couple of sweet, retired ladies that they want to destroy them. Isn't there some way we can turn the tables on these creeps?"

"We can beat them … at their own game. The Wiccan circle has been doing it for several years now," Lars said, "but that doesn't mean there haven't been casualties. People's reputations and relationships have suffered. This time the Manroots are involving the police, and if they get their way, the women could be arrested and convicted of murder or kidnapping. Angry, scared people have been known to destroy property or use violence when they believe lies, especially lies spread to cause fear."

"How do we keep Fisby's church people from spewing horrible stories about my wife and her friends?" Samuel thought about possible dark days ahead and having to move away from Elmira, leaving their home and friends behind.

"What they're planning is defamation of character," Lars explained. "It's against state and federal law. It's against the more universal laws of morality. If we must, we can sue to make sure authorities enforce that law. We can make public the truth about the good characters of Kitsy, Fayette, and Sheila for those who are willing to listen. We might even be able to take the Manroots to court and get financial compensation. We know something about the Manroots' plans to use churches and police. What we don't know is the extent to which they plan to use low magic."

"There's someone who does know about their magic-making plans," Leo put in. "That Lantern Man fellow. Why was he at the coven meeting in the first place? What can he tell us? Do those warlock devils know who he is? Was he followed? Can we find him?"

"Yes. It would be prudent to locate Alfred and talk with him. In the meantime, we have magic on our side, too." Lars nodded, offered a sideways grin, and chuckled as if to acknowledge that Leo and Samuel probably didn't want to believe in magic. "It would help to know more about the kinds of wizardry the Manroots expect to use, but even without that knowledge, we've got some powerful shields and defenses. Magic protection spells are often effective if created and used correctly."

Samuel remembered how Pastor Fisby admitted Sheila's protection spell knocked him out. Was the short, plump, former church secretary able to put a man in a coma with a spell? For that matter, was Fayette so adept at creating a truth charm that Pastor Fisby couldn't shut up about the Guild of the Supreme Brotherhood of Manroots? And what about Samuel's good-natured wife, Kitsy, former second grade schoolteacher? She was mostly responsible for freeing The Lantern Man from his book prison. Samuel felt a cold chill move down his spine from the top of his neck to his lower back. What else was she capable of doing?

Lars' phone buzzed. "Excuse me, gentlemen." The co-leader of the Waterleaf Fen Circle, answered the call, listened, and then frowned. "Chief Castillo wants to bring Fayette in for questioning? Why?" Leo and Samuel watched as Lars pressed his phone tighter to his ear. "Yeah. Okay. We'll be there right away. If the police chief sees us all together, he'll at least know Fayette's got a crowd of people watching out for her."

Inserting his phone into a back work-pants pocket and grabbing the notes Leo and Samuel made about the Manroots meeting, Lars stood. "That was Abigail. Fayette needs our help. My truck's right out front."

"What's this all about?" With effort, Samuel pushed himself from his chair, realizing he was bone weary.

"Police came to examine the curse left in Fayette's yard. On the ground not far from the curse site they found a pocketknife with Fisby's initials. The knife apparently vanished from Fisby's hospital room the night he disappeared. Chief Castillo seems to think it's more evidence that Fayette had something to do with the pastor's kidnapping. He wants to take her into the station for an interrogation."

"More likely Fisby was the one who left the curse and the knife, or his brother Elden." Samuel scowled.

"There's no question about it." Leo, eyes unfocused, grabbed his hat and wallet. "We know who fetched Fisby from the hospital and why. We ought to tell the chief."

"I suggest we tell deputy Bruce and deputy Noah." Lars started for the front door. "As I understand it, those two are more open minded about the case than their supervisor."

Three men fit across the spacious seat of Lars' pickup cab with room to spare. The Wiccan co-leader insisted they buckle up. Samuel, next to the passenger door, turned sideways to locate the shoulder belt and glanced at the side mirror. He did a double take. About three houses behind them he made out the ominous profile of an ochre-colored Corvette sedan.

In Fayette's driveway, Samuel and Kitsy's SUV and a police cruiser parked side by side. Lars parked his truck along the sidewalk behind cars belonging to Abigail and Estra of the Waterleafs. Between the cars and the house, Police Chief Castillo and Kitsy, Sheila, and Fayette exchanged words in a tense, tight circle.

"How do I know you didn't contrive this so-called curse in your yard and plant Fisby's pocketknife nearby to confuse our investigation," Castillo said as the three men climbed out of the pickup cab. "Do you have any idea how many calls we got this morning demanding that we arrest Ms. Fairlight and Ms. Pinker? Folks from Pastor Fisby's church, Fisby's brother, friends of Fisby … concerned citizens want to know if he's still alive, where in Hades he is - excuse my French - and why our suspects are still walking free."

"How many calls did you get this morning?" Lars' question rumbled across the yard and startled Castillo.

"More than 40 by the time I left the office to report here." Castillo looked hard at Lars, switched his glower to Fayette, and then turned his face toward a spot in Fayette's yard where Abigail and Estra poured bottles of sweet-smelling liquid over a hole in the ground filled with fresh, new potting soil. Beside them was a lead-lined box containing the soil removed from the hole, a burned doll, and a length of barbed wire.

Leo and Samuel joined Kitsy and Sheila, taking their places behind and on each side of Fayette, who seemed to stand straighter, as though comforted. She drew a deep breath. "If those phone calls are the main reason for taking me to the station, then that smells like mob rule." Fayette's arms, one encased in a sling, joined each other in a stiff fold across her midriff, her back straightened another degree, and she spaced her spandex clad legs in a defiant stance. "Maybe you haven't found the missing pastor because you haven't asked the right questions. I want to know why someone put a curse in my yard. I want to know who left that pocketknife near my front walk. Find the answer to those questions and you'll probably find Fisby Parkinson." Fayette scuffed the toe of one shoe on the cement. "Holy Frijoles, Chief Castillo, this isn't fun for us. This isn't a game. This is bull-snot harassment." Fayette pointed to the site of the mostly dismantled curse and the strangled doll.

Kitsy stepped forward. "And I want to know why those horrid posters keep popping up with my friends' faces on them. Why aren't the police doing something to stop it?"

"The posters are unfortunate, I agree, Ms. Browning, but we cannot stop or arrest the person or persons hanging them in public places. If you want something done about them, you'll need to sue the people who made them and prove to the courts that their statements are false," Castillo said. "Only then do the posters become illegal. As it stands, we at the police department don't know for sure who poisoned Pastor Fisby or who took him from the hospital. From our point of view, the posters may or may not be true." Castillo swiped a palm over tired eyes. He turned to face Fayette. "I may be back later today for further questioning, so don't leave town. As for Fisby's disappearance, your name is at the top of our suspect list, and my suspicions just magnified a hundred-fold after this morning."

"That's not fair." Kitsy's declaration was almost a shout.

Sheila put a comforting hand on Kitsy's shoulder and turned to Castillo. "If Fayette's not at home, Chief, you can find her with us at the River Surge Plain Preserve. We've got a fieldtrip planned to learn more about local plants and their uses."

Chapter 29

Five women, including two Waterleaf Circle Wiccans and three members of the Reading Club of Retired and Capable Ladies, piled out of Abigail's car at the beginning of a three-mile-long footpath. This was to be a workshop on mindfully and honorably gathering materials for shield charms. It was to be a lesson on focus, intention, and the kind of straight thought that renders the cleanest protection spells. Sheila hugged herself in nervous anticipation. This was going to be about magic 101.

The hiking trail meandered through a protected river surge plain and preserve, where salt and fresh water mingled for miles through muddy sloughs and plant-rich soils. Tidal influences pushed up the river from the ocean, feeding slough grass and sedges in the marshy wetlands and Sitka spruce and red alder in the forested groves.

Estra's jeep waited at the other end of the trail so when they finished, they could call it a day and ride, rather than walk, back to the trail head and Abigail's car. They started their trip a few hours later than planned because of the curse discovered in Fayette's yard and the lost time spent dealing with the police chief. Of course, once chief Javier Castillo left, everyone had to hear what happened to Leo and Samuel the night before. As a group, they agreed that Lars, Samuel, and Leo could take copies of the Manroot-meeting phone recordings and their written notes to deputies Bruce and Noah while the women went ahead with their herb-gathering expedition at the preserve.

"My strewing protection spell really worked," Sheila repeated with bewilderment for the tenth time that morning. Elden's admission the night before, that the women's protections were powerful, took the three friends by surprise. They were still adjusting to the news. Once out of Abigail's car, Sheila grabbed Fayette's uninjured arm and pulled her friend close. "Your truth spell must have been dynamite. Who knew we could actually do magic?" she whispered. Fayette patted Sheila's hand. "Blood and sand, I'm still not sure I believe it. What if I get wrongheaded and it all goes to piffle?"

For her part, Kitsy wondered if she was a misfit in the group. Everything that happened to her magic-wise, especially regarding The Lantern Man, seemed accidental. Her affinity or skills for spell-making were yet untried except for the scarves she made, which hadn't proven useful. Plus, she'd caught Samuel looking at her with a wary expression, as though he didn't really know her anymore, as though she might sprout warts on her chin or conjure up a frog. That hurt. Besides, had he forgotten that it was his whistling that called Alfred from his book prison?

Estra, short red hair sticking out in a fringe from under her gray, El-Pacca-woolen cap, interrupted Kitsy's thoughts by thrusting a pouch of pungent tobacco into her hands. "We each need to carry something." Estra's severe blue eyes, her slim pointed chin, and her set jawline portended a no-nonsense approach to their expedition. To Sheila, Estra handed long-handled plant clippers and to Fayette, she gave a six-inch knife in a sheath. "Put those in your backpacks with your water and sandwiches." Estra's deep-toned orders intensified her commanding demeanor. Her stiff posture smacked of seriousness, from her heavy rubber boots to the pom of her hat. "Now, get a grip, ladies. So, you crafted some magic. Big deal. You're in the most precarious position a magic maker can find herself. You are accidental magicians who could really cause mayhem right now, mostly for yourselves, but for others too."

Sheila suffered a pang of shame over her excitement, and Kitsy sighed, reminding herself for the hundredth time that she had little control over magical experiences, especially when they involved witched objects like *The Book of Forbidden Knowledge*. Fayette felt herded toward the trail head with the stinging whip of Estra's voice.

"All of us in the circle were beginners once." Abigail's patient words caught their ears and drew their attention. Her sage green, Merino wool fisherman's sweater and wide-legged jeans looked so comfortable that Sheila coveted a similar sweater of her own. She admired Abigail's long fingers and darker skin tone. The circle leader tied her graying black hair away from her face in a thick ponytail.

"Before we enter the woods, let's prepare ourselves." The Waterleaf priestess smiled, looking into each woman's eyes before speaking again. "Remember, we are entering a sacred place. Magic is all around us in the form of natural energy. This woodland and wetland are full of lifeforces belonging to each living being and each native object. Everything here deserves our respect. We must clear our minds of old and unwanted energies before we enter. This takes training. I recommend that if you want to continue performing the direct movement of energy to fulfill a purpose or intention, what we call magic, that you practice meditation on a regular basis. For today, focus on the beauty of this place and the uniqueness of every twig, leaf, and stone."

Abigail led a deep breathing exercise and a short, guided meditation that included shaking negative energy from their fingers. They knelt and pressed their open palms into the cool, damp earth to replace the negative energy with Earth-connected vitality. That finished, the women stepped one by one from the parking lot onto the trail.

Over the path, fall leaves from alders and big-leaf maples amassed in a thick, layered collage of greens, yellows, and browns, soft and spongy under their boots and shoes. Tree trunks dressed in moss, their branches almost naked in their fall sleep, stretched toward the mostly gray October skies. Everything in the forest was damp from a recent rain shower.

"Very little gathering happens here in the fall," Abigail called back to them from the front of the line. "But we come here for inspiration in every season, and today we will harvest a member of the ginseng family, *Oplopanax horridus*, to help protect your homes."

For several minutes none of the women said anything, and the rhythmic thuds of shoes and boots hitting the leaf cushioned ground added percussion to the forest sounds they heard. A crow declared herself and another answered. The wind rustled what October had left of fall leaves on shrubs and bushes, or green leaves on plants such as salal or evergreen huckleberries.

Whenever her mind wandered to worries about Samuel or fears about the consequences of magic, Kitsy worked hard to concentrate on the gray and black limbs of tall trees silhouetted against the sky or the toasted-bread colors of leaves turning to soil on the path. Making an effort to take deep breaths of the cool, fresh air, Kitsy focused on appreciating the moisture dripping in suspended time from the moss that hung from tree trunks. She had a lump in her throat, and if she remembered right, it had been there since the events at Fayette's house. Among the forest plants, the lump seemed to dissipate.

Sheila felt her shoulders relax as her legs moved her deeper into the peaceful woodland. When the path brought them in view of the muddy banks of a slough, she felt little spurts of gladness at the wispy mist coming off the water. She had a long nap the day before, and maybe that was why she couldn't sleep in the early hours of the morning. Her mind was on Darwin. There was an enormous hole in her chest, she realized, that seemed to grow from missing him. While she felt helpless to control what the Manroots did to her reputation, it was the loss of Darwin that kept her mind reeling in the wee hours.

Kitsy had already gone to bed. Unable to sleep, Sheila rummaged through her bookshelves for something soothing to read, a hopeful romance maybe, or an inspiring biography. In a stack of miscellaneous folders and coffee table books, Sheila re-discovered a notebook her parents kept that contained remembered bits and pieces of their lives in the Koya tribe. Memories flooded back of her parents singing a song to her as part of their bedtime ritual. Might the song calm her after all these years? She found the page with the words, grabbed her guitar from the corner of the kitchen, and sat on a stool to sing the sweet, resonant folk tune.

Siran Uge: The Magician's Song.
O Goddess
Invest all knowledge and power
On this novice
O Kondagadbo and Bandimadio
Bless her, bless her
Awaken the latent power
The power that is sharp and cutting
As the barba grass-blades
Teach her
The secret powers of the gods of

Instead of feeling calmer, singing the song stirred prickly sensations. A light flashed before her eyes. Her fingers tingled. Sheila worried that she had a stroke, but minutes later, her vitals were fine. She could walk straight. Her words when she sang the song again were crisp and clear. Strange, though, that a breeze seemed to catch and lift the corners of the song page on the table as she sang.

Sheila brought with her into the woods all her anxieties about Darwin and worries about old songs, but every step she took diminished their hold on her mind. Like Kitsy, she took deep breaths and felt calmed. Quiet energy from the sleepy plants on each side of the trail seemed to sharpen her confidence and sense of self.

For her part, Fayette brought neither fear nor anxiety to their nature preserve circle lesson. Anger was her go-to emotion in times of stress. Speeding down backroads on her Harley or whipping around corners in a roller rink, those were the kinds of distractions that helped her work off heated passions. On the trail, it was the wind that caught her attention as it moved through her hair and lifted the dryer bits of large, golden, vine maple leaves at her feet. A gray squirrel chattered at her from the side of a large cedar trunk and then skittered higher, looking down from a lofty branch as if tempting her to follow.

"If I knew how, I would," she called up to the little face with bright, interested eyes. For at least a mile, Fayette forgot the dull pain of her broken collarbone and the irritation of having to carry a side pack rather than a double-strapped daypack.

Often Abigail stopped to point out the seasonal appearances of individual plant species, some with and some without greenery. About one and a quarter mile into their walk, Estra and Abigail halted, picking up sticks from the brush and using them to poke through the ground matter a few feet off the trail.

"There," Estra said in her booming, bass voice. Abigail bent to look and then nodded. She motioned for Kitsy, Sheila, and Fayette to come closer. On the moist ground at Estra's feet was a scaly, tannish lump of rounded shell, about eight inches across. It was a decomposing gourd. One, large, punctured hole gaped through the thin, brittle gourd surface near what looked like an old stem. With her stick, Abigail traced a brown, dead looking vine that climbed high in a nearby maple tree.

"It's a manroot, *Marah oreganus*," Estra said. "Somewhere around here, underground, is the manroot tuber. These tubers can be quite small or weigh as much as 220 pounds. They're called manroots because the lobes and extensions of the tubers often look like arms or legs."

"Yes. That's right." With a kind, half smile, Abigail examined the weather-disintegrated remains of the manroot gourd. "This is not a plant that we harvest, but we wanted you to see what one looks like after summer. This is the plant for which Fisby's coven named itself."

"Believe it or not," Estra added, "the above ground parts of the plant, the gourds, and the large-leafed vines, die back in the summer. The tubers send up shoots in the winter, which begin to grow in January and February during the rainy season. At that point, the vines can crawl up to several inches a day, and as the vine grows, it feeds its tuber. Sometimes botanists call the manroot fruit wild cucumber, but the spiky gourds repel most people. They look a bit extraterrestrial."

Sheila's gardener-self wondered if she could grow the plant for medicinal purposes. "What is it used for?" she asked.

"We Waterleafs don't use it." Abigail smiled. "And

I wouldn't advise trying to grow one as its vines have exceptionally large leaves which can overwhelm the trunks of trees or bushes. Every part of the plant is poisonous, though native peoples had some uses for it. I once heard that some Native Americans used it to commit suicide. But the tuber can become a kind of soapy extract, and there are users who soak the fruits to make loofas. I read that people used to make a poultice from the gourd or mashed the upper stalk in water to dip aching hands."

"I've heard of the tuber being mixed with bear grease to apply to scrofula sores and a decoction was created by the Coast Salish to treat venereal disease," Estra said. "In January, we can show you what it looks like after its vines start growing again. That way you can better identify it. Some people find the manroot tubers to be sinister or disturbing to look at, but tubers mostly stay under the ground. We rarely see them."

Abigail put her arm around Estra and gave her an affectionate squeeze. "Manroot plants don't hurt the environment. They're just part of it all. If people use the name manroot to scare or harm people, that's about human ugliness, not true to the traits of the plant itself." The Waterleaf women led them back on the trail. "Just around the corner is the little deer path that passes by a large patch of *Oplopanax horridus*. Let's find the path and have our sandwiches," Abigail said.

Kitsy was relieved to see that the path was easy to identify, crossing the main trail in a place where deer habitually moved through a ground cover of vivid green maidenhair ferns. The five women seated themselves on two largish cedar logs to dig into Estra's sandwiches, homemade sourdough bread holding together cucumber slices and dried, roasted red tomatoes, marinated in garlic and oregano-spiced olive oil.

"Where's the roast beast?" Fayette murmured, poking the vegetables with a dirt-smudged finger.

"We are sorry to start your education with such a serious outing," Abigail told them between bites. "On most visits, this place inspires a sense of play and joyful discovery. But you're under siege, right now, and there's urgency in the need to help you safeguard yourselves. We must hurry through some of our lessons as we ask the land for strong protections. If you decide to learn more about channeling and directing energy, we'll have plenty more circles and outings."

"I'd like that, and I'm grateful for the help." Kitsy savored the taste of marinated tomato and wondered how the sandwich would taste with hotdogs included. Might make a good recipe for her cookbook project.

"I've learned a lot already," Sheila said, thinking about the notes she would take when she got home. "I'm excited for future lessons about these plants and these wetlands."

Fayette nodded in agreement. "Yup. But I've learned all I want to know about manroots, human or otherwise."

Clouds above the preserve thickened and darkened.

"Rain soon," Estra announced. "We'd better get to that thicket of *Oplopanax horridus* as quick as we can."

"We can call the plant by its common name, if that's easier." Abigail winked at Kitsy, who was trying to repeat Estra's pronunciation of the plant. "It's usually called devil's club."

"Woah. Is this a dark magic plant?" Fayette's eyes narrowed under the rolled edge of her denim blue rag wool stocking hat.

Estra clicked her tongue with impatience, and Abigail reassured the group. "Someone must have named the plant devil's club because of its sharp spines. It's a member of the ginseng family, like we said before, and really an extremely positive and helpful plant, used for thousands of years as Indigenous medicine and for hundreds of years in western herbalism. Devil's club is a sacred and protective plant, and its essential energies boost the spirit, sharpen the mind, and ease stress."

Abigail explained that the patch down the tiny path was a large colony of devil's club, spreading out between ferns and grasses for more than an acre. "It's never a good idea to take from a smaller patch, and it's never right to take too much. We harvest from the middle of the patch where the plants are overcrowded. And we follow the rules of the honorable harvest, as explained in the words of Indigenous leaders such as Robin Kimmerer."

Ask permission of the ones whose lives you seek.
Abide by the answer.
Never take the first. Never take the last.
Harvest in a way that minimizes harm.
Take only what you need and leave some for others.
Use everything that you take.
Take only that which is given to you.
Be grateful.
Reciprocate the gift.
Sustain the ones who sustain you, and the Earth will last forever.

"Ohh. I wish I'd heard those reminders all my life." Sheila spread her arms as though taking in the whole forest and spun herself in a full circle. "It's glorious to feel closer to all of this."

Kitsy laughed and reached out to touch a moist, moss-covered fir trunk.

"Time?" Estra raised her thin, spiky eyebrows in Abigail's direction.

"Time." Abigail got up from her log, stuffed the remainder of her sandwich in her pack, and pulled out a pair of thick, leather gloves.

Estra pointed with her right hand up the trail. "Follow," she said to the newbies, "but stay quiet and respectful."

The tiny path entered a wooded area and then led to

an open area thick with leafless stems, some close to the ground a foot to three feet tall, but others as high as six to eight feet tall, arched and leaning in all directions. Piles of brown and tan leaves, larger than maple leaves, carpeted the ground around the stems. Upon closer inspection, Kitsy, Sheila, and Fayette could see that each stalk supported hundreds, maybe thousands of thin, sharp thorns.

"Watch from here," Estra instructed.

"Intention is everything from this point on," Abigail said. She began to sing in a soft, lilting chant.

Thank you. Thank you.
Thank you for being here.
Thank you for listening.
We have come not to hurt but to help.
The purpose of our harvest is to protect buildings and people from evil spirits, from bad energy.
Your medicine is powerful and much needed.
We will take only what is needed, with your permission.
You will not be hurt. You will keep growing strong.
You will help others.
We thank you again for your strong medicine.

When Abigail stopped singing to the devil's club, she and Estra bowed their heads, and while their three students watched, the Waterleaf women initiated the same deep breathing exercise and short, guided meditation they performed at the beginning of the trail. First, they shook negative energy from their fingers and knelt, pressing their open palms into the cool, damp earth to replace the unhelpful forces with earth-connected vitality. Rising to their feet, they bowed again to the well-armored plants before them and then put on their gloves.

"Tobacco, please," Estra motioned to Kitsy, who handed her the pouch she'd been carrying. Sheila passed the long-handled clippers to Abigail, and Fayette gave the knife from her side pack to Estra.

"We need about fifteen pieces." Estra stepped with care around the spiny talks toward the middle of the patch. "Five for each of them."

Sheila noticed that the Wiccan women whispered to each plant they approached and then strewed tobacco as a gift around the stalk. "We're cutting 10 inches from the top of the plants for our protection pieces," Abigail called to the three watching at the edge of the clearing. "We leave the thorns on except to scrape a few inches from the ends to make handles for holding. When we give them to you, you'll be able to smell the spicy, pungent odor from the plant cuttings. There's nothing like the fragrance of devil's club to clear the mind."

Fayette, shuffled her feet and watched for several minutes, but soon impatience got the best of her. What, she wondered, was beyond the devil's club patch? She took measured steps along the path toward a section of trees on the other side of the clearing. No one protested, so she continued. As she entered the trees, she could see that they formed a narrow line of thick shade that separated the devil's club from another clearing. The path ended under the trees, and as Fayette approached the new clearing she could see why. From the wooded hill, she looked over an opening full of blackberry brambles. Masses of armored canes seemed to guard an old cabin, serving as a barrier between the edge of the preserve and the cabin's back deck. Or was it the other way around? Did the blackberries guard the preserve from the cabin? On the other side of the cabin, Fayette could see a highway that ran along the preserve boundaries.

A long time ago, someone had cut a crude trail through the blackberry jungle, but it was poorly maintained, so blackberry thorns would be constantly grabbing at anyone who ventured down the path. Fayette stood close to a large cedar trunk under the thick tree canopy and scrutinized the rustic cabin. What would it be like to live so near to a protected, wild area? What kinds of wildlife ventured onto the driveway, and what was it like to be in a snowstorm in the woods?

In the middle of Fayette's brazen snooping, someone pulled the curtains open in the back window. A face peered out. A hand wiped moisture from the glass. Fayette gasped and shrank back, taking cover in the tree shadows, moving herself further around the trunk for shelter. Had those piercing eyes seen her? She didn't think so. But she had seen Pastor Fisby Parkinson's eyes staring out at the blackberry brambles, scanning the tree line of tall cedars. Fayette recalled the tense moment in Fisby's hospital room when she'd taken one last look behind her only to find those same hyena-like eyes glaring into hers.

The face in the cabin window was there only for a moment and then the curtains slid closed again. Fayette breathed in, held it, and then backed slowly from the tree. She felt disoriented yet managed to find the little forest path again and retrace her steps to the devil's club gathering spot, relieved to see her friends and teachers still busy with the harvest. Estra and Abigail collected and wrapped all the required pieces of devil's club in paper sacking, five each, ready to distribute into their packs.

"Where did you get to?" Sheila gave Fayette's right arm a peeved shake, but remembered it was important to keep her energies positive throughout the gathering process for the sake of successful channeling.

"I'll tell you when we get to the car," Fayette hissed, unsure if she should share stressful news right yet. She breathed in a deep lungful of air and decided to try and wave negative energy from her fingers as the Waterleafs showed them. She squatted down and pressed her hands into the damp leaves on the ground, willing good energy to enter her. Estra, cleaning her cutting knife with a cotton rag, watched Fayette with interest but said nothing.

After a final ritual of thankfulness to the clearing and the plants, the Wiccan teachers led the way back to the main trail. They had about a mile to go before the end of the journey. Each hiker kept to herself and said little during the last stretch, gazing in wonder at flooded areas of wetlands, water nearly breeching the wooden bridges and walkways. The ever-darkening clouds finally let go of concentrated levels of moisture, and the women endured a heavy shower for the last ten minutes.

All at once, the parking lot was in view, Estra's silver jeep a welcome site and the only vehicle left waiting. They made mad dashes to the portable toilets, stripped their wet gear before taking seats in the jeep, and settled in for the ride back.

"Before we start back," Fayette said, adjusting her sling, "I've got something to say that you all need to hear."

"You want to bring the food next time?" Kitsy guessed.

"Your shoulder hurts?" Sheila reached and to try and help Fayette secure the buckle on her sling strap.

"Holy buckets!" Fayette's feet were wet, and her soaked pants clung to her like a wet towel. Her patience was thinner than embroidery thread. "Can you just listen?"

From the driver's seat, Estra snorted. "By all means, tell us what's been eating at you since you sneaked off while we gathered devil's club for you."

This elfish woman with toothbrush-textured hair had the manners of an ungrateful raccoon, Fayette thought, but she bit back a snarly retort. "I saw Fisby." Fayette said the words and then sat back glowering between Kitsy and Sheila in the back seat. Stunned silence greeted her revelation.

Abigail reacted by reaching into her backpack and pulling out a cardboard box. "Lucinda baked these for us. I almost forgot. Let's get some energy into us and then hear out our ever-observant companion."

Lucinda's generous supply of brown butter, toffee, chocolate-chip cookies were exactly what the travelers needed to ease the tension in the moment.

"Mmm. Walnuts," Abigail said as she chewed. "Lucinda likes to add walnuts to her recipes when she thinks her goodies might help with mental powers."

Finishing one cookie and taking a second, Estra sighed. "Okay, Fayette. What makes you think you saw Pastor Fisby near the devil's club clearing?"

Fayette's doctor warned her years ago that anger could raise a person's blood pressure. Every time Estra spoke, Fayette felt her blood pressure spike. She'd have to steer clear of the woman in the future. Right now, she'd focus on Abigail as her main audience. "There's a cabin on the other side of some trees near the clearing. I was looking out from the trees to the cabin when someone peered out a window over the back deck. I know it was Fisby. After casting my truth spell over him in the hospital room, I'd know that face anywhere. He's hiding out in that cabin."

"I forgot there was a cabin so close to that spot in the preserve." Abigail tapped her nose with the first finger of her right hand as she munched another bite of cookie. "Farmers built the cabin along the public road long before the area became a wildlife and ecological preserve. The property is not in the preserve boundaries, just along the edge."

"Did this person in the window see you?" Estra sounded critical.

"No. I don't think so. I stayed behind a tree trunk and in the shadows of the trees." Fayette leaned her head against the back seat. She started the day deflecting police allegations for things she had no fault for, and now she felt unduly accused again.

"I believe you," Abigail said, "and I suggest we keep an eye out for this cabin. We'll drive right by the front side of it on our way back to the trail head. Let's see if we can determine the house number so we can report its location to the police."

"Well, I just wish you two would knock on the door and put the guy in magical deep freeze, or something," Kitsy said. "I'm tired of him and his manroot minions."

Estra started the jeep engine and snorted again. "Magic doesn't work like that in the Wiccan world. Even if we could control people using magical energies, we don't work dark magic. We Waterleafs protect ourselves by using intentionally focused energies, but we're guided under the premise of 'do no harm.' "

"Whatever we do with guided energies," Abigail added, "we must always remember that it takes energy to use energy. If we hurt others, or force something on others against their will, it comes back on us three or four times."

"A body can wish, though, can't they?" Kitsy laughed.

"I'm with you, Kitsy." Sheila leaned over to give her friend a thumbs up. "We can hope for just deserts, can't we?"

"What goes around comes around, of course. Deserved punishment is certainly part of universal law, but just deserts often come later rather than earlier, unless you use magic. If you're a magic practitioner, what goes around seems to come around rather quickly." Abigail offered Kitsy a rueful smile. "That's why focusing on protections and positive outcomes is the best kind of magic."

"So, is my broken collar bone deserved punishment for getting Fisby to confess the truth against his will?" Fayette rubbed her shoulder with doleful massage strokes. She'd been asking herself that same question since the accident happened.

"Hmm, I'm not so sure of that." Abigail was thoughtful. "The spell seemed unusually strong, according to what Fisby's brother Elden said at last night's meeting. It may very well be that some part of Fisby wanted to confess. If so, your spell simply unblocked a strong desire. It might have been a positive result rather than negative. Your broken collar bone might just have been an accident; or it might have resulted from negative energies directed your way by a member of the Manroots, in which case, the energy will come back on that spell maker four times the strength experienced by you. Manroots seem to think they are impervious to the laws of the universe, that they can protect themselves from themselves. In the long run, they cannot."

As Estra guided the jeep out of the parking lot, Sheila asked a question that had nagged at her for a while. "You showed us where a Manroot grows in the preserve. Are there waterleaf plants here too? Did the circle name itself after a local plant?"

"Indeed, yes," Abigail said. "Waterleafs are perennials that mostly die back by this time of year. They're hard to point out right now, but we will show you the green shoots of our namesake in the spring when we can eat the young leaves in salads or steamed as greens. They remind some of us of eating Bok choy."

"Their species name is *Hydrophyllum tenuipes*," Estra added. "Nothing ugly about waterleaf plants. We call the ones here slender-stem waterleaf."

When crumbs were all that remained, Abigail folded the cookie box with care and slipped it into her pack. Even though it was only 3 o'clock, the light dimmed in a sky already dark with heavy rain clouds. Shadows blended into one shade of darkness under the trees on both sides of the road. The ditches were half full of standing water.

Estra's jeep passed homes separated from each other by acres of grasslands and forest. Sheila thought she might enjoy the isolation of life near the preserve but wondered if it was lonely to live so far from town. They all felt the jeep slow and Estra looked over at Abigail and then in the rearview mirror at the women in back. "Okay. We're coming up on a mile from the parking lot. Shouldn't that cabin Fayette saw be around here somewhere?"

A mailbox served sentry for a gravel driveway leading to a barn-red, 1960s ranch style house to the right of the road.

"Wrong side of the road," Fayette said. "Our cabin would be on the left, right next to the preserve trail."

"Bingo," Kitsy said as the jeep turned through a tight, left-hand curve. They eyed a shabby brown structure with its sagging front porch and moss laden roof. Whoever occupied the cabin kept their burlap curtains drawn tight at the windows, and blackberry brambles seemed to surge like a frozen waterfall, obscuring the fence on the left side of the cabin. On the right, stairs led to what must have been the back deck Fayette talked about.

"Anyone see a house number?" Sheila asked as the jeep slowed to a crawl in the middle of the road.

"That mailbox has a faded number on it," Kitsy answered, "but I can't make it out."

"I believe it's 1478," Estra said. She'd stopped the jeep in the middle of the road and was taking pictures of the mailbox and the cabin. At that moment, a flash of gray and black tore from the overgrown brush in the front yard and lunged for Estra's open window with a raging snarl. The beast's jaws grabbed Estra's coat sleeve and pulled. Fayette heard the quilted fabric tear, but she was already grabbing from her pack the unfinished veggie sandwich with its heavy, thick, whole grain bread slices and was able to throw it across the front of Estra's torso toward the dog's head. To her relief, the sandwich landed on the long nose and over the eyes of the German shepard. Confused, the dog let go of the sleeve long enough for Estra to pull her arm inside and shut the window. She gunned the jeep motor so fast the tires skidded but managed to propel the jeep into a quick getaway, leaving rubber beside the German Shepherd, who gobbled the bread without delay. Another car turned the corner and barely missed hitting the poor brute, who high tailed it to his jungle yard. As the jeep turned another corner, away from the scene, Fayette saw the cabin door open onto the rickety porch and a second German shepherd cross the threshold.

Holy perdition. Fisby's guard detail? Fayette shuddered, thinking about the dog's massive jaws and tearing canines and what might have happened if the two dogs had been out and about just an hour ago, when she'd peered over the top of that overgrown bramble patch to see the back of the cabin. Maybe that's why Fisby looked out the curtains in the first place. The dogs might have warned him of her presence.

"Park over here in this turnoff," Abigail ordered Estra. "I want to look at that arm."

"I'm okay. The dog only got my sleeve. There's no real damage." Estra sounded impatient. Fayette decided Estra wasn't one to tolerate fussing. Apparently, she wasn't one to say, "thank you," either.

Chapter 30

When Sheila returned home, she found Darwin waiting on her porch steps. When Fayette unlocked her front door, she discovered a note from Leo, and when Kitsy entered her kitchen for the first time in more than 24 hours, she found Samuel sharing bottles of craft hard cider with The Lantern Man, who had come to find his tin lamp.

"Got any more of these shortbread cookies?" Alfred took the last one from the rose-patterned plate between himself and Samuel.

"Better ask Darnelle to stock up." Kitsy strode into the kitchen and hoisted her pack onto the counter. She felt exasperated at how quickly The Lantern Man's initial, thick accent and use of language had given way to a twenty first century version of English. The creature had, of course, used his Old British English as a ploy.

The Parkinson brothers kept him trapped in the family bookshelves for how many years? He'd heard Northwest Coast English for at least 40 of them. Still, the linguistic change seemed remarkable. He could switch with ease between 500 years of linguistic change. With Samuel, Alfred talked like any old someone on Elmira's streets today. His mannerisms and habits were still suspect, such as his frequent tendency to spit on the ground, but there were a lot of quirky people in the modern world.

He wasn't that far out of place. He still wore Samuel's borrowed clothes, but they looked washed and pressed. No doubt Darnelle took good care of him.

Alfred turned his face toward Kitsy and eyed her damp coat and mussed hair. His hard-set jaw and aggressive smirk told Kitsy that the ill-mannered Lantern Man of a few days ago was back. It was hard to keep track of who was in control of this ancient body from one minute to the next, Alfred or The Lantern Man. Had her presence caused him to revert to his more sour self?

"Trying your hand at pseudo magic?" The Lantern Man's tone was sarcastic, and his nostrils flared. "Are those Waterleaf Circle hags making believe they can teach you anything about spell work?" At that moment Marmy leaped to the edge of the counter so she could stare down at their seated guest.

"Hold on," Samuel cut in. "Kitsy hasn't done anything to warrant that kind of criticism. Leave her be."

The Lantern Man snickered. "One of the best conjurors in history trained me in magic for many years. I know sham artists when I see them."

"Things are different now than they were four hundred years ago, Alfred." Kitsy pointed at a stack of Samuel's folklore books. "Most of us read, and every generation builds on the knowledge of the last. Because of books and public education, we don't have to rebuild the wheel. With practice, we can each learn new things, no matter what age." This was a speech Kitsy gave time after time as a teacher, especially to parents who claimed that you either had talent or you didn't, and that education was a waste of effort for some people.

A mean chuckle exited The Lantern Man's throat. "Are there any real magicians anymore? The Manroots." He shook his head and frowned. "A few are perilous and powerful. I plan to avoid them. Mostly the Manroots are amateurs who know just enough to be dangerous to themselves. I sat in a circle with them last night to hear what kinds of magic they planned to use against you and your friends, and I had to laugh. That's what gave me away."

"Yeah. I saw you riled them," Samuel said. "What happened? What kind of magic do they plan to use against us?"

"They're resorting to curses, poppets, spell coins, fire, war magic, and fateful bottle magic to silence you and make you afraid. Their use of low magic is repugnant because it's done so poorly. They seem to favor Voodoo without understanding it." The Lantern Man spat on his empty plate.

Samuel rubbed the space between his eyes and above his nose as if to soothe a migraine. Kitsy grabbed a notepad and titled the first page "The Lantern Man's warnings."

"And how did they find you out?" Samuel asked.

"I laughed, like I told you. Then I accused them of being light weights who needed to get out of the game and leave magic to the heavy lifters. One of them called me an imposter, and that led to other accusations. I discovered that my magical abilities are returning. I was able to throw flames at the bottom of their robes and start some fires." With glee, Alfred recounted his escape from the Manroots meeting. He grinned at Kitsy and Samuel like a dog returned from chasing a squirrel. Then he sobered. His eyes softened and the frown was gone. Alfred was back. "But the lantern still has a hold on me. I feel more human than I have in centuries, yet I'm not free. Sometimes I am Alfred. Other times I am The Lantern Man, compelled to lead people astray. I feel the lantern's pull. I must find that damnable, tin-plated lamp and its piece of coal and do what I can to release myself from it."

"And what must you do?" Kitsy asked in a soft whisper.

"When my teacher forced the lantern on me, he said

there was only one way to free myself. I must sacrifice myself or my desires for someone else out of love. A lantern man does not have any desire to find love. The Lantern Man does not want to be free." Alfred's eyes filled with remorse. "I think I need to go out into the marshes again as The Lantern Man and fight the urge to lead people to their deaths. I must find a way to feel a sense of love for humanity. But when I have the lantern, my mind only knows the need for revenge and for power, the power to mislead people to their end. Once I have the lantern back, I do not know if I will remember my desire to be free of it."

"What if we help you?" Samuel considered the possibilities.

"You are a fool if you think you can help." The Lantern Man shot out his words with a hiss. Alfred was gone again. Marmy hissed back.

"We cannot assist The Lantern Man, but we may be able to help Alfred." Kitsy moved close to the table and placed her hand on top of Samuel's. "We should go to the bookstore with Alfred and talk to the circle, see if anything can be done."

"Your pack is full of something that leaks power." The Lantern Man got up, kept his distance from the orange kitten, and poked a finger at the pack buckle. He pulled his hand to his chest and stepped back; his eyes pinched into suspicious slits. "Are you planning to restrain me again, keep me in this house. I won't stay."

"Don't worry. We're happy you live someplace else." Kitsy began to clear the glasses and plates from the table. She was already tired of talking to The Lantern Man in all his ill-mannered glory. "I forgot for a moment. Those are pieces of devil's club in my pack. They're for installing above the doorways and at the beginning of our walkway because they absorb any bad energy or evil before it can come into our home. We gathered the pieces from the nature preserve this afternoon. I just need help securing them in the right places before it gets dark."

"What do we need to attach them to the house?" Samuel stood to get the tool kit.

"Maybe nails. Maybe hooks to lay them in?"

The Lantern Man stood outside and watched as Kitsy held the ladder for Samuel so he could arrange the lengths of devil's club above their doorways. This creature from the sixteenth century felt pain and even fear from the thorny plant when he was in his lantern man form, but it dissipated when he was Alfred.

"I forgot to tell you," Kitsy said to Samuel, "we found where Fisby is hiding."

Alfred straightened and walked closer.

"Where is he? Are the police going to check it out?" Samuel felt no sympathy for the phony pastor who spent hours each day manipulating people in the most insidious way possible, through religion.

"He's in a cabin on the edge of the preserve, about a mile back from the end of the main trail. OUCH!" Kitsy's thumb had slid down the length of the knife-scraped, devil's club handle and into some of its thorns. She let Samuel take the devil's club stick and then put her thumb in her mouth. "As for the police, someone's going to inform them. I don't know what they'll do about it."

"Give me a chance to lure him out before the police come." Alfred was in control of his body, the sneer gone, and he was begging. "Give me back my lantern and let me use it to bring Fisby out into the wetlands near his cabin."

"Why?" Kitsy was puzzled but also alarmed.

"I think being freed from the lantern is somehow tied with being freed from him. His father was my old teacher, the one who put me into that book as a lantern man and sealed me in my prison. Then, Fisby kept me a prisoner on his bookshelf for more than one hundred years. I've got to settle things with him, and it's got to be at night when the lantern is hottest."

"I don't follow." Samuel stood next to Kitsy and focused his full attention onto Alfred.

"I can't explain. It's a knowing, a feeling I've had long before you whistled me out of the book. It's because Fisby, through his father, controls The Lantern Man. He controls power over the curse that banished me into *The Book of Forbidden Knowledge*."

Kitsy glanced up at Samuel and shrugged. "We don't have the lantern, Alfred, but let's take you to someone who might be able to help figure things out. If you need to confront Fisby in the wetlands, I think it has to be tonight. The police will check on the cabin soon, and then who knows where Fisby will go. Let's ask Abigail and Lars what to do."

They finished installing the devil's club, grabbed their flashlights, coats and boots, and tried to coax a protesting Alfred into the SUV. "This world of yours is full of demonic metal insect creatures that fly down your roads. I do not want to be inside the stomach of such monsters again. Darnelle's van was bad enough." He growled out a Lantern Man obscenity and spit on the driveway.

***

While Kitsy and Samuel dealt with their ancient guest, Sheila walked with reluctant, step-by-step wariness up the footpath toward the porch steps where Darwin waited. Was this going to be the end of their new relationship? Was Darwin there to accuse her of being an unfaithful woman who entertained other men in the evenings? Would Sheila have to protect her broken heart by asking him to leave for good?

Sheila stood within two yards of Darwin's booted feet when he looked up to meet her eyes with his. She could see he was whittling a little wooden bird, a wren. He put his carving knife down and stood. The wren sat cradled in his two large hands, which he cupped together as though holding a live bird. Without a word, Darwin, hair askew and bits of wood falling off his work vest, stepped off the porch, and then, to Sheila's utter surprise, knelt in front of her, offering the bird for her to take. Confused, Sheila reached out and lifted the miniature figure, warm and smooth, from Darwin's hands. It was a pretty little likeness with alert eyes and a gentle face.

"Sheila." Darwin's voice came out in a croak. He cleared his throat and started again. "Sheila, I've been a fool. I mean a real schmuck, a bozo, a halfwit, a numbskull, a rat, a real wanker. There's no excuse for what I thought and did and for the way I hurt you the last couple of days. I know you might not be able to forgive me just yet, but I'm asking if you might try to forgive me someday. And then, when you maybe think you can trust me again, I hope you'll marry me. I've loved you for more than ten years but was too stupid to do anything about it. Now I'm tired of being stupid. I'm tired of being a halfwit. I'd rather stop wasting time and be the one you share the rest of your life with."

The hole in Sheila's heart ached. She wanted to trust Darwin again, but she knew she needed to give herself time just to make sure. So, she said nothing and did the only thing she could think of doing. Sheila put the bird in her coat pocket, lowered herself in front of Darwin's kneeling form, grabbed his face, and kissed him. They stayed in a tight embrace until their knees and backs started hurting. When they could no longer ignore the pain, Darwin stood and helped her to her feet.

"Come on in and I'll make some cocoa." Sheila's heart was gladder and lighter than it had been for days.

Patches rubbed against Sheila's legs as she piled lemon cream cookies on a plate and set the table with mugs. When the little calico rubbed against the bottom of Darwin's Carhart work pants, Sheila thought things might just turn out after all.

Once they'd settled over their hot chocolate, Patches made herself comfortable on the chair between them and Sheila told Darwin about the day's outing, the devil's club she needed to hang, and how they'd discovered Fisby's hideout.

"I realize, Darwin, that you're caught in the middle of something you have nothing to do with." Sheila leaned in and touched his shoulder. "I know you were taking down those awful posters when that trickster pulled you into the middle of a fiasco that I helped cause. I'm just so glad that you're better now."

"I'd take those posters down again and again." Darwin pushed his mug away and leaned his elbows on the table, determined to show his loyalty. "I'm a wiser man, less naïve than I was a few days ago. I'm better today because our friend Lars helped me create what he called a binding spell that protects me from the negative energy caused by that Manroot con artist. I'm able to separate myself from the lies he told me. Lars and I melted that hexed suggestion coin."

"But you never asked to be yanked into this magic mess," Sheila said, her face a study in grief and concern.

"I'm going to be fine," Darwin said. "I'll be fine because you've let me back into your life again. We're in this together, even though I don't understand what *this* is."

Sheila closed her eyes, glad Darwin was talking with her again, sad that she'd exposed him to such worry.

After cocoa and cookies, Darwin helped Sheila hang her devil's club protection sticks above her front and back doors, her greenhouse doors and on the top of the trellis over the front gate.

"If this devil's club works anywhere as well as Lars' binding spell, it's going to make a big difference." Darwin looked up at the prickly stick above the front door with a sense of relief and hope. "I trust it'll keep out any nighttime visitors." He looked shocked for a minute. "I didn't mean it the way it sounded."

Sheila laughed and then they both laughed and then their laughter swelled because it became a catalyst for releasing stress that built up over several days, stress about events they couldn't stop or control. They had to sit on the steps and hold onto the railings to try and keep their sides from hurting. A neighbor looked over the fence and asked if they were okay.

"Better than okay," Sheila gasped, wiping tears from her cheeks. "We're going to be just fine."

***

While Sheila and Darwin knelt across from one another in front of Sheila's front steps, Fayette read the note from Leo asking if he could bring another casserole, Chinese chicken this time. "After all, we've only had one meal together. Let's make it two."

As tired as she was, Fayette decided she could use some masculine company and a hot, homemade meal. If their first casserole together was any indication, Leo was an accomplished comfort-food cook. She texted him. "How about 6 p.m. I'll heat the bread and pour the beer."

"I'll bring road maps," he texted back. "We can start plotting our first road trip for when your collar bone is healed."

"Oh, my sainted trousers," Fayette said to herself. She relished a good Harley road-trip plan. What she wouldn't give to inhale a lungful of fast-moving air perfumed with fir boughs on an old-growth-forest highway.

After the rainstorm, her backpack needed to dry out, so Fayette, without touching the masses of spikey thorns, laid the sticks of devil's club side by side on the kitchen island. Maybe Leo would help her hang them above the outside doors. One-handed and one-armed, she slung her pack over the shower curtain rod and then sank onto the couch for a cat nap with her tuxedo boy Max curled up in the crook of her knees. Her house was toasty warm with a new heat pump installed, and over the next few hours, Fayette was able to savor the comforts of home. For the time being she enjoyed a false sense of security in a blissful state of ignorance.

***

Also meeting that afternoon, over a full pot of Earl Gray at the Lucky Cup Café and Bakery, were Elden Parkinson and genealogist Betts Harvey. Over the course of three weeks, Betts used up five precious vacation days trying to track down either Elden or Fisby. Finally, she was going to get some answers.

"As I told you, Mr. Parkinson, this is my first case since starting my new genealogy business, and it would be devastating to get nowhere for my client. He's very enthusiastic." Betts handed over a picture of her 57-year-old customer. "If I'm right, he's your grandson, Peter Parkinson Elliston. Mr. Elliston came to me a month ago highly puzzled about his heritage and asked me to sort things out. I must tell you; the genealogy data I discovered is mystifying. No wonder Peter is puzzled."

Elden sat back with impatience and surveyed Betts with a withering look. "Lady, I have no grandson."

"Well, that's what I thought at first because of the numbers. Because according to church records and birth certificates and whatnot, you're way too old to be alive, let alone Peter's grandfather. But, you see, and I do hope you will forgive me, I snatched a hair from the back of your coat one day in the hospital. That was after I nicked a hair from your brother Fisby's pillow in the same hospital. And, to my surprise, after submitting the hairs for genetic analysis, along with one of Peter's hairs, you came out as Peter's grandfather, and Fisby came out as Peter's great uncle."

"But that's impossible. I have no children." Elden leaned back in his Windsor chair with a dismissive wave of his right hand. His eyes shifted to the front door, and he picked up his bike keys as though ready to leave.

"Well, I'm pretty confused, too," Mr. Parkinson. Betts pushed a genealogy chart across the table to the man in front of her. "Here's my rough heritage map that connects the relationships. It seems impossible because you are still alive in 2023, and you were born in 1889. Your brother was apparently born in 1883. That makes you 134 years old and your brother 140 years old. How can that be?"

Elden's eyes glittered and he shut his mouth, glancing over Betts' chart with sudden interest.

Betts continued. "According to my research, a daughter was born to you and a woman named Annie Covington in 1915. Annie named her little girl Bianca. Your daughter, at the age of fifty-one, had a baby in 1966, a boy. He's the Peter who is your grandson. None of the people I've named in this line of Peter's family tree are deceased. Peter looks to be in his thirties and yet he is 57. You look to be in your late forties, not 134 years old. Please explain where I've gone wrong."

"This Peter … his grandmother is still alive?"

"That's what I've discovered."

"Annie had a daughter in 1915?"

"That's what the records show."

Elden banged the table twice with a clenched fist, drawing the attention of other seated bakery patrons, and causing Betts to startle and jump. His lower jaw moved forward and then he shut his mouth. He appeared to grind his teeth until his jaw, along with his eyes and mouth, seemed to harden into stone. He spit out a wretched volley of words. "He knew. He's known all this time."

"Excuse me?" Betts looked more confused than ever.

"Fisby knew. My father knew. The two of them pushed Annie out of my life. They said I could not fulfill my destiny if I married and had a wife and family. They both destroyed my hopes of ever being with her. And they must have known she was with child, my child."

Elden stood, grabbed Betts' chart from the table and folded it into his front jacket pocket with shaking hands. Without asking, he confiscated the picture of Peter.

"That'll be all, Ms. Harvey. I have a job to do that necessitates confronting my brother Fisby." He strode out of the bakery, his breathing ragged, like someone working hard not to cry or scream. His eyes burned, unseeing, dilated with anger.

Betts sat stiff and motionless in front of her still-full, Italian Faenza Carnation teapot. What did Elden's off-the-wall reaction mean? She had her list of queries when she first sat down with Mr. Parkinson, but instead of decreasing, the number of unanswered questions had grown. In the last three weeks, Betts wasted precious days trying to get to the bottom of this baffling genealogy commission. She'd driven an hour each way from her ocean-side hometown to Elmira. On one occasion, Elden pushed her out of his bead and coin shop after he'd gotten into a snit with some biker woman. The next day, Elden once again ignored Betts at the hospital. The two other times she'd come, she could find neither Elden nor Fisby to talk with. This trip, she'd somehow succeeded in getting Elden to sit down with her. And after all her trouble, the only thing she'd learned was that there existed a dark family secret having to do with Peter's grandmother, Annie, and his grandfather, Elden.

"Glipperfiggetfumblepiston," Betts said to herself to try and feel better. Word salads always helped raise her spirits. Next day off she would get up early and once again drive the forty miles to visit Elmira. Elden was a stone wall, but Betts could try again to find Elden's brother Fisby and show him the inexplicable family tree. By gum, she was going to get answers. Someday somebody had to crack.

"I'm not going to fail my first case," she said to the cooling teapot. How many weeks had she waited for her first customer after starting her new genealogy business? Two months of weeks, and then, out of the blue, Peter Parkinson Elliston brought her a doozy, a real brainteaser. "No quitting," she told herself. "I'm duty-bound to give him at least some answers."

CHAPTER 31

From her back porch, Kitsy watched the beginning of sunset, unaware of just how uncanny the night would become, oblivious to the twists and turns some people's lives would take before the sun rose again.

She'd agreed to go with members of the Waterleaf Circle into the wildlife preserve to give Alfred moral support. Lars and the others concurred that Fisby might, indeed, have power over the lantern man curse. Alfred insisted he needed the lantern to lure Fisby into the wetlands, where he would confront the pastor. To help Alfred, Kitsy would join the others in lending positive energy to protection charms and binding spells.

The skies were clear, which meant the night would be chilly, probably frost-freezing cold. Instead of bundling up in boots and mittens, Kitsy would much rather stay home and relax with a mug of mulled wine in her favorite chair, but the whole business wouldn't take long, she told herself. Alfred would try fighting the curse for a few hours and then they'd pile into their trucks, cars, and vans and slip back into their regular nighttime routines.

"You've gone over and above the call of duty," Kitsy told Samuel when he offered to come along. "It's not your fault I got involved in all this. You deserve a night home after what you went through last night. You've been wanting to study more folklore from Alfred's time of origin. This is your chance."

"But I'm invested." Samuel looked pensive and then excited. "I want to see Alfred free himself if he can. And what a once in a lifetime opportunity to witness firsthand an honest-to-good fight for freedom and be able to separate that from what's been made up about a paranormal creature who lived in the East Anglia Fens from the late Middle Ages to the Renaissance."

"Alright then. You were at the bookstore this afternoon when Estra and the others talked about what we'll have to do. Ever since our first meeting with them, the Waterleaf Circle members have been building a range of binding spells to discourage the Manroots from harming any of us. To push the binding energy along, are you up for reciting the words for charms, and wearing a Laurel Bay wreath around your neck, and sitting in the middle of a devil's club patch?"

"If you can, I can." Samuel winked at Kitsy and went to gather wool socks, long underwear, and other heat-trapping items of clothing.

Fayette called to ask for a ride to the preserve. Leo wanted to keep his truck hidden in his garage, and motorcycles were out of the question with Fayette's healing collarbone. The Harley ride to Fisby's house the day before had been too much for her.

"Darwin offered to drive Sheila," Fayette said. "Sheila says he's joining us. She also said that after what happened to Darwin, he believes in the existence of witching and wizardry, and he approves of the parts that safeguard against mean magic. He wants to help shield others from dark arts like that jinxed coin he picked up and put in his pocket."

"They're back together, then." Kitsy was glad to hear it.

"Holy gaboly are they." Fayette sounded nauseated. Kitsy could just picture Fayette rolling her eyes on the other end of the phone call. "I had to hold my phone ten inches from my ear while Sheila blurted out words faster than Bugs Bunny on speed. She's so happy. I could barely keep up," Fayette complained.

As she and Samuel headed out the front door to meet the others at the preserve, Kitsy spotted her stack of reading-group books on the tiny table in the foyer. There on top was *The Magic of Starting Something New in the Age of Retirement*. Who would have guessed that a book on aging and keeping the brain healthy could inspire a month littered with one puzzling crisis after another? Folded next to the stack of books was the scarf Kitsy made herself days ago, the one in pink colors and embellished on the seams with witch stitches, the one her rose bush tore in several places. She had repaired the tears with new witch stitches soon after the thorn incident and before cutting out fabric for new scarves. On a whim, Kitsy picked it up and tied it around her neck before following Samuel to the SUV.

"I'm preparing for battle," she murmured.

Seven vehicles were parked side by side in the trailhead parking lot, once Kitsy steered their SUV to a spot next to Lars' pickup. They were all there: the six members of the Waterleaf Circle; Kitsy, Sheila, and Fayette; Samuel, Darwin, and Leo; Alfred, and Darnelle. As they gathered behind their vehicles, Gilda passed out bay Laurel circlets to put around their necks.

"Bay is a powerful herb for protection and strength," Gilda whispered each time she released a circlet to a recipient.

"I'll be craving spaghetti sauce the whole time," Samuel said, sniffing the spicy leaves.

"Fourteen of us, then." Seth Green nodded in satisfaction, his ears covered with a fuzzy, sage and wheat colored wool hat and the rest of him enveloped in a navy, wool long-coat over shiny, black, knee-high rain boots. He carried the straps of a backpack in one hand and a flashlight in the other. "Numerology is one of my specialties. The qualities that go with fourteen are resourcefulness, independence and adaptability, all good things for someone working to free himself from a curse. Fourteen strengthens energies for fearless transformation and for embracing change." Seth finished his speech by slapping Alfred on the back in encouragement. Kitsy winced, realizing she'd been with Alfred long enough to diagnose some of the triggers for his personality changes. Seth's back slap startled Alfred so that he lost concentration. His Lantern Man side took hold.

"Get off me, jerk." The Lantern Man turned and snarled in Seth's face. "Maybe I don't want to transform into a gormless, simpering, prat of a humanoid. Maybe I want to be famous for haunting these wetlands and drawing people into these cold sloughs until they step in the wrong places and drown."

The fiend's words echoed in the woods beyond their parked vehicles as the magnanimous moon, hanging low, began to rise above the far-off hills. Darnelle stepped closer to The Lantern Man, holding Alfred's pack. He reached out to grab it from her.

"It'll wait till Alfred is here," she said, batting his hand away.

He bared his teeth at her then puckered his lips and hooted. "You be a witch."

"You know, in the last few days I've decided to take that as a complement. Alfred, I know you're in there." Darnelle's voice broadcasted disapproval and a warning. She hoisted the pack onto her own shoulders and buckled the front harness to keep it secure. "Remember what happens when you act like this? You sleep on the couch. There are no blueberry pancakes with maple syrup for breakfast. No TV shows. No lessons in how to use an electric stove or lawn mower or espresso machine. No backrub. No foot massage." Her words appeared to inflame The Lantern Man rather than encourage Alfred.

"How did Darnelle become so devoted to such a wretched being in such a short time?" Fayette muttered in Sheila's ear. "I'd have thrown his ass out the first day I met him."

"She's no fragile flower. She can give out dirt the same as The Lantern Man, but yes, she must see past the cursed man into the heart of Alfred." Sheila thought about Darwin's mistake and his apology. It wasn't quite the same, though. Darwin was usually Darwin, steady and even tempered, not opposite personalities locked in one body. "Alfred wants to get free of the curse, and that's Darnelle's hope. If he can't, she'll have to release him for her own good. Living with The Lantern Man would be impossible."

At Abigail's quiet suggestion, everyone circled Alfred and Darnelle and then sat in the cool, gravel-covered parking lot to join their energies. Estra took a thin stack of notes from the front pocket of her red and black checked fisherman's jacket. She kept one piece of paper for herself and passed the rest to her left and right. Each person took a note until all twelve in the circle had one. Estra stood, secured the remaining two slips of paper, stepped into the middle, and handed them to Darnelle and The Lantern Man. Darnelle studied her copy. The Lantern Man crumpled his into a small paper ball, dropped it on the ground and pressed it into the mud with his worn hiking boots, the ones he'd borrowed from Samuel.

"You see, we can't return the lantern until the time is right," Lars said to the still-standing Lantern Man. "But we can help you focus, Alfred, to find yourself again until you remember your purpose for being here. Lucinda will lead us in centering and in grounding our energies to support you."

Sheila thought of Lucinda's delicious brown butter, toffee, chocolate chip cookies, the ones shared in Estra's jeep only hours ago. She couldn't see Lucinda's dimpled warm smile in the dark, but when their meditation leader spoke, she knew by her honey mead voice it was there.

"First, let's center our energies, find our balance and alignment. If you feel excess energy, you can release it. If you feel low energy, borrow some from the earth. Everyone, take a slow, deep breath through your nose and release it from your mouth. Draw peace and calmness in as you inhale. Release tension and stress when you exhale. Now… Breathe out, slowly and evenly. Breathe in, slowly, evenly." Lucinda guided their breathing five times and then sat in calm stillness. In the quietude, Sheila took in the sound of rustling leaves as the night air moved over them. She heard water running in the distance, maybe from a stream or creek. How had she not noticed those sounds minutes before?

"If we want to focus our energy on helping Alfred regain himself, we need to ground our own vivacities and bond our bodies and minds to Earth's energy," Lucinda said. "Tonight, it will be important to stay connected with our Earth as a way to focus on right intention and to be present in the moment. After we are done here in this circle, if you begin to feel disconnected, place your hands on a tree or sit by a pool or body of water to help you stay grounded. For now, we will ground ourselves with the energy of the earth together. Place both hands palms down in front of you onto the cool dirt. Take deep beaths and visualize vigorous roots extending through your hands into the soil. Release old, tired energy into Earth from your roots. Earth knows how to heal and recharge worn and tired energy. Breathe deeply. Bring your roots back to yourself and move your hands to your sides. Place your palms onto the earth. Extend your roots into the soil and visualize clean energy moving from Earth through your roots to your hands and from your hands to your whole body. When you finish, bring your roots back to yourself, full of bright, positive energy; take two deep breaths." Kitsy felt Lucinda's warm, low voice wash over her as she closed her eyes and breathed in the kindly night air. "Put your hands in your lap," Lucinda purred, "and sit in the calmness of your connection with Earth's balancing energies."

In a way, Sheila thought to herself, once she finished the meditation, *I connect with Earth's energies each time I stick my hands in the dirt around my garden plants, but I never realized what I was doing. I never focused on my intentions.* She felt grateful for Lucinda's guidance and pictured herself exchanging energy with Earth, focusing on intention each time she planted seeds, weeded, or harvested. *Life just might feel lighter, freer, if I share energy with the earth and do it with positive awareness.*

"So be it," Lucinda said, ending the grounding meditation. She instructed the circle to say together the words on their pieces of paper. Since it was dark, and their flashlights were off, they followed her lead and repeated after her.

Two minds struggle in one soul.
The fabricated mind devours.
The genuine mind is lost.
True mind Alfred awake, stay steady.
Overcome The Lantern Man.
True mind Alfred awake, persist.
Overpower the devourer.

An anguished sob startled Sheila. It came from the middle of the circle where Darnelle had her arm around Alfred.

"The Lantern Man has gone into hiding within Alfred's body," Darnelle said.

"He's afraid. The Lantern Man is terrified of dying." Alfred choked out his words to Darnelle. "What should I do?"

CHAPTER 32

Just as the meteorologists predicted, the skies were clear enough to see the stars, and, yes, the night was crisp, transforming the moisture on the ground into tiny ice crystals. The circle of Wiccans and friends became a line of walkers, some with flashlights, marching on the trail toward the place where the devil's club grew behind Pastor Fisby's cabin. It was in the devil's club clearing that the Waterleaf Circle would return Alfred's lantern to him.

Unbeknownst to the Waterleafs, in Fisby and Elden's out-of-town cabin, four Manroot members, including Fisby, prepared weapons for war magic. Manroot disciples intended to leave these low magic weapons for Waterleaf Circle Wiccans outside the Forever Reading Bookstore in downtown Elmira.

"Wasn't Elden going to help with this?" The heftiest Manroot sat on a bar stool in which the stuffing was visible through a crack in the ragged upholstery. The man's jaw worked a piece of gum in his mouth as though it was a piece of gristle. He hunched his barrel frame over the worn kitchen island, picking at one of the spots where the Formica was especially pocked.

"Yeah. He said he'd be here." Fisby scowled, his face still pale from the effects of rosary pea poison. "It's possible he got a shipment of gemstone beads and is doing inventory, but a few days ago he did provide the materials for our project, our little effigy poppets." He gestured at the tray of flat head pins, eye pins, crystal beads and doll-sized knives and swords; Fisby picked out a fresh tuber from a plastic bowl smudged with streaks of mud. The whitish tuber presented outgrowths that looked like human arms and legs. "I think I'll call this one Lars Columbus."

Fisby proceeded to pin crystal eyes onto the tuber head and to draw on a thick, frowning, black-marker mouth. "Did you know Columbus was a reconnaissance plane specialist during the Viet Nam War? Yeah. North Korean troops shot him down in the most southern province of North Vietnam in 1968 when the U.S. bombed that area. That's where he learned about magic, from a shaman in the mountains. Too bad he's a traitor. He's lowered himself to be part of a Wiccan group led by a woman. He'll have to learn his lesson." At that, Fisby stuck a miniature knife into the tuber, right where the heart might have been.

"Really, it's genius to make effigies from manroot tubers," said the coven member with the bushy gray mustache. "We've all heard of mandrakes used in magic rituals in the old days. I read that mandrakes from the Mediterranean and manroots from the Northwest Coast are both from the same plant family, the Curcurbitaceae. They're curcurbits, and they're also both poisonous."

"Does that make us Manroot coven members poisonous?" The gum-chewing Manroot thumped his chest and laughed.

"No doubt. That's the point, isn't it?" Fisby finished his effigy with a pin through the stomach.

"A big difference between mandrakes and manroots is that mandrakes supposedly scream when you pull them out of the ground and the sound kills everyone who hears it." The tallest Manroot finished his sentence and ran a tiny sword through his effigy of Seth. He set aside the effigy with its screaming red mouth and grabbed a second tuber from the bowl. "Manroots are quiet when you dig them up. I should know. I'm the one who harvested these yesterday, out there in the preserve."

"Why in hell's name did you only bring six." Fisby looked the man up and down with a critical stare. "This is enough for Waterleaf Circle effigies, but we should have six more to scare off those three revolting women and their snooping friends. We'd scare the shikaka out of those biddies if we left effigies in their mailboxes. A few injuries and sicknesses connected with effigy stab wounds, and they'd give up any thoughts of conjuring ever again."

"Meaning no disrespect, sir, but you try locating the right-sized manroot plants at this time of the year. They're rare, even when you can see their vines. We're lucky to have these. But sir, genius to think of using these in our war spells. Genius."

The light over the kitchen island cast dim shadows over the grungy room, with its worn, scratched cupboard doors and vinyl floors, peeling from the baseboards in the corners. The Parkinson brothers bought the cabin a few years ago, just as it was, furnished with 1970s, musty-smelling carpet and furniture. They had yet to make improvements, and the whole house felt dingy, uncared for, and gloomy, especially the rooms with floor-to-ceiling, imitation paneling. Fisby's guests fidgeted on their stools, looking at their watches, saying little, and eager to finish and leave.

When the men completed six effigies, one for each Wiccan member, Fisby turned out the electric lights and lit black candles in the middle of the island. Four Manroots slipped on their robes and even donned their masks before the ritual. They chanted words over their little tuber poppets, calling on forces who specialized in causing pain, suffering, and fear. Fisby ended the spell.

"Oblige our enemies to understand that power is for men to wield. Women are to serve men's power."

"Make it so," the other Manroots answered him.

Fisby blew out the candles, turned on the kitchen lights, and stripped off his robe and mask. His followers did the same.

"Deliver these babies early tomorrow morning." Fisby handed the bowl of little tortured tuber bodies to the tallest Manroot, who took them, wrapped them each in newspaper, and tucked them in the large inner pockets of his raincoat, which hung on a hook near the front door.

"Hey. Good to know you're not hurt or dead." Bushy mustache tried *apple polishing* Fisby to start a conversation. "We wondered if we might have to take more extreme measures to get those women to confess."

"Are the women still on our police chief's radar?" Fisby's head shot up in suspicion. "No one's talked, have they?"

"Not us. Police still think the women did something to you. We left that pocketknife with your initials near the curse we set up on that biker woman's front lawn. Once the chief found the knife, he was certain that the women perpetrated your disappearance."

It was then that the four men heard voices, not near enough to understand them, but close enough they each knew someone was out back, somewhere in the preserve. Fisby approached the rear window, pulled open the burlap curtain and slid free the glass panel. Past the blackberry patch and beyond the little wooded area he could see the erratic beams of several flashlights but only for a moment because in the same instant, the lights disappeared. Everything went still except the movement of air through evergreen trees, directed by a night breeze.

Five minutes passed. Had he imagined the lights and the voices? The rosary pea poison led to daytime dehydration-hallucinations and 3 a.m. nightmares. Had his waking delirium returned? And then he saw it, a longish strip of wavering, white luminosity that seemed to hover beyond the trees like a spook light. Fisby last saw a similar ghost light more than one hundred years ago, when his father banished The Lantern Man into a copy of *The Book of Forbidden Knowledge*. Could there be the same kinds of cursed spirits carrying sinister lights in the marshes of America's Pacific Northwest? He'd never heard of them in this area of the world. This strange, ominous glow required an investigation.

"We're following that light," Fisby ordered his Manroot disciples. "It appears to be other worldly, a paranormal phenomenon."

The four Manroots rushed to put on coats and then strode, one by one, out the back door, across the deck, down the steps, through the rough-cut trail between the brambles, and into the little grove of woods. Unbeknownst to them, other figures followed. Elden, who half an hour ago parked his motorcycle on a trail entrance two hundred feet down the road from the cabin, was willing himself to wait in the trees until the time was right. He planned to confront Fisby after his guests left. When Elden saw Fisby and the others leave the house by the back door, and when the three Manroot devotees failed to return to their monster trucks, he decided to shadow them.

Two others followed behind Elden. Because the driveway was already full of cars, deputies Bruce and Noah parked their police cruiser at the next available pull out and walked to the cabin. Despite their chief's incredulity, they wanted to investigate the report that Fisby hid himself in the cabin. "It's a diversion," Chief Castillo told them, but since things were quiet at the station, the deputies had taken off for the preserve. They arrived at the reported address just in time to see Elden follow four men into the woods, and since nobody answered the front door, Bruce and Noah agreed they should check out the activity behind the cabin.

"What's that freaky light ahead?" Noah pointed to the wispy glow flickering through the trees.

"Campfire?" Bruce guessed.

"Naw. It's traveling." Noah stepped into the forest grove with Bruce. From their position behind two firs growing close together, the deputies could see a group of four men gathered at the far edge of trees wearing what appeared to be calf-length, city-style trench coats. Unseen by the group of four, another dark figure in a storm-shield, motorcycle rain suit and bearing a backpack leaned against a tree between the long coats and the deputies. Bruce and Noah were unable to make out the source of the strange light, but they could see it moving to their right in the direction of a creek gully. They knew about the creek. It extended from the east into a culvert that brought the water safely under the road and then drained out on the preserve side near the cabin. From the culvert, the creek moved west into the wetlands through a shallow gully that would take it to a slough. All sloughs led to the river, and then on to the ocean twenty miles away.

"I'm thinking we need to announce ourselves and then investigate that light. What if it causes a fire?" Noah whispered to Bruce.

"I doubt anyone's going to start any forest fires tonight. It's too wet. Let's stick to our original purpose and find out if Fisby is hiding out in the cabin. But we could announce ourselves and see if one of those men is our target," he conceded.

A sound that the deputies had never heard in a wild forest on a fall night interrupted them. It was a chant, people singing together on the other side of the cedar and fir trees.

Two minds struggle in one soul.

The fabricated mind devours.
The genuine mind is lost.
True mind Alfred, awake, stay steady.
Overcome The Lantern Man.
True mind Alfred, awake, persist.
Overpower the devourer.

Fisby's mind thrashed through a firestorm of suspicion and confusion to make sense of the words that came from the middle of a grove of devil's club stems. He knew the patch with its upward growing prickly spires, fed by rooted rhizomes in the moss-covered ground, but he mostly ignored devil's club magic because it was about healing and protection, two purposes he considered weak, a waste of time.

The chant named someone called Alfred. Fisby distinctly heard the name. The chant identified The Lantern Man; Fisby was sure of it. But how was it possible? Could Alfred, transformed centuries ago into The Lantern Man, have escaped from the book that Fisby hid in his own library? Who besides Elden had access to his books? Elden had never double crossed him, but there were a few Manroots with the skill to detect a magical artifact. Did Manroots enter his house without permission? But then, why would there be people chanting in support of Alfred's release from Lantern Man captivity? That was more of a do-no-harm focus on magic, not typical Manroot intention.

Fisby breathed hard. His anger roared in his ears. His blood pressure escalated until he truly did see the trees as a thicket of shimmering red beacons. Yes. He would act. Fisby would stop the attempt. His own father passed the power of the lantern man curse to him, Fisby Parkinson. He would re-energize the spell and force Alfred Dowsby, born 1616 in the Wiken Fens, to carry the lantern into another book. And then he would kill Lars Columbus and handicap the rest of the Waterleafs.

As for the three newbie witches, he would destroy their lives. The Manroots would help ruin them.

"I'm following that light down there." Fisby growled, turning to his companions. "Those singers are Waterleafs. Stay here for now, and if they try to stop me, cover me. They think the devil's club protects them but throw those effigies into their midst while they're singing. That ought to shake them."

For a moment, Fisby studied the light from the cursed lantern as its holder wound his way through vine maple, lady fern, and salal. The spurious pastor wondered at the light's essence, shaped as a long, thin, translucent figure with wispy, root-like arms and legs. The shapes reminded him of the tubers he and the other Manroots made into effigies. Shaking his head, Fisby made his move, slipping further right among the trees so that he would be downhill from the Wiccans and screened from view in the creek gully as he came out from the trees.

Fisby, the leader of the Manroots and owner of The Lantern Man curse, needed to stay unseen. His brother, Elden, watched and followed. He kept himself shielded in deep shadows, far enough behind that Fisby was unaware of his presence. The other Manroots directed their energies onto the clearing and the chanting Waterleafs.

"Isn't that guy who just left the group Fisby? I couldn't tell for sure, but I think it might be." Bruce took a step in the direction of the gully. "If we could identify him, we could get out of here and go home."

"Yeah. But don't you think some weird stuff is going down?" Noah grabbed Bruce's arm and pointed to Elden's shadowy form slipping from tree to tree behind Fisby. Then he pointed to his left. "What are people doing in the preserve chanting? And what about that light? And this here is public property, so we don't need a warrant or permission to check it out."

Bruce reasoned that if these people weren't breaking

any laws, he wanted to leave them and all their creepy nuttiness and go back to the office. "Biggest priority for me is identifying Fisby, and if we corner him where there's more light, we can at least take pictures or video so we can show the chief." Looking up at the moon through the treetops, Bruce sighed. Moonlight brightened the meadow beyond, but darkness remained heavy under the trees.

"Let's follow that Elden fellow, then. I don't think anyone else knows he's here, and he'll lead us to Fisby," Noah said.

In the meantime, dispersed between devil's club stems, the six Wiccans and their six companions stayed focused on Alfred's light as it moved down the shadowy, brush-tangled gully toward the creek. They sang the awake-and-overcome chant every five minutes and directed their supportive energy between chants. The Waterleafs were aware of the Manroots. The rising moon revealed silhouettes of figures in long coats at the edge of the trees, and the Wiccans could feel the men's efforts to block their encouragement spells.

"The enemy is here." Seth pointed out the men to Gilda, who stuck out her tongue in their direction and forced a laugh.

"Ground yourself when needed," Lucinda's reassuring voice called to them. "Center yourself. Think of Alfred. Think of Darnelle."

Darnelle had insisted on staying with Alfred in his search for freedom from the lantern. How that freedom would manifest was unpredictable.

"Alfred thinks he must confront the man who kept him prisoner for so long. He has to come face to face with Fisby," Darnelle had told Estra.

"Be careful where he leads you when he becomes The Lantern Man." Estra pointed the first fingers of both her hands at Darnelle's chest for emphasis. "In his cursed form, his intent is to use his lantern light to lead people to the brink of tragedy, a precipice, the edge of a vast chasm, a steep muddy slide into deep, cold, rushing water. And then he extinguishes the light and leaves them alone in their precarious circumstances. If you find yourself lost, stay put and call for us."

But The Lantern Man never got the chance to lead Darnell or anyone else to a dangerous, wet place. Fisby was on him before he could cross the creek. Only a few dead snags away, Elden watched the meeting of prisoner and jailer, cursed and curse-owner, conjuror and conjuror.

Yards behind, Noah and Bruce scrutinized Elden as he watched the meeting of Fisby with Alfred. Noah pressed the video function on his iPhone and pointed the lens toward the two men and one woman below Elden, a scene illuminated by the uncanny lantern light. "It's Fisby, alright." Noah sent a copy of Fisby's picture to the chief and kept on filming.

"I don't have time for baloney or gibberish," Chief Castillo texted back. "Just take care of it."

Uphill from the creek-side meeting, the awake-and-overcome chant filled the air once more. Darnelle grabbed The Lantern Man's fisted hand as Alfred struggled to regain mindfulness within his own body.

Fisby grinned at Darnelle. "How did you know to be here? I can always count on you. Your devotion to the church is admirable. We will reward you for your help with this cause. Yes. Hold him for me as I get control of him." For a moment Darnelle's face twisted in confusion. Then it dawned on her that Fisby knew nothing about her friendship with Alfred. Fisby assumed she was still ignorant of his duplicitousness and was there to help the anti-magic cause. Fisby still believed she supported his fraudulent church leadership.

"The Lantern Man in the flesh and in person. I don't know how you escaped your banishment, boy," said Fisby, son of Alfred's teacher, "but I own the curse that connects you to that lantern. You, freak of nature, will never break free without my permission, and I can think of no reason to grant you freedom."

Darnelle whispered in Alfred's ear. "Pastor Fisby thinks I am still his disciple. He doesn't know that I know all about him now." With that piece of assurance, Alfred struggled through the lantern man haze. He was alert and himself, but unsure how long he could maintain his clarity.

Fisby muttered something about chains and binds, a spell to take someone prisoner. Alfred would have to think of a quick defense. He searched in his memory for his teacher's lessons of resistance. A boomerang or ricochet spell came to mind. He sensed the energies of Wiccan encouragement in his surroundings and felt Darnelle's hand on his now open fingers, and then Alfred focused all his will and intent on the remembered rebound spell. When Fisby's imprisonment spell hit him, he was ready.

"When a spell is meant to hurt and injure, let it fall fourfold on its conjurer." Alfred called out the words, holding his arms stiff and straight. He felt Fisby's spell along the full length of his body, as though iron shackles grew around his wrists and ankles, as though iron chains weighed him down around his neck and torso. Alfred heard in the distance the awake-and-overcome chant and did not give in. Darnelle's warm hand touch his splayed fingers. He repeated, "When a spell is meant to hurt and injure, let it fall fourfold on its conjurer."

A wrenching, prying suction drove Alfred, reeling, to his knees. Darnelle closed her eyes and screamed, but a louder, higher-pitched squeal drowned out her cry. When she opened her eyes, Alfred was still by her side, now on all fours. Only feet from Alfred's hands, Fisby, too, was on the ground, on his back, writhing and cursing, his face full of surprised rage. Alfred's counter spell had, indeed, reversed Fisby's attempt to chain him. The seventeenth century warlock's powers were returning.

"I don't know how long the reverse spell will hold." Alfred got to his feet, squeezed an arm tight around Darnelle's shoulder, and then let go. In his attempt to concentrate and keep The Lantern Man at bay, Alfred brought the palms of both hands to his temples and pressed hard.

"It's time, then." Darnelle slipped off Alfred's pack and began digging inside it. She pulled out a book, a jar of gray powder, a candle, matches, and a piece of paper covered with hand-written words. She arranged them on a naked tree log that stretched across the creek. "You can do it. You can banish your jailer in his own prison. It's time to exile him into a book like his father did to you."

"I have dreamed of doing this for many long years." Alfred panted, trying to stay focused. He set the lantern on the ground, not far from Fisby. "Did you know Pastor Parkinson taunted me almost daily, especially when something had gone wrong for him in his so-called ministry and in his clandestine life."

"Just stand next to the log, Alfred. We've got to do it now." Darnelle's voice sounded desperate. She reached for Alfred's hands to pull him toward the book and the bottle, but his expression stiffened into frosty hostility while The Lantern Man fought to take hold. They needed to do the spell before Alfred's demonic alter ego returned. The Lantern Man was unpredictable. What if he proved unwilling to die to free Alfred's humanity? He might decide, out of self-preservation and out of spite, to release Fisby. If that happened, not only would the Manroot leader imprison Alfred again as The Lantern Man, but Darnelle knew Fisby would punish her to satisfy his deepest need for vengeance. Before she could help pull Alfred to his feet, someone grabbed her from behind.

"I'll be doing that," said a voice in her ear. "I've fantasized about banishing Fisby for years and years, but today my reasons multiplied, and there is nothing to hold me back."

"Elden?" Darnelle stiffened with surprise and fear, unable to move in the man's nutcracker-like grip. "But I thought you were devoted to Fisby."

"I was as devoted as a bitter hostage can be," Elden answered, his tone sour like rotting rhubarb.

Noah nudged Bruce as they crouched behind their vine maple lookout several yards up the hill. "Look. That Elden's got a knife and he's holding the woman against her will. It's gotta be time for us to make a move."

"Hold on." Bruce remembered that acting too soon could push a hostage holder into violence when a different tactic might result in release of the prisoner or at least fewer injuries. "Let's see if that other fellow gives Elden what he wants so he lets the woman go. They still don't know we're watching, so we don't want to force the issue if we don't have to."

Five sets of ears waited for Alfred's answer. The deputies, Elden, Darnelle, and Fisby watched Alfred grab the upper side of the log for leverage. As he worked to steady his feet, he panted with the exertion of directing a reverse spell, but also with trying to push down The Lantern Man's potency. For Darnelle's sake, his Alfred self wanted to let Elden have his way. Alfred was willing to give up the dream of banishing Fisby. He understood Darnelle was more important than an act of vengeance.

His louder Lantern Man voice pushed to the surface, speaking to his Alfred self. "We have always done the bidding of others. It is our turn to win the war and take our due. It is our turn to show the world that we are our own man, powerful, someone to reckon with. I will make the spell and banish Fisby."

"Darnelle has no part in this." Alfred breached to the surface of his being and gasped out words to Elden. "Do your worst. Take over the spell."

Even as Alfred asked for Darnelle's freedom, The Lantern Man took control and grabbed the matches to light the candle.

CHAPTER 33

Uphill, in the woods bordering the devil's club clearing, the Manroot with the bushy gray mustache set to bellowing. His comrades howled like manic teenagers, the kind who get a thrill out of watching a bully.

"You fellas over there hiding with the women in the devil's club? You must get off on ball-busters and man-haters pushing you around. You dudes are real mamma's boys." Bushy gray mustache wheezed with laughter. He normalized his voice so that only his fellow Manroots could hear. "Sometimes you don't even need spells or magic to rule." They slapped him on the back.

Squatting on the ground next to Fayette and Sheila, working to avoid devil's club thorns, Leo and Darwin gritted their teeth. Samuel, who was busy holding a pen light between his teeth and writing notes in a notebook, seemed oblivious to the noises around him.

The Manroots continued to direct their mocking energies toward the Waterleafs. Each of the Wiccan protectors could feel their intentions divide. They struggled to deflect the negative objectives of the Manroots and at the same time send positive energies to help Alfred and Darnelle. Dispersed between erect wooden stems within the devil's club colony, they could not see what was happening near the creek, but they knew a struggle was in progress, so they lit candles to aid in centering their wavering energies. The merry, flickering lights offered hope and cheer to ease the stress, and then the flames quivered and almost blew out when a Manroot lobbed newspaper-wrapped packages into their midst.

"Leave them be. Focus on Alfred," came Lucinda's reassuring voice.

Kitsy, who believed the group would not miss her energies, decided to gather the packages and examine their contents. She felt her contribution to the chanting was an unpracticed weaker link, but maybe she could help by taking the newspaper wrapped bundles away so that they would not be a distraction. There were six compact parcels on the ground. She gathered them and took them to the back of the devil's club clearing, in the opposite direction from the creek, and toward a small stream.

There, on the edge of the devil's club colony, by the light of the moon, still rising, Kitsy opened the paper. Tears filled her eyes at seeing the little tortured tuber bodies, each with crude, black or red mouths and eyes made of pin piercings and sharp crystal beads. With tender care, she pulled out the pins and the sharp miniature weapons. Taking a plastic sack from her pack pocket she stuffed it full of the newspaper, the pins, the small-scale knives and swords, and the crystal beads. They could destroy these ugly things, she figured, or secure them in lead-lined boxes like the items that were part of the curses left in Fayette's and Sheila's yards.

Gathering the tubers, Kitsy wrapped them with compassion in her homemade scarf. Next, she made her way to the stream and laid the young tuber bodies on soft moss. She retrieved her first aid kit from her backpack and set to work.

"Here you are little one," she said to each tuber as she bathed it in the stream, washing off the obnoxious marker mouth, cleaning the pin and toy weapon wounds, and letting the water flow over the tender body to sooth the drying tuber skin. "Heal my little one. Take no hurt from this night." She laid the tubers, with their arm-like and leg-like outgrowths, onto her scarf. Combing out their hairy root extensions with her fingers, she applied aloe gel to their cuts and punctures. Kitsy had nothing to dig with, but she was determined to replant the tubers in the ground where they belonged. With the aid of moonlight, she found a strong, short stick, and using it and her hands, managed to dig six, moist holes in the underbrush not far from the stream.

Picking up the first tuber in gentle slow motion, she took it to the first hole. "Grow strong. Feel loved. So may it be," she told it. She almost dropped the little body in its planting hole when it seemed to bow to her from the palm of her hand and then lifted its arm-like roots to hug the first finger of her other hand. She could not hear a voice but instead felt an inner communication from the baby root. "Thank you, dear lady. You could have thrown us in the brush as trash, but you gave us the means to live. I will always remember." Tears dripped down Kitsy's cheeks as she placed the rhizome into the loose dirt where she could swear it wiggled just slightly, as though burrowing into a fuzzy blanket. She covered the tiny tuber with wet, dark, earth, making sure the top of the tuber body was near the surface. With each tuber, she received the same warm thanks, and when they were all safely planted and her work done, she sat on the banks of the stream, washed her muddy hands, and cried at the cruelty and horror the baby root bodies endured.

Little did Kitsy know that her kindness to the tubers triggered the rules of enforcement for a basic law of magic. Conjurers get back what they intend in a magic act. The Manroot coven members intended harm to the Waterleafs and used the tuber babies to cause damage with their spell. They believed they had done enough to protect themselves from such reversals of power, but in fact, they would feel the repercussions for their hostile intents several times over. Before Kitsy finished tucking them into their soil beds, the little manroot tubers cast off the negative energy that the Manroots' spell forced them to contain in their bodies and sent it back. Six tender bodies sent a four-fold reversal of negative energy to their Manroot torturers.

Fisby felt the reversal of power first and all at once. His ethereal chains hardened and tightened as the first wave of negative energy hit him. His eyes burned, and sharp metal punctured his stomach and side. His lips turned black. The others who tortured the baby tubers would experience a different fate during the first wave of reprisals.

"Help me," Fisby gasped out to his brother. Elden witnessed Fisby's heightened powerlessness and heard Fisby's pleading words. He wondered at his own lack of caring or concern, realizing just how deep his resentment and hatred escalated since meeting with Betts Harvey, the genealogist. Elden looked away from Fisby. As Fisby's book prison, Elden had chosen and brought the classic description of a path through Hell, *Dante's Inferno* by Dante Alighieri.

Unaware that a reversal of power was on its way that would change their plans, bushy gray mustache Manroot, the tallest Manroot, and gum-chewing Manroot stayed sheltered under cedar trees as they worked to interfere with the grounding and centering efforts of the Waterleafs. Abigail and the others knew the devil's club deflected the greater part of the Manroots interference, but it still took energy from all of them to protect themselves and each other.

The Manroots' delight at causing mischief kept them focused on the devil's club clearing, and they snickered over the mayhem their effigies were likely triggering even as they conjured binding spell after binding spell to weaken the Waterleaf chant meant to support Alfred.

Behind the Waterleafs, manifestations of negative power reversal moved with stealth through the trees. Punishment for the three Manroot coven followers would come from wild creatures native to the Northwest Coast mountain environment, and while these animals rarely roamed together, this night, Earth energies called on them to join forces. Sleek, graceful, and silent, two tawny females and a male stalked their human Manroot prey only feet away.

It was not in a cougar's practical nature to kill humans, and slaughter was not their intent this time. The forest cats would simply match the injuries that the baby manroot tubers sustained and then leave their arrogant victims in pain to rethink their place in the world. Remorse and empathy might not be possible for these men, but episodes of negative power reversal would increase over the years if they failed to see the error of using and abusing the lowest, meanest forms of magic.

While the cool yellow eyes of cougars watched the three Manroots bellow out menacing and demeaning phrases, words they called war spells, Elden, from over the top of Darnelle's head, ignored his brother writhing on the cold, muddy creekside. He pulled Darnelle's arms tighter behind her, pushing her to her knees and pulling her hair back and down until her anguished face looked up at him and he could draw his knife easily across her throat. Darnelle's body shook, and she squealed when Elden yanked her arms back further to tie them with the draw string that he pulled from his rain hood.

"Leave her be." Alfred held momentary control, panting with the exertion of staying conscious.

With curiosity and professional interest, Elden watched the struggle on Alfred's face. He'd always known there was a book in Fisby's library that contained a creature called The Lantern Man. He'd known The

Lantern Man was a cursed wizard of some sort.

"You know, I never supposed that you could escape from that book, Alfred Dowsby. But what's more astounding is that someone else shares my ambition to banish Fisby. I never imagined I'd be competing for the right to destroy my brother." Elden revealed his knife, then, and aimed it at Darnelle's throat. "You won't be the one to do it, though, not unless you want me to stick this into Darnelle, here."

In their hiding place, Noah and Bruce both tensed, ready to spring into a run. Noah pointed to a tree closer to Elden and Darnelle. They edged their way past a vine maple, stepping with as much stealth as was possible.

The four humans at the creek were at a temporary impasse. Fisby lay groaning and struggling, weighed down by invisible restraints.

His teeth bared and his eyes tormented slits, The Lantern Man's hand shook as it prepared to set lit match to candle wick. Elden had Darnelle constrained as a hostage with a knife near her throat, and between defending themselves from negative energy directed by the Manroots and trying to reclaim their focus to help Alfred, the Waterleafs' energies diminished.

The moon continued to rise. It was three days on the waxing side of its full stage, and on such a clear night, its light intensified to reveal shapes, shadows, and movement.

Chapter 34

Exhausted from centering, grounding, and focusing intent, Fayette nudged Sheila and pointed to Darwin and Leo. The men were on their feet and moving toward the edge of the devil's club clearing in the direction of the Manroot taunts and interruptions. Samuel remained seated, absorbed with pencil and paper, taking notes as fast as he could.

"Where's Kitsy?" Sheila scanned the clearing and could see no sign of her.

"She got up to pick up those packages the dolts in the woods threw over here. She must have taken them someplace." Fayette stretched her good arm and her back to try and work out kinks that settled in her muscles from sitting on the ground for so long; then, with effort, she maneuvered herself into a standing position. "I gotta see what's happening down there in the creek. The lantern is still there. I can see its glow. Why isn't it moving? What's happening with Darnelle and Alfred? Why are we just sitting here?"

"You might mess things up," Sheila protested. "We're supposed to stay where we're protected and can help."

"I'm just going over there to the outcrop over the creek bed and in those bushes. No one will see me. I just want to look over the edge. What harm would that cause? Aren't you curious? Don't you want to know what's going on? I'm tired of doing nothing. I want to help if I can."

Sheila, feeling torn, watched the silhouettes of Darwin and Leo edge closer to the woods on her right and Fayette start toward the underbrush on her left. *Am I too much of a scaredy-cat?* It was something she'd wondered most of her life. *Or am I smart to stay safe and not take risks?* Sheila's thoughts got the best of her. *You're not completely useless. You know how to take risks. You experimented with magic. Yes. And those experiments are why you're sitting next to thorny, spiky branches in the middle of a frosty clearing. Sure, you've been trying to help. But maybe there are better ways to help.* Her last rumination got Sheila to her feet. Half reluctant, half eager, she followed Fayette in a crouched stance, knees bent, back horizontal to the ground, much like a knuckle-walking great ape. Fayette led the way to the thicker underbrush downstream from the glow of the lantern and closer to the creek bed.

When they reached their destination and looked across and down the slope toward the light, Fayette made a growling sound in her throat. Sheila gasped.

"Holy botulism," Fayette whispered. "I never thought I'd feel sorry for Darnelle. Is Elden trying to defend his brother from The Lantern Man? Is that why he's got Darnelle tied up and locked into a death hold? What in perdition happened to Fisby? Where did he even come from? He looks like he's dying."

"Look." Sheila pointed past the scene at the creek bottom. "See over there past the lantern light? It's the deputies, Noah and Bruce, hiding behind those alders. What are they doing here?"

An agonizing, guttural groan, swelling to a roar, interrupted the two spying women looking down over the creek. Alfred lost his battle in that moment. The Lantern Man took power over their shared body causing the Waterleafs to reel at the change of force.

"You can't end me. I know now that if I sacrifice my vengeance for the sake of another, I die, I lose my lantern." The cursed fiend chuckled to his inner self, taunting Alfred and then focusing his scrutiny on Fisby. "But I can end you without dying. I can use my power to curse you into a book, and I will put that book in a place no one will ever find. I brought a book that I believe will torture you into the inferno of insanity, you who hide behind a judgmental version of Christianity. You call me evil while you teach your own ugly rendering of scripture for the sake of personal power. We are not much different you and I." The Lantern Man giggled, a hair-raising, putrid titter. "The book Alfred and I chose is called *Invitations to a Wiser Scripture: Equal Value and Shared Dignity for Women and Men in Biblical Interpretations.*"

"That book doesn't sound so bad," Sheila murmured to Fayette, but even as she said it, Fisby sat up through his pain and grabbed for The Lantern Man's legs.

Fisby spit out one word at a time, "There is no equal anything for women compared with men, not when it comes to religion. Not when it comes to magic."

Darnelle screamed, interrupting Fisby. Involuntary terror saturated her cry as Elden used his knife to cut her. "Her arm now, but her neck and jugular soon if you do not stand down, Alfred Dowsby." Elden stood over Darnelle's neck, pulling her hair, his knee in her back. He lifted the knife, now tinged red at its point. A spot of blood flowered and grew on the light blue fabric of Darnelle's upper right coat sleeve.

The words of the Waterleaf chant seemed to glide within a quickening breeze into the creek hollow. A short distance above the creek, Fayette and Sheila spoke along with the Wiccans.

Two minds struggle in one soul.
The fabricated mind devours.

The Lantern Man hissed in the direction of the devil's club grove and its occupants. He turned toward the log, grabbing the paper copy of his spell to banish Fisby. He lit the candle.

"He's going to go ahead with the curse." Sheila leaned further over the embankment. "What will happen if he goes through with it?"

Darnelle screamed again as Elden pricked her other arm with his knife. "I'm warning you, Alfred, your friend will die if you go ahead with this."

It was as though The Lantern Man had shut out the rest of the world. He ignored Elden and reached for the spell bottle and its powdery ash-like contents.

Fayette grabbed for a branch to pull herself to her feet. "I'm going down to help. We can't let Elden go through with torturing Darnelle. We have to help Alfred." As she turned to lower herself down the embankment, her boot slipped on a thin, mossy log and she went down, landing squarely on her injured shoulder.

In the moonlight, Sheila saw her friend's face contort from the pain and whispered, "Oh gawd, oh gawd, oh gawd." Fayette reached for Sheila's leg, and Sheila became a support post so Fayette could pull herself into a sitting position.

"Damnation, we've got to go down and help." Fayette winced as she felt her arm and shoulder with her good hand. She tried to get up and follow through with her plans to jump into the fray, the pain in her shoulder causing her to close her eyes and grit her teeth.

"Hold on. You're not going anywhere." Sheila pushed Fayette back to a sitting position.

"Then it's up to you." Fayette narrowed her eyes at Sheila.

"And do what?"

"Either find a way to help Alfred overpower The Lantern Man and save Darnelle, or save Darnelle yourself."

"Me? I'm no good at being a one-woman calvary."

"Either do something or spend the rest of your life feeling like a coward." Fayette pulled no punches. She felt little sympathy for what she considered selfish insecurities.

Sheila rummaged through her pack to try and find something to help her distract Elden or The Lantern Man. Her hands shook as she grabbed a package of something without looking at it. Her legs felt numb as she forced them to move one step at a time toward the edge of the embankment in front of Fayette. She stood there frozen. "I don't have a plan," she complained. And then Fayette gave her a push.

Stumbling, Sheila worked hard to keep her balance as momentum forced her legs down the slope, toward the log where The Lantern Man worked. Her boots filled with wet, sandy soil. Her arms windmilled, but she had little control over her destination. Though she tried to veer to her left, a low place in the slope determined her direction. Fairly flying, Sheila's feet found the creek bed where she crashed full force into The Lantern Man as he held his lit candle up to the night sky.

The collision was stupefying, spectacular, sensational, like a bowling ball striking a bowling pin square on. The Lantern Man lay on his back, his head in the gravel near the running creek water. Sheila extricated herself from the top of him and stood.

"So sorry, Mr. Lantern Man," she said, breathing hard. "Can I help you up?" Sheila located the candle and put it back on the log. "There. It's back where it should be. You can try again."

Elden, holding his knife to Darnelle's throat, appeared frozen to the spot as he watched Sheila reach out her hand to help The Lantern Man rise to a sitting position. Flustered, she gave her crash victim the package she'd found in her backpack. "Here, take this."

Dazed, The Lantern Man tried to shake off his confusion, examining the package and finding it to be an assortment of shortbread cookies. The knock on his head from hitting the ground and the unexpected gift were distraction enough for Alfred to break through and push down his Lantern Man alter ego.

"Blood and bloody ashes." Alfred bawled out the words with such force that his speech muscles tore and inflamed his throat. "Take the potion, Elden. Take the candle. Remove Fisby from this world. For Darnelle's sake, I will not fight you." His last words, "fight you," were a croak.

"I do not need your candle or potion. I have my own." Elden stepped aside for Alfred to grab hold of Darnelle and bring her to her feet, and Sheila let out a glorious sigh of relief, only slightly aware that her left foot, boot and all, was sinking in a mud hole.

As he untied Darnelle's arms, Alfred could only get out a hoarse, "I'm so sorry."

Impatient to get his deed done, Elden strode to the log. In seconds, Fisby's brother had his own candle, potion, and book arranged on the log next to Alfred's conjuring supplies. He set *Dante's Inferno* next to the book Alfred brought.

"Step aside," he told a bleeding Darnelle and an exhausted Alfred. They did as he demanded.

Torn between extricating her foot from the mud, and keeping her eyes on the hostile brothers, Sheila braced herself for possible bloodshed. She could detect nothing sweet or tender between Elden and a wretched Fisby, shaking with pain in the dirt next to The Lantern Man's spectral light.

"Why?" Fisby's voice was hoarse and his breathing shallow as he watched Elden prepare the powder and light the candle.

"Because you and our father took the only thing from me that would give my life meaning. You chose a hollow existence for me and demanded I follow your creed." Elden turned toward his brother, his face so full of fury and venom that Fisby winced. "I remain dominated, subordinated under your position as older brother until you are gone. And so, you must go."

"What brought this on?" Fisby was reduced to gasping out his words. "It has always been the duty in our lineage to be loyal to the patriarchy. That is how our magic stays strong. You know that." Fisby coughed through the pain of his tightening shackles. "We have a duty to the house of Wehha of the Wiffingas dynasty."

"I never felt that our lives had a real purpose," Elden said, straightening his back. "You and our father claimed that our mother's death was for the best. A petty excuse for our father harassing her to the point of suicide. And then, when I fell in love, you forbade the marriage. You drove Annie away, and then you told me she died."

"People die, and sometimes that is for the best." Fisby looked away from his brother. "We maintain the laws of Wiffingas conjurors and the male lineage. Loving a woman makes a man weak. You know that. Your fellow magicians and the men of your lineage can no longer trust your allegiances and loyalty to the wolf dynasty once you marry. A woman will require devotion to her so that your father and uncles and brothers can no longer count on you to work with absolute faithfulness."

"Annie Covington is not dead. You knew that all these years. You hid from me that I have a daughter with Annie. Her name is Bianca. And now I know I have a grandson, Peter, Bianca's son." Elden began to weep, even as he prepared the spell.

Her heart skipping beats out of sympathy for Elden,

Sheila gave a last pull, nearly falling over as the mud released her boot. She took a step toward the grieving brother. He glanced her way but turned and spit on the ground near Fisby's feet. "Years wasted, years when I could have been with Annie, could have had a life with purpose, not one that feels hollow. You sacrificed me for the sake of power that I don't care about. If I remain with you as a younger brother, you will compel me to continue this empty existence, and for what? The only way to stop this pain is to banish you. And so, I must."

Elden took a piece of paper from his pocket, grabbed his bottle of lead-colored powder and stepped closer to his struggling brother. Sprinkling the powder over Fisby, he recited words in a language Alfred, Darnelle, Fayette, Sheila, Noah and Bruce did not understand. As he repeated the words over and over, Fisby faded bit by bit, his color turning as gray as Elden's curse-fueled powder. He seemed to steam, like water rising from a hot pan. His body formed a trail of vapors that caught light from the lantern and then vanished like rain drops on a puddle. Fisby worked to grab onto something that might keep him anchored to the ground. His wispy hands seized the lantern. In the next moment, the steam trail that was Fisby rose in the air, and with the speed of a tornado, dove for one of the books on top of the log. At the same time, they all heard a piercing, shrill-ish scream from the direction of the woods near the devil's club grove. Elden turned toward the scream just as his brother's stretched and translucent form, holding the lantern, entered the pages of his new, hard-cover prison.

Torn between moving downhill to confront Elden and moving uphill to investigate the scream, Noah and Bruce stood frozen for a long moment. For one thing, neither wanted to ask the other if he'd seen a human person, Fisby to be exact, melt into a comet of steam and seemingly disappear in thin air. Another scream, this time a shriek within a growl, resonated through the woods and marshlands. All who heard it felt the fight/ flight response of instinctive human fear.

"I know that sound. That's a cougar," Bruce said. And then a man's bawl of terror echoed the mountain lion scream. The officers sprinted toward the cry, leaving the scene of the vanished Confess and Reform Church pastor. After all, Darnelle was no longer a hostage, and the need for help uphill seemed more immediate and maybe less mystifying. They could explain cougars. How would they ever rationalize seeing Fisby, suffering and alive, beg for mercy from his brother Elden, whose anger fostered no pity. How could they describe Elden's behavior and then the transition of Fisby as solid substance melting into thin air? They had dim pictures on a video, so they could prove to Chief Castillo that Elden knew exactly where his brother was. They'd get Elden to come down to the station and answer questions and likely arrest him for assaulting the woman called Darnelle, if she wanted to press charges. In the meantime, cougar screams flooded the night troposphere of woods and clearing. So did human yelling and shouting.

"Judas Priest. There's more than one mountain lion here." Bruce forgot Fisby and Elden as he patted his gun holster for reassurance and then unsnapped the cover.

Several people from left and right ran towards the direction of the screams, coming from the edge of the forest trees. While Waterleaf witnesses saw the leaping and running forms of three large cougars leaving the glade, by the time the officers arrived the cats were gone. Three prone figures lay groaning, crying, and begging for help. They were the Manroot disciples who worked so hard to put a crimp in the Waterleafs' efforts to help Alfred. Bushy mustache, the tall one, and gum chewing Manroot sustained several injuries and were overwhelmed with pain. Noah determined that none of their wounds were life threatening, but the EMT's were on their way to shuttle them to the hospital for treatment and observation.

"Did you notice that the cougars wounded those blokes in exactly the same places?" Darwin shook his head in wonderment. "I mean, they could have killed them with one nasty bite and a shake, but they didn't." He and Leo came upon the Manroots with a fight in mind, but just as they'd gathered gumption enough to step out of the bushes and confront them, the mountain lions charged in.

Lars heard Leo and Darwin talking. "You saw it all, then? The cougars attacked just enough to administer very particular wounds and then disappeared?"

"You could say that." Leo patted his own heart and torso as he recalled the effectiveness of cat claws and incisors to mete out the injuries he witnessed. "I can hear the deputies over there planning a cougar hunt to roust out the cats."

"They won't find them," Lars said. "They're long gone. I doubt they're even local cougars. They're passing through, and they won't hang around."

Emergency crew headlamps and police-issued electric torches illuminated the wooded grove and devil's club meadow with funnels of light bouncing off the trees and shifting in the night-ether like a whole convention of will o' the wisps.

Over on the other side of the creek, the trees and hillside were dark, and only Elden knew he was the last human to see the mountain lions that night.

He'd run up the hill, aiming himself in the direction of his hidden motorcycle as he crashed through the brush. Breathing through long, hard heaves, he pushed away branches and hauled himself up frosty, slippery slopes as fast as his one-hundred-thirty-four-year-old body could manage, determined to leave before the chaos settled. The creek bed was his guide, past the open area, the blackberry brambles and up through trees to the road that ran in front of the cabin. There he found his Chieftain Elite Indian cycle, hidden just where he left it on a short, dirt trail. With care, Elden rechecked his backpack for the book containing his brother. He secured the pack onto the Chieftain.

Just as he steadied the bike to climb aboard, three swift, golden shapes brushed past him. One snarled a warning, stopping to sniff his pants and hand. And then they were gone. Elden felt a prickle of fear cloud his mind and move down his spine as the powerful felines passed close enough to touch him. He carried the scent of a man who used low, malicious magic, but his fate was not the cougars' concern. They'd done what the baby tubers called them to do and that was all. Elden understood they were more than wild animals, that they'd come for a purpose. When his heart slowed to a tolerable pace, and when each breath was normal again, he started the engine of his escape cycle and was on the road with one, quick acceleration. He'd stop long enough to batten down his shop, Brilliant Things, and then Elden would be long gone before anyone started looking for him.

Moonlight often gives the world a bluish cast, and it was through a pale cerulean glow that Fayette, still above the creek bed, watched Alfred tend to Darnelle's arms, wrapping the cuts in strips of cloth torn from the bottom of his undershirt.

"We should have those cuts looked at," Alfred said.

"Not tonight. I just want to go home." Darnelle slumped to the ground, and Fayette, her shoulder pain subsiding, realized the woman was in shock and decided to reveal herself and join the couple next to their log.

"Come on, Sheila," Fayette yelled down the slope. "Do you still have that blanket in your pack, the one you brought in case you got cold? I think Darnelle needs it." Fayette pulled out her pocket flashlight. From her vantage point she'd seen the silhouettes of Waterleafs moving about among the devil's club. She'd heard the sounds of the animal cries and the yells of scared men. Now she could see the hodge-podge of headlamp and flashlight beams in the distance.

Sheila reclimbed the slope, gathered her pack and Fayette's, and, on her own steam this time, descended the slope back to the creek bed, providing a supporting arm for Fayette. Locating her red and black, gingham car blanket, Sheila wrapped it around Darnelle's shoulders, tight as a baby swaddle.

"That was an awful scare you went through," Sheila soothed. Darnelle leaned to one side, on the point of falling over. Her strong-jawed face, usually ruddy, looked ashen in the moonlight; her eyes, typically fierce, were dull with exhaustion.

Fayette turned on Alfred as though he was one of her children at the infuriating age of sixteen. "Alfred, are you okay? What in the name of Merlin's pink tutu were you and Elden playing at?"

But Alfred wasn't listening. He was patting himself all over, his chest, shoulders stomach, head, and legs. "My God. I'm me."

"What do you mean, you're you?" Fayette's impatience pumped up a notch. She wanted to slap some sense into this confounded, weak-willed creature.

"I mean, that's all I am, me, Alfred, and nothing else." The man from the seventeenth century, re-awakened in the twenty first century, whooped and jumped around like a bead of water in a hot oiled skillet. After yelling and leaping in a circle clear around Fayette, Alfred dropped to his knees in front of Darnelle, hugging her close, blanket and all. "Honey, it's me, Alfred, and that's all I am. The Lantern Man is gone. The curse is gone. Even the lantern is gone." She laid her head on his shoulder, too numb to speak but blinking back unshed tears.

Sheila and Fayette looked around. He was right. The lantern was gone. Fisby grabbed it in his last-ditch effort to hold onto something that would keep him grounded. He carried it with him into his new prison, to be confined in the pages of a book. Both women knew something that Elden apparently missed. Had Alfred and Darnelle missed it too as they reacted to the piercing screams coming from the cedar grove? Elden imprisoned Fisby in the book that still lay on the log in front of them, not the book he snatched up when he exited the scene. The red, leather-bound *Dante's Inferno* was empty of everything except paper, words, and type. Instead, Sheila and Fayette had watched Fisby's essence pour into the pages of the large-print, hard-backed book Alfred brought, *Invitations to a Wiser Scripture: Equal Value and Shared Dignity for Women and Men in Biblical Interpretations* by Felicity P Sawyer.

"Fisby's in there." Fayette whispered to Sheila, pointing to the book laid out next to the cream-colored pillar candle and bottle of drab, dusty looking spell powder.

Sheila nodded and smiled. "Bless him."

Sheila's sweet sarcasm triggered in Fayette an insane and powerful urge to yell, to hoot at the sky. Once started, she couldn't stop. Howling at the moon seemed incongruous to the serious situation, but Fayette's exuberance infected Sheila. They both giggled, and then hooted, and then howled with relief till tears slid down their cheeks, and they had to sit down gasping. Even Alfred and Darnelle joined in, though they weren't sure why. It just felt good, and it had been a night beyond imagining for them all.

Chapter 35

Elmira's police station might never have been as full as it was 3:30 a.m. the morning of the cougar attack and Fisby's and Elden's disappearance. Fourteen people crowded together behind the front desk, waiting to give statements. When Chief Castillo heard about the goings on at the preserve, he insisted that Noah and Bruce waste no time in getting to the bottom of what the chief called "highly suspicious shenanigans."

Waterleaf Wiccans, Darnelle and Alfred, Leo, Samuel, and Darwin, and Kitsy, Sheila, and Fayette either leaned against the waiting area wall, assembled on the bench, or hoisted themselves to sit on the front desk to await their turns to explain what they knew. No one had a complete picture of all that had gone on near the devil's club glade, in the cedar grove, and by the creek, and they had a hundred questions to ask each other.

"No matter how crazy you think those police officers will find your story, tell them the truth," Abigail advised. "They need to know that magic was involved whether they believe in it or not."

Gilda and Lucinda brought in carafes of hot chocolate from their vehicles while Seth supplied a pastry box full of fruit-filled muffins. Instead of settling into the silence of a gloomy police interrogation line, the waiting "suspects" threw an impromptu party. One by one the deputies escorted them to the back room and asked each witness to describe everything they saw and heard in the wetlands and wildlife preserve. As soon as their turn was over, they had permission to go home, but each one returned to the front lobby to find out what they'd missed.

"Where is the book?" Lars asked, sitting up straight when he learned it contained the banished Fisby.

"I've got it," Alfred said. "But I don't want it. I don't even want to touch it. Can you take it? Are you going to try to release Fisby?"

"You escaped *The Book of Forbidden Knowledge* because someone whistled you free. In a spell like this one, each cursed individual will have their own personal means of breaking out of their prison. No one knows what the key is, except maybe the prisoner, and then again, he might not know. So, even if I wanted to liberate the man from the book, I wouldn't know where to begin," Lars said. "And I'm glad I don't know so I won't feel obligated to try. But that doesn't mean we shouldn't work to protect the book. Who knows what trickery a desperate Fisby might cause locked in the pages of a feminist theology treatise." Lars' grin was wide and mischievous when he learned the title of Fisby's new home. "Whoever picked that book is a mastermind, a devious mastermind."

"It's from Darnelle's bookshelf," Alfred admitted. "From her college days before she met Fisby."

The report Leo and Darwin gave of the cougar attack and Darnelle's description of the liberation of Alfred from The Lantern Man were stories that the magic community would retell, chew on, and analyze for many months to come. Alfred found himself inundated with hugs and handshakes from everyone. At least a dozen times, Samuel breathed a sigh of relief knowing the stringy-haired, vulgar Lantern Man would never ask him for shortbread cookies again. Still, he'd gathered intriguing materials for a folklore research article.

To Sheila's embarrassment, Fayette told a riveting tale of how Sheila raced down the creek bank, knocked The Lantern Man to the ground, and saved the day by helping Alfred take control over his body once more and rescue Darnelle from Elden. Alfred backed up Fayette's rendition.

"For a church secretary, you pack a mighty punch," he told Sheila. "I'm grateful."

"Here's to Sheila saving the day. If she hadn't crashed down that hill, Alfred might still be The Lantern Man." Seth raised his cup of cocoa, and everyone lifted their mugs to honor the toast. After that, it was hard for Sheila to resent Fayette for pushing her down the embankment, but that didn't mean Fayette got a free pass. Sheila had a long memory.

But it was Kitsy's narrative about the baby manroot tubers that seemed to touch everyone, first in heartbreak for the infant tubers, and then in gratitude for their rebirth.

"Your care for those tortured babies resulted in much more than I think we'll ever understand. I believe you started a kind of positive domino effect." Estra told her. "The effigies were meant for us Wiccans, and if we had opened the packages and touched the tubers, the negative repercussions would take months to reverse. You did, indeed, save us from harm as you were saving the babies from pain."

"There may be a link between freeing the tubers from the effects of low magic and the arrival of the cougars." Lars tugged on his short beard. "I can't say for sure, but it seems to me that Earth energies punished the Manroots. The wounds were unusual for cougar attacks, and they were too similar, man to man, not to be purposeful."

Kitsy shivered at the memory of the wounds on the baby tubers that matched the Manroots' injuries. Lars had a point.

Abigail, with a soft, sympathetic nod of her head said, "I think that you learned tonight what your gift is, Kitsy." She paused to make sure Kitsy was listening. "You, my dear, are a healer."

They all clapped while Kitsy escaped her embarrassment by leaning into a one-armed hug from Samuel.

By 6 a.m., the group left the police station to find warmth beneath comforters and to drift into safe slumber in their beds at home. What the police made of their reports and descriptions didn't concern them. They'd done what had to be done, and that was that.

Before leaving with Leo, Fayette asked for Bruce or Noah as she had one last worry.

"Fisby has two dogs in his cabin, big German shepherds. I don't know if anyone knows about them or will think to care for them."

"Right-o." Noah yawned and rubbed his tired eyes. "We'll send someone over to check it out." Unsaid was Noah's hunch that the strange disappearance of Fisby was a magic performance stunt, a trick of the light.

"Fisby will be back in a matter of hours or days, ready to pick up his dogs from whoever volunteers to foster them," Noah told Bruce after Fayette was gone.

"Yeah. That's got to be what happens," Bruce agreed.

"Otherwise, what we saw might have really gone down," Noah said.

"And that can't be." Bruce looked fiercely pleading in the aftermath of Noah's matter of fact tone. "I mean, if what we saw was real, that'd mean a shake-up of all I've learned is true about the world, and I don't want that kind of burden. It's too weird."

"Nope. Me neither." Noah considered their options. "What we gotta do next is find Elden Parkinson and bring him in. Darnelle wants to press charges for the knife wounds, the threats, and the harassment. We're witnesses, and we need to process his arrest. Also, he's got the answers to what happened to Fisby Parkinson."

"Right now, I don't care what happened to Paster Fisby, and I won't start caring until I get some sleep." Bruce grabbed his jacket and slung it over his shoulder. "Even if the Hells Angels, or Billy the Kid, or King Kong shows up in town, I'm still going home."

CHAPTER 36

A few days after their adventure in the preserve, the Elmira City Herald, a weekly newspaper, came out with two front page headlines. In bold print, the top headline proclaimed, *Cougars Injure Three*. The second headline declared, *Brothers Missing: Police Stumped*.

"Look here." Leo pointed to a paragraph on page two of the paper. He sat at the kitchen table waiting for their food to brown in the oven. Italian sausage casserole was the main course for their third home-cooked dinner together. "It says here, *'Deputies Bruce Peabody and Noah Lakoff saw Elden and Fisby Parkinson together behind the brothers' cabin the night they both disappeared. Witnesses confirm that Pastor Fisby Parkinson had been staying at the cabin since the morning he vanished from Elmira Regional Hospital. For several days, police conducted an all-out search for Mr. Parkinson, believing him to be kidnapped.'"*

A loud banging at the sink interrupted Leo, who looked up from the paper to witness Fayette standing over a gallon container of mint chocolate ice cream, frozen hard. She'd removed her arm sling, and with vigor, she beat the handle of a large knife with a hammer, trying to force the knife blade to break through the double churned dessert so she could serve it.

"You alright?"

"If Sheila and I are mentioned in that article, stop reading right now."

"No worries. They got it right this time. This is what it says. *'The pastor was admitted to the hospital Oct. 16 suffering from a coma caused from Abrus precatorius poison. Police were at first concerned the poisoning was the result of foul play and were collecting evidence on two suspects. Deputies Peabody and Lakoff determined yesterday that Parkinson's condition was, in fact, induced through accidental self-poisoning, according to Police Chief Javier Castillo.'*"

"Well, funky nuggets." Fayette's shoulders relaxed, and she put down the hammer and the knife. "It's a story to rival that mysterious town legend about a spectral figure trapping teenagers with a fire wall up on the Elmira water tower 35 years ago. It'll be fun to see what town gossips make of the Fisby and Elden disappearance. Maybe now Chief Castillo can spend more time with his baby twins and less time interrogating us." Fayette grinned before leaning over to give Leo a kiss right on the lips. "Maybe I'll have time for more important things, too." She winked, and Leo put down the newspaper to return the kiss. It was the first of many.

***

"Maybe now they'll stop putting up those awful posters," Sheila said after she and Darwin read the same story in the same issue of the *Elmira City Herald*. The two started their day over breakfast and spent much of the rest of the morning talking, which led to a late afternoon harvest of Sheila's garden pumpkins. A collection of drawings cluttered the table with Darwin's plans for carving Jack O' Lantern faces.

"Let's hope," Darwin said about the posters. He was half listening and half speculating. "Say, you don't suppose Jack O' Lanterns are any relation to The Lantern Man, do you?"

"Oh, la," Sheila laughed. "I don't even want to go there."

***

Kitsy and Samuel were just too tired to worry about what was in the local newspaper. With careful precision, Kitsy cut out jewel colored cloth pieces for a new scarf. As she constructed her new scarves, she would include the witch stitches, but this time she would prepare ahead of time. Abigail, Lucinda, and Estra were good teachers, and Kitsy paid serious attention to their advice about grounding and centering, focus and intention. She would think with care about the exact words to use over the stiches. Even when good intentions were behind the words, unintended consequences could occur if the words left too much for the universe to interpret.

Leaning against the wall next to the front door of their home was the ash-handled broom Sheila had given Kitsy. Earlier in the day, using Sheila's recipe, Kitsy conducted a strewing spell, using her broom to cleanse and brighten her whole house.

While Kitsy cleansed her home of lantern man energies, Samuel organized his lantern man notes. He wanted to share his lantern man experiences with the folklore world, but the academic community would see his work as outlandish if he wrote as though what happened was truth. He'd need to write it out as a story told to children. These days he'd begun to wonder how many stories told to children had more literal truth in them than he'd imagined.

In the middle of Samuel's unruly stack of notebooks and scattered papers, *The Book of Forbidden Knowledge*, The Lantern Man's long-term prison, drew his constant attention. He needed to find a place for it, someplace where the book couldn't distract him. The morning when they were all gathered at the police station, Samuel asked Alfred if he wanted the book.

"Burn it." Alfred did not hesitate. "The very thought of seeing those prison pages again turns my stomach."

Now that he was putting his office and his notes in order, Samuel wondered if it was prudent to keep the book. He wasn't ready to burn it, so he decided the wall safe was as good a storage place as any.

Samuel knew that Alfred gave Lars the book containing Fisby's essence. Where would the bookstore owner store such a thing? Would Elden come looking for it someday? Samuel's musings shifted to the Guild of the Supreme Brotherhood of Manroots. How was the coven handling the loss of its leadership and the strange cougar attacks of three Manroot disciples? Considering the Manroot creed, Samuel hoped the group realized the cougar wounds were a warning, at least that's what the Wiccans believed. He crossed his fingers that the narrow-minded Manroot group would flounder in chaos for many months to come.

***

Downtown Elmira, at the Forever Reading Bookstore, Lars installed acoustic sound barrier panels on every inch of the inner walls of a hidden cubby constructed in one of the store's bookshelves. For the time being, the locked cubby would house Fisby Parkinson's new home, an abode begotten through bibliomancy with an address titled *Invitations to a Wiser Scripture: Equal Value and Shared Dignity for Women and Men in Biblical Interpretations*. Lars pondered the situation. As a Wiccan, Lars hid strange artifacts of power throughout the store, but this enchanted item was more concerning than most. The bookstore owner felt obligated to take it. Alfred had yet to prove himself a trustworthy guardian.

"I'd rather throw the book into an active volcano," Lars confided to Cathbad and Freya, as he secured and locked the door of the cubby. Freya yowled as though in agreement. Cathbad offered a soft growl.

***

Free of worries about haunted books and biblio-prisons, Alfred and Darnelle sat close together on Darnelle's Tyrian purple Chesterfield sofa in front of the crackling fireplace talking to each other about their childhoods.

"Somehow I knew when I was a girl that I was destined to meet you," Darnelle announced. "And I always thought I'd learn about magic, too."

"I never dreamed I would find such a perfect companion." Alfred, eager to start on a new life path, took Darnelle's hand. "My teacher said many times that a conjurer should never marry. A woman and family would complicate his work. But I can see in this time and place that he was wrong about that. Teach me how to live in your century, and I will show you everything I learned from my teacher."

"We'll make a powerful union." Darnelle's calculating hazel eyes looked into Alfred's cunning brown ones. They were sealing a conspirative lifetime arrangement.

Chapter 37

Werewolves, dragons, vampires, princesses, pirates, and, yes, witches bumped shoulders, stepped around each other, and sat crowded together sharing peanut butter spider cookies, pumpkin bundt cake, hocus pocus Binx cookies, vampire poke cake, and dirt pudding with gummy worms. It was midafternoon, and the All Hallows Eve celebration was in full swing at the Lucky Cup Café and Bakery.

At their usual round table in the corner, near the window looking out on Main Street, the Reading Club of Retired and Capable Ladies gathered around a pot of Egyptian Licorice tea and a plate of mini apple cider doughnuts. They wore regular everyday clothes, no costumes. But then, each woman was a real, honest-to-goodness, newbie witch; the Waterleaf Wiccans welcomed them as such. It seemed like overkill to dress up like one.

The women spent the first half hour sharing their critiques of the newspaper articles from the week before and agreed the news reports exposed more questions than answers.

"Do we really need to do a critique and assessment of our October reading materials? I mean we lived those books. Do we have to talk about them too?" Fayette was ready to move on and pick a book for November.

"I bought some more, you know." Sheila gave them a sheepish half smile.

"More what?" Fayette took an impatient bite from a buttery doughnut.

"Books about high magic, good magic, helpful magic. I went back to the bookstore in Olympia. They've got an enormous collection of new and used. Personally, I like the used copies because I like to imagine who the previous owners were, and I wonder if they tried some of the spells and recipes, and I wonder what happened. Did they make the same kinds of mistakes we did?"

Fayette, who was looking around the crowded room, noticed the woman she'd been curious about, the one who witnessed her confrontations with Elden at Brilliant Things and at the hospital.

"There she is. That woman I told you about." Fayette pointed to a figure near the bakery display case wearing black leggings, ankle-high leather boots, a royal blue boot skirt, and a hand quilted red vest over a long-sleeved, light blue cotton shirt. The woman was about their age with round cheeks, wavy, short-cut, gray hair, and bangs set over a dignified, open face. Her friendly, approachable, brown eyes looked over the crowd with composed scrutiny.

"Should we ask her to join us?" Sheila threw her arms out to her sides as though to embrace the whole world.

"Yeah, lets. I want to know who she is and why she keeps showing up and watching me." Fayette got up to do the asking but Kitsy put a gentle hand on her friend's healing shoulder.

"I'll go ask. Right now, you look ready to bite her." Kitsy wove her way through the ghosts and swashbucklers to the front where the woman paid for her muffin and a mug of tea. As the woman turned, Kitsy approached and pointed to their table. "Say, if you don't have a place to sit, we'd like to invite you to join us."

"You bet I'd like to join you." The woman's voice

was low and clear. "I've wanted to talk to you three for ages. My name is Betts, Betts Harvey."

They found a chair for Betts and shared introductions all around.

"Where are you from, Betts? Are you new here in Elmira?" Sheila offered her a doughnut.

"I don't live here, but it seems like I've spent every one of my days off in Elmira this past month, and I like the town. I live about forty miles from here, out on the coast. I retired from teaching recently and just started a business as a genealogist. My first customer's background investigation needed some face-to-face research with a couple of Elmira residents. I still haven't been able to talk to the people who could help me. I visited with one man but got next to no information from him. I'm afraid this investigation may be a bust, and I so wanted to have my first job be a success."

"Who are these people? Maybe we can help." Kitsy gave Betts a curious sideways look.

"Their names are Parkinson, Elden and Fisby, and they're brothers, I think. I talked to Elden several days ago, right here in this bakery, but I'm afraid my questions and my discoveries upset him. He took the family-tree chart I made for his grandson and got out of here fast. Now, I'm looking for Fisby as my last possibility."

"I saw you." Fayette's voice carried an accusatory edge. "In a few places."

"That's right. I think that's why I wanted to talk with you. Seemed as though whenever I caught up with Elden, you were there, too. I thought it was more than a coincidence, and it seemed as though some kind of confrontation was going on. Elden was either angry or leaving, so I couldn't talk with him."

Fayette pushed a copy of the Oct. 25 issue of the Elmira City Herald towards Betts, the one with the stories about the cougar attack and the missing brothers.

"Oh, my. They disappeared?"

"There's reason to think that the information you gave Elden last time you talked with him had something to do with their vanishing." Fayette's brows raised, and she looked Betts square in the eyes. "Would you mind sharing what you told him? It might help us locate the man."

So, Betts pulled out of her bag another copy of the Parkinson family chart and unfolded it in the middle of the table, pushing aside the tea pot and near-empty doughnut plate. She pointed to the brothers' birth dates. "You, see? This can hardly be accurate. Yet, Elden didn't deny that he might be more than 134 years old. And he seemed shocked to know that he had a grandson and a daughter and that the mother of his daughter still lives. Really, they're all too old to be alive except for Elden's grandson."

"How open minded are you about magic and the paranormal?" Sheila asked. Something about Betts, maybe the mischievous sparkle in her eyes, caused Sheila to think she could tolerate a paradigm-shattering revelation or two. "We can tell you what we know and some of what has happened this October, but we don't want you to go away thinking we're loony bins."

"I've wondered about a few things over the years, and this chart has had me questioning some of my basic beliefs and assumptions. I'm up for hearing your story."

And so, they told her most of what they knew about the Parkinsons and a little about what they'd learned on their own about the magic world.

"So, you see, it seems very possible to us that Elden Parkinson is more than 134 years old and that his brother Fisby is older." Kitsy sighed. "I tell you what. Give us your phone number and email address and we'll keep you updated. If we hear anything about the brothers or Elden's whereabouts, we'll contact you."

Betts did just that, handing a business card to each of

them. "Poor Peter, Elden's grandson. It looks as though I won't be able to finish the job for him."

"Elden left right after he heard he had a grandson," Sheila said. "I'll just bet he went to find his family. Peter will get a firsthand account of his family history from Elden, and that's because you told Elden he had a family to find. That means you accomplished what Peter asked you to do. He'll get the answers he wanted, just not from a chart."

"I love that idea. Thanks, all of you." Betts got up to leave. "So glad to have met you. If you're ever in Brocklebrook, stop in at the Dirty Dozen Bakery. Coffee brewer and baker is my post-retirement, part-time job. I'd love to catch up on your adventures. I have a feeling there's a lot more coming your way."

They were quiet as they watched Betts wave before opening the café front door. She needed to get her car on the road to beat the coming snow.

"Time to talk books." Fayette's mind was on her scheduled casserole dinner date with Leo. In the last week they had supper together every other evening.

"I want to know what Fisby is learning these days inside that book Elden forced him into." Kitsy grinned. For some reason, she didn't feel sorry for the pseudo pastor, and she wondered about her lack of empathy. "I want to read *Invitations to a Wiser Scripture: Equal Value and Shared Dignity for Women and Men in Biblical Interpretations* by Felicity P Sawyer."

"I've already got my copy," Sheila said laughing.

"Feminist theology it is, then," Fayette agreed, taking the last doughnut hole. After all, she wasn't one to leave leftovers.

THE END

APPENDIX

Supplemental history of Alfred Dowsby

The Story of The Lantern Man
by Samuel Browning and Alfred Dowsby

*Note to the reader: Samuel Browning's summaries
are in regular print. Quotes from The Lantern Man,
otherwise known as Alfred Dowsby, are in italics.
Alfred Dowsby's story comes entirely from the
imagination of this book's author.*

Alfred Dowsby was born in 1616 in a herder's cottage within the Great Fens of East Anglia, England. His life began in an untamed country where the marshes, tidal creeks, washes, meres, and rivers helped rear him to be as wild as the land. He was an untamed innocent who was to become a reckless monstrosity due to the greed and avarice of men who would destroy the Fens.

"Like most of the Fenmen, my father herded cows and sheep. He fished and trapped birds when he wasn't chasing livestock. My brothers, and sisters, and I milked the cows and made cheese and butter. We cut the tall grasses for hay, and we gathered peat for fuel and sedge and reed for thatching. My mother grew

vegetables in the high places, where the rising waters in winter deposited soft, fertile silt."

The reader can get a picture of the Fens wilderness from Todd Andrew Borlik's description in his 2021 article *Magic as Technological Dominion*. Borlik portrays the Sixteenth Century English Fens as stretching 1300 square miles. It was a region that, "in most parts, barely rises above sea level, and in 1600 consisted of a mixture of shallow lakes, mudflats, sodden peat, and tidal creeks, dotted with uplands known as 'edges' and 'islands.' "

Several sources concur that before the 1620s and into the1630s the people living in the Fens knew how to make the best of their environment, working with the landscape rather than against it, functioning in harmony with nature in ways we might envy. Theirs was an example of sustainable land-use. The grasslands, woodlands, bogs, reed beds, and fens were sources for a bounty of food and other resources.

"Our life was fixed in the hinterlands on an isle often cut off from others during the winter. But in the summer, the waters retreated, and we had access to towns and villages, where there were cathedrals, churches and abbeys, and all manner of marketplaces."

The Fenmen and Fenwomen understood and taught their children local knowledge about the ways of water, plants, and animals. They gave certainty to magic long after people in the cities considered the idea of magic to be unsound and indefensible. "The Fens fostered a microculture where greater credence in magic might linger, even well after the Reformation," Borlik points out. "It was a magic-ridden place." Even outsiders thought that the Fens were breeding grounds for demons.

"My mother was a cunning woman, a wise woman. People came to her for cures and advice to help them manage sickness in body and in heart. I knew about the

Fen bogies, imps, familiars, and the spirits that lived in the marshes and meres. Sometimes, when everyone was asleep, and the moon was high, I went looking for them. I would see lights in the distance, dancing over the water and bogs. I'd follow the lights but couldn't catch them. Once I discovered an injured otter by one of the main paths. I decided that it must be the dying familiar of a fairy. I killed it with a stick."

In the Fens, boat craft was a way of life, and Alfred, like his brothers, sisters, and parents, often traveled by punt from cow and sheep grazing places, to wood gathering spots, to herb and fruit gathering niches, and back to their thatched-roof hut and the winter barn. Tied to daily chores, but free to explore, Alfred knew of the old Roman causeways and roads that were scattered in parts of his home country.

"The older I got, though, the more I felt drawn to the town of Ely. It is north of Cambridge and near the towns Witcham and Witchford. Our home place was slightly north of Ely, and a few hours away by punt on the river Ouse. I thought it was in town that I could make something big of myself. One day I went to the Ely market and stayed. After that, I only went home for special celebrations or to bring presents from the market. I was a young lad then."

At the age of fourteen, Alfred could earn enough for food and a place to sleep by doing odd jobs for the monks, clerics, and people setting up and taking down market stands. He solicited town visitors for small jobs, and he swept up and ran errands for shop merchants.

By the time Alfred left home, it was 1630. Venture capitalists, seeking land and the means to get rich, decided to drain the Fens of water to make new farmland available for themselves and other investors. What the local people thought, whose livelihoods depended on the wetlands, was of little concern to the developers. Except, local people made it their concern.

"My family was against the Fen drainers. We all joined the protests. I know that my brothers helped sabotage some of the dikes and pumps that were built. The Fen people made up songs and curses to taunt and scare the engineers and workers. My mother was among the women accusing the outsiders of witchcraft. Wealthy men from the cities were robbing the Fen people of their common area and of their livelihoods. They needed to be stopped. Drainage was big business. Its purpose was to create new farmland, not for local people but for major landowners, and it meant depriving Fen people of rights to fish and hunt."

Contracted by King Charles I, Fen drainers arrived to build cuts in the Fens to join the Great River Ouse to the sea along with the Old Bedford River and the New Bedford River. This was known as the hundred-foot drain. Until the joining, these rivers drained into the Fens. After the joining, windmills pumped water away from the newly drained areas. "Gentlemen Adventurers" funded the construction while engineers directed the draining. Many called the destruction of the Fen wetlands the greatest environmental disaster executed in English history.

"In the meantime, my family and my neighbors were up to their knees fighting for their Fens, rebelling against changing the course of the rivers, struggling for their livelihoods. But I wanted in on the riches, and the drainers needed workers. I knew that the outlanders saw my people as heathenish yokels. I knew my people saw the drainers as diabolical. Both sides accused the other of witchcraft and sorcery. I was so set on making myself useful to the engineers and the rich landholders that I willingly warned the drainers, for food and money, when my people planned raids and protests. I pointed out the local Fen leaders."

No one knew of Alfred's duplicity for many months, except for the engineers and developers who received his news gladly. They encouraged him to return home and learn more about Fen organizers and their plans to destroy pumps and dykes. The gentleman adventurers treated Alfred to sumptuous meals, gave him new clothes, and deluded the young traitor into believing they admired him. By accident, he discovered they despised his deceitfulness and laughed at his willingness to let them use him for so little reward.

"I heard some men laughing behind a curtain in the Abby. I heard my name mentioned, so I listened. They called me a worm, the lowest of low, a quisling, and a spy. And then I knew I was never to be one of them, never to become an estate holder, never to be brought into the royal fold. They had simply used me. My heart blackened. My mind felt hot, like the coal in a lantern, always burning, burning with hate."

Full of resentment and shame, Alfred returned to his family's home one dark, wet night. He invented a story about the draining engineers as conjurers and spell makers. People of the Fens were willing to believe his story. They'd suspected magic all along. After all, intermeddling with the natural order of things was, to them, a clear indication of magic.

The conflict between the fen people and the capitalists intensified.

During the years of re-routing rivers and interfering with the natural water flows, draining engineers accused the Fenman fathers of inciting the destruction of draining works. One of the Fen men threatened to bury a draining project supervisor "in one of his own ditches." To discredit the local people, the venture capitalists and their engineers used the superstitions of the Fen people as an excuse to drain the marshes, washes, tidal creeks, moors, meres, and rivers. Outsiders portrayed the Fens as heathenish backwaters in need of destruction. Society in the big cities dreaded the creatures that could be living in the hinterlands. Outsiders especially feared fairies. When the Fen rioters and protestors tried to stop the draining projects, the developers from the cities charged them with using black magic and witchcraft.

"It's true my people understood the importance of folk magic. They were motivated by a desire to maintain equilibrium and not to practice domination over the Fens. We knew of Fen magic. We knew of the Tiddy Mun as a peculiar Fen bogey. Our Tiddy Mun was a short goblin in a gray cloak who lived in the meres. Some said they saw him on misty nights. Occasionally, the flooding got high enough to reach the uplands. When that happened, cottagers, led by cunning women, marched outside during a full moon and chanted spells asking the Tiddy Mun to make the waters withdraw. It was a way of managing our environment with the help of a bogey."

A malady spread through the Fens that we in the modern world call malaria. The word mal-aria means "bad air." Unaware that a parasite spread by mosquitos caused the disease, people told themselves that the wetland air was the reason for the sickness, so the venture capitalists said they should destroy the wetlands to rid the land of malaria. Local Fen people, over time, acquired some resistance to malaria, but the newcomers had little resistance. More often than not, the newcomers associated the disease with demons or Fen witchcraft used to torment engineers and developers.

When local people came down with malaria, they often called for cunning women to help, like Alfred's mother. Alfred remembers his mother staking rods into the ground, lighting them on fire, and chanting: "as the rods burn, so let the ague burn too." Sometimes cunning women advised people to swallow a spider tucked inside a raisin, to eat cobwebs, or to drink urine. These were local remedies connected with wise women's knowledge. The people outside the Fens saw these practices as witchcraft.

James I was king of England until 1625, and he believed witches tried to kill him several times, so Parliament passed a Witchcraft Act in 1604 that was a charter for an English witch-hunt. Puritans, who despised witchcraft, were gaining power. Alfred's mother was in danger.

"In the meantime, I came to believe that I could grow in power and wealth with the help of the demons, fairies, and bogies, rather than with the help of mortal men of high social standing. Those men had one kind of power, but the magic folk had greater power. At night, I sought out the ancient supernatural beings who dwelled in the thick brushes and hidden places of the Fens. My mother was a cunning woman, respected by her community because her purpose was to help, never to hurt. My mother was a wise woman, not a witch, but I sought a different path. I wanted the power to punish the cold-blooded venture capitalists and their engineers draining the Fens. I wanted control over those who humiliated me. When I turned twenty, I sought out a diviner or sorcerer, wicca [masculine] or a wicce [feminine], male or female. It didn't matter to me."

When Alfred talks of wicca or wicce, he refers to a type of person as perceived in the 1600s. The goals of Wiccan witches in our own United States in the Twentieth and Twenty First Centuries do not align accurately with the perceived ambitions of so-called witches in Alfred's time. To Alfred, wizard meant 'a wise man.' A woman wizard was a wise woman, not a witch. Wizards and wisewomen could practice magic by manipulating nature to produce miracles. They were thought of as people who combined natural aptitude and learned skill. In contrast, a witch, they thought, was someone who had the uncanny ability to cause harm to others, just by wishing it or thinking it. In Alfred's time, people mostly thought that witches differed from wise men or wise women because witches, they believed, were motivated by envy. In truth, individuals labeled as witches were simply people others could blame if things started to go wrong. During the famous witch hunts of Europe, witch hunters often accused wizards and wisewomen of witchcraft. Most people suspected of being witches did not fit into the witch category as envious people causing harm to others.

The current Wicca religion is new since the 1950s. A civil servant named Gerald Gardner published a book called *Witchcraft Today* in 1954. He theorized that the church persecuted witchcraft, an ancient pre-Christian religion, but that it survived underground. However, most evidence shows that in the past, wizards, wisewomen, and people called witches were largely solitary individuals who did not organize themselves as part of a religion.

In contrast, the new religion of the Twentieth and Twenty-First Centuries, called Wicca, has attracted many followers, and developed its own traditions. Wiccans, often, but not always, organize themselves and meet in covens. They teach and practice shared knowledge and ideals. Today, Wiccans' first and primary ethical principle prohibits harming another human being. 'An' ye harm none, do what ye will.' Wicca is a young religion indigenous to Britain. Wiccans of today identify through empathy with the people of the past who Protestants and Catholics persecuted and charged with witchcraft.

Just the same, there were (and still are) a few who practiced dark magic against the creeds of "do no harm."

"One night, when there was no moon, I saw a fire in the distance as I punted through a marsh, dense with great Fen sedge. It was late fall, and the frogs were hibernating. All was quiet except the sound of my oar as I used it to feel a way through the reeds, making room for my passage. I moved closer to the fire, docking my watercraft at the foot of an island. As I climbed a

short distance uphill, I could see a figure, a man cutting segments of his hair and throwing them into the fire. He picked up a shirt, tore it into pieces, and threw the sleeves and then the rest into the flames. Each time he added to the fire, it burst upwards in scorching surges, and then he talked the fire down, his voice soft and then loud and then soft again. I thought I recognized the full-sleeved silk shirt and the jacket of pomegranate-patterned linen that went piece by piece into the fire. They belonged to a draining engineer who was particularly eager for information about the Fen people. Remembering his false, covetous smile, I felt deep satisfaction at seeing his clothes burn.

By the look of the fire raiser's hooded cloak, he was no benevolent wise man. He'd made his shroud from red, tanned leather, close-fitted with back and front hemlines plunging downward like the points of arrows. A thread and needle artist embroidered the collar and hem with images of frenzied monsters. I was in awe. This was the kind of conjurer I sought, unshackled from the bounds of sympathetic humanity. Long brown hair, streaked with gray, straggled down his back in clumped strands. Pieces of cut hair hung uneven in front. In strange contrast to his unruly locks, the man trimmed his salt and pepper beard with even precision. His eyes mirrored the flames in the fire as he shouted and murmured, shouted, and murmured long streams of words that I could not decipher. I watched, so fascinated that I was unaware of the four-foot-long black and yellow serpent that slid from the water and settled over my left leg. It was only a grass snake, but it surprised me, and I let loose a yell. The conjurer's head turned in my direction, but he kept on with his spell work."

That night began Alfred's apprenticeship with Wehha. Alfred calls him 'The Teacher,' but the man's family named him after the earliest Anglo-Saxon ruler of East Anglia, the father of the Wiffingas dynasty, whose name meant 'descendants of the wolf.' Wehha told Alfred that Wiffingas descendants went underground after the Danes took control. Neither the Danes nor the Romans, who arrived later, knew of the hidden remnants of the wolf dynasty. Wehha saw himself as royalty and rightful king of the Fens. He spent his days manipulating politics in secret, and, by using supernatural energies, he earned favors from the fairy folk to call upon when needed.

"The Teacher told me that night he was expecting me. My mother, he explained, was a descendant of the Wiffingas clan, though she did not know it. The magic that was strong in her passed to me. The Teacher said, 'Those rods she lights to burn away the malaria work sometimes, but not if my magic is causing the illness. Her magic is undisciplined and simple. Mine overpowers hers.' He told me he could help me control and focus my magical aptitude, but I must never question him if I wanted to stay with him. 'Never cross me, son, or you will live to regret it.' I didn't realize living to regret would mean lamenting my very existence, bemoaning even my birth, for hundreds of years."

It turned out that the draining engineer whose clothes Wehha cast into his Fen fire died the next week in a house inferno in Ely. Alfred was terrified of The Teacher then, too afraid to think of leaving his side as errand boy and student. The conjurer was as powerful as he claimed to be. For nine years Alfred served The Teacher and learned the Wuffingas methods and rituals for conjuring and spell-making. He also learned to be disdainful of wizards and wisewomen, like his mother, who used their skills and talents to cure and make peace, to do no harm. They wasted their aptitudes, he believed, and the energy they put forth to help ordinary fishers and farmers kept them from achieving the status and wealth they deserved as superior beings. The Teacher modeled for Alfred a particular philosophy about the most valuable uses for magic.

"The Teacher lived in a tall stone tower on his own island deep in the Fens. I slept in the damp basement underground, tending to the fires in the morning and preparing The Teacher's ingredients for his work each day. Many times, he refused to tell me the purposes for his conjuring. Often, he showed me how to gather ingredients, prepare them, and then use them in various rituals and spells. Sometimes The Teacher instructed me to use his rowboat and take items to Ely to leave on people's doorsteps or windowsills or to exchange at a market stall for goods or money. Some so-called gifts that I left on doorsteps had been commissioned. Some were from The Teacher himself to influence people's thinking, and, in that way, to direct political decisions. A few items were meant to cause punishment to a family. As I delivered the spells, I sometimes saw one of the dandies who used me in my younger years. I spat on the ground behind them and uttered spells to bring them misfortune. Then, when I was almost 30 years old, The Teacher set me free. 'You're ready, Alfred, to make your own future. But beware; if you ever try to use your magic in opposition to me or to counter my magic, you will wish you were never born.' I thanked The Teacher and left his tower with only the clothes on my back."

It was 1646 when Alfred became a free and educated conjurer. By then, although they hated the monarchy, Puritans adopted King James's ideas about witchcraft from his book *Daemonologie*. Witch hunts were in vogue, and people hired professional witch hunters. Some came to Ely and the Fens. Witch hunters were sure that villages around Ely protected people whom the Puritans thought were religious radicals. The hunters were set on rousting them out. In addition, developers and witch finders targeted families who resisted the drainage of the Fens as possible witches or as harboring witches.

Having learned reading, writing, and bookkeeping

from The Teacher, Alfred set up shop in the town as an accountant. Clients could go to him if they were illiterate or needed something read or written. Alfred was careful to hide his second occupation as a witch or warlock.

In his family's eyes, Alfred had finally grown up and was taking responsibility for himself. They brought him milk and cheese from the pastures and spent hours in his company talking about the draining of the marshes and the subsequent loss of fish and other species that made it harder for them to find enough food to supplement the grazing. Each time she came, his mother asked him when he intended to start a family of his own. Alfred believed a family would interfere with his ultimate goals to dominate the people in charge of business and politics.

"Each night, when the doors of my shop closed, I descended to a basement I dug out in secret. It was damp, of course, like the one I'd occupied in the tower for eight years. You can't really expect basements in the Fen to be dry. But it made a good workshop for my real work. I began to manipulate my neighbors through magic. I worked magic to sway the clergy and bishop in the monastery and cathedral. In secret, I influenced the businessmen and engineers trying to make farmland out of the Fens, and the people who ran the weekly markets. When my magic required me to make talismans or potions that I needed to place near houses, chapels, or shops, I donned my darkest wool cloak and soft shoes and slipped in and out of night shadows as I made my clandestine deliveries. Sometimes Ely residents discovered my spell-bound gifts. I tried to prevent the discovery of my spell receptacles because, when found, they fueled and intensified searches for local witches. When the witch hunters came to town, I focused my magic on spells I could conduct from my basement, but those were never as effective as spells delivered directly

to the intended recipient."

Reveling in the increasing levels of power he built through his conjuring influence on the town administrators, Alfred thought of himself as a puppeteer and the people around him as puppets. They acted out a play he created, better than Shakespeare's plays, he told himself. Whether he had much if any influence through his spells is questionable, but he believed he was directing lives and decisions. When the notorious witch tracker, Matthew Hopkins, came to Ely, the city officials hired him to find witches in the town and surrounding area. Alfred thought himself clever enough to try and bewitch Hopkins the witch hunter. One dark night, a time of the new moon, Alfred set out to install a spell receptacle behind climbing ivy at the witch hunter's doorway. He charged his spell with a suggestion incantation. The idea was that if the witch hunter heard Alfred's voice suggesting something, Hopkins would feel compelled to act on it.

"That night, as I worked to insert a tiny clay spell pot into a crevice under the ivy near the witch finder's residence, I felt a cold hand on my shoulder. The hand roughly spun me around, and the pot flew from my fingers and landed on the ground at my assailant's feet. The witch hunter, Hopkins, picked it up, and I muttered a short incantation under my breath. I knew I had one chance to save myself. If the spell worked, I could offer the right suggestion. I had to think of something plausible on the spot, and I had to think of it fast.

An idea came to mind, and I acted on it. 'I am a witch hunter, like you Mr. Hopkins. I have been tailing a known witch. He put this spell pot here. I assume it contains a spell that needs nullifying.'

I'm not sure the witchfinder believed me, but he played along.

'You are the accountant with an office down the street,' Hopkins said, twirling the left side of his long

mustache. 'No one told me you are a witch hunter. What witches have you turned in for conviction?'

'None, yet, sir,' I said. 'I am new to this and want to make sure I have the best of proof.'

'What makes you qualified to identify a witch?" Hopkins' tone was surly and full of suspicion.

'I grew up with a cunning woman, my mother,' I confessed. 'She used magic for her neighbors' problems and to help cure people of sickness. I know some of the signs from her.'

'So, your mother is a witch.' Hopkins' eyes narrowed. 'She will be questioned and brought before the court.'

'No, sir. She is a wise woman, not a witch,' I was quick to say. What had I done, I wondered, and how could I distract him from my family? I decided to take a chance. 'No, she's not a witch, but the man I followed tonight is one. He lives in a tower on an island in the Fens. He's the one you want to focus on. His name is Wehha, and he keeps alive the magic brought to this area through the earliest Anglo-Saxon rulers of East Anglia, the Wiffingas dynasty.'

The witchfinder's eyes widened with interest. Tracking down a witch connected with the Viking invaders of old would be a master coup.

'You must show me how to get to this tower and this witch called Wehha,' Hopkins said. 'If you take me to him tomorrow, I will have your mother watched rather than put in custody before her trial. But she will undergo examination and a trial at the Ely Quarter Sessions.'

The witch hunter regarded me with pursed lips nearly hidden by his heavy beard and mustache. 'I will commandeer a skiff and then find you at your place of business early in the morning. Be there.' He turned, then, and entered the place he rented.

I stood in the street, frozen, remembering the final words of The Teacher only months ago. 'But beware, if you ever try to use your magic in opposition to me *or to counter my magic, you will wish you were never born.'"*

Alfred could think of only one thing to do. He untied his own punt from the edge of the waterway and rowed with all his might for hours to get to the tower and warn his former master. Would forewarning him be enough to gain The Teacher's forgiveness?

No one ever saw Alfred again after that night. He was not at his place of business when the witch hunter came to get him. Of course, Hopkins conducted a thorough investigation of Alfred's sleeping quarters and office. The witch hunter found the basement and let it be known that the young man was under suspicion of witchcraft, much to the surprise of Ely residents who used his services. Hopkins and his allies never found the tower Alfred spoke of, however long they looked for it. In Hopkins' anger at being thwarted, Alfred's mother was to be the brunt of the witch finder's wrath. She endured months of depravity and unsanitary conditions waiting for trial and died of disease before her trial date. According to historians, she was one of many who suffered the same fate. Judges usually acquitted people like her in court during the Puritan witch hunts, but many defendants died in custody awaiting their trials.

"I came to the tower that night and woke The Teacher, explaining what happened and that men might come for him. I expected him to be angry, but I had never seen the true power of his wrath until the wee hours of the coming morning. He looked at me as though I was the lowest of worms or an insect he wished to crush under his heel. 'I warned you never to cross me,' he said, his voice at first cold and hard and then rumbling low, like the start of an avalanche. 'The searchers will never find me, and neither will they find you, Alfred of the Fens. When I finish this spell, you will be but a shell of a man, no longer human. Your destiny for as long as marshes exist on this planet will be to haunt the wetlands. Your

only possession will be a lantern with a coal for a light, and as much as you might chase the people who come close, you can never be one of them. You are alone, Alfred of the Fens. People will come to fear you, as they should. Not even your mother can trust you now, and no one should trust you in the future.'

'Is there nothing I can do to earn your forgiveness,' I pleaded.

'You are a traitor, full of avarice, caring only for yourself,' thundered The Teacher. 'Should you one day care enough to sacrifice yourself for the sake of another, then you might break from the torment you are about to begin.'

'I don't understand,' I said.

'I know,' said The Teacher.

And that is how I became The Lantern Man, cursed to carry a light in a metal box and wander the marshes. I came to hate humans and animals alike because they were free to live and free to die."

By the time the sun came up that morning, Alfred was no longer Alfred. He was The Lantern Man. Over time, stories emerged about the man who carried a light, tempting people to follow him to their deaths in the reed beds of the Fens. His was often a lone light, shining over the darkness, luring people in. As the stories of The Lantern Man spread, so did advice for how to avoid him. Experts on the Fen wild areas counseled people not to carry torches or lights at night in the Fens because the Lantern Man followed such lights. Never whistle was another piece of wisdom because The Lantern Man runs towards a whistle and will kill the whistler if he can. Never mock the Lantern Man or he will follow you all the way home and try to torch your house. As one old man said, 'Hold your breath. If The Lantern Man is upon ye, throw yourself flat on your face and halt ye breathing.'

Even as the incidents with The Lantern Man increased

and the stories spread, the Fens shrank because of the drainage. The Lantern Man's territory for wandering withered. He even began to hope that developers might drain all the marshes in the world, that wetlands might disappear so that he could be free of his torment. By the end of the 1800s, almost 99 percent of the Fens were gone, and The Lantern Man found himself haunting the Wicken Fens near Cambridge. It is in this vicinity that The Lantern Man stories are most common and persistent.

"I spent more than 250 years wandering through the Fens, constantly moving as the drainers rerouted the waterways, set up pump stations, and turned the wetlands into farm country. I was a shell of my former self, no longer human, no longer feeling much that was good. My memories of my family and the people of Ely faded. My jealousy and anger grew to include every human in the world. I became ever reckless. I didn't care what happened to my victims, the ones who followed my light into the bogs and rivers. I relished chasing travelers with my lantern until they were lost and scared. No one cared for me. Why would I care for them?

"In time, my loneliness got the best of me. It had taken more than two and a half centuries to begin feeling remorse, even empathy and to wish I had a woman to love and a family to raise. I had begun to lead the people lost in the Fens to their safety rather than to their deaths. But just as I was learning to feel for others, and just as the heat of the coal in my lantern began to cool, a delegation of Wicken Fen neighbors visited the home of an ancient man called Wehha."

In the early 1900s, people living around Wicken Fen decided they were fed up with the old bogies and the spirits and the magic folk thought to be haunting their bogs and wetlands. Most people in Britain gave up believing in such things by the early Twentieth Century.

In contrast, Fenland communities remained isolated, which meant that Fen folk whispered about bogies and lantern men and other Fen fiends long after the rest of Britain decided paranormal creatures were mere superstition.

By 1910, a delegation of Wicken Fen neighbors visited the home of an ancient man called Wehha. He called himself a fiend hunter who could rid the countryside of unwanted creatures of the night. The people wanted lantern men and all manner of will o' the wisps to disappear.

"You guessed right. Wehha was The Teacher, so old he neared the end of an exceptionally long life as a conjurer and wizard. Since it was his spell that formed me into the monster I am, it was easy for him to commandeer my essence and imprison what was left of me into the smallish book, just published that year and sold in city bookstores. Wehha trapped me between the pages of The Book of Forbidden Knowledge for a hundred and thirteen years, until you, Samuel, whistled me free.

"Wehha had two sons. Their cunning mother left them as boys because she could no longer endure the cruelty of being with their father. I suppose she felt they were all better off without her, as Wehha degraded her day after day until she no longer believed she was capable of much. I understand she eventually took her own life. Wehha believed that women were less than human and that wise women of the Fens could never reach the knowledgeable heights of male necromancers and warlocks. He taught his sons his prejudices, and because they believed their father and blamed their mother for leaving them, they degraded women and their magic. Like Wehha, these sons are long-lived for humans. When Wehha died at the age of 637, the sons inherited their father's fortune as well as his conjuring tools and books. 'The Book of Forbidden Knowledge,'

my prison, is part of one of his son's collections.

"Wehha's sons brought their history, their conjuring tools, and their book collections to the Americas in 1983. East Anglia in Britain, their ancient birthright, is largely tamed. The wild energies of the fens and forests are shadows of their former glory, so the Wiffingas Clan descendants were attracted to the deep forests and powerful rivers of the Pacific Northwest, still full of untamed potencies.

"Pastor Fisby Parkinson and Elden Parkinson are Wehha's long-lived sons, and now that I am free, I plan to take revenge on them for the pain they caused me for more than 100 years and that their father caused me for nigh unto 377 years."

Bibliography

Borlick, Todd Andrew. 2021. *Magic as Technological Dominion. John Dee's Hydragogy and the Draining of the Fens in Ben Johnson's The Devil is an Ass. Neophilologus.* 105: 589-608.

Coward, Matt. 2014. *The Witch from "His-Story" to "Her-Stories": Changing Contexts.* Paranthropology: Journal of Anthropolgical Approaches to the Paranormal. Vol. 5, No. 3 10

Meeres, Frank. 2019. *The Story of the Fens.* The History Press.

Saxena, Jaya. 2015. *There's a Sexism Problem in the Modern Witchcraft Community.* Boston Globe. 11/19/2015

Young, Francis. 2013. *Witches and Witchcraft in Ely: A History.* Cambridge Print Solutions. Cambridge.